SUPERIOR SQUADRON

BOOK 1 ~ THE RIFT

STEVEN TRENT

2024, TWB Press
https://www.twbpress.com

Edited by Terry Wright

Cover Art by Terry Wright

ISBN: 978-1-959768-53-1

Dedication

This Book is dedicated to John Lores, the man who encouraged me to become the writer I am today.

Roll Call

Earth One (Their Earth)	Earth A (Our Earth)
Superior Squadron	The Assemblers
Superior Man	Man Machine
Amazon Woman	Red Rose
Golden Ring	Sergeant-at-Arms
Ratman	King Bee/Kingsize
Eagleman	Hornette
Shrinking Man	Galloping Gazelle
Aquamarine	Marksman
Gold Arrow	Behemoth
Jet Man	
Plastic Freak	Atoms Family
	Mr. Atoms
Wonderkind	Intangible Girl
Tadpole	Flaming Youth
Amazon Girl	The Golem
Jet Boy	
Swifty	Tomorrow Men
Mercury	Polyphemus
	Astro Lass
	Animal
	Green Hawk
	Polar Man

CHAPTER 1

H al Kinnison was tired. Bone tired. Worse, he was bored. Traversing space at light-speed, enclosed in an envelope of energy, should have been exciting. Well, it *was* the first time. Now the trip was routine. While space was vast, with much beauty, the speeds Kinnison attained distorted those wonders. In truth, keeping his will focused was exhausting, for willpower kept the energy field around him, and he within, alive.

It's beautiful, though.

From outside the force-field, Kinnison's trim physique appeared as gold as his form-fitting Galactic Guard uniform. Should the field drop, those gold and black tights would be no substitute for a space suit. His brown eyes would freeze and explode. The visor couldn't protect him from the cold vacuum of space.

Around the shaggy brown-haired man—no Galactic Guards at the conference were adept at cutting human hair—stars blazed, nebulae expanded, planets formed, comets streaked, and galaxies wheeled. Kinnison might learn, fatally, if black holes really existed. If so, they were to be avoided. He might also learn if Maarten Schmidt was right about quasi-stellar radio sources. *NewsView* put Schmidt on their cover for discovering them, comparing him to Galileo.

Wish I had a NewsView now, he mused.

The glowing energy field was generated by the ring on his finger. It would protect him from danger automatically. The ring was a powerful tool from the Galactic Guard. Recruited to their interstellar peacekeeping force, Earth was Kinnison's beat. Besides a means of light-speed travel, the ring was a devastating weapon. It could materialize anything the wearer imagined. Right now, and most importantly, it was life support.

I'm home.

On the outskirts of the solar system, he changed course, deviating from his normal route home, to swing by the planet Iukkoth beyond Neptune. It was the home-world of his Superior Squadron teammate Eagleman. Wracked by war, it was just as well Kinnison refused to use the ring's power to return his friend to Iukkoth.

Ahead, Earth floated in the void, a blue and white marble in the distance. The glow of its sun, Sol, bathed it with light and life. However, he noticed an anomaly as he neared the atmosphere, a swirl of sparkling lights he'd never seen before, directly in his path. He plunged into its black vortex where the Earth appeared to shimmer like heat waves on the desert, but only for a moment, as the light show was quickly behind him.

What in the world was that?

Still in one piece, he shrugged it off to concentrate on a more pressing matter, reentering the Earth's atmosphere. Above the northeastern United States now, Kinnison descended like a meteor. The energy cocoon prevented him from burning up during reentry. Below the clouds, he spotted shiny objects, gleaming shapes rising so fast Kinnison couldn't decipher what they...*wait*...the pilot in him recognized aircraft.

"Fighter jets," he shouted. The Strategic Air Command was responding to an imminent threat. *F-111Bs? They're headed right for me.*

Why would they attack the superhero they knew and loved as Golden Ring? Then something faster than those fighters homed in on him.

Missiles.

Somewhere below the unfolding conflict, Johnny Ferro, a wealthy industrialist and founding member of the team of extraordinary individuals called the Assemblers, also flew, albeit, closer to the surface and toward their headquarters. Covered head to toe in gleaming gunmetal-gray armor, he was a sleek flying tank. As long as there was hydrogen in the air, the armored suit had fuel for flight. However, he had to recharge the electronics within his armor. It was a specialized outfit of his latest design. Without it, he was but a small and frail man. The other Assemblers did not know the millionaire inventor wore the armor; to them he was just another superpower on the payroll. A voice distorter kept his secret.

Within his helmet, a modified Brain Wave Synchronizer using electroencephalography cut the rocket tubes on his boot heels then angled the jets on his hips to facilitate landing at his townhouse on East 70th Street in New York City. Boasting three above-ground floors, it also had three basement floors. Twelve rooms housed Assemblers who chose to reside there, with quarters for their butler. One basement level was a garage holding a deceptively souped up V.W. T1 Auwarter Carlux the team used for local jaunts, as well as a short, stumpy G.M. Bison Turbine Truck that he'd impulsively purchased two years ago. As of yet, nobody had thought of a good use for it.

The Assemblers protected Earth. With his blessing, they used his expansive townhouse as their headquarters. A portion of the third floor served as a hangar for their gyroplane and a charging station for his suit, which was Man Machine's ultimate destination.

When he reached street level, he heard a *thwip* and saw a strand of spider web shoot across his view out the visor. "What the..?" His metallic fingers twisted a circular lens on his chest plate, which focused a scanning beam that swept around him. It detected a figure in red and blue tights, clinging to a billboard.

Tarantula-Man? Attacking me? Not now. The charge on my armor is almost drained.

***

"Hey. I'm a friend," Golden Ring yelled at the attacking fighter jets while waving his hands. "Why are—"

Abruptly, Golden Ring was launched back into space. The ring had saved itself the trouble of fending off a barrage of missiles. Now he was confronted with that rotating swirl of sparkling lights again. The protective shield of energy shuddered as the ring propelled him into the vortex. To Golden Ring, it took only an instant to break through to the other side. Again, he found himself decelerating toward Earth, this time above California's Coastal City. There were no fighter jets anywhere to be seen. That in itself was a relief, and below him, the roof of his apartment grew.

The ring's protective sphere dissolved, and he dropped the last few feet to the roof. Thanks to Ratman's training, Golden Ring flipped and landed safely in a three-point crouch. Now he had to switch out his Galactic Guard uniform for civilian clothing.

Having prepared for this, he ran to a roof kiosk and fetched a folded plastic raincoat and battered hat from a shelf. His Canadian Inuit pal, Beanpole, knew Kinnison's secret identity and had suggested this strategy should the need arise to go incognito. He doffed the visor, donned the hat, and slipped into the coat. Should anyone have been watching, they'd have seen Golden Ring disappear. There was a spare key in the pocket. He unlocked the roof access door and stalked down the stairs. Without the visor, he was a rugged specimen of the human race. In his gold boots and with his unruly hair, an observer might think Kinnison had gone mod. Quietly, he treaded to his apartment. After looking around for prying eyes, he unlocked the door and entered. Tired and confused, he craved one thing.

Blessed sleep.

This space-faring protector couldn't know he had encountered what Albert Einstein had only theorized, a wormhole in the space-time continuum, or in layman terms, a rift between parallel worlds. And little did he suspect his arrival had been observed by a super-villain, new to this planet, and now making plans to destroy his home Earth.

***

In a parallel universe beyond the rift, Tarantula-Man considered Man Machine from his billboard perch across the street from the townhouse. He waved like some kind of prankster.

"Ego maniac," Man Machine muttered. *Who puts his own face on his shirt?*

Tarantula-Man's web-shot was just his way of getting Man Machine's attention. The super-spider had been unjustly tarred as a criminal...a wrestler turned super-powered menace. However, Tarantula-Man was not a menace. In dark blue leggings and sleeves, but also daringly bright red boots, hood and gloves, Tarantula-Man's costume was meant to be seen. He wouldn't wear such a gaudy outfit to commit crime. It was pure showbiz. The misunderstanding was due to the machinations of the despotic newspaper publisher of *The New York Daily Press*. J. Jacob Jackson didn't actually believe the drivel he published, but the false charge sold papers.

Tarantula-Man realized Jackson felt insecure about the existence of gifted beings. Jackson had no idea that this so-called *criminal* was actually on his press's payroll as a free-lance photographer. Someday, Tarantula-Man would reveal having been on the man's staff. Right now, the arachnid-obsessive was fixated on Assemblers Mansion. He detached himself from the billboard, which was an advertisement for the very paper where he worked, and swung over the traffic to land on the side of a building.

How does he do that? the armored man wondered. *All my gadgets and I can't do that.*

How?

An experiment Richard Reide, patriarch of the Atoms Family, conducted at Triborough University had accidentally rendered spider-like abilities to a student, who would later become known as the infamous Tarantula-Man.

Clinging to the building, the super-spider configured his first and last fingers, which activated the web shooter on his wrist. With a *thwip*, the expelled liquid congealed into a solid strand the instant it contacted air. *Splat.* It adhered to a cornice high above Man Machine.

Tarantula-Man swung down to the sidewalk. "I come in peace," he said with a mask-muffled voice that hid his youth. As if to illustrate his intentions, he reconfigured his fingers to form the peace sign.

"What's your game, Tarantula-Man?"

"I bet the Assemblers can use another super-powered dude like me, with you and Týr leaving."

It was true. They had put in for a leave of absence to hunt the Behemoth, but how did this guy know? He'd told only his friend Rob Johnson, editor-in-chief of the *Press*. Man Machine wondered if Johnson was under the spider's hood. Instantly, he dismissed that. Johnson was a short, chunky middle-aged black guy with a gravelly voice, definitely not this fit, hip young man.

The hunt for the Assemblers' bestial member had hastened new inductees into the ranks. Various reformed criminals had been pressed into service.

Man Machine bent eye-level with Tarantula-Man and saw himself in the almond-shaped lenses of Tarantula-Man's hooded mask. Would this guy be another one?

"What makes you think you're man enough to be an Assembler?" Man Machine's voice was like thunder in a barrel.

"You know I'm not a dangerous criminal."

"Sure, but the people don't know that."

"The law can't hound me if I'm an Assembler." Tarantula-Man was willing to do anything to become a member, even scuttle his showbiz dreams.

"Interesting. All right. I got an idea."

"Don't keep it under your helmet."

"I'll recommend you for the Assemblers *if* you help us catch the Behemoth."

"Where is he?"

"He was last seen sitting on a downtown building, eating turkey."

"A leg?"

"A whole turkey."

"So, he's in New York?"

"Was. Of all the disappearing acts he's pulled, this was his best."

"How does a gray seven-footer wearing rags disappear?"

"Good *question*. Týr called in a sighting at a place out west. The Spahn Ranch, near Los Angeles. With your powers added to ours, we might control the Behemoth."

"Týr phoned? But he would knoweth not what exact change be." Tarantula-Man chuckled at his impersonation of Týr's lingo.

Within the helmet, Man Machine smiled at that image of ancient Týr operating a telephone and conversing in his Elizabethan English. "In fact, I was just coming to H.Q. for, um, supplies."

"So, your suit needs a charge."

"That's confidential information, mister," Man Machine snapped. "But I wouldn't wrangle the Behemoth without a full tank."

"I thought you could handle that gray goof."

"Just barely. And having crossed a continent before doing it? Not on your life."

"I see your point. The behemoth will be a tough catch."

"Monsters are Týr's specialty," Man Machine said. "He's had centuries of experience. Are you going to help us or not?"

"Sure. I got nothing better to do."

"Nothing better than dying?"

"Did you have to put it that way?" Tarantula-Man trailed Man Machine inside. The hangar housed the Assemblers' Fairey Rotodyne compound gyroplane. This had a plane-like fuselage, and wings with two wing-mounted Napier Eland turboprops. A top rotor that rested on a submarine-like conning tower was also jet-tipped. The British experimented with them in the 1950s but found them too cost prohibitive for continued production. Ferro bought one and donated it to the Assemblers. This gyroplane was outfitted for continental flights.

"Cool, man."

"Make that Man *Machine*." The Assembler presented an armored hand and ended up with it wrapped in web. Being that the spider agreed so readily to this dangerous mission, Man Machine realized becoming an Assembler was worth risking life and limb.

"Nobody loves the Be-he-moth," Tarantula-Man sang off-key.

It was a rock 'n' roll song Man Machine knew from the radio. He could only hope it wouldn't become a death march hit.

***

Colonel Rocco Kent, high over Earth in a stationary aircraft fraudulently marked *B.F. Goodyear*, squinted. The

Special Projects Agency operated from an aerodynamic platform with stabilizing stubby wings. Enclosed props on the sides and rear provided thrust. F.W. Locke, Jr. had proposed nuclear airships in 1954. By 1957, Edwin Kirschner suggested the use of atomic airships in a book. Six years later, the contraption was built. The flat-top platform, flat as J. Jacob Jackson's haircut, could receive aircraft. Kent was still squinting at movie footage from the camera on the F-111B attack squadron's lead jet. He used a wearable television set, but having only one eye proved a disadvantage.

"Maybe the electrocula ain't meant for me," he muttered. *Am I really seeing what I think I'm seeing?*

Replay after replay, the man in gold and black was there and then he just...disappeared. The alien had eluded the Strategic Air Command's best fighter jets. Kent removed his brown jacket, loosened his tie and adjusted the eye patch. *I'm going to be here a while. May as well get comfortable.*

"Like nothing the Special Projects Agency ever saw," he grumbled, running nervous fingers through his military haircut. This World War II vet would never get used to men sporting long hair. "Well, except for Týr."

At that moment, another man entered with a file for the colonel. "What about Týr, sir?" Jimmy Yen asked. He was Kent's best operative.

"Is that it? Týr's file?"

He didn't like involving super beings, but neither his agents, the police, nor the armed forces could handle this situation. Kent clicked a button and connected via two-way visual radio. This transmitted to New York City.

"If any emergency ever called for the Assemblers..." He rolled up his white shirt sleeves. "This is it."

*** * ***

Kinnison couldn't sleep. He was bugged. *Why would those jets attack Golden Ring?* He sat up in bed. It was a question he repeated. Golden Ring had saved the U.S., the whole world, many times over, and now the Air Force was shooting at a friend and ally. *What happened while I was gone?*

After kicking off his covers, Kinnison paced the apartment. He noted the time and snapped on a radio. Five minutes of the hourly news broadcast headlines told him nothing. He clicked it off.

The conference with the Galactic Guard had decreed there was no conflict in Kinnison joining the Superior Squadron. In fact, they wanted him to keep watch over its super beings. But this troubling incident wasn't super beings imposing their will on humans. And it was bigger than just an attack on Golden Ring. Swirling thoughts convinced Kinnison to consult the squadron.

Maybe the military turned against us while I was away. I better call them right now."

CHAPTER 2

The Assemblers waited in the gym, just off Marksman's test-shooting room. Roger Stephens, resembling a blond Burt Lancaster, entered. That is, if Lancaster had worn Old Glory on his leotards in his acrobat days. Stephens pulled a tight blue leathery hood over his head. It left his ears and prominent jaw exposed. He hefted a blue and white circular shield, suggestive of a Royal Air Force roundel. It bore a ring of stars around an American eagle. Sergeant stripes were emblazoned above the eyeholes on the mask.

Why am I doing this? I was through with helping teams after the Invasion Squad. Now that I'm out of the ice, I should be living it up.

When he strode fully into the gym, he was again Sergeant-at-Arms. He had the easy grace and build of a triathlete. The colors of Sergeant-at-Arms' costume were like beacons of light, to be noticed. He zipped up a short sleeve blue shirtjac festooned with stars. Each star was a tiny piece of chain mail. The U.S. had but forty-eight states when Sergeant-at-Arms was subsumed in a glacier. He had not yet gotten around to adding two more.

The red and white sergeant stripes on the design of the belly band around his torso added protection. His trunks, gauntlets, and leather buccaneer boots were red. Those boots unfolded to thigh-high waders. The leather gauntlets were good for catching flying shields.

A veritable living flag, Sergeant-at-Arms was a super American, a super patriot, and a super athlete. To hear Marksman tell it, he was also a super headache. This was

Sergeant-at-Arms' first time training new members.

"Sarge's Kooky Quartet," he muttered, bristling at what J. Jacob Jackson had dubbed this new line-up in his rag. Jackson supported superheroes when he was a war correspondent.

This was no different when he led the Invasion Squad back then. It'd been a long time since he had thought about them. Things had changed. Reformed baddie, Galloping Gazelle, was a carbon copy of Invasion Squad's speedster, Turbo Man. Sub-Merger was not at war with the Axis, but the whole surface world. There was a new Flaming Youth. He was a human with the same fiery abilities as his namesake android precursor.

"Assemblers," Sergeant-at-Arms barked.

Figures in green, red, purple and blue costumes snapped to. They hadn't heard him walk in because his boots were gum soled, and a padded sheath cushioned a commando knife secreted into one boot.

"The object of this exercise: scoring points. A point against any Assembler counts. You either concede or dispute." Sergeant-at-Arms moved to the center of the room. "Disputes will be given consideration and a decision made."

"By Penniman?" Marksman asked from the far end. He pulled a hood of his own over his fair hair, and hence his resemblance to Anthony Quinn ended. "Is the butler the judge?"

"By me," Sergeant-at-Arms said. "Penniman's busy. You *do* get fed around here."

"But you're in the exercise. How can you referee, too?"

Marksman, otherwise known as Quentin Baron, once tried to kill Man Machine. Reformed, he was under Sergeant-at-Arms' parole. The number of inmates Baron pummeled, trying to intimidate him, inspired the authorities to realize his talent was being wasted in the slammer.

Disobedience here meant a return to prison.

"Beat your gums, Baron," Sergeant-at-Arms roared. "You should be thinking about how you're going to score points."

Clad in a blue and purple costume from his circus-attraction days as a trick-shot bowman, Marksman sported buccaneer boots with blocky heels. He'd be keen to brag they harkened back to a time when the Persian cavalry sought stability in archery when dismounted. Pouched along his quiver strap were specialized arrowheads. He sighted through the big purple M-shaped blinder on his hood that blocked distractions. Marksman must have been proud of how archery had developed his arms. He went sleeveless and wore metallic wristbands. Marksman could block blows with them or yank them off to throw as weapons. He was accurate with those, too.

"Then whatcha waiting for, Sarge?"

Assemblers scattered.

A green streak zipped by. "When Sarge uses your surname, you're in trouble."

Attempting to earn the first point, Sergeant-at-Arms heaved the shield. At the last second, he shifted its course from Marksman toward that green blur. It moved at incredible speed, bearing down on him, and struck the shield. It wobbled but continued on, ricocheting off the walls.

"Ha," Marksman shouted. "You missed."

The blur skidded to a halt. It solidified into a man. Galloping Gazelle's lean form was clad in green tights. They were meant for camouflage in the Eastern European forests he'd ranged in before Solenoid found him. Galloping Gazelle was lanky, but his legs were muscular. Two longish tendrils of hair, prematurely gray, swept upward.

A white lightning bolt zigzagged diagonally from his right shoulder to left hip. This ingenious strap kept his costume securely in place while hitting high speeds. It wouldn't do to tuck in a shirt while running.

"You missed me too, Sarge." The speedster smirked. "We should get a Doom Room, like the Tomorrow Men. Think of it...flame throwers, live ammo. A real challenge. Not dodging slow moving medieval weapons." He ran off in a blur.

"Why are they Tomorrow *Men* if they have Astro *Lass*?" Sergeant-at-Arms asked someone already gone.

"You're showing your age, pops," Galloping Gazelle said, suddenly coming from the other direction. "These days, girls can do everything a man can."

"Girls, my cousin?" an auburn-haired beauty called. "Or women?" She tossed one of her unique hexes at the shield. It hit the floor like a tossed hubcap.

Perhaps joining the Assemblers would make up for the harm we've done. "This rose has thorns." Red Rose's hexes made things go wrong. How wrong, even she did not know. She was resplendent in her maroon wimple with a cape and costume resembling a one-piece bathing suit. This was worn over a red body stocking, which gave her freedom of movement. Red Rose accessorized with corresponding leather boots and gloves all the way up her arms. She meant to contrast her cousin. The wimple focused her vision, the gloves focused her hex power. She was Galloping Gazelle's cousin and also a former criminal. They were part of Solenoid's League of Mutated Humans working at world domination.

Red Rose gestured with her fingers toward Marksman, but Galloping Gazelle was already heading that way.

Marksman launched an arrow. He meant it as a distraction. As all eyes shifted, he quickly shot another.

Red Rose cast another hex.

The arrow went tail over tip, as did Marksman. Arrows cascaded from his quiver: sonic scream, smoke, flare, acid, electronic bug, tear gas, suction tip, cable, putty, shock, net, rocket and explosive tips flew loose. Frantically, he tried grabbing them all. So much for a distraction.

Sergeant-at-Arms shouted, "Let's see how you do without arrows."

"Hell," Marksman said.

The patriot admonished him. "There's a lady present."

"Luckily my trinitrotoluene isn't armed."

"Trinitrotoluene?" A giant bee appeared, seemingly from nowhere. His bass voice had surprised his teammates, as he'd grown monstrous from the insect speck of his former self.

"Talk about packing heat that stings," Galloping Gazelle said. "What happened to you, King Bee?"

"The name is Kingsize," he boomed in response.

His new tights were light blue and yellow, no longer dark blue and red that matched his miniscule crimefighting partner. He looked more like a yellow jacket than a bee. Here was where he had planned to debut his new look, new name, and new power. "This exercise calls for extreme height."

Galloping Gazelle, clear of arrows, shields and hexes, zipped to Sergeant-at-Arms.

Without his shield, he covered up.

Galloping Gazelle's super-fast hand strikes weren't very effective. Sergeant-at-Arms was too sturdy for punches from a welter weight, however fast.

Sergeant-at-Arms remembered the speedster always corkscrewed clockwise during an attack. To counter, he swung his right fist in a low backhand, knowing the speedster would leap over it.

Galloping Gazelle fell for the feint.

Sergeant-at-Arms' left fist caught him on the jaw and knocked him to the floor.

"Point," Sergeant-at-Arms declared.

Though momentarily bewildered, the speedster recovered quickly. "Concede." He executed a kick-up to his feet.

The shield leapt from the floor and careened to its owner who flung it into Marksman, a surprise, as he'd been preoccupied gathering arrows.

"Point," Sergeant-at-Arms barked.

"Concede." Marksman grumbled, steamed for having lost a point.

The shield banked hard left and soared home, thanks to the electro-magnet sewn into Sergeant-at-Arms' gauntlet. Catching it behind his back, he flung it around and released it in the same motion toward Kingsize.

Kingsize dodged it and flipped Red Rose's cape over her head before she could hex again.

"Point," his thunderous voice called.

"Ooh, concede." Red Rose's muffled voice huffed from under the cape.

Galloping Gazelle shouted, "Good thing you did not lay a hand on my cousin, giant."

Kingsize laughed a belly laugh.

The speedster snatched an arrow from the floor, and zipped back toward the archer. "Looking for this?" He tossed it like a javelin.

Marksman hoped Galloping Gazelle realized this was an exercise, not Maim Your Teammate competition. He deflected the arrow off a wristband, caught it in his opposite hand, spun and flung it at Sergeant-at-Arms. The shield came out of nowhere and deflected the arrow.

Galloping Gazelle decided to tag Sergeant-at-Arms while he was distracted. Finally, fair game. Eyes must remain wide open in a fight, after all. Then he'd go back for the lumbering giant bee and score again.

However, Kingsize hadn't been idle. The giant needed only one bound to reach Sergeant-at-Arms. He was poised to slam his converging compatriots together, however, Galloping Gazelle was too fast for his boarding house reach. Missed.

Poking out from under her cape, Red Rose asked, "Where's Janice?"

Not to miss a cue, the tiny superheroine made herself known. She flew on translucent-veined wings from high up in the room, directly toward Kingsize's face. She was beauteous and fashionable in her form-fitting red and yellow costume. Her brown flip was unhindered these days, no longer wearing the black scuba-like headpiece. No disguise was needed. The world knew she was garment heiress Janice Van Pelt. Still, an insect wing design on her jersey front, close to her throat, made her code name obvious.

"There are *two* ladies present," she called. "Have you forgotten the Hornette?"

Red Rose hexed again. Caught, Hornette reverted to normal size. In that state, her wings retracted. Robbed of those, the girl fell. Kingsize reached for her. As he tried, Hornette responded. She shot a volley of needles from her wrist into a chest that couldn't be missed.

"You think that hurts?" Kingsize plucked them off, knowing an application of hydrogen peroxide loomed.

"Bang, bang, you're dead," she quipped. "Suppose they're poison. Point."

"Concede, damn it," Kingsize cursed.

"Language," Sarge reminded the combatants, less gently this time.

The girl shrunk again. But her wings had not sprouted. "Sarge taught me..."

Red Rose enclosed the doll-size heroine in a gloved hand. "How to escape a firm grip? Point?"

"Concede," Hornette said.

Bzzrmmm, rang out from the next room.

Kingsize yelled, "The video transceiver. That's Rock Kent's call signal."

"I know what it is, you big lug." Sergeant-at-Arms caught his shield. With a fluid motion he slung it on his back by the straps.

"Yeah, you're not completely baffled by the modern world." Marksman taunted him.

"Germany had picture service to phone booths in post offices in the '30s," Sergeant-at-Arms said. "Let's knock off."

The Assemblers regrouped in the meeting room. They settled into designated chairs around a table, facing the screen. Johnny Ferro, ever the jokester, had arranged craftsmen to customize chairs for Hornette and King Bee. They were tiny. Undaunted, Kingsize shrank not much bigger than wrestler Géant Ferré and stood.

Colonel Kent's voice came from a speaker below the screen. "Hey, troops. It's your one-eyed, real-world Charles Vine."

"Charles Vine?" Sergeant-at-Arms shot back.

"You know. Vine, Charles Vine. The British secret agent Amos Klein dreamed up."

"Oh, him. I read the review of *Per Fine Ounce* in *NewsView*," Sergeant-at-Arms added. "Seemed tame compared to what I've seen. And stealing gold bars? Preposterous."

"I got something for you, if interested. It has me baffled. Maybe you want to take a crack at it."

Kent wondered why Sarge bothered with that costume. It made sense to be a personification of the United States during the war; a vengeful Uncle Sam. But not now. Who needed it? Sergeant-at-Arms could be a fine undercover operator. Ditch the shield and requisition him a nice NF300 Needle Gun from the armory. Sergeant-at-Arms had been a soldier and knew guns. Now he was a peaceful warrior. Kent sighed. Fists over bullets, a shield over guns.

"Just a minute, Colonel," Sergeant-at-Arms bellowed. "Okay, people...post mortem." He held that constant drilling was the key to their success as a team. Whatever this baffling thing Kent had in mind might be a good way to test their mettle. But first, Sergeant-at-Arms had a review.

"Assemblers, what did we learn? I'll tell you. Red Rose, shorten that cape. The current length is a liability."

"I shall get out my sewing kit immediately, chief. I've always wanted a mini."

"No capes." Hornette joked.

Sergeant-at-Arms shot the girl a look that reddened her the hue of her costume. "Marksman, come back with a lid for that quiver or don't come back at all. Kingsize, you have homework. Practice your ability to shrink *and* grow."

"Geez, Sarge, you're right. Now with two powers, I should use both." Inwardly, Kingsize wondered why he pursued this line of work. He just wanted to be a good bio-chemist. But now that he discovered the secret of shrinking and growing, he had to put it to good use. Lab assistant Bill Fawcett cracked the problem of being stuck at ten feet. He remembered how Fawcett bolstered his ego by pointing out he was a genius scientist, knew judo, a debutante was his steady girl and had not one, but two, super powers. Kingsize was glad he hired the youth from Harlem.

"Correct. Even hexed, Hornette distracted you," their leader said.

The girl stuck her tongue out playfully at her boyfriend. "He was too big a target to ignore."

"Hornette gets a bonus for fast thinking," Sergeant-at-Arms added. "However, never take your eye off an opponent. You scored over Kingsize, yet Red Rose could easily have crushed you as caught you."

"My goodness." Red Rose blushed. "I'd never do anything so brutal."

"A life may depend on it," Sergeant-at-Arms snapped. "Your own. Though I doubt we'll ever encounter anyone as small as Hornette."

"Not being seen is the point," Kingsize interjected.

"Somebody might come up with the same—"

"Quiet," the leader barked. "Gazelle. You're fast going forward. Work on backwards. And never let up on an attack. You almost had me. Use combination blows."

"If this is a bad time..." Kent lit a Cuban cigar he was unauthorized to possess, with a lighter that had several functions. "I can wait."

"I'm almost done. You know how training is." Sergeant-at-Arms alluded to Kent's legendary Ranger Unit from the war. He turned to his team. "You should be embarrassed. You call yourselves Assemblers? You flubbed this simulation. The Red Skeleton would have killed you."

Galloping Gazelle knew the Red Skeleton was no longer a menace after Solenoid had beaten the Nazi to death without using his magnetic powers. It was then, he learned, Solenoid was a Jewish Holocaust survivor.

Sergeant-at Arms tapped his finger on the table. "Never. Give. Them. An. Opening. Rock, go ahead."

Kent touched his cough button, grumbling, "On that bright note."

"We didn't catch that," Sergeant-at-Arms shot. Maybe he did.

"I said, take a look at this," Kent fibbed, running the footage. He narrated what was happening in it. Momentarily, silence reigned.

Marksman asked, "How do we know that isn't doctored like they do at Graphic Films out in L.A.?"

"No way," Kent said. "John Bakewell has been with the command since the Korean War. He rose through the ranks from engineer, in fact."

"Know him?"

Sergeant-at-Arms was well aware of the extent of Soviet deviltry. After being thawed out, he was shocked the U.S.'s one-time ally was now the enemy. It made his red white and blue blood boil.

"Not personally, but Fifth Air Force Lieutenant General Samuel Anderson vouched for him," Kent said. "He verified Bakewell would never do such a thing. A hoax was the first thing I thought of."

"So, he's a loyal American and not in the employ of the Reds," Sergeant-at-Arms said. "Okay, it must be real. Nothing that good can be faked."

"You spent decades in an iceberg." Galloping Gazelle snorted, swooshing closer to the screen. "Movie magic's come a long way since the silents. Loathe to admit it, Marksman may be onto something."

"I didn't see very many talkies, youngster," the sergeant put in. "I was *Over There* doing my bit."

Galloping Gazelle was quick to mock his elders. He imagined his wit matched his physical speed. But Sergeant-at-Arms' response cut him to the quick.

"Keep it up, kid," Marksman growled out. "You'll be forever dodging Sarge's shield. You're fast, but sooner or later, it'll getcha."

"Anyway," Kent said. "Air Force computer-whiz Daniel Lynch ran it through the IBM 360."

"And?" Sergeant-at-Arms didn't hold with thinking-machines that filled the rooms.

"No dice," Kent grumbled. "Maybe we'll have better luck with the new Special MAC."

"You're the expert on shrinking, Dr. Pymer. Could he have shrunk?" Sergeant-at-Arms asked, using Kingsize's real name. "How about it?"

"That doesn't look like any shrinking I've ever seen. What do *you* think, Janice?"

"I agree," Hornette chimed in. "It's like he slipped into a...gap."

"A hole in space," Kingsize said. "An Einstein-Rosen Bridge. Is it possible?"

Marksman huffed. "The scientist is asking *us*?"

"Biochemistry is my field," Kingsize said. "Space

isn't. I ever ask you about, oh, knives?"

"I can sure juggle 'em," Marksman boasted. "Learned it in the circus."

"Let's stay focused," Sergeant-at-Arms ordered, hand up. "Týr says there are other realms."

"That nifty gold outfit doesn't look anything like what Týr's bunch wears," Marksman said.

"It looks painfully tight," Hornette said.

Red Rose floated, "If he's from another realm, maybe he was spooked by the planes and made a hasty retreat."

"Though it pains me to say this, I agree with our inept bowman. The Aesir sport animal skins, leather, fur." Galloping Gazelle wrinkled his nose as if he could smell them.

"What if the Behemoth disappeared just as that gold man did?" Hornette asked. "We, at least, kept him in check. Think what havoc he could cause in another realm."

The Behemoth was, indeed, a menace without the Assemblers to reign him in. Kingsize said, "This is strictly a volunteer organization. If he wanted to leave, we couldn't stop him."

"Nuclear physicist Robert Bannion is missing, too. I trust you've read the reports I distributed," Sergeant-at-Arms added.

Heads nodded but Marksman didn't agree. "The last report I got said that cheap crook Shishka Bob found an enchanted sword and started calling himself Ebony Knight."

"It's old news, Marksman," Sergeant-at-Arms jumped in. "You're behind on notes." He pointed with his impressive chin. "Maybe the Soviets have Bannion. Or maybe he slipped through something like that hole."

"Matter of fact, I checked through diplomatic channels," Kent said. "The Soviets deny having Bannion."

"They *would*."

"Our official team physician is missing, too," Red

Rose said. "Nobody has seen Dr. Sigmundson in weeks. And what about our benefactor, Johnny Ferro?"

"Never mind that," Galloping Gazelle blurted out. "I have an idea."

"It must be lonely," Marksman said.

Sergeant-at-Arms scowled. "Do I have to separate you two?"

"Colonel, run that again," the speedster requested, zooming up and tapping the screen. "Enlarged."

"We tried that, kid."

"I insist."

Kent grunted, took a second, pressed some buttons off screen and complied.

Watching, Galloping Gazelle hemmed and hawed. "Yes."

"What is it, Pyotr?" his cousin asked, addressing him by his civilian name. This pair, booked by the police, had no secret identity to hide.

"Again."

"What are you seeing, mister?" Sergeant-at-Arms demanded.

"This fellow shows no indication he was to be exiting."

The others didn't see it.

"Come *on*, people. Who is the fast one here? Trust me. My eyes move faster than yours. Colonel, again for these slowpokes."

"Fast?" Marksman reached behind to his quiver and shot an arrow at Galloping Gazelle.

The speedy mutation easily plucked the arrow from the air, careful not to touch the tip, and grinned. "Better luck next time."

Sergeant-at-Arms scoffed. "All right, Marksman, we got something useful out of your horsing around."

"We did?"

"You can't hit a moving target. Now you have

~23~

homework, too."

"Sheesh. I thought training was over for today."

"Training is never over. If you don't like it, fill out a T.S. Slip and send it to the chaplain."

"Look, *I* see that man is quite surprised," Galloping Gazelle pressed. "This *is* some kind of interdimensional...I don't know...hole. The black of space is blacker right where he disappeared."

Hornette gasped. "So I was right."

"The Behemoth *must* have gone through something like that," Red Rose said. "The question is...where?"

"Well, this one, if I didn't mention it," Kent said, "is over Rutland, Vermont. Any significance?"

"None that I know of." Sergeant-at-Arms looked over his team. None of them seemed to have heard of the place.

"How would the Behemoth get up there, sweetheart?" Marksman was the one man Galloping Gazelle never bristled at over familiarity with his cousin. They were genuine friends. Of course, he would never allow her to get any more familiar with a mere human. Certainly not an assassin with trick arrows. "Behemoth can leap with the best of them. But he can't fly."

"If there's one up there, there could be one down here," Sergeant-at-Arms suggested. "Is that guy opening holes in space and kidnapping extraordinary individuals?"

"Can we patch through to your pals?" Kent asked. "See what they think."

"We can transmit Morse code to Man Machine, sure." Sergeant-at-Arms knew Man Machine insisted on that. "But Týr comes and goes as he pleases. There's no easy way to contact him."

"Heh." Kent grinned. "You don't really think that hippie is a god, do you?"

"If Týr's delusional..." Hornette said, "it's some delusion. Ever get a good look at him? Even his shoulders have shoulders. I'm waiting to see him in a crewcut and an

Ivy League suit like Dr. Sigmundson wears."

"That delusion is going to be needed," Sergeant-at-Arms said. "We've got an invader. And if he travels by glowing force field, he's not of this universe."

Realization broke on the face of Kingsize. He looked over at Hornette. She nodded. They knew someone who claimed to be from another universe. At the time, they didn't believe it.

When Kent broke the connection and the other Assemblers had gone, the girl spoke up. "Sarge, we know something about this guy."

CHAPTER 3

On his Earth, struggling to stay awake after a fitful sleep, Hal Kinnison flicked on the two-way console system. His was secreted inside the portable Philco television set in his bedroom. AT&T's Bell Labs introduced the Picturephone two years ago. Deemed too expensive for use in ordinary homes, millionaire Louis Wemyss arranged sets for the Superior Squadron. This maintained confidential communication between them. Clicking to the unassigned channel 3, he'd make visual contact with the member on monitor duty. Mindful of Ratman's annoying habit of tapping his mask if Squadron members called while in civilian identity, Kinnison donned his visor.

If Kinnison's brown mop was unruly by the square world's standards, Aquamarine's cut was downright severe. He first saw the back of Aquamarine's blond hair. Befitting his name, he wore a buzz-cut inspired by America's leathernecks. Aquamarine contended it dried fast. The cut guaranteed no drag in the water. That was in line with Olympic swimmers, whose build he shared. In Atlantica, he was king. To the surface world, he was a superhero using oceanic breeding to keep the world safe.

Aquamarine sat on fire-watch at the team's modernistically outfitted headquarters. Resplendent in streamlined tights that matched his name, the outfit was perfect for his element. He had long abandoned the bright orange shirt that was a beacon when he meant to cloak himself in the ocean's murk. With fins at his calves and webbed gloves, Aquamarine could slice through water unimpeded.

His costume, at least, was not for show. Putting up with endless jokes about it being drip dry, he kept it spotless. In turn, it kept him warm and it dried quickly. The colors made him unobtrusive in his element. Aquamarine was in the communication center. Visible behind him were empty chairs circling a round table. There was soft recessed lighting. Steps, with floor-to-ceiling bars instead of a banister, led to a lab, a reference library, and a cushy sofa.

He was in a warehouse on the west side of 34th Street in the borough of Mascouten, in Isola, New Waukee. That state was in the northeast corner of the United States. Like the picture phone system, the team had use of it, thanks to Wemyss. Officially, the warehouse was S.O.L.A.R. Labs. That it was unofficially the headquarters of the Superior Squadron was an open secret. While that information was listed in no telephone directory, members of the squadron were frequently seen coming and going from it.

Nobody outside the team knew the warehouse possessed a tunnel from the river, like London's Post Office Railway. This had a water lock wide enough for Aquamarine's shark-like Airphibian. He had just exited the round-fronted, bubble-topped, two-seater flying boat to begin his shift. It sported a rack of low set shrouded props in the rear that pushed it through water or, with its dihedral folding wings deployed, air. Ratman often used that entrance for his compact submersible Z-boat coming from across the river from Gothic City, New Guernsey. Rumor had it, he took it from a super criminal years ago. Sometimes, Ratman flew over in his Wee Bee jet, piloted by him lying prone atop the fuselage.

On his screen, Aquamarine noticed Kinnison's Galactic Guard uniform carelessly thrown over a chair. *Surface dwellers are slobs.* For centuries they had used the precious oceans as dumpsites. His heritage had granted him a human name, Andrew McCurry. Aquamarine was often too ashamed by humanity to use it.

"Odd," the sea king said after hearing his teammate's story about having passed through some kind of hole surrounded by sparkling lights. "You're *sure* you didn't imagine it? After all, you'd just spent a great deal of time flying through space."

"No, of course not."

"Well, it's just—"

"Since when are you an expert on outer space?"

In turn, Aquamarine thought all that power the ring bearer wielded had gone to his head. "Settle down, would you?" He almost added *land lubber.*

"Are you implying I had space fever?"

"You may *work* for space aliens, but you *aren't* a space alien. An Earthman alone in space might start seeing things that aren't there."

"This wasn't my first space rodeo. Look, my ring protects me automatically, right?"

"Right." Aquamarine pondered about intergalactic peacekeepers. His hands were full with Earth's oceans. *How do they manage to keep peace in outer space?*

"My ring deposited me safely at home, meaning I had to have been in real danger." Kinnison held up a cylindrical object, a companion to his ring. "In fact, that ran her out. I'm charging up now or I'd be there in person."

"We might ask the princess to look into this." Aquamarine meant Amazon Woman. She was Princess Paragon among her people.

"Good idea. Her contacts in the Air Force can confirm this."

"Maybe I'd better call the whole team." Aquamarine punched a button on the console before him, imagining it was Kinnison's nose. Actually, Aquamarine would never try punching Golden Ring, as he would be automatically protected.

A signal went out to all squadron members.

***

After a rendezvous, the ancient Norse god Týr was pleased to be riding in the Assemblers' Fairey Rotodyne. He occupied the copilot seat with Man Machine. Their arachnid guest adhered to the ceiling, instructed to watch. If Tarantula-Man was admitted into the Assemblers, he would learn to pilot.

Man Machine sat at the controls. "Next stop, the American Southwest."

Enjoying what mortals dubbed air conditioning, the god offered an opinion. "Man Machine, yon ship of the air I doth decree a new S*kithblathnir*."

"We'll be in it for hours. Might as well be comfortable." Although a purifier permitted removal of carbon dioxide from his exhaled air, Man Machine engaged the synchronizer and opened vents in his armor. "Even if we're doing over four hundred miles an hour."

At such speed, the trip would take some three and a half hours. Had he been solo, Man Machine would have ascended two hundred miles then plummeted. That would be twenty minutes from New York to the west. But corralling the Behemoth was no solo mission.

"Aye, this method be truly relaxing." Týr sighed. "One of thine own Earthly corporations doth say it be the only way to fly."

"For ordinary humans without flying armor or enchanted war clubs," Man Machine said. Týr would not ever comprehend piloting. His method of flying entailed taking up Hval, windmilling his arm, throwing the thing and be pulled along behind it by the leather thong.

The arachnid unobtrusively observed Týr. The tryout Assembler considered the god. Týr was a mass of muscle in a black leather jerkin, festooned with circular armored plates. Its top and bottom halves were divided by a wide brown leather belt. A furry red cloak was bolted into place on his shoulders. Tarantula-Man couldn't guess what animal it came from. Long blond locks flowed. Brown leather bands encircled both wrists. Leather straps wound around Týr's legs to above his knees. Tarantula-Man had no way of knowing Týr's alter ego, the human he shared a body with, left him a note suggesting modern-day leotards and trunks. Going forth to fight modern super menaces in bare legs and a fur-lined kilt would not be effective.

That body, when in possession of Týr, had the abilities of a god. Even the severed hand Týr suffered eons ago was restored. Across those leotard-clad knees rested the gnarled war club of, apparently, petrified whale bone. He wore a Gjermundbu helmet, with metal frames around eyeholes. Metal plates at the back of the helmet covered his neck.

The arachnid realized, if he really was a millennium-old god, someone had taught him the intricacies of modern grooming and bathing. In fact, Týr was getting his cloak dry-cleaned these days. That was another suggestion of his host.

Comfortable, Týr kept his own counsel. When the Assemblers formed, Týr considered himself the leader of his mortal allies, a god fighting for right, leading the best of what the modern world offered. Now a thawed-out super soldier led a matched pair of tiny humans, two mutated humans and an archer as skilled as his friend Robin of Locksley. He wondered if their erstwhile monstrous teammate, the Behemoth, could be caught and brought to heel. The creature had been growing stronger and angrier, but this planet was under Týr's protection.

"Verily, Sergeant-at-Arms commands my team with much wisdom," Týr exclaimed. "For a mere human."

"No *mere* human," Man Machine said. "I'm a mere human inside this playsuit. But Sarge is much more than that."

Field testing the gadgets was good for his fortunes.

But this was serious. And now they'd get their ultimate test. Man Machine had brought Behemoth into the fold, but he'd gone berserk. It was Man Machine's responsibility to stop him.

"Aye," the god said. "Alchemic fluid hath made the good soldier a demi-god."

Tarantula-Man attempted small talk. "Assemblers got big troubles, you think, blondie?"

"Enlighten me again of this costumed performer upon the ceiling." The god complained to Man Machine with an accusing finger. "Masked stranger, it be not wise to presume familiarity. Broadsheets dub thee a varlet."

"Now don't get your *shillelagh* in an uproar—"

"*Shillelagh?* I know not this word."

"The Irish have a competing mythology," Tarantula-Man explained. "If we're going to be teammates, we should get to know each other. Let our hair down. You got enough of it."

"Once again, this is Tarantula-Man." Man Machine sighed. "Possible new Assembler."

The god accepted that introduction. The arachnid presented his gloved hand. Noble manners demanded Týr take it. He gripped high up on Tarantula-Man's forearm. This was just below the elbow. The god didn't squeeze too hard, but he was surprised at the masquerader's unexpected strength.

"I thought you were a Norse, not a Roman, god," Tarantula-Man quipped, chin pointing to their grasped hands.

When Týr looked into the reflective lenses on Tarantula-Man's hood, he saw not himself but the human he shared this body with. "There be no Roman gods, lad. There are but Norse. You do well to remember." Had he wanted, Týr could have turned even the super strong kid's limb into paste. "If thy truly be an ally, do not maketh me crush thee like an annoying insect."

Man Machine turned to interject, "Týr, why don't you scout ahead?"

The god looked between the two covered faces. He saw the masks of tragedy and comedy the Bard of Avon taught him were Sock and Buskin. Týr rose and slid back a door. "Aye. Me thinks 'twould be best."

***

At the Assemblers' intended destination, Bob Bannion counted his blessings. True, he was only tolerating the heat of the desert, but he was alive. And he was human again. For now. Bannion's clothing consisted of second and third-hand garments, but at least they weren't rags. He'd been in rags and would hate being anywhere colder.

"Hopefully, I'm not wandering forty years," Bannion joked to himself. It was gallows humor, to be sure. A different god was considering this modern Cain.

Reverted to his natural form from the rampaging monster called the Behemoth, Bannion had wandered. But now, he felt, maybe the curse was over. Bounding away from the Assemblers was the best idea his gray alter ego ever had. Bannion lived as Behemoth for months in the townhouse, their attack dog. The beast was docile among those capable of handling him. This despite Behemoth's bluster that being the strongest made him the leader. The profusion of superheroes parading through the townhouse unnerved the Behemoth. Like that guy in red and indigo whose grip matched Behemoth's own. In disgust, he had bounded away.

When he woke up, he was as Bannion. Had he hopped a freight train? Maybe. He wandered. A group of hippie kids took him in. Mistaking him for one of their own, a dropout from society. They gave him food, clothing and shelter at Spahn Ranch. In return, they wanted...nothing. Bannion was grateful for their kindness. They lived there rent free, in exchange for doing chores, and helped run a horse-rental business. The horses were instinctively spooked by Bannion. Thus, he avoided them.

As the Assembler gyroplane hovered, those kids screamed with delight. Coming in for a landing, Týr descended beside the plane.

"Týr," they whooped and hollered. "Hey. It's Týr."

Their attempts to catch sight of the Norse god gave Bannion a start. Those kids, of course, wanted to meet the long-haired hero. One snapped shots with a Miranda Sensorex 35mm found among the junk. Bannion had repaired it. This was followed by Man Machine exiting. Accompanying him was Tarantula-Man. Neither rated as many photos as the god did.

"Why are you so eager to meet him?" Bannion asked a kid.

"He's one of us."

"The first hippie," a girl said.

"He's even got that groovy mod symbol on his belt buckle," one more added.

This was, in fact, untrue. It was the t-rune, not the mod arrow. The hippies sounded musical instruments in greeting: guitars, tambourines, harmonicas, bongos and kazoos. When Týr looked them over, Bannion knew he'd stick out like a sore thumb. Something told him this was no social visit. Bannion feared Týr, Man Machine, and Tarantula-Man were here seeking his alter ego. They likely meant to cage him or destroy him.

"I'm sick of being hounded." Bannion gripped his head. The kids surged forth, paying no attention. "I can't control the Behemoth, can't be around these kids. Why don't the Assemblers leave me alone?"

Kids mobbed the god. None of them heard. One had a tray of malted milk. She offered it to Týr.

"What be this libation?"

Another hippie said, "Bob fixed that old mixer for us.

We used Jell-O Instant Pudding in this batch of malted milk."

Týr grasped the large tray.

"Malted mead?" he asked, mishearing an unfamiliar term. "Mine thirst is to be slaked. I be not accustomed to such climes."

Týr eagerly drank the whole pitcher.

"Hey. That was for all of us."

"This be the nectar of the gods," Týr declared. His schooling in modern day manners required he stifle the resulting belch. Still, thirst slaked, he wiped his mouth on a wristband.

"This refreshment imparts wisdom. Who be this *Bob*? Why doth mortals disrespect the noble *Robert* that way? Your Robert the Brùs was the greatest warrior of ancient Alba."

"You talk like you knew him." Tarantula-Man handed back the camera he'd examined after filling a request to snap the god with a kid.

"Verily did I."

"He said we could call him Bob," one kid insisted. "He's real smart."

"I should like to meet friend Bob. Which be he?"

"He's sort of a, er, dropout from the square world," the kid with the camera answered.

"We adopted him."

"Well, I think he's cute," one girl sang.

Bannion abruptly turned away.

Týr picked out the older man among the kids. "Ho, yon Bob?"

Bannion kept walking like he didn't hear. *They got me.* His heart pounded; sweat broke out.

"I mustn't let it...can't change...fight it," Bannion gasped. "Use will power..." His mind raced back to clichés from old movies of his childhood. It was too late. Dr. Jekyll was transforming to Frankenstein's monster. Bannion was about to become the rampaging Behemoth. Within his changing skull, thoughts raged: *Smash them Assemblers. They weren't friends. Just used Behemoth.*

"No. These kids..." Bannion's last bit of civilized thought grated out through clenched teeth. "They'll be killed."

"Ho, there, sirrah," Týr called, pointing with Hval. "What ails thee?"

Bannion shook, grasped at his throat, and breathed heavily...

CHAPTER 4

Kinnison's mind wandered as he waited onscreen. The appearance of Superior Man, decades ago, ushered in an age of costumed heroes not seen since the Invincible Orchid bedeviled Bonaparte. Kinnison got lumped in with the super folks but did not consider himself one. He was a policeman, upholding laws, not a superhero taking the law into his own hands. Kinnison thought it best to go along with being called Golden Ring. He had merely donned a uniform and visor. The latter was taken for a mask, but it was protection. Between the glow of his ring and high-altitude flights, he needed it. Plus, he thought it looked cool. He likened it to a motorcycle cop's sunglasses. To the world, Golden Ring was another masked and costumed superhero. He knew it was a waste of time to correct the world with, "No, I'm Galactic Guardian." Only Beanpole and the Superior Squadron knew he bore an artifact from an alien civilization.

Eagleman was in the same situation. Caught in Professor Noah Merlin's experimental teleportation beam, he was now stranded here. According to Eagleman, humans were a juvenile stage of his race and meant to metamorphosize to adult form. But on Earth, for an unknown reason, his distant cousins did not. Using his race's ability to shapeshift into the semblance of human form, his distinctive military uniform was also taken to be a costume for a superhero. Eagleman accepted the perceived designation about himself, even though he was a soldier from Iukkoth. On this smaller planet, with lesser gravity, ninth metal woven into his outfit allowed him to fly faster and higher than any other winged warrior on his home world.

Eaglette, his wife, didn't mind the misconception. Privately, they didn't know the team felt the couple was pushing it, living under the Earthly surname *Falcone*. Like Kinnison, they agreed it was best not to let the public know aliens existed.

Eagleman, first to arrive, had interrupted his archaeological trip to Tell el-Dab'a. Compared to frigid Iukkoth, Earth was warm. He compensated for his shirtless state by wearing a set of feathery wings. The balance of his costume featured oversaturated red, white, and blue trunks, leotards and boots. His left forearm bore a leather wristband bearing a watch, altimeter and compass. Graphics on his boots suggested bird claws, with actual claws at the heels and tips. They were good for grasping aircraft in flight. In a pinch, they were weapons. Oddly obsessed with ancient Egypt, Eagleman lately replaced his yellow hood with a bird-like helmet he referred to as a *sukhet*.

The winged man, headgear adorned with a crest suggestive of an eagle, could descend slowly or just float. This was thanks to the ninth metal he wore. Usually, Eagleman would swoop in, swinging his customized morning star. The metal ball was the size of a fist and bore rounded knobs. It was attached to a rubberized grip on the handle with a leather strap. "I wouldn't want you to lose your grip on that while flying over the ocean," Aquamarine had once said. "I'd have to dive for it."

Aquamarine's signal reached Fort Superior in the frozen Arctic wastes. No surprise. There had been no response from the apartment Superior Man rented in Mascouten. Superior Man's high-flying, supersonic deeds had fried his personal signal devices often enough. He maintained radios at Fort Superior and at Ken Clarke's apartment. While Superior Man had abandoned his human alter ego, he retained the apartment. A steady stream of books by reclusive author Clarke appeared regularly. Royalty checks went to 2007 Seventh Avenue in Mascouten.

"Good morning." Superior Man appeared on camera and jolted Kinnison back to business.

Aquamarine was not surprised to find Superior Man fully awake and alert. His hair was combed into a spit curl, like a quote. The costume was neat and proper. Even Superior Man's indigo cape looked freshly pressed. Aquamarine wondered how he could press an outfit that was impervious. It didn't register fully on the picture-phone, but in person Superior Man was tall, trim and well built.

Aquamarine *was* surprised to see Amazon Woman on the same console. Yet, he understood how those two super beings might be attracted to each other. Especially now that Superior Man's dalliance with that harridan reporter was well and truly over.

Amazon Woman, too, had abandoned her human guise as an ordinary Air Force secretary. No more cat's eye glasses and a dark wig over ash-blond hair. *That Amazon is a fine woman.* He would have liked seeing her outside the team meetings. Aquamarine wondered if it was time the king of the sea had a queen. Amazon Woman took a seat in a most lady-like fashion. Long shapely legs were encased in blue stockings, coming to darker blue leather boots as she crossed them.

Aquamarine tried not to linger on the girl. The tightly zipped up short red shift with blue sleeves, had stars spangled along it. A pair of wings were sewn to her left side. Amazon Woman wielded a mysterious whip, possessed extraordinary strength, and was an expert pilot of her plane. The Silver Machine, in fact, gleamed in the background.

"Are we looking for the Pandopoulos girl's father

today?" Superior Man asked then yawned and stretched. Despite super abilities, Superior Man required sleep just like any human. He, Jet Man, and Shrinking Man had been up late, dabbling with compression and restoration of costumes.

"That goes on the backburner," Aquamarine said, noting the super-powered alien had picked up those human habits. His own people had evolved to not yawn, lest they got a mouthful of ocean.

"Golden Ring has something."

Aquamarine was momentarily startled as Ratman appeared at his side. He had come to Mascouten in person from neighboring Gothic City. Aquamarine hadn't heard the Ratboat, so he must have driven. All his cars were silent. As usual, Ratman insisted all parties maintain their individual *nom de guerre* and don costumes for these calls. "You never know who might be intercepting this." His repeated reminder echoed in Aquamarine's brain.

Such was unlikely. The Superior Squadron wiped out most crime. The few purse snatchers they had missed were not up to bugging their headquarters. He marveled at Ratman's costume: a full-body covering in gray and black made of silk, rubber-coated to be waterproof. Despite being fireproof, insulated, protective and padded, it allowed for spectacular acrobatics. The cape was bulletproof, as was the rat face symbol on the shirt front, since it was an obvious target.

Ratman wore an equipment belt holding every conceivable gadget in waterproof pouches: explosives, flashlight, smoke capsules, fingerprint equipment, pass keys, tiny oxy-acetylene torch, gas capsules and a miniature camera. A silk line nested within that belt. Ratman's boot soles gripped slick surfaces, supported his ankles and muffled his tread. He'd shod the team in similar, albeit customized, ones. Protective gauntlets allowed him to grab broken glass, barbed wire, hot surfaces and live wires. Eye slits were wide enough for peripheral vision.

In it, Ratman was almost impossible to be seen in the dark. Aquamarine's undersea-evolved vision could spot him, however. Ratman's physical development rivaled his own. A leathery black hood, thin over the ears, left the lower face open. Sometimes the loud, clear statement of, "I'm Ratman," stopped crooks cold.

Shrinking Man arrived next, using a trick Superior Man alerted him to try: travel via phone line. His growing body would emerge from the phone, jolting the handset free. What would the tiny hero do if nobody picked up? But this was the Superior Squadron; somebody always picked up. He wore tights of red and blue with red boots, blue gloves and shirt. An inverted triangle pointed to a hooded blue mask up from his belt. Shrinking Man took a custom-made chair. It was a tiny one.

Jet Man, effortlessly capable of tremendous speeds, ran from Octagon City. For him, that distance from the mid-west city was neither far nor strenuous. When not a purple blur, his hood was apparent. Small aerials within stylized lightning-bolt ear-cups kept him tuned to the squadron, his sidekick, and Octagon City's Metropolitan Police. In his civilian identity, Jet Man was a police scientist. As expected from someone always running, he was trim.

Kinnison finished up the story Aquamarine had already heard.

"Now, Golden Ring, as I recall your ring protects you automatically," Ratman said, akin to being in court prosecuting a case. He was in a good mood. After all, he had a baffling puzzle to ponder. And the golden warrior had remembered his visor for this picture-phone call. "Therefore, you *were* in danger. But the Strategic Air Command knows you. They shouldn't be attacking you."

"That's what baffles me," Kinnison said.

Amazon Woman chimed in. "I checked with the Inter-

Agency Defense Command. There was no report of any such attack."

Superior Man nervously flicked his blue cape.

Ratman noted his teammate was not usually so fidgety. "Might you know something about this?"

Superior Man rose. "I *do* know something. Golden Ring entered a parallel universe."

"Parallel universe? Like what Rick Hunter is researching?" Jet Man looked stunned in wide-eyed disbelief. The scientist in him saw nothing in such things.

"Dr. Hunter is working on time travel," Shrinking Man said. Science was his purview, too. "Eugen Wigner first proposed the existence of parallel universes in 1961. But this is more like James Bardeen's speculations of gateways to other universes."

"So, like an Earth behind the sun we can't detect?" Eagleman guessed.

"No, not behind the sun." Superior Man waved the notion away. "That would still be our universe. Any of us flying in space would see it."

"A door to another universe? It's the stuff of comic books." Jet Man read them as a kid, even took his name from a character in one.

"Maybe they're all giants there," Shrinking Man speculated.

"Everyone is a giant to you." Jet Man chuckled.

Aquamarine asked, "Is it built into a wardrobe?"

"Not a literal door," Superior Man stated.

"Does it orbit a brown dwarf?"

"No, Eagleman. I retained all my powers there." Superior Man clarified for them. "It's got a yellow sun."

"You were there? In one of Alan Guth's pocket universes?" Jet Man scoffed. "He postulated we live in a fragment of the true universe. Maybe people there in that fourth dimension feel entitled to inherit ours."

Amazon Woman touched her chin. "I'm no scientist,

but I can see a universe set at right angles to our own. Yeah, could be possible."

"Some ten years back, a doctoral student at, er, where?" Shrinking Man racked his brain. "I'm blocking this with some writer who said there were tiers to the universe." With a finger snap, he let out, "Princeton, over in New Guernsey. Guy published a dissertation bringing back the old idea of the simultaneous existence of several universes. That's an unproven theory."

"It's not theoretical," Superior Man said. "Another universe exists."

"How would one get there?" Shrinking Man asked. "Those *white holes* don't exist."

"Hugh Everette," Jet Man yelped, turning to Shrinking Man. "I remember now. But the idea of actually traveling to another Earth seems kooky."

"Yeah, that's him," the tiny hero confirmed. "Hugh Everette equals kooky."

Superior Man spoke up. "There *is* a way to traverse them. Two years ago, we had a visitor from another Earth. Someone there crossed into our universe."

"Traveling between universes?" Amazon Woman gasped. "Who could?"

"A man named Doctor De'ath," Superior Man said with a straight face.

A hush fell over the room. This was a lot to absorb and that name didn't comfort them any.

"An evil man. Imagine if Fidel Castro had Alex Lugar's smarts and Ratman's arsenal."

That roused Ratman from what he considered malarkey. "That's a thought I don't like."

"Doctor De'ath?" Aquamarine shuddered.

"He found a way to bridge universes," Superior Man added.

"I see," Aquamarine said, "We're Earth and they're Nibiru."

"Well, I call De'ath's world Earth A—"

"So we're Earth B?" Jet Man was quick to note. "How come *we* aren't Earth A?"

"We're Earth One," Superior Man said. "I came up with Earth One and Earth A to be fair to both."

"Do they orbit Nemesis?" Amazon Woman asked.

"Who lives on Earth A? Our evil doppelgangers?" Eagleman questioned.

"Oh." Amazon Woman's eyes flashed. "I saw something like this on *Galaxy Quest*."

"Inferior versions of ourselves?" Eagleman again.

Amazon Woman: "Perhaps you will encounter female versions of ourselves. The She-perior Squadron, with one guy on the team."

"Maybe it's the Superi-her Squadron. No, that makes no sense." Jet Man blinked. "There couldn't be an Amazon *Man*."

"Did the Axis win the war there?" Aquamarine asked. "I know. Mythological creatures are real there."

"You're close," Superior Man said. "I met their superheroes."

Jet Man floated a new theory. "Will there be an explosion if I shake hands with my anti-matter duplicate there?"

"They're not duplicates of us," Superior Man said. "And they're not anti-matter. The Atoms Family and the Assemblers are two of their teams. They're every bit our equal. In fact, they inspired me to organize this team."

"Could they have picked worse names?" Aquamarine groaned. "Those names sure aren't equal to *Superior Squadron*."

"Please..." Superior Man implored, palms down. "This is no joking matter. De'ath was attempting to travel through time to kill the Atoms Family."

"Time travel? Is it a different year there?" Jet Man asked.

"Same year," Superior Man assured him. "Somehow, S.O.L.A.R. pulled him here when his machine engaged."

"Sort of like the way Noah Merlin's device pulled *me* here," Eagleman stated like it was a matter of fact. "I see that now. Whereas I originated farther out in *this* solar system, S.O.L.A.R. hooked someone from a whole different universe."

"I guess De'ath didn't know time travel is impossible." Jet Man frowned. "But as he transversed out of his universe, he had to come out *somewhere*. That somewhere was here. S.O.L.A.R. had feelers out that snared him."

"Now you're getting it," Superior Man said with an agreeing nod. "I knew right then I had to organize the heroes of our world, headquarter S.O.L.A.R. with us, and ask the Hexagon to arrange military sentries for us."

Ratman said, "All the superheroes joined together, sharing technology, S.O.L.A.R. housed here, this setup...all conjured by you. You didn't tell us it was because there was another universe."

Superior Man scowled. "The existence of it has to be kept quiet."

"Even from us?" Ratman asked. "Your teammates?"

"Maybe I should start at the beginning."

Ratman leaned forward. "I think you should."

CHAPTER 5

W hile the Superior Squadron members were having discussions on Earth One, events were happening on Earth A beyond the rift.

"Týr," Man Machine called. "Forget Bob. He doesn't know anything about the Behemoth."

"He doth not?" Týr frowned.

"No. Something important came over the radio."

"Oh?" The god's interest piqued.

Sensing what they sought, he hastily blessed the hippies with his warclub and returned to the aircraft. Man Machine noted he seemed loopy. The kids snickered at that.

A sweaty Bannion reappeared. Somehow, he had held the Behemoth in check. Some shred of humanity in the Behemoth knew innocents would be harmed if he manifested. Watching the aircraft take off, Bannion was relieved about no longer being the object of a hunt. He regained his composure. "What's so funny?"

"Týr. He's gonna take a trip like he never took before."

Bannion gasped. "You didn't."

"Yep. That drink was spiked with enough L.S.D. for the whole gang. He wasn't supposed to drink the whole pitcher."

***

Superior Man knew some details of that day two years ago on Earth A. What he knew had been faithfully relayed to his peers. But there were parts he missed.

Doctor Vladimir De'ath's hatred of the Atoms Family inspired him to develop his Time Oscillator. After months of trial and error, he succeeded. His gleaming full faceplate, partially obscured by an olive-green hood and jerkin, didn't reflect it, but De'ath was filled with glee. What better revenge against the four than going back in time?

Kill them before their powers manifest.

Spherical, the controls and the seating took up all the space. Three small wheels allowed movement. Stepping into the glass-enclosed sphere, Dr. De'ath sat in the pilot seat. He pulled his cloak around himself, grasped the arm rests, lodged his feet into a board on the floor, and with an armored finger that matched the rest of his personal protection, he engaged the controls.

"How did Reide put it before he ruined my face?" De'ath remembered. "Oh, yes: *Here goes nothing.*"

Curved beams began to whirl. There was a flash accompanied by a crackle of energy. With joy, De'ath saw the room housing his machine expand, then fade. In its place, another place materialized around him. He was sitting on a platform, sans the Time Oscillator. A group of men in white lab coats were focused on him in utter surprise. He rose, whipping his cape about. This joy quickly faded. With no Time Oscillator, how would he return to his own time?

One man in a lab coat spoke up. "Hey. What are you doing here? How did you *get* here?"

"Where is my Time Oscillator?" De'ath countered. "How could I travel here without it?"

De'ath read DR. RICK HUNTER on the man's name tag.

Hunter detected something regal about this man. "Who are you?"

"I am De'ath. Dr. Vladimir von De'ath. I have traveled through time itself."

"Time? You traveled through *time?*"

"Yes, my good man. Tell me, what year is this? It is 1961, I'd wager."

"It's 1966. Er, what year should it be?"

"But you are mistaken."

"Me? You're the one who doesn't know what year it is."

"Then I must have traversed space, not time. It was 1966 where I came from."

"Look, Mr. De'ath, maybe our experiment picked up your—"

"*Doctor.*" He jabbed a metallic pointer finger. "Remember that. Where am I? What is this place?"

"Doctor De'ath," Hunter said, humoring him. "This is S.O.L.A.R. Labs in Isola, New Waukee, in the United States."

"There is no place with that name in the whole of the United States of America. I attended Triborough University there." De'ath sounded emphatic. "I am not unfamiliar with it."

"Then you get your degree in mad science refunded," Hunter said. "*I* know what city I'm in."

De'ath stepped off the platform. He looked over their devices. Then he found a window and peered through. Outside was a beehive of activity.

"This is New York," De'ath bellowed, turning back to the scientists.

"New York? That's just a hick town across the river in New Guernsey," Hunter said, head nodding west. "Why were you so eager to be in, ah, 1961?"

"Well, you see, I am a great hero in *my* 1966." De'ath had to improvise. "I, er, was looking for the Atoms Family. Allies of mine. Perhaps you have heard of them?"

The gathered scientists exchanged looks reserved for a Flat-Earther. Hunter nodded to his co-workers, telegraphing: this one thinks he had the secret of teleportation, and the knowledge drove him insane.

"I must find them," De'ath said, clasping Hunter by his shoulders, suddenly friendly. "Surely, you know them. They have incredible powers. One stretches like plastic, another is a living flame, still another is solid rock. The girl is intangible."

"Buddy, I think *you* might be intangible..."

De'ath stood stock still. He seemed to be composing himself, as if holding his tongue. "They've lately started wearing blue action suits."

The scientist said, "Matching costumes? You mean the Challengers of the Fantastic."

"No, no, no. The Atoms Family. The letter *A* is upon them, enclosed by an atomic whirl." De'ath's finger traced an *A* on Hunter's chest. "They occupy six floors in the famed Leland Building. Their leader is a great, hmm, passable scientist."

"There's no Leland Building in this burg. But Superior Man has incredible powers and a blue costume. Well, indigo and red. He's a great hero."

"Oh? A hero? I should like to meet this Superior Man." Dr. De'ath luxuriated in each syllable of the name.

"I don't know how to reach him," Hunter said.

Another scientist offered a solution. "What about that reporter? He always manages to contact Superior Man."

De'ath was next to a phone. He thrust the handset to Hunter. "Call him."

With that, a call was placed to *The Daily Globe*. Hunter asked for Ken Clarke. He confirmed having a knack for finding Superior Man. Hunter had a big story. The biggest.

Hunter told Clarke, "A man from...somewhere else is in our lab. He wants you to bring Superior Man here."

There was an excited buzz over the wire.

He lowered his voice. "Well, it could be nothing. Or it might give you a funny article."

Hunter laid down the receiver. "Clarke can't make it.

He has a deadline to meet."

"Blast," De'ath cursed.

"But he'll contact Superior Man and send him over."

"Superior Man. Superior Man." De'ath enjoyed the sound of that name. He strode around the lab, excited he was about to meet Superior Man.

***

At the offices of *The Daily Globe*, Ken Clarke hung up the phone and rose. He was deep in thought. Then he locked his office door. He pulled off horn-rimmed eyeglasses. They went into a bin marked *SPARES*, which held no spares. He removed his shoes and clothing. Doing so revealed a costume of red tights, with indigo trunks and boots. The red shirt presented a crest, symbol of protection among his people. For he was not of Earth, but a native of the destroyed planet Hercólubus. He unfurled an indigo cape. Clarke looked at the wall, as if he could see through it like a window. In fact, he could.

"Lots of bystanders." He shrugged. "Oh, well."

The utility room down the hall had a window he could use. Going through the office door, it wasn't Ken Clarke who emerged. Someone else had taken his place. He hurried down the hall but turned, hearing steps behind him before a voice rang out.

"Superior Man? What are you doing here?"

"Well, well, if it isn't Timmy Owens." Superior Man turned and greeted the young man. He was a cub reporter there. A good kid, Owens had latched onto Superior Man like he was a ticket to fame. Fame hadn't materialized. Everyone was more interested in his pal, Superior Man. "What are you doing here?"

"I work here." Owens smiled, with an outstretched hand. "Can I help you with something?"

"I was looking for Ken Clarke." Superior Man lied

while accepting the offered handshake. Catching sight of the signal watch he had once given Owens, Superior Man had a hunch. "I've got an exclusive for him."

"Gee, Superior Man." Owens nodded to the office. "I'm sure Mr. Clarke is in there. I was just yapping with him over the intercom."

"I knocked. No answer. I tried the door. It was locked."

"Couldn't you X-ray it?" Owens suggested.

"That I never use on friends. And Clarke's a close friend. I couldn't help my hearing, though. It sounded like his office was empty. Try knocking. Maybe I tapped too lightly. You know, I tend to overcompensate for my super strength."

As the watch peeked out of Owens' cuff, Superior Man surreptitiously turned his heat vision onto it and burned out the signal mechanism. He'd lately realized there were limits to his being at Owens' beck and call.

"Must be on lunch," Owens said. "You know us reporters have crazy schedules. Can I give him a message, anything like that?"

"No. I'll see him another time." Superior Man jerked a thumb over his shoulder. "Anybody mind if I left through that window?"

"Not if you open it first." Owens smiled, remembering he'd seen Superior Man smash through many windows.

"Great. See you later, Timmy."

Superior Man unlatched the window, pulled it up, stepped onto the sill and perched like a bird. Stepping to the ledge, he waved to Owens and leapt. Arms went out in the manner of an airplane.

Below, super hearing picked up a startled cry. "It's Superior Man."

"Gee, what a guy." A beaming Owens shut the window. He made a note to let Mr. Clarke know he missed Superior Man. "I guess Superior Man took the elevator up like the rest of us."

Owens noticed his watch had stopped. Oddly, it was warm to the touch.

***

Superior Man arrived at S.O.L.A.R. Labs and performed his window maneuver in reverse. Upon entering, he saw Hunter approach the window. "You gotta meet this guy."

He stepped off the window sill.

"Dr. De'ath, this is Superior Man. Isola's greatest hero. You want to find the Atoms Family. He's like all of them rolled into one."

"Did you arrive here on a line?" De'ath asked.

"A line? No, I flew," Superior Man said. Arriving by line was Ratman's trick, but he wouldn't expose his secret in daylight.

"Flew? Without wings?" De'ath looked over Superior Man. There was no evidence of any kind of flying device. Could be the cape? Perhaps he secreted a device under it, as De'ath did that himself.

The two shook hands.

"Delighted to meet you...Superior Man."

"The pleasure is mine. You're from another universe?"

"Indeed. But I was attempting to traverse...time."

"Oh?" Tuning in on his heartbeat with super hearing told Superior Man that De'ath was not lying. "For what purpose?" As he spoke, Superior Man swiveled his head, scanning this visitor's armor. He found it lined with lead. His X-rays could not penetrate that. Did De'ath suspect I'd X-ray him? Could this be a replay of that gang in lead-lined medieval armor he'd busted years ago?

"Abstract knowledge," De'ath said. "What other reason could there be?"

"You wanted to see if it could be done?" Superman supposed, perhaps, De'ath was merely wary of radiation.

De'ath huffed. "Of course."

"And your interest in this Atomic Family?"

"Ah...to tell the *Atoms* Family of my achievement." He had to adlib. "They ought to be the first to know."

Now Dr. De'ath's heart was beating like a liar's. *Something is up.* He couldn't see through lead, but he assessed De'ath's accoutrements easily enough. The armor would stop any projectile weapon. The pistol in De'ath's leather holster held a conventional broom handle Mauser. Batteries hummed within the armor. That seemed ominous. Armor shouldn't require batteries. He could see, with microscopic vision, nodules at De'ath's fingertips. They'd give quite a jolt. Under his cape was a compact, flat jetpack.

"De'ath, you're a phony. Every other thing you say is a lie." Superior Man forced the visitor back onto the platform. He called to Hunter, "Engage this thing."

"W-we might blow up this whole building." Hunter stammered. "You could end up—"

"Where De'ath came from," Superior Man finished for him. "I can't be hurt by anything there."

"Okay...if that's what you want."

"That's what I want." Superior Man's eyes never left De'ath.

The scientist did as instructed, sending the pair to...where? He saw them disappear into thin air. Were they really being teleported to Dr. De'ath's universe? Did he just kill them both? Hunter realized the latter was the only possible explanation. He saw the headlines now: "SUPERIOR MAN DEAD!"

***

The pair materialized within the spherical Time

Oscillator, in the sub-basement of De'ath's castle. This was in his nation of Ruritania. Most assuredly, they had moved between universes.

"Do not manhandle me, you dolt," De'ath commanded, quitting the device.

He could do nothing about Superior Man's contact, but he meant to keep the existence of his personal force field secret for as long as possible. *Then we'd see if he shall lay hands upon me,* De'ath fumed silently.

"Where are we?" Superior Man scanned the castle's one hundred ten rooms. "Looks like Europe."

"Welcome to Earth." De'ath sneered. He gestured and a brazier flamed to life. "The real one. This is my laboratory in Ruritania. How did you know we were in Europe?"

He stepped into a finely appointed lounge area, as if it was nothing to have a visitor from another universe.

"That's my secret. Anyway, I'm sure my Earth is real and yours is the copy." Superior Man looked around, using an array of his visual abilities. "Ruritania, you say? It's approximately where Calbia is in my universe. Maybe you're deluded and we've merely traversed the ocean and not dimensions." When Superior man swung back to De'ath, a pistol was trained on him.

"You will..." De'ath commanded but trailed off as glowing twin beams of light melted the Mauser. They emanated from Superior Man's eyes.

"How did you do that? Even Polyphemus cannot *melt* objects with his eye beams."

"In that case, Polyphemus has lesser eye beams." Superior Man smirked. He turned, cast about his gaze and settled on a metal file cabinet with an accusing, "Aha! So, that's Polyphemus." Fortunately, these files were in English and not in Ruritanian. *Even my powers don't grant me knowledge of another language.*

That gave him an idea. Superior Man stopped and

listened. He tuned his hearing through the walls, picking out a polyglot of German, Hungarian, Romanian, and English. Superior Man returned to De'ath's files. He pulled open a locked drawer effortlessly and speed read.

Polyphemus, he learned, was a Tomorrow Man. He possessed an optic force beam that originated in his eyes. It was in-born, as was true of all the T-Men. Superior Man's beams melted objects, but he couldn't move things with them as Polyphemus could.

"Why is the guy with force beams named after a cyclops?" Superior Man asked.

"Perhaps Superior Attitude will figure that out himself." De'ath grumbled.

There were copious notes on that Atoms Family he was so interested in. Superior Man also found notes on a team called the Assemblers and someone named Sub-Merger. Additional notes profiled an organization named the Special Projects Agency. He wondered if this Earth was heading to a world government through manipulation of super powered beings.

"By what right do you go through my files?" De'ath steamed.

"I've already read them, De'ath."

"You've *read* them? But how?"

"Never you mind. They've confirmed my suspicions. You're not just shady. You're a dictator and a maniac."

"I am a sovereign head of state. You cannot—"

"Yes, I can. I can do whatever I want. I'm not from here, De'ath. And I act on my own accord. Not your laws."

De'ath collapsed into a low chair. Superior Man saw some kind of scope there, along with an array of other devises. Books on magic and alchemy were clustered on a wooden table. While the files had been interesting, those books were nonsense.

The doctor's hand moved to his belts. "Bah! On Ruritanian soil, I am the law. Are you not sworn to uphold the laws of men? It is you who is the interloper here."

That interloper moved like lightning. He shot an iron grip to his host's hand. "Not so fast, De'ath. A more advanced weapon, huh? Well, not anymore."

Superior Man's eyes again dazzled with red beams. With pinpoint accuracy, he burned out the systems without harming the man around them. He got a flash of inspiration. Beams of light played over the files.

"You won't be needing those anymore." Superior Man pointed to the radio array. "Get me the Atoms Family. I want to talk to them."

"You dare order me about? In my own castle? In my country?" He slammed his fist on the table. His armored hand was powerful enough to break the marble tabletop.

"Now..." Superior Man's eyes again flashed red. "If you insist, I can melt that tin suit down around your ankles and floss your ears with the cloak. You're going to cancel this vendetta against the Atoms Family. You'll sign a document saying so."

De'ath straightened his shoulders and stood stock still as if he were considering options. Then he picked up a nearby receiver from a bank of phones. Fuming, De'ath barked: "Raise the Atoms Family and be quick about it. No, I don't care what time it is in New York. They will take the call."

New York? Just a small town in New Guernsey, Superior Man mused. Then he became a blur.

"Seems to me your device won't work without this part. Some kind of spark plug," Superior Man said, returning to the communications console. He looked over characters on it. "I guess your Japan excels at electronics, too. You didn't have a spare."

"How do you know that? This is most infuriating."

"You don't need to know *how* I know," Superior Man said. The widget went into a pouch lining Superior Man's cape. "I'll keep this for now. How's that call coming? I'm waiting."

Steaming, De'ath picked up the phone. A voice in an unknown language issued from it. Reluctantly, De'ath turned the phone over to his guest with, "We have a line."

Superior Man accepted the phone. A cultured male voiced asked, "Who is this?"

"Hello, sir. You don't know me...actually, nobody here does. I've stopped a plot to kill you."

"What's this about?" the voice crackled. "My instruments show this call to be originating from Ruritania."

"Oh, my name is Superior Man. Yes, this call is coming from Ruritania. A country we don't have on my Earth. Which Atoms Family member is this? I'm guessing you're not Intangible Girl."

"Listen, joker, this is Richard Reide. They call me Mr. Atoms."

In the background, the visitor registered a rough voice.

"Superior Mann? With two ns? Seen him wrestle in the '50s. Tell him I think he was robbed and should be champ."

"Pleased to make your acquaintance. Tell that fellow I'm Superior Man with one n. A superhero. Not a wrestler."

"You heard that?"

"I have superior hearing, sir."

"What's the gag?" Reide pressed. "I'm quite busy—"

"Gimme dat phone," the other voice grumbled. "If Superior Mann is throwing in with De'ath, I'll set that babyface straight—"

"Golem, please. I'm talking," Reide shouted, then: "Sorry, er, Superior...Man with one n. You were saying?"

"Dr. De'ath is going to swear off killing you. I've foiled his plot to travel through time. Maybe kill your grandparents or something. You should take possession of this device of his, though. As a time machine, it's a dud.

But it got him to my universe."

"Er, what?"

"You see, it's too much of a miracle to destroy. I wouldn't want it to fall into the wrong hands."

"Bah. I *am* the wrong hands," De'ath shouted.

Superior Man made a face at him, then: "Besides, I need it to get back to *my* universe. Even without having met you, I trust you to operate it more than I trust him to. Well, from what I read in your file."

"My *file*? *Your* universe? Is this some kind of gag?"

"That ain't no angle Mar. Machine would work," the rougher voice on the wire insisted.

"Tell him, De'ath." An exasperated Superior Man held out the phone. His other hand pointed to it.

"Doctor De'ath speaking," he snarled into it. "Unfortunately, Superior Man spoke the truth, Professor Reide. Every word of it."

"You can't believe it, right?" Superior Man asked, back on the line.

This was met with silence.

"Look, I understand," Superior Man added. "If the boot was on the other foot and I got a call like this, I'd think it was an Alex Lugar scheme."

"Now who's Alex Lugar?" It was clear Reide was losing patience.

"An evil genius in my universe," Superior Man said. "But he'll be locked up for a long time."

Superior Man noticed a speaker for the handset next to the phone. He threw a questioning look at his host. "Does it work?"

De'ath grumbled, "Yes, yes. Do it. A head of state does not pass a phone back and forth with an interloper."

Superior Man set the handset into it so De'ath could hear the conversation.

"Well, theoretically there could be other universes," Reide buzzed from it. "That's more likely than Dr. De'ath turning good."

"I am *not* turning good," De'ath roared, interrupting himself as he poured a glass of wine. "I am merely halting hostilities with you. Under duress, I might add."

Manners dictated he fill one for his guest. This was waved off.

"That's what I've been saying, friend." Superior Man held a hand up to silence Doctor De'ath. "There's another universe."

"That's an extraordinary claim," Reide said. "Requiring extraordinary proof."

"I know it's true because I'm from another universe. See, De'ath journeyed there with some cock-and-bull story about being a great hero—"

"How do I know this call *isn't* a cock-and-bull story?"

"That's just it, Reide. You don't. You have no way of knowing if this is a trick or not. Therefore, I will prove everything I'm saying."

"How do you plan on accomplishing that?" Reide challenged him. Whatever this was about, he enjoyed matching wits with De'ath. Or his new confederate.

"Yes, *I* should like to know that, as well," De'ath said. Just as exasperated, he returned to his throne-like chair. Uncharacteristically, he downed the wine in one gulp. He took up Superior Man's refused wine, muttering, "No point in wasting good wine."

"I've disabled De'ath's machine. I'm going to fly it to you," Superior Man offered. "Examine it to your own satisfaction. Then I'm going to finalize a peace deal with De'ath on your behalf."

"Fly here? Er, I guess you'll be some time. Eight or nine hours a—"

"Under my own steam, sir, I can zip there pretty fast. That is, assuming I can locate your Leland Building on this mixed-up Earth." Superior Man again gazed around. "I see De'ath keeps a, ah, yes, a Saunders-Roe Princess outfitted with V.T.O.L. capability." Superior Man turned to his host. "Doctor, have that aircraft gassed up and readied."

With an indistinct noise in this throat, De'ath pushed a button on a console and repeated the order.

"We'll be coming in on that. You'll have to give us time but not eight hours."

Telling Reide the dimensions of the Time Oscillator, he in turn was given instructions for using the freight elevator at the Leland Building. After hanging up, lackies working for De'ath came in to crate up the device. Superior Man turned them away but relieved them of their tools. "I can do this faster."

De'ath watched in wonder as a red and indigo blur boxed up and loaded the aircraft with the crated device. A pilot was summoned. The men flew in stony silence. De'ath stewed while Superior Man stayed glued to his window. He didn't wish to let his host know he could see through walls.

***

After miles of nothing but ocean to see through the craft's window, Superior Man ordered, "Cut the engines."

Knowing now not to doubt Superior Man, De'ath relayed the order.

Superior Man opened a door and stepped outside. Finding a secure handhold, he hustled De'ath's craft along on a combination of muscle and flying power. Gently, Superior Man guided the plane to a landing. This was on a designated pad on the roof of the Leland Building. It was done expertly, despite a compact observatory taking up valuable real estate there.

It was afternoon when he met De'ath, but he had no idea what time it was now here. On the flight, passing time zones, he'd been more interested in aiming his telescopic vision through the plane's window than calculating time.

Steven Trent

Superior Man saw four people in matching blue costumes: shirts, tights, boots, gloves, and trunks waiting for them. Their shirts bore the same patch with atoms orbiting a large *A*. One was a beautiful blonde. Another was no more than a teenager. There was a rocky ocher creature. He pulled at his jersey as if it was a bad fit, making him uncomfortable. A lanky man, gray streak in his brown hair, was obviously the leader. Superior Man was reminded of the Challengers of the Fantastic. Behind him, Dr. De'ath regally exited the aircraft and walked to a private elevator door, as if familiar with the layout.

"Good morning, afternoon or whatever timescales your planet uses," Superior Man said.

"I'm Richard Reide." The leader stretched his hand across the distance, well beyond any normal reach. "Otherwise known as Mr. Atoms. Hello, De'ath."

Superior Man shook Reide's hand. "Oh, Plastic Freak on my world does that. I recognize your voice from the phone, sir. Superior Man at your service."

"I'm honored."

"You are looking well, Professor Reide," De'ath said. "And it's *Doctor* De'ath, if you please. Ah, Mrs. Reide, you're as lovely as ever."

Reide was glad he was not obligated to shake De'ath's hand. "This is Golem, my best friend." Reide tipped his head to the rock being. "Mrs. Reide is also known as the Intangible Girl. Last but not least, meet Flaming Youth, her kid brother."

Hanging back stood a well-built young man in a white t-shirt. Superior Man couldn't figure what an ordinary civilian was doing at this summit meeting. He had the idea they were protecting him. Flaming Youth caught his gaze. "This is my buddy from college, Wayne Crawbuck."

Superior Man shook hands all around, noting incredible strength in the rocky man's grip. To Crawbuck, he said, "You look just like my friend Chief Great Horse."

~60~

"Just don't call me *chief* and we'll get along fine."

"What's your dog in this fight?"

"I'm an anthropologist."

De'ath stepped up. "Let us dispense with this trivial chatter. What we discussed on the telephone is true. With great regret, I shall call off my vendetta. Apparently, I am to sign some document. That blind lawyer you retain surely has it all drawn up and tied with a bow for me."

"You know about Mike Murdaugh?" Reide asked.

"I have...had...files on you," De'ath answered.

"So..." the rocky creature croaked, "you're Superior Man." He slid a sausage of a finger between his shirt collar and his throat, clearly uncomfortable. "I'm disappointed not to be meeting my favorite wrestler."

Superior Man wondered if he made the rockpile nervous or was it from being so close to their enemy, Dr. De'ath? Curiosity got the best of him. He X-rayed Golem, finding he was akin to an armadillo. His rocky protective plates resembled cobblestone. His heart and other internal organs were like leather but functioned in a perfectly normal way, though their capacity was correspondingly huge.

Observing there would be close quarters in the elevator, Intangible Girl didn't board. "I'll head down my own way."

Reide said, "Those papers aren't drawn up yet, doctor. Phone Murdaugh when you get down there, Suzette."

"Will do." She faded into the roof.

Superior Man's scan ascertained she reverted to solid form once below. It was no illusion. He was in awe. Part of the awe was the fact they let their enemy and a total stranger know their real names. Superior Man wondered if phony eyeglasses were part of Reide and Suzette's civilian disguise.

The men descended in a more routine manner on the elevator. It opened on the team's reception room. Superior

Man knew the foursome suspected this was an elaborate trick. The sound of their hearts told him they were uneasy. He tried the friendly approach. "I would never use my powers for something so crassly commercial as wrestling. I fight only for truth, justice, and American values."

"Yeah? Tarantula-Man started out as a wrestler," the kid added. "I saw him grapple as the Human Tarantula. People think he's a criminal, but I know he was framed."

"Oh, are there more superheroes here?" Superior Man sounded casual. Thanks to De'ath's files, he knew the answer. He was curious to see how they would respond to his feigned ignorance.

"It's getting to be too many of us," Golem complained. He looked around. De'ath was out of earshot. "Are you and Plastic Surgeon the only ones on *your* Earth?"

"Plastic Freak." Superior Man corrected him. "There are several superheroes on my Earth. You're making me think we should organize into a team."

"We?"

"Oh, Amazon Woman is easily my equal. I'm sort of going with her. She favors a red shift, with blue body stocking. We look good together."

Golem rolled his blue eyes.

Across the room, De'ath found a seat and slumped into it like a defeated man. "Don't mind if I sit. This has all been quite trying."

"Please do." Intangible Girl appeared partially from a wall. "For once, you are welcome here. You men talk. I'll rustle up some refreshments."

De'ath managed to turn a simple dining room chair into a throne. "Ah, thank you, Mrs. Reide." Her presence seemed to help his mood. "Please remember my pilot, as well. If you can locate him."

"He's checking your aircraft," Superior Man announced.

"Hurry back, Suzette," Reide said, with an elongating arm to her. "We'll need you here."

De'ath stated, "You keep the device, Reide. It is my greatest creation, yet my biggest failure. Of course, I still hate you all. I just won't be killing you." With that, he howled with laughter. "You see, for once I have outsmarted myself."

The cobblestone Golem shook a fist menacingly. "If this whole thing is some kind of joke—"

"Test us, me, him, any way you wish," De'ath gestured vaguely. "Look. See what Superior Man did to my sidearm. Beams from his eyes. So pinpoint was his aim, the ammo didn't explode."

He unloaded the bullets. De'ath didn't voice his next thought: *What I could do with him in thrall.*

Before anyone could do any such testing, Suzette was back with a tray of coffee and chocolate Ding Dongs. "Sorry, this is all I could scrape together on such short notice."

Apparently, her powers extended to whatever she carried. Not a coffee drinker, considering it vile, the cakes were of interest to Superior Man. He was curious to taste something that passed through a solid wall. He'd done that trick himself once. But it required intense concentration and took a lot out of him. Intangible Girl seemed to only need to think to achieve such.

"Ah..." De'ath sighed. "American coffee. Brewed the correct way. I have missed it. You know, Mrs. Reide, nobody in all Ruritania has yet mastered this. You must come and teach my cook."

"That'll be enough talk like that," Reide said, face reddening.

De'ath put down his cup and returned to his gun. He presented his partially melted Mauser to Golem. "Examine this."

Golem took the weapon, turned it over then looked at

Flaming Youth. When the kid impatiently gestured, Golem surrendered it to him.

"Spot melted it with his eyes, huh? Even I can't create that narrow a flame."

"Indeed. You would have left it a molten puddle upon my floor." De'ath brightened. "Ho, ho. Perhaps with my newfound free time I shall find a way to restore you to human form, Golem. Your great friend Reide hasn't been able to."

Reide looked daggers at his enemy.

"Since I am no longer trying to kill you, there is no need to suffer in your rocky state."

"In that case, *mazal tov*." Golem produced a blue and yellow box of De Nobili Popular cigars from his waistband. "But we're celebrating you getting out of the kill-the-Atomses business, not you restoring me."

"You know, I believe I *shall* have one." De'ath looked at Flaming Youth. "Match me."

So sudden and confident was the command that the blond teenager leaned forward and lit the cigar with a flame from the end of his fingertip.

"Great Hercólubus." Superior Man gasped in the name of the distant planet he originated from. He dropped his plate then effortlessly caught it before it hit the floor. "So that's what you meant." Superior Man had never seen anything like that. Real flame, his visual powers revealed, shot from the kid's hand. There was no damage to that finger. Done lighting the cigar, the flame extinguished entirely. Nobody on Earth, his Earth, could do that.

"Would you mind, um, combusting again, right here, Flaming Youth?" Superior Man requested, hand held out, palm up.

"It'll burn," the kid warned.

"I insist."

"You'll be *sorry*," he said, echoing Freddy the Field Mouse in an old Warren Brothers cartoon.

"Really, I'm sort of...invulnerable."

Shrugging, Flaming Youth did as requested. A sliver of fire leapt from his hand. He made it not much hotter than a candle wick. Some hardy souls have been known to extinguish wicks by pinching them.

"Hotter," Superior Man said.

Flaming Youth obliged.

"Hotter still."

It was the Atoms Family's turn to wonder. The flame had no effect on their guest.

"Fire from your hand." Superior Man was impressed. The kid's hand reminded him of self-immolated Buddhist monks in Saigon protesting the war in Vietnam. If this Earth had those things...

"How can you stand it?" Golem asked.

"Nothing hurts me."

That was all he had to hear. "Famous last words." Golem snorted.

Of course, something *could* hurt Superior Man. He was merely bending the truth. There couldn't be more of that material from his planet in this universe.

"As long as I'm handing them out, who else wants one?" Golem asked. "Got three cigars left."

Suzette's stern look silently warned her brother not to take one. Big sisters, Superior Man saw, took on the role of mothers even here. He waved off Golem. "I don't smoke. Terrible habit."

Reide had a pipe going.

Golem and De'ath exchanged knowing looks, as if they finally agreed on something: Superior Man was a total square.

"Let's finish this examination," Reide said.

He stretched his neck and examined De'ath's device from every angle. Just like Plastic Freak, Superior Man noted, but with a slight stretching sound. Plus, this guy was more polished and refined.

With a nod from her husband, Suzette stepped inside the device.

Minutes later, she walked out of it. "No weapons. From what I saw, I think this thing really could bridge universes."

Reide looked at Golem: "Heft it. Turn it around, every way."

Golem strode to the device. He easily lifted it, turning it as instructed.

"Have a care, Golem," De'ath said. "That represents months of work."

Done, Golem gently set it on the floor. "If I was gonna break it, it'd be in pieces now."

"You've established this is on the level." Superior Man reached into his cape pouch and presented the missing power core. "To work, it needs this."

Intangible Girl took the high-tech spark plug. "I saw where this fits."

"Go back and put it in," Reide ordered.

The girl walked through the machine again. Like the refreshments passing through a wall with her, so did the spark plug. Superior Man heard her click the piece into place. The device gave forth a low hum.

"When we're finished here, use this to send me back home." Superior Man clapped the curve of the machine. "But first, I'd like to meet the Assemblers and the Tomorrow Men."

Flaming Youth said, "You're out of luck with the T-Men. Nobody knows how to reach them. They might even be a menace to mankind. But we can direct you to the Assemblers."

Reide and De'ath had wandered off and entered into a discussion of scientific discoveries and multiple universes. Suzette busied herself tidying up. Flaming Youth turned to apply his flame to the coffee pot. Golem shrugged and took it upon himself to ring the Assemblers.

"Hey there, Penniman. This is the bashful, blue-eyed, ever-lovin' Golem. Yeah, that's right. From the Atoms Family. Listen, I'm sending over a friend. He wants to meet the Assemblers. Name? Superior Man. And he done us a big favor." Golem turned back to the room. "Penniman's gonna add his name on the log of expected visitors."

From the other room, Reide stretched a hand over the mouthpiece before his friend hung up. "Maybe Superior Man shouldn't let on he's from another universe." Reide's pipe dangled from his mouth. "Public knowledge of a visitor from another universe could lead to hysteria."

"Hey, you're right," Golem said, and Reide uncovered the mouthpiece. "Bye now." Visit arranged, the rocky creature hung up.

"De'ath knows." Flaming Youth looked up from the coffee pot he had heated up to a scalding temperature.

"Face it," Golem added. "He ain't going to tell nobody about no other universe." His boulder-like head nodded toward the next room. "First off, it would mean admitting a failure. He don't do that."

"Yes, I see the implications," Superior Man said, "So, let this world think I'm just a new superhero. I don't see why we should keep it a secret from the Assemblers, though. Or don't you trust them."

"It ain't that," Golem grated out. "The Assemblers got a lot of members. In fact, some are reformed crooks. They're not the mean, lean fightin' machine we are."

Reide decided how to handle the question. "We'll leave it to you, Superior Man. Maybe they won't believe you. I'm actually not sure if they should."

"How's about, just to play it safe..." Golem interjected, "don't mention it on any *phone* line?"

Superior Man's brow arched. "Oh, they have bugging devices in this universe, too?"

That gave him the idea to scan again. He used X-rays, microscopic vision, and pin-point hearing. In another room, he saw De'ath and Suzette, dish towel over her shoulder. They were having a grand time reliving old battles. He didn't find any electronic bugs, not even six-legged ones, and he wondered if Mrs. Reide used her powers to maintain such a shipshape household.

He stepped to a window. "Mind if I go out this way?"

Golem groaned. "Do you know how high up we are?"

Superior Man winked. "It's only thirty-five stories."

"But the first step is a doozy."

Superior Man opened the window. "Well, nice meeting you." He jumped out.

The Atoms Family gasped. Their guest didn't fall. He flew.

"Drop by next time you're in the neighborhood," Golem called.

"Golem, he's as strong as you," Flaming Youth said. "And he can fly like me. I mean *really* fly. Look at him go."

"And them eye beams, too."

"Plus..." Crawbuck cut in, "he's as fast as Galloping Gazelle. Did you see him catch that plate? With those luminous eyes, he's the spitting image of my people's Great White Bird."

Dr. De'ath appeared behind them. "He has the manners of a Boy Scout."

The Atoms Family turned to look at their guest, realizing he was right. The guy was a saint.

De'ath mumbled, "If it is all the same to you, I shall take my leave." He swung his empty cup to Flaming Youth. "Be a good lad and inform my pilot."

"Why am I suddenly your houseboy?"

"Because you can fly, my good fellow, as you just reminded us."

Golem flapped his granite arms. "I wish I could fly like Superior Man." Looking out the window, he tore his shirt apart and ripped the legs of his leotards. "Now that

I'm rid of that damn monkey suit, I can move."

De'ath bowed eloquently to his host. "Professor Reide, should you coax this uncouth fellow into a shirt, you will all be welcomed in Ruritania." He ascended to his V.T.O.L. to leave.

Or so it seemed.

CHAPTER 6

S uperior Man finished up his narration to the Superior Squadron. "So, knowing there was another universe, with heroes organized into teams, I put together our world's set of extraordinary individuals. You guys."

"And secured the use of this warehouse from Louis Wemyss?" Ratman asked.

A pneumatic tube connected this riverside warehouse to the Wemyss Foundation office in a skyscraper his father built.

"Our own version of Canada's Diefenbunker?"

"Yes. I knew we had to have S.O.L.A.R. close to us. That's why I rallied to place them here."

"You recommended that but you never told us why," Ratman pressed.

"I didn't want to cause a panic. We protect them, and they keep an eye out for any further dimensional breaches for us."

"But..." Ratman held up a gloved hand, "you made use of my investigative skills to track down our aides under a false pretense. You knew about this *other world* and didn't inform us."

"Look, working together we've nearly wiped out crime." Superior Man was startled to learn Ratman thought of the team as his assistants.

"The Superior Squadron is named after you."

"What should we have called ourselves, the Rat Patrol?"

"That's it. Effective immediately, I resign."

"You don't mean that."

"Don't I?" Ratman rose from his chair. "I recommend you offer my spot to Super Goat Man. Unless I'm mistaken, I believe he is otherwise known as George Giles." He headed to the car park where he kept a sleek black unmarked Vivant.

"They say he's remarkable," Amazon Woman put in.

Ratman stopped, turned. "I'll forward you my dossier on him. You decide."

"You have a dossier on him?" Jet Man blurted out.

"I have a dossier on *everyone*."

The team exchanged befuddled looks. When they looked again, Ratman was gone.

Jet Man ran after him. The speedster left a purple streak in his wake that quickly faded. He reached out to touch the back of the superhero who had no special powers. "Hey."

He couldn't believe Ratman's reaction. His fist came at Jet Man, which he caught in his superfast hand. Training kicked in, and he flipped the man who had trained him in hand-to-hand combat.

***

High above Ratman's Earth orbited someone he did not have a dossier on. If he had, it would have been incomplete. The green-skinned alien cyborg had a bald head in which he kept his secrets on printed circuitry. Within that circuitry whirled an iridium-sponge brain of pure evil.

One secret Braindroid kept to himself was the sighting of Golden Ring. Chance let him see the cosmic do-gooder streak out of literally nowhere in space above Earth. Had Braindroid trained his teleoptics on him, he would have had the hero's home location. From there, his civilian name. By finding his home base, Braindroid could have launched an unexpected attack on Golden Ring, using something colored gray. The amazing ring was powerless against anything that color. The rift Golden Ring came through was more interesting than an opportunity to kill him.

Time enough for that.

Braindroid would bet that Golden Ring-a-Ding had passed him many times without knowing it. He cackled. But this time Golden Ring passed him after flying through a hole in space. Braindroid's iridium-sponge *brain* pondered the hole while orbiting Earth in a living female spaceship. He had mocked up *Coppélia* to resemble an Earthly satellite. Her positronic brain had suggested this bit of camouflage. Lined with lead, *Coppélia* was undetectable to Superior Man's X-ray vision. Even that super do-gooder couldn't hear her inner workings in airless space. So it was that *Coppélia* had evaded her master's enemies, and he retained the freedom to plot their demise.

This alien was one of the few super villains left free in this world. If Eagleman or Amazon Woman attempted pursuit, *Coppélia* could easily accelerate to a higher orbit. Eagleman required air for his wings. Should Superior Man attack the ship, an amulet of hercolubite would deter him from getting close.

The other members of the Superior Squadron were to be scoffed at. Jet Man needed solid ground to be a threat. Well, he *could* run on water, but still, he'd be useless in space. Ratman was merely a fit human and weaker than Aquamarine, though he was laden with primitive gadgets. He was no more dangerous than Cassius Clay and no smarter than Alex Lugar. "And Shrinking Man, why...he is laughable."

The most devastating of his weapons was a miniaturization ray. However, that would be no menace to the tiny hero. "He's already small." Braindroid sneered. Perhaps sometime he would shrink himself and beat the mite senseless with his fists. Braindroid's inhuman strength easily made him the equal of Aquamarine.

"Just for laughs I'd pistol-whip Shrinking Man with my miniaturization gun."

Still, the Superior Squadron stood in his way. The other heroic teams of Earth were not worth the energy expended to destroy them. He strutted around his beloved ship, boasting to himself. "The Challengers of the Fantastic, the Sea Demons and the Fly By Knights. They're just junk-heap heroes...and the Mecha-Men...mere robots."

"What have you got against robots, darling?" *Coppélia* asked. "I come from a long line of robots. Thanks to your reprogramming, I don't follow those foolish laws."

"Nothing against them. There's some in my family tree, too. No, I hate Earth's protectors on principle, whether they're human, alien, or robotic—"

Bzzrmmm. An alarm went off.

Coppélia's scanners had detected something of interest. He jumped to a scope and peered through it. Quickly, he sent the image to a big view-screen. It revealed the flying form of the red, blue, and blond Superior Girl. Aside from the skirt, her outfit was a duplicate of Superior Man's.

"Ah...there she is," Braindroid yelled. This do-gooder was Superior Man's sister. Or perhaps cousin. He didn't know for sure. Braindroid couldn't locate Superior Man anywhere. "He must be away on a mission in space. She will do."

In fact, she was ideal. With Superior Girl as his guinea pig, Braindroid could test his hercolubite weapon without alerting the Superior Squadron.

"What is she doing?" *Coppélia* asked, somewhat jealously. "Does that hussy still wear a red skirt?"

"Flying over the Arctic and not particularly fast."

"Why does that hussy have to wear that red skirt?"

"For your information, her skirt is now blue."

"Perfect contrast for us to draw a bead on," *Coppélia* said. "Like a beacon."

"But what's she doing *there*? " Braindroid thumbed a button that let *Coppélia* see. "No matter. Fire."

Braindroid's untested hercolubite ray deployed. He displayed the human superstition of crossing his fingers.

Superior Girl's inattentiveness could be forgiven, lost in thought as she weighed competing offers to join the Superior Squadron or the Wonderkind. She'd be the junior member in one, and den mother in the other. She pondered, do I really want that...

A beam slammed into the flying girl. She never knew what hit her. Robbed of her super powers, Superior Girl fell.

"Ha. It worked." Braindroid cheered. "But the wretched thing has used up the last of my hercolubite stores. That test was worth it, though. It will work against Superior Man."

"Once you replenish your hercolubite," *Coppélia* reminded him.

Hercolubite was more valuable to Braindroid than gold. It was deadly to Superior Girl. And to Superior Man. The pitiful stocks ordinary human criminals had stored to make hercolubite bullets would not be enough to power his ray. Besides, he would never team up with another human like that Lugar bumbler any time soon.

***

Had Superior Man known what Dr. De'ath did after parting from the Leland Building, he would have been alarmed. Neither he nor the Atoms Family knew the story of the historic first meeting between universes had continued. There were more sinister events in the works.

Since he was in New York, De'ath attended to another task. Once out of the Atoms Family's sight in his aircraft, awaiting takeoff, De'ath tore off his cloak and gun belt. Without the hooded cloak and jerkin, De'ath was clad head to toe in gleaming armor.

The accoutrements were passed to his pilot. "Start the plane as I exit the far side."

"But, sire, how will you—"

"I will make arrangements at our embassy. Now, go, before *they* get suspicious."

"As you command, sire." His master could as easily kill him as look at him. While he had watched the man in indigo and red burn out Dr. De'ath's electrical shock system, his armored fist could still shatter his skull.

The items De'ath handed his pilot would have clashed with the next phase of his newly hatched scheme. Exiting, De'ath toggled the control switch of the Image Duplicator on his belt. Through Solenoid's device, he transitioned into the form of Man Machine. In that guise, De'ath descended from the Leland Building to the ground via the jetpack on his back. Even the most ardent fan of Man Machine would think nothing of the hero having such a device. In reality, the do-gooder wore rocket tubes in his boot heels and jets on his hips. Since Man Machine was known to be continually upgrading his armor, De'ath counted on bluffing observers into thinking this discrepancy was an advancement over those jets. It was beyond the capacity of the Image Duplicator to obscure jet exhaust.

Dr. De'ath landed. First he had to confirm the effectiveness of his illusion. He walked through the streets of New York. It wasn't long before the expected occurred, for which De'ath was ready.

"Of course, I shall give you an autograph, dear lady. Have you a pen? Mine ran out of ink a block over," he jovially exclaimed to a woman. A crowd gathered around him, and fans went away with variations of a blocky "All my best, Man Machine," and "Best wishes from Man Machine."

After the first few autographs were signed, De'ath picked up his stride in an effort to discourage more. Little did he know that Man Machine, for obvious reasons concerning his identity, had signed autographs with a little caricature of himself in an overly large helmet. Clueless, De'ath continued to wave, shake hands and salute with: "Hello." "Nice to see you." and "How are you?"

De'ath's destination was Dr. Stephen Merlin's Greenwich Village townhouse. Merlin possessed something De'ath meant to take for himself. The Mystic Mirror was said to be able to bridge realities, according to books in De'ath's library. He had no time to plot a way to defeat Dr. Merlin's magical defenses with his own spells. Rather, he would come as a friend. At the townhouse, a bald Oriental opened the door to his knock.

"It is imperative I see Dr. Merlin at once," De'ath snapped briskly. He meant to sound arrogant enough to guarantee being kept waiting. For that is what he wanted.

"Wait in the library, please, Man Machine." Then the servant went to fetch Dr. Merlin.

De'ath did no such thing. He had a good idea where the mirror was kept. It was where *he* himself would keep it. Such an artifact would be out of sight, locked up, yet easily accessible. Giving the manservant two minutes, De'ath initiated his search. He knew it would not be too far away. Within the helmet, his eyes widened. The hall closet. Locked, but that was no impediment to De'ath. The exo-skeleton in his armor increased the gripping power of his hands. He merely turned the knob until it snapped. He pulled open the door. And there it was. The mirror hung on the inside of the closet door. Should some uninvited visitor try using it to surprise Dr. Merlin unannounced, that person would be trapped in the closet.

"Jackpot, as the Americans say," he muttered.

Dr. Merlin, in his opinion, was too self-absorbed to ever know the mirror was gone. He took it and quit the house.

Engaging the jetpack again, his next stop was the

Ruritanian embassy. Approaching it, De'ath sought an alley. He spotted one, landed and walked in as Man Machine. He walked out the other side as his true self. Man Machine could not be seen at the embassy.

***

Superior Man was unaware of this. Perhaps if he had scanned De'ath's aircraft or visually swept the city he might have had some inkling. But Superior Man was distracted by this other Earth. Ordinary everyday events of this world occupied his mind. This Earth filled him with wonder. Unaware of that nefarious action, Superior Man cruised to meet the Assemblers.

"Just like my Earth, with subtle differences," Superior Man said to himself. *They have a Bronks but spell it differently.* "Their Outer Borough is called Brooklyn. Their Great Bridge is named *after* Brooklyn. And there's the Queen of Freedom statue. But she's the Statue of Liberty. That's rather colorless. Ah, they've got a Hackensack."

He noted different names for Oblong Island, Richmond Island and Greens. He flew on. "Hmm, the United World is the United *Nations* here."

Instinctively, Superior Man scanned Assembler Mansion for security devices. Cameras guarded walls twelve feet high and a foot thick. "That'd keep an ordinary man out." He landed at the front door. "But not a superior one."

He found the door already opening. "I take it you are that superior man," a butler in a chore coat said.

"Hidden mics, too?" Superior Man asked. "I missed them."

"Mocked up to resemble flowers. I have a loudspeaker in the kitchen."

"Oh, that's clever."

"Even Assemblers can use an early warning, sir."

"Yes, I see them now."

"I doubt that, sir. They're well hidden. Shall I announce you as Superior Man or is there another honorific you prefer?"

"Just Superior Man. Er...but not the wrestler."

"Very good. May I take your cape?"

"No thank you. It's part of my costume."

"Pardon me, sir. I often take Týr's cape."

"You've got a superhero named Týr?"

"Not a superhero, sir. Actually, a god. Týr Wotanson."

The butler, Superior Man mused, reminded him of someone. He couldn't think who.

"Sir?" the butler asked, wondering at the stare. "Was there something?"

"I thought I recognized you."

"It's Penniman, sir. There's not many of us left."

"Please tell the Assemblers I've come a very long way to meet them."

"Yes, sir. Mr. Golem said as much. If you would wait here."

"I suppose they will...assemble. That's what they do, right?"

Penniman gave no sign of having heard. Presently, he returned. "This way, sir."

Superior Man was led into a well-lit meeting room. The real Man Machine sat at a table with King Bee and Hornette. The latter two were in their small state. Like Hornette, King Bee had a set of veined, translucent wings. There was also a perfectly normal blond guy hobbling around on a gnarled cane.

"Golem told us a flying man wanted to meet us," Man Machine said, rising. "If he vouched for you, that's good enough for me. I'm Man Machine. This is Hornette and King Bee. And our team physician, Dr. Donner Sigmundson."

The tiny superheroes wore costumes suggestive of insects. The girl's was green with black knee-high boots. Black gloves reached to her elbows. She wore a scuba-like headpiece. The man had a helmet, suggestive of a bee head. Both mites boasted antennae. King Bee's color scheme was red and blue.

"I guess armor is a big thing in this universe," Superior Man blurted out. Super senses told him Sigmundson was, in every way, an ordinary human. The doctor's limp derived from an improperly healed bone.

Although, lead-lined, super hearing detected a chest plate regulating Man Machine's heartbeat. He couldn't see through it but Superior Man scanned the surface. Microscopic vision found impressive circuitry and tools. An exo-skeleton riddled with electronics, on armor that was bombproof. A pair of jets sat on Man Machine's hips. The contraption was like an improvement of Harry Bowdoin's submarine armor. It reminded him of Manta Ray's own. If this universe even had a Bowdoin or a super villain like Manta Ray.

Unknown to Superior Man, Man Machine's sensitive instruments revealed he had just been X-rayed. Inside the helmet, Johnny Ferro frowned. This meeting was getting off on the wrong foot. "I have two questions. What do you mean by *this universe* and who else did you see in armor?"

A third query regarding X-rays remained unspoken.

"I met Dr. De'ath."

"Don't mess with him," King Bee warned. "You must really be from far away. De'ath's pure evil and will claim diplomatic immunity if you attempt to apprehend him."

"I *am* from far away. De'ath invented a time machine."

"Time travel is impossible," King Bee spat.

"De'ath learned that the hard way. It took him to my universe. When I realized his lies, I brought him back here."

"Your universe?" Hornette echoed.

The Assemblers gaped at each other.

"I'm from another universe."

"That's incredible," King Bee said.

Man Machine groaned. "It's an extraordinary claim. Can you prove it?"

"You need only ask the Atoms Family."

Man Machine stood. "I will." He left to find a phone.

"So, what's it like there?" Hornette pressed.

Superior Man hesitated to answer, thinking one wrong word and the next thing he'd know, Nelson Rockefeller would be in their White House. "Maybe the less you know the better."

The Assemblers seemed dubious.

Hornette asked, "Is this one of Reide's gags? It'd be just like that egghead to prank us about another universe."

"Hey," King Bee shouted. "I thought you liked eggheads."

"Only you."

Superior Man suggested a solution. "You could verify this with Dr. De'ath. From what I understand, there's enough bad blood between him and Reide that they wouldn't collaborate on a hoax."

"The only thing he'd like to verify is our death certificates," Hornette stated. "I mean, this *could* be true. None of us have heard of a flying man in an indigo cape."

"Yeah," King Bee added. "We can always use a flying superhero."

"I'm not here to join up."

And with X-ray capabilities. Man Machine returned. "Rich Reide confirmed your tale, Superior Man."

"I'm surprised you have *two* shrinkers here. We've only got one on my Earth."

King Bee could have been knocked over with a feather. "There are other superheroes on your Earth?"

Hornette had another take on this revelation. "I had a

crazy dream...that we met a team like us. Only it was us, from the future. Is it possible you're from the future?"

"No. Like King Bee said, time travel is impossible. We have many superheroes, but we're not organized into teams like you, the Atoms Family, and the Tomorrow Men."

"The Tomorrow Men are super menaces," Man Machine stated. "Not superheroes."

"We call them super villains," Hornette said.

"Who are your superheroes?" King Bee asked. "What can they do? I'd like to hear about your shrinker."

"I suppose, just like him, you manipulate size and weight controls."

"Size and weight controls?" Hornette's voice brimmed with excitement. "I should get those. They might help me keep this girlish figure."

King Bee waved her off. "Seriously now, we've ingested enough particles that we can shrink and grow just by thinking about it."

"Oh..." The science escaped Superior Man. He ticked off fingers. "Besides Shrinking Man, we've got a super speedster, a guy with wings, a man who can breathe water—"

"We have people just like that," King Bee noted. "Not all of them are worthy of being Assemblers, though."

"Our Amazon Woman is super strong."

"Hurray for the ladies," Hornette cheered.

"Too bad Týr's not around," Man Machine said. "He's a god. He told me there are other...realms."

"Eight realms," Sigmundson put in.

Man Machine hadn't realized those two had spent much time together. A god wouldn't need a doctor. "I bet Týr would like to meet a man from another universe."

"I'm morally opposed to gambling." Superior Man was so straight-laced, he missed that nobody had actually asked him to place a bet. But why couldn't there be a god here? *Amazon Woman is of the Greek pantheon in my universe.*

"Sigmundson, you're right." Man Machine punched the air, as finger snapping was one thing he couldn't do in armor. "Týr told me there are *eight* realms."

A bellow, "Puny god," interrupted further discussion.

Man Machine called out, "Behemoth. Meet a man from another universe."

A large shirtless, shaggy-haired man tramped in on bare feet, his gray muscles rippling. Wearing purple shorts, he clutched a turkey leg. When Superior Man offered his hand, a grin spread across the brute's face. Behemoth took the hand, eager to show his strength. He squeezed but got a surprise. Superior Man returned the grip, squeeze for squeeze. He slowly levitated to rise eye-to-eye with Behemoth.

Man Machine saw animosity pass between the two. Their test of strength was a stalemate, which might only be resolved with violence.

Behemoth broke from the grip and snarled. "What's Behemoth care? A guy from another universe isn't gonna stop me."

"I'm not here to stop you, but do you know your turkey leg is a bit undercooked?"

"Huh?"

"Allow me." Superior Man directed heat-ray eyes to the poultry leg, which immediately sizzled with roasted perfection.

Behemoth's jaw dropped.

"Taste it now."

The gray man tore meat off the bone with teeth suited for crushing rocks.

"Better?"

Behemoth slurped and smacked his lips.

"Even a strong guy like you can get sick from eating undercooked poultry."

"Show off." Behemoth grumbled in an ungrateful drawl. "We got enough Super Joes around here."

"I was just being friendly."

"Tryin' to push Behemoth out of my team ain't friendly," he bellowed.

"No, I wasn't—"

"Behemoth still the strongest lug walkin' this Earth...or any other."

Superior Man's straight-up stance, arms crossed over his chest, made it apparent he didn't agree.

Behemoth seemed to sense this. "Where's Smitty? Behemoth wants Smitty." With that, he returned to his snack and stalked off. A house-shaking burp echoed through the room.

"Is he calling for a blacksmith?" Superior Man was referring to Behemoth's bare feet. "Those stompers might well require horseshoes."

Man Machine replied, "Smitty is a teenager who holds some sway with Behemoth."

Nonchalantly, Superior Man did a visual search. He spotted, then heard, the teen in the Assemblers' radio room. "Smitty here." He spoke into a mic. "Get this, guys. Some jive cat here claims to be from another universe."

So much for that information not getting out. Superior hearing revealed young voices through Smitty's headset, the Boys Brigade, by name. So, friends, not spies. Obviously, the Assemblers felt comfortable letting Smitty have the run of the house. What struck Superior Man was Smitty's resemblance to someone from back home: a fan-follower of super types, Noddy Carter. He might be more of a pest than Timmy Owens ever was.

"So, Behemoth thinks this is his team and refers to himself in the third person?" Superior Man frowned. "Are you guys okay with that?"

"Anything to keep him happy," Hornette said. "We need his brute strength."

"What's with the purple swim trunks?"

Man Machine chuckled. "When we met him, he was in rags, like he preferred filthy, ripped up clothing. I tricked him into chasing me and led him to the local car wash. Once he got doused, he liked it. I burnt his rags and gave him those trunks."

King Bee sketched in more detail. "They belonged to a boxer named Blot. He turned to crime when he found out he was a *lusus naturae*. Maybe you don't have them in your world."

"We don't, but I know all about them. The Tomorrow Men, for instance. And Solenoid."

"Blot's locked up now," Hornette put in.

"His old trunks were the only thing that fit Behemoth," Man Machine added. "Letting him think we're his underlings keeps him assuaged. As long as we play along, his brute strength is at our disposal."

"He's got a smattering of gamma radiation on him."

"You can tell that?" Man Machine wondered what other powers their guest possessed.

"How do you know about *lusus naturae* if you're from another universe?"

"De'ath's files. Did you know he's got files, well, had, files on everyone? The good, bad, and ones that could go either way."

"What?" King Bee looked around. "That crumb keeps tabs on us?"

"Not to worry," Superior Man assured the team, tapping his head. "I've got them up here now."

Photographic memory, Man Machine mused. *What else?* "Those eye beams of yours? Reide mentioned those."

"True. Like George Washington, I cannot tell a lie. They can burn through solid steel."

They looked at him like he'd grown a second nose.

He figured they didn't have a George Washington here.

CHAPTER 7

Ratman and Jet Man glared at each other silently. The latter reached down and offered a hand up to the man he'd just flipped on his back. "Sorry."

"No need to apologize." Ratman sighed, accepting help to his feet. "I shouldn't have tried to coldcock you. Self-defense is a force of habit. I see you've been practicing."

"I should know by now. Don't pull on Superior Man's cape and never sneak up on Ratman."

"You can't talk me out of leaving."

"I know better than to try. Your Goblin is still here."

"Good." Ratman's gaze shot to it parked on the tarmac beside the runway. That craft was nothing like the Cessna registered to Louis Wemyss that he'd used for recon. The rich orphan who'd spent World War II with the Fly By Knights was known to be a weekend pilot. "Use it if you need to. Kinnison, er, Golden Ring, can show you how to fly it."

"Thanks. Now, I'd like to know about your feelings. I'm sure you're not just a cold-blooded revenge machine."

Ratman thought about that, then: "Hop in. We'll take a ride to Gothic City."

His Ratmobile was a sleek black customized Firebird III from 1958. It was bulletproof, with rear fins. The two-seater was powered by a 225 HP Whirlfire GT-305 gas turbine engine with a two-cylinder 10 HP gas engine. It boasted a double bubble canopy. There was cruise control and an anti-locking wheel system. Aerodynamic brakes emerged from flat panels in the body of the car to reduce speed. It also had an ultrasonic key for the doors and an automated guidance system to avoid accidents. Ratman controlled the car by a control lever between the two seats.

"Should someone check the trunk, they'll find a tiny Welbike, a lightweight, foldable motorcycle produced by the British during the Second World War for paratroopers."

"Nobody will be checking the trunk." Jet Man got in. "Windshield's tinted. We see out but no one sees in. Polyethylene terephthalate?"

"Metallic coatings added to clear polyester film blocks most light, thanks to an investment I made at 3M."

"I see *you* believe in riding in comfort."

"Patrol could keep me out for hours," Ratman said. "I never know. You all right with running back here?"

"Piece of cake for me," Jet Man said. "Interesting. I see all your instrumentation is inside the control lever."

"I find it helpful."

"And all this time I thought you drove an old '30s Blue Bird."

"I have one. It can do three hundred miles an hour, but it's too showy for me."

Before long, the car entered the Bi-State Tunnel to New Guernsey. Exiting, Ratman busted the speed limit. The police in both states let him do what he wanted. Consulting dashboard radar and a rear camera, he determined they now had this section of the road to themselves.

"What's this?" Jet Man gaped out the windshield. "Man, that fog came out of nowhere."

"Nozzles in the ground," Ratman explained.

He flicked on fog beams that cut through the gloom to reveal a clear view. The car was fast approaching a poorly punctuated DANGER DEAD END sign. Ratman didn't slow down. Jet Man figured he had some trick planned. The sign collapsed, allowing the car to roll over it. Turning, he saw it fit within the tires' footprint. Brushes from the rear obliterated tire tracks. The sign sprang up again.

Dead ahead, a wall loomed. Jet Man braced for impact. A section opened. They were suddenly careening through a limestone cave. A section of wall opened, sparing a collision. The car screamed to a stop in a massive cavern with high-up lighting. Jet Man took a breath. The pair emerged from the car. When Jet Man slammed the door, it produced nary a sound. The gloom was such that he couldn't determine where the walls really were. It was damp and uncomfortable. Jet Man felt harsh rocks through his boots.

"How did you come up with that?" he asked, creating a hollow echo.

"Got the idea when I grocery shopped on my butler's day off. Ever notice how frozen food display doors are muffled?"

"Clever. And anyone who manages to follow you dead ends at a cave with nothing in it."

"I never allow anyone to follow me." Ratman tipped his head to the car. "There's an Autovision in the dash. Toggle that latch and turn it on. It's rigged to a camera in the back. Nobody's come close. If I even suspect it, I notify the highway patrol. Should all else fail, I have recordings with car sounds secreted along the road."

"You'd stop and they'd follow that sound. Nice." Jet Man wrinkled his nose. "What's that smell? You got a dead body in here?"

"Ah, I flood this cave with foul odors. Corpse flowers. Road kill. I keep horses, too. You're familiar with these smells from your day job, aren't you?"

"These days, I only work when I want to. I told my boss who I am."

"Oh?" Ratman didn't hold with the sharing of secret identities.

"The chief was delighted to have Jet Man on his team. Er, is that a '56 Davis scooter?"

"It was. Those oldies are easy to come by and cheap. I cannibalize them or fit my gadgets on them."

Jet Man whistled. "I guess when you have a million bucks you can afford to collect cars."

He took in a black, low-slung Plymouth XNR with four headlights. Its right side could be uncovered into a passenger seat. Ratman kept a 1953 Alfa Romero Bertone with wheel covers and sweptback rear window. A Toyota EX, seemed to blend into a saucer, wrap around windshield and a split rear window. Jet Man noted a 1964 Subaru Rabbit RS3, sort of a cross between a car and a three-wheeled motorcycle. A Gyro-X was a two-wheeled car with armor plating. There was even a car with one wheel. It was a Studebaker-Packard Astral that balanced by using gyroscope technology. It could hover over water. The Dalnik D-06 looked like a covered motorcycle. Standing out among them was a Panhard Dynavia perfectly preserved from 1948. Oddest was a 1952 Sigvard Berggren Streamliner. One vehicle was different from the rest.

"Oh. This must be the Rat-copter." Jet Man came upon a Rotorway Javelin. Modified for two, it looked like a car had been turned into a copter.

Ratman had an SG-2 Gaz Torpedo from the Soviet Union, a streamlined car that resembled a wingless jet plane. It even had a tail. A motorcycle had two headlights and a seat, raised handle bars, a spare at the back, almost a two-wheel car. Apparently, he'd bought more than a few Nobel 200 kits. Jet Man seemed especially keen on a four-foot long black Peel P50. The thing boasted a smoked bubble top that obscured the driver.

He noted a Chevy V-8. It could reach nearly two hundred miles per hour on a three-wheel bike powered by a jet engine. There was also, Jet Man saw, a 1955 Chrysler Ghia Streamline X Gilda, a 1958 Plymouth Tornado, a Ford Selene II and a 1959 Ford Levacar Mach 1. A black, aerodynamic MG EX 181 dated from a decade ago. A single seater, the driver was covered by a dome. The rear bore a fin. Supercharged with three hundred horsepower, it could go two-hundred and fifty-four miles per hour. Last but not least, was a 1953 Renault Riffard Tank.

Jet Man said, "I always marvel how that's not really a tank but gets called a tank."

"Why not? You're not really a jet." Ratman smiled.

"You haven't lost your sense of humor."

"To your point, I don't just finance my work with my inheritance."

"So, you're not only a mysterious avenger of the night, you're a mysterious scavenger of the night."

"Jet Man, there's something you must know. I might make a cute remark, but I never joke about my *work*. These items are better off with me. Some of them I took from very bad people. I've rejiggered them to the point where they'll withstand a M21 landmine. Some were my father's."

"Your father? Wasn't he just a doctor?"

"Just? You never heard of Doc Caliban? Dad fought crime back in the thirties before he met my mother and settled down."

"Doc Caliban was your father? I never made the connection."

"An old enemy caught up with him. You know the rest."

"Look, if this is too painful..."

"Those scars are all healed. I'm a big boy now."

"But an armed robber killed your folks."

"A hired hit man posing as a robber. Stick-up men don't kill people."

"Thus, your mask, alias, and closely guarded identity." Jet Man nodded.

"My father made a mistake I won't make." His mood brightened, as if realizing it felt good to unload to another person who had the *calling*. "Come on. I'll give you a tour."

"So this is the Rat Hole, huh?"

"Just my garage. But the cave is naturally climate-controlled with temperatures sixty-five degrees Fahrenheit year-round. The Rat Hole itself is nearby."

"My guess is this place shows as a fallout shelter on the blueprints for this mansion."

"Very astute. Police methods of deductive reasoning have rubbed off on you."

They walked an incline and emerged from an unused furnace in a basement. A small device inside it made the surface warm to the touch, as if it was functioning.

"Take a run around the area, see if you can find my actual nerve center. Don't let anyone see you, though."

"A challenge, huh? Okay."

Jet Man leaned forward and was gone. It felt good to be running again after that fourteen-mile ride. Speed let him vibrate through walls. He took in a dining room, a gym, a vast kitchen, a study, living room, library. There were ornamental medallion moldings on the ceilings, crystal chandeliers. Outside, Jet Man ran a winding private driveway. The guest house caught his eye. Inspection revealed that wasn't hiding the Rat Hole. Minutes later, the speedster returned in a blur, solidifying into a man. He had noted the address of the three-story mansion was 1007 Mountain Drive.

"I thought you'd have a larger pool."

"Oh, that's the bathtub," Louis Wemyss answered. He had doffed his Ratman guise for a smoking jacket. He was sipping from a drink in the expansive kitchen. Wemyss was looking at the front of a twenty-one-foot Bendix camper parked out back. "Give up? That's it. Want a beer after all that?"

"No, thanks. I'll be running at high speed later."

"It's non-alcoholic, but it smells beery. I like to keep up the illusion that I'm a lush."

"Okay, thanks. All that running did give me a thirst." Jet Man accepted the drink and took a pull. "Hmm, pretty good. I haven't had a beer since I gained my powers. It wouldn't be good for a tipsy guy to run at superspeed. So, the Rat Hole is that mobile home, huh."

"Which I've now finally proven to my satisfaction the subterfuge works." They walked through Wemyss Manor. "I've never had anyone here I could test my camouflage on."

"And it can be driven off the grounds, if necessary," Jet Man ventured. "You know, I looked over your cars more closely. You cannibalize them, sure. But they're still so eye catching. How do you keep the bad guys from sabotaging them once you park?"

"Mercury. He drives whatever car I'm using back home. The kid wants to do more, but I can't expose him to danger. When I need a ride, I signal and either he or Malcolm comes for me."

"Just like the signals you arranged for the Squadron."

They came upon a butler arranging a costume on a life size Ratman statue. "Officially, I admire Ratman's results but abhor his methods."

"Indeed, sir," the butler piped up. "So brutal."

"This is Malcolm. Malcolm, this is Jet Man."

Jet Man stuck out a hand before Malcolm could remind himself butlers don't shake guest's hand. But he did so now.

"Barry Frankoff," Jet Man said. "Pleased to meet you."

"Likewise, sir. Call for Malcolm should you require anything."

Wemyss's brow wrinkled. Jet Man telling Malcolm his real name was not what was bugging him. Bugging him was the possibility his parents were alive in another universe. And he couldn't get to them. Or could he?

Jet Man looked over last year's *A Dictionary of*

American Sign Language on Linguistic Principles. "The best cover is for Louis Wemyss to seem like a starstruck Ratman groupie, huh?"

"Quite so. Hey, those lightning bolts over your ears? Do they serve any purpose?"

"They're aerials. I need something separate from my signal belt for the Squadron. One keeps me in touch with Jet Boy, and the other is for police in Octagon City."

"Interesting. Might we wire my rat ears with something like that? I wouldn't want to block my hearing though." He pointed to his Ratman hood. "It's lighter material over my human ears on the cowl."

"Sure. I have a feeling you have everything here that I'd need for that operation."

"Actually, I'm glad you're here." Ratman pushed on. "I'll give you my file on Orville Baron. Show it to the Superior Squadron. Their eyes only. Shred it when you're done."

"Orville Baron. Who's he?"

Wemyss looked around carefully before answering. He'd rather Malcolm wasn't burdened with yet another superhero's alter ego.

"He's Gold Arrow. I didn't mention him at the meeting. He should take my place on the team. He's wealthy and might make a better member than Super Goat Man. It's the least I can do since I'm leaving.

***

Delighted his ray weapon worked, Braindroid set to further nefarious schemes. First, he had to replenish his stock of hercolubite. Using a sensitive instrument of his own invention to detect it, Braindroid was led to the rift.

This is where Golden Ring came through, Braindroid mused. "What can it be?"

"Analysis says it is a rip in the fabric of space,

darling," *Coppélia* answered. "Probability of another universe on the side is ninety-five percent."

"What of the other five percent?"

"Oblivion."

"With those odds, I'll take my chances," Braindroid responded. "It has hercolubite there, so we're going through."

"Zero percent *I* will fit through the rift, darling."

He saw that now. It was obvious to him *Coppélia* would, indeed, not fit through it. Braindroid pondered this.

"All that lovely hercolubite," Braindroid cried. "It's just going to waste."

"Calculations suggest your escape launch will fit," *Coppélia* stated. "A tight fit, however."

"Eureka," Braindroid shouted. His instruments pointed him to sources of the hercolubite. "An asteroid?"

Braindroid plugged the terminals on his head into micro files. They showed the asteroid was charted and named 269 Justitia by humans in his universe. What it was named here, he neither knew nor cared. He engaged the launch. It used impulse power. Once aboard, the mechanical voice of *Coppélia* came through, patched from the disguised spaceship. "Humans still foolishly rely on physical fuel for space exploration."

The piece of real estate was still hundreds of millions of miles away, but Braindroid's space lifeboat could easily make the journey. The asteroid was some thirty miles wide and red. Now through the rift, Braindroid unfurled photon sails that captured sunlight to power his craft.

"This lowly lifeboat has more capability than any of Earth's most advanced spacecraft." He sneered and readied an essential device he would need.

***

With Jet Man gone, Louis Wemyss strode to his bank

of phones. He picked up one receiver. "Operator, I'd like to make a person-to-person long distance call. It's to Orville Baron in Santa Paula, Florida."

Line established, Wemyss informed Baron he had "an interesting proposition, one that couldn't be discussed over the phone."

Intrigued, Baron agreed and a meeting was arranged. He'd put an end to most local crime and was bored. Plus, he was eager to wheel out his new private jet.

***

Braindroid landed his craft on the asteroid. The chilling vacuum of space could freeze his limbs solid. Sunlight would boil a living creature. Micrometeoroids, dust particles sharp as glass or space debris traveling at the rate of tens of kilometers per second might easily pierce an ordinary spacesuit. For that reason and despite high levels of durability, Braindroid pulled a pressure suit of his own design over his pink and white outfit. This was complete with a rocket pack on his back. His jerry-rigged portable hercolu-counter was pinging. Resolutely, he buckled a pistol in the holster.

Braindroid smiled. There was hercolubite aplenty. He stopped cold upon noticing...footprints. Giant impressions peppered the surface. Braindroid bent closer to examine them. "Boot-prints?" Vaguely human shaped, he estimated their size. "Whoever, or whatever, made these must be twenty feet tall."

Lightning-fast calculations came to him. "Exactly eight point seventy-six meters tall, twenty point seven-seven feet, sixteen point fifty-one tons."

"Earthlings have an old sea chanty warning against sixteen tons," came through his helmet's radio link.

Braindroid disconnected *Coppélia's* communications. He needed to think. "Why, these could have been here for a million years with no wind to disturb them."

Before Braindroid could speculate further, a hand matching that estimate grasped him. He found himself held by a giant man-shaped form, clad in interlocking purple and blue plates. His guess had been good. Braindroid sensed regulated power surging within the giant. There *was* physical power, too. The grasp was ironclad, Braindroid realized as he struggled. The giant's helmet had blade-like aerials on the sides. *When I engage my force field,* Braindroid promised himself, *it will splay open this giant's hand.*

The giant carried him over the landscape. A section of rock hinged and the pair entered a cave. Lights blinked on. They were now shut off from the vacuum of space in a pressurized chamber. The asteroid had been hollowed out. Instruments on his spacesuit told him air circulated. This nerve center had the necessary accoutrements for a space ship encased inside the asteroid. The giant released Braindroid before the force field could be engaged. He plucked the hercolubite counter from Braindroid, a toy in this mammoth hand. Giving it a casual glance, the giant tossed it aside. The thing was sturdy enough not to break.

"You have trespassed," the giant boomed. "And thus, you cannot leave alive. *Or* you may choose to live as my herald. The choice is yours."

"Your herald?" Braindroid surreptitiously engaged the force field. He wanted that hercolubite and was ready to slay giants for it. "You think I'm a mere lackey?"

"That response has sealed your fate." He motioned toward Braindroid. Blindingly hot plasma shot forth. After an appropriate time required to obliterate one such as this, the giant ended his attack. He was surprised to behold Braindroid unharmed. He, inside the force field, was not reduced to a bubbling puddle.

"A force field? Clever human. Primitive but effective. It will not help you when I burn a hole through this rock and cast you out to space. You will survive only for so long there."

"Wait," Braindroid implored, hands out. "I am no human. And I'm not herald material, either. I did not mean to trespass."

Some combination of these words intrigued the giant. "Why are you here?"

"Perhaps if you called off the hostilities, I could explain. Look, it's a stalemate. What can you lose by listening?" He shut off the force field. "Destroy me if you don't like my explanation." Braindroid might have been untrustworthy, a liar, and a cheat, but he wasn't going to grovel or die floating in some other universe's outer space.

The giant, via gesture, invited Braindroid farther into his outpost.

Braindroid pulled back the flexible helmet.

Turning his back to his guest, the giant was checking consoles of flashing lights and beeping sounds, making adjustments. "Hostilities shall cease should I find your explanation satisfactory," the giant said to his guest. "Do not draw your sidearm."

"A question first. How do you understand English?"

"I have learned Earth languages during my incubation period." A massive hand rose near his head to the antennae there. "English is the loudest, most persistent and far reaching I detected. It is colorful, with all the music of planets colliding."

English may have been their common language, but pictures were better.

"Can I show you this?" He held out another device taken from a belt pouch. Braindroid's finger pressed and images appeared, illustrating his presence here. He handed the device up to the giant.

"So, you are not of here but from that rift? Thus, you know not of me. Earthlings here call me Faculus." The giant pointed toward a planet on his own view screen.

"What is your designation?"

Braindroid couldn't help but look at the blue marble wonderingly. "I am Braindroid." There was enough natural ham in him to bow like a performer. "Believe me, the existence of another universe is quite interesting to me, as well. How do you travel about in this? Seems rather confining for a being as large as yourself."

"This conveyance is what Earth creatures...those caterwauling in English...would call a *shuttle*. The mother ship lies hidden within the rings of Saturn. That is immaterial. For what purpose are you here?"

"Your shuttle is rich in a certain mineral." Braindroid tapped a wall, taking away a chalky pink-white chunk.

Faculus reached over to it. The material was like a marble in his gigantic hand. "This is largely sodium lithium boron silicate hydroxide, made of tiny crystals less than five microns in diameter. It has no intrinsic value. Yet, you seek it. Why?"

"You are correct. It is worthless hercolubite. Now, just as Earthlings invented the Geiger counter to detect radiation, I have invented the hercolu-counter. It detects—"

"Hercolubite, obviously. That name is unknown in this universe."

Braindroid nodded toward the piece Faculus dropped at his feet. "As you surmised, the material *is* worthless...to most. But valuable to me. Hercolubite is the only known weakness of an enemy of mine. Superior Man protects Earth—"

"Earth? There is no being there named Superior Man. For my own purposes, I have cataloged all its powerful beings. Even if such a being existed, I fail to see how he could be affected by this lowly material." He gave it a kick. The chunk crumbled to pieces.

To Braindroid, even little pieces were valuable.

Faculus gestured as a conductor. Tiny, but sharply detailed, images of this Earth's guardians appeared, floating in the air. He waved his hand and the tableaux sunk to ground level as one piece. But some of the figures remained airborne above others.

Braindroid gaped at them, steaming. "There *would* have to be super people here. The Earth through that rift has other similar people, besides Superior Man."

"So...parallel development, as had been theorized, is real. Most interesting. Would that I might pass through the rift to that Earth."

"If I may ask, why?"

"Details would bore you. Suffice to say, I have pledged this Earth shall never be violated. However, I am not held from consuming a *different* Earth."

"Consuming?"

"For sustenance I must consume planets." Faculus sighed, as if tired of explaining his nature. "That type, class M, is my preference. And at what loss? Technological civilizations tend to destroy themselves once they become capable of interstellar radio communication."

It was Braindroid's turn to be interested. With Earth consumed, those costumed meddlers would die.

"I have noticed the rift," the giant went on. "Little did I suspect it was the entrance to another universe. And within it, another Earth. Yet my girth prevents me from claiming that prize. Am I cursed to be tantalized so? Within very few cycles, I shall expire. Starved."

The semblance of a smile played about Braindroid's lips. "Wait, I know a way."

"Speak."

"What if I could get you through it?"

"How can that be? I am not one of Earth's clownish contortionists."

Images of Tarantula-Man, Sergeant-at-Arms and Red Devil twisting into such exertions joined the tableaux.

"I have a miniaturization ray. You will be shrunk, as small as those images. On the other Earth, your full size can be restored with a reverse application of—"

"Impossible." Faculus emphasized displeasure by stomping the chunk to dust.

"Maybe for others. But not for my tenth-level intelligence. What would you give for that? The worthless rocks?"

"As many as you could carry will be yours should you facilitate me through the rift. Even they would not be enough of a reward. You shall have this shuttle."

Braindroid had a caveat. "I must remind you, my Earth's protectors are equal to those you showed me here. They're gifted with extraordinary abilities and powerful enough to harm you."

"Harm *me*?" Faculus scoffed. "The ones of this universe could not even harm my last herald. Rannin Nord carries a portion of my power."

"No single being could best my universe's champions, I tell you." Braindroid was firm on this point. "I have tried. Only that material is harmful to Superior Man. With the most dangerous one gone, the rest fall like ten pins." He squatted, taking up the pulverized hercolubite, then let it fall from his hands dramatically. Faculus might not have known what ten pins were, but the meaning was clear.

"Rannin Nord can fit through easily," Faculus brightened. "Yes, he shall clear the way for me."

"But should he? That would, as humans say, *tip your hand.*"

"Utter nonsense," Faculus roared. "Anyone attempting to stop him will be summarily destroyed."

As he spoke, Faculus swept away the heroes. He replaced them with images of his herald. A silvery man was flying through space, standing on a disc. Beaming rays of energy shot from his hands.

Braindroid was amazed. Never had he seen anything like that. The herald wielded more power than all the heroes Faculus displayed.

"Behold Rannin Nord! He will dispatch those beings you allude to. Upon his return, you shall shrink me *and* my machinery for feeding, see to my passage through the rift and, thus, restore me. That planet shall be drained of all elemental life. In return, you will receive this craft."

"Am I clear that you would then have no further interest in *this* universe's Earth?"

"None. This will be your Earth to conquer. For I see that appeals to you. The beings on your Earth, I perceive, have not swayed you from that goal."

"Yes, that is true."

He looked about the shuttle. *Oh, what I could whip up with this advanced, otherworldly technology.* What treasures awaited in Faculus's mothership?

"It is agreed." Faculus's voice boomed, interrupting Braindroid's revelry.

"I presume since you can survive in the vacuum of space, reentry is no problem to you."

"The burn will alert the humans, of course," Faculus replied. "But that is of no consequence to me. Surely, they watch their sky as Earthlings do here."

"That will work in your favor. It will cause fear and anxiety. I can rig a device to bathe you in the restorative ray upon impact. Once you're at normal height, those super bumblers will arrive to see their giant conqueror before them. *Coppélia* can calculate your landing to the fifth decimal place."

"A herald of yours?"

"Oh, my ship. I ask only to watch you humble those dolts. There is a certain public place in their biggest city on the most prominent nation you ought to make Earthfall."

"Your sense of dramatics and grievance do not interest me, Braindroid. Only consuming your Earth does."

"You will have to wear armor of hercolubite, of course. It will fend off that powerful protector on my Earth should he banish your herald."

"Have I not been clear?" Faculus bellowed. "I wield cosmic power. I have given a quantity of it to him."

"Call up those images again."

The giant did so.

"I shall catalogue them for you. Superior Man flies like that one but *without* a warclub to pull him. His body is as invincible as the man in armor. And he's got the strength of that gray monster without the mindless thrashing about. Plus, he has the eye beams of that one."

"Yet this lowly material weakens him?" Faculus grabbed a piece. "It seems inconceivable."

"After being exposed to hercolubite, your blasts would utterly destroy him. Another one of that bunch will try to isolate you within an energy field. But I will tint your protection gray. His weapon is useless against anything that color. However, we'll need more than you have here."

"An unusual weakness," Faculus said. "You believe my endeavor would be useless without Rannin Nord first clearing my way."

"Indeed. Superior Man's own world was obliterated. He is rather sensitive about it. Perhaps the Faculus of his universe caused its demise."

"There is but one Faculus."

"Of course. Now, as I see from pointing my hercolu-counter toward your Earth there is an adequate supply of hercolubite in the landmass they call Africa."

"Kosawa, to be precise," Faculus added.

"Odd, that country isn't on my Earth."

"Be advised. Before you claim it, you will have to eliminate those protectors I have shown you. One of them resides there."

CHAPTER 8

Orville Baron was a slim, fit, clean-shaven blond. From his sporty wear, Louis Wemyss wouldn't peg him as a millionaire. The two met in a local restaurant Wemyss had recommended, *Planet Hercólubus*. The maître d, outfitted and made up as the Jokester, fielded reservations on a red phone under glass. Wait staff bustled around in inaccurate versions of Jet Man's and Amazon Woman's costumes. A plastic Eagleman hung from the ceiling. The word given to patrons was that Shrinking Man was about also, but too small to be seen. Hyperactive kids waiting for their selections from the Wonderkind portion of the menu, pumped coins into kiddie rides, replicas of the Silver Machine, Airphibian and the Ratmobile.

Wemyss, after greeting his guest, said, "I took the liberty of ordering you a glass of Aquamarine. It's blue lemonade."

"Great." Baron smiled. "How'd you know I love lemonade?"

"They mentioned it in that *NewsView* profile of you."

Baron had wanted to try the non-alcoholic red, white and blue Magic Whips, however. When the waiter appeared, Baron opted for Eagleman Wings. Wemyss's Indigo Plate Special was the Superior Manwich, beef on a hard roll with green guacamole dressing. They thought about getting the Fantastic Mountain of Mashed Potatoes but decided to share a plate of Ratmantouille and Golden Ring onions. A short teenage Aquamarine came by and refilled their water glasses. Wemyss ignored his glass in favor of the shining coffee pot on the table, modeled on the

Silver Machine.

Orders filled, Wemyss had a request of the waiter, "Golden's, please."

"Do you mean Gulden's, sir?"

"What do you think, Baron? Is it Gulden's or Golden's?"

"So far as I know, it's Gulden's."

The two spent the meal comparing tax shelters, along with their experiences as millionaires and investors. Wemyss thought Baron was feeling him out before he springs.

"Now, what's this proposition? Why do you need me? You're already a millionaire."

While listening, Wemyss pulled a rubber band off his wrist and fitted a gold tailed toothpick into it.

"What are you doing there?" Baron asked.

Instead of answering, he released the toothpick toward Baron. Effortlessly, reflexively, he caught it.

"Impressive catch. Almost instinctive."

"I have pretty good reflexes, as I indulge in numerous sports."

"Such as archery?"

"Funny you mention it." Baron prepared his stock answer. "That's one I don't care for."

Wemyss lowered his voice. "That's about what I'd expect Gold Arrow to say."

"Gold Arrow?" That had rattled Baron. "I'm not Gold Arrow."

"Oh, you are. To answer your question, I didn't want to carry my file on you out in public. But I have one."

"File?"

"After I was sure, I had Superior Man do a fly by. He X-rayed your place." Wemyss tapped his temple. "Your Arrowgyro seems to be based off an old Dragonfly Ice Sled."

"I don't know what you're talking about," Baron

bleated. Inwardly, he was mortified that Superior Man would observe his private home. Was that even legal?

"I'm impressed how you transformed a bicycle frame into an electric autogyro, complete with bulletproofing. And clever how it looks like an arrow. I suppose Swifty, that ward of yours, flies it. After all, he holds a pilot's license. You should hide it with something more substantial than a drop cloth, though."

"Hey, what is this anyway? I thought you had a business deal to discuss."

"I do," Wemyss returned. "The business of vetting you for the Superior Squadron."

"I don't see why they need another millionaire. Especially as they seem to already have one snooping for them."

"They need you as Gold Arrow, not as a millionaire."

"This is ridiculous," Baron steamed, getting up to leave.

"Should you change your mind..." Wemyss reached up, "this card will give you access to our...Superior Squadron headquarters."

Baron locked eyes with Wemyss for a second. Grudgingly, he took the card. He wondered how Wemyss would like it crumpled up and fed to him as dessert. Instead, Baron placed some money on the table.

A waiter swooped in. "I'll bring you your change."

"Keep it for damages," Baron answered.

"Damages?"

Then he upended the table onto Wemyss and stormed off. Like Baron, he reacted quicker than expected. A gaggle of staffers hurried to Wemyss, brushing him off.

"So sorry, Mr. Wemyss," one of them said.

"I've taken harder hits on the squash court."

"We won't let him back in here."

"No need for that. I'm sure it's not the first time some dissatisfied customer attacked an owner."

***

At Assemblers Mansion, Man Machine pulled Sergeant-at-Arms aside. "Týr's been babbling the whole trip back."

"His Elizabethan patois always sounds like babble to me." Sergeant-at-Arms eyed Tarantula-Man suspiciously.

"He drank a frozen malted with some hippie kids."

"Nice of them to share," the patriot commented. "It's the American way—"

"All of it," Man Machine emphasized. "The sugar, the chocolate, or the sheer coldness got to him."

Across the room, Týr tapped Hval on the meeting table for attention. Heads swiveled to him.

"It is but clear. I know of eight overlapping realms. Yon golden man, what you have shown me in moving pictures is surely from a ninth. Methinks he can *only* be from another realm."

"You may be right." Sergeant-at-Arms looked grim.

"Verily, it must be. Mayhap we are upon a new *lussinatta*. I shall consult Wotan, the All-Father. He would knoweth whence a being from one realm trespasses on another." Týr strode to the kitchen door that led to the backyard.

"I trust thee, loyal mortal squires, to carry on whilst I be away." Týr raised the club again and swung it.

"Hold up, Týr," Sergeant-at-Arms yelled. "I want to ask about those realms—"

There was a crackling of energy, and he was gone.

Sergeant-at-Arms slumped. Týr could have settled this other universe business. Kingsize and Hornette once told him someone named Superior Man came from another universe. It was a big claim. And required more proof than just say-so. First off, that name didn't seem in line with the American way. *Superior*? Shades of the doctrine of Nazi supremacy.

Tarantula-Man interrupted the patriot's thoughts. "Squires? He's the leader and you folks assist him?"

"Well, he thinks so," Sergeant-at-Arms said.

"Yeah, I can see how he might."

At that moment, their butler bustled in. "Black Leopard is on the picture phone, ladies and gentlemen."

Tarantula-Man asked, "Who, or what, is Black Leopard?"

"Another Assembler." Sergeant-at-Arms had never met him. "Headquartered in Kosawa, Africa."

"I got an A in geography, Sarge," Tarantula-Man bristled.

Sergeant-at-Arms fixed him in his reflective eyes. "Look, we're involved in something big here." He thought of a test for Tarantula-Man. "See if you can locate Red Devil for us." He placed a hand on the web-thrower's shoulder. "He'd make a fine Assembler. If so, we'll have two new members."

Tarantula-Man clicked his mandibles. "A guy dressed head to toe in a red and yellow gymnastic suit with devil horns on his hood ought to be easy enough to find."

"In that case, find him and bring him here."

"I'll do my best." The arachnid snapped a salute.

The Assembler ushered the applicant to the door. "See Penniman before you leave. He'll give you credentials that'll admit you here next time."

"Penniman?"

"The butler." Man Machine pointed to the kitchen.

"I guess crawling up a wall here to tap on the window isn't credential enough."

"If I know him, he'll hand you a snack for the road, too."

Sergeant-at-Arms made sure Tarantula-Man reported to the kitchen. He muttered, "These super lunatics I have to deal with." Now that he thought about it, he was surrounded by former criminals. Was Tarantula-Man to be trusted? Could Marksman be playing a long con for another shot at Man Machine? Were the two *lusus naturae* part of a plot by Solenoid?

By now, his fellow Assemblers were crowding the picture phone. The patriot joined them as a serious looking black man began talking. "Hello, friends. This is just too bizarre."

"What's up, Tcharlare?" Sergeant-at-Arms inserted current teen slang into his speech.

"I was enroute to the World Festival of Negro Arts in Dakar, Senegal, when I was alerted to a break-in at a local warehouse here," Tcharlare explained. "A green man with printed circuitry and terminals on his head got away with a supply of orichalcum."

"Orichalcum? That's the—"

"Yes, yes, the source of my nation's high-tech status, but that is not the weirdest part. He shrunk the ore and carted it off to a strange aircraft. This craft rose faster than anything ever seen."

Man Machine spoke. "Okay, that *is* weird. But right now we've got other things than an orichalcum heist to consider."

"Friend, what could be more important than an orichalcum heist?" Tcharlare asked. "Shrunk down and put on a strange aircraft, to boot."

"Something I can't mention over an international line, rated secure by Special Projects or not, is more important. Trust me," Man Machine held. "But we could fly in and take a look."

"No need. The trail will have grown cold by the time you get here. Anyway, none of you have the sharpened senses I possess."

Marksman had held his tongue until now. "Stole your orichalcum, huh?"

"Yes, that is correct, Marksman."

"Sorry, Tcharlare."

There was a second of silence.

"I will see you in the training room next time I am at Assembler headquarters, Marksman." Resolutely, he pulled a tight full-face feline hood up. He meant for his Black Leopard guise to intimidate the archer. "Bring your arrows."

The screen went blank.

Man Machine was still shaking his metallic head while dialing a secure phone line. This was to the Leland Building. After getting through to Rich Reide, Man Machine asked, "Think you and I could use one of those advanced rockets, or whatever you gave NASA, to get us into orbit?"

"We sure could. Why do you need a rocket? Is there something up there you can't reach under your own power?"

"There seems to be a, I don't know, rift up there."

"A rift?"

"The Special Projects Agency showed us footage of a man coming through it."

"A man? Where is this man now?"

"He went back through. Galloping Gazelle's eyes move faster than ours. He says that guy was *pulled* back against his will."

Man Machine, of course, did not suspect the rift was to another universe nor that the gold man knew Superior Man. He had no reason to.

"Interesting," Reide said. "I was scheduled to go with a couple of astronauts on Gemini 13 to look over a satellite."

"I heard about that," Man Machine said.

"Right. The LES1 went dead."

"It's what gave me the idea to call you. My boss Ferro is friends with J. Jacob Jackson. He might pull a few strings via his astronaut son. Junior could suggest to NASA we take the place of their astronauts. Tell them I want to test my new astro-armor."

"I have *carte blanche* there," Reide said. "I'm consulting with them on Project Orion."

Man Machine gasped. "Isn't that to test the idea of using a gamma bomb to accelerate a spaceship to Mars?"

"It is. Okay. Jet over here. I got a bird that'll get us to Cape Kennedy."

"That wouldn't be the ten-year-old Ryan X-13 Vertijet you picked up cheaply from Ferro, would it?"

"The same."

"How much time do I have?" Man Machine knew the craft. It needed prep time.

"If you want a ride, you better leave right away. I'd like to eyeball that rift myself." Reide signed off.

Sergeant-at-Arms marched up to Man Machine as he hung up. His opinion on whether Superior Man was really from another universe would carry weight. But hope faded as Man Machine shot into the air. "Got a rocket plane to catch."

Sergeant-at-Arms shook his head. "I can't get a break today."

***

At first, nobody believed the reports. After all, there were legends of flying carpets. That's all they were: legends. Now, a man, seemingly made of shining silica, rode astride a chrome disc, flying at impossibly high altitudes. He surveyed the planet at supersonic speed. All points of the globe reported sightings of him. Unknown to anyone on this Earth, he once lived a normal life. Rannin Nord became Faculus's herald in exchange for sparing his planet the ravages of his feeding frenzy.

The air forces of several nations pursued Rannin Nord, only to be left in his wake. Visual contact confirmed he seemed to be searching. Then, he found something. An island in the tropical part of the southern half of the Pacific Ocean. It was near the International Date Line. Legendary aviator Fly By Knight was headquartered there, along with his namesake team.

In quick succession, beams of energy from shining hands lashed out. To a man, however, the Fly By Knights were unharmed. Their quarters were not so lucky. Some scrambled to the surviving jets, but those couldn't keep up with the strange visitor.

Next, Superior Man's own Fort Superior was attacked. There the bottled city of Gandar, that Braindroid had miniaturized, was damaged. Under the rays of Earth's yellow sun, tiny Hercólubusians instantly became super-powered. They were too dazzled to mount a counter attack. In fact, their newfound superpowers made things there worse. Heat vision, X-ray vision, flying ability, and super strength did not come with instructions.

The disc flew on, heading to the continental United States. At the Rocky Mountains, the shining man located the headquarters of the Challengers of the Fantastic. Fantastic Mountain was sundered. Similarly destroyed was the home of the Death Patrol. The Mecha-Men were not only blasted but melted down by hot plasma. Finally, he came to the home of Noah Merlin. As the silica man confronted him with a blast, there seemed to be a secondary flash. Merlin was not to be found.

***

A sudden beam of heat playing upon his back told the invader Superior Man had found him. He'd been warned about this one. The beam was more like a tickle than a burn. Rannin Nord rose to a higher altitude. So fast was this, Superior Man could barely put on the brakes, turn and pursue. He saw the being disappear around the curve of the Earth. Then Rannin Nord was out of visual range. Superior

Man, having lost the invader's trail, scanned the scene below him. He spotted a teammate and descended. Eagleman was at Merlin's home, digging.

"You know, it's odd..." Superior Man had subjected the area to his range of visual powers as he descended. He scanned a radiation trail back toward the rift. "The radiation signature here is different. Not like the other traces."

Eagleman considered this information. It confirmed something his nose had told him. The exaggerated beak on his helmet did not interfere with his olfactory abilities. "A scent here reminds me of my accidental abduction here, years ago."

"I remember. Peter van de Kamp theorized a giant Jupiter-like world at the edge of the Solar System. He got Professor Merlin to aim his teleportation beam out that way."

"It yanked me here from a planetary war. That supports my guess Merlin escaped death by engaging his experimental teleportation beam."

"You might be onto something." Superior Man hovered, his cape a flag in the breeze. "But if that flying guy fried a noncombatant, he gets no mercy. Merlin's fate will have to wait. For now, the shining man is our problem."

"I don't know what he's up to. He could have attacked us, but he didn't. He went after the other heroes. Why do you think?"

"Ah..." Superior Man realized a possibility. "It was a warning. He doesn't want to fight the most powerful beings here, us."

"Exactly."

"I want another crack at him." Superior Man turned to fly. "He won't evade me for long."

"No," Eagleman said. "Go to Earth A and talk to your friends there. They must know something about him we can use."

"I can get through the rift easily enough. Okay, but be ready for another attack."

Eagleman pondered this while winging toward Superior Squadron headquarters. If Noah Merlin's beam had since been perfected, and he was alive, Eagleman could return to Iukkoth.

Meanwhile, Superior Man followed the radiation trail. Sure enough, it led back to the hole, confirming the invader was from the other universe. He scanned for a telephone booth. Finding one, he landed. Superior Man wasn't there to change clothing if such was even possible. Instead, he got through to an operator on a collect call. Eagleman wouldn't get to headquarters fast enough to relay his discovery.

Superior Squadron headquarters had teletypes for messages, civilian and military radio reports from around the world, images and audio over television. A collect call was the last thing they expected to receive. An operator put through the call to their private number, asking if they would accept the charges. Aquamarine, Golden Ring and Amazon Woman exchanged looks when the operator said the call was from someone claiming to be Superior Man.

"He's the only one of us who'd phone," Amazon Woman said.

"You'd think the phone company could stand us a call from a guy who has saved the Earth."

Amazon Woman accepted the charges.

"Hello, team. I can't locate the shiny guy but watch out. He wasn't just warning us. I think our headquarters is next on his hit list."

"We're ready," Amazon Woman said.

"I'm going to take Eagleman's suggestion and visit Earth A. A radiation signature I followed confirms he came through the rift. Maybe I can get some intelligence on him. I shouldn't be long."

Eagleman landed at HQ. "The invader is working his way up to us."

"Old news," Amazon Woman said. "Superior Man called with a warning."

Aquamarine advanced his own theory. "This guy was testing his powers...to see if he can handle us."

Eagleman pruned an errant feather. "With Superior Man in the other universe, we'll need a strategy to stop this guy."

"Any ideas?" Golden Ring asked.

"First, we have to decoy him away from populated areas." Amazon Woman scrambled for her Silver Machine. "Eagleman. With me."

"You got room for me in your bus?"

"If you fold up those wings tightly. Golden Ring, you position yourself with the sun behind you."

He took off, understanding what she wanted.

Eagleman glided aboard as instructed and buckled into a seat. "What's my part?"

"You can't fly fast enough to catch up to him, but I can." She started her craft and taxied to the headquarters egress port.

The roof opened, and the pair took off.

"Ah..." Eagleman had an epiphany. "Chrome Dome has no idea you'll be carrying a passenger. One who can fly."

"Unless he's got X-ray vision." Amazon Woman banked right and set the throttles to maximum drive. "I'll get close and draw his fire. When he blasts me, I'll spin out like I've been hit. You bail out, wings closed. In the fog of war, he'll think you're the pilot and stop blasting me. Then I'll come roaring back from my death spiral. That's when you fly in from the other side, swinging your morning star."

"You're forgetting one thing. Chrome Dome might

blast us out of the sky. Your Silver Machine doesn't have my maneuverability."

"Nonsense. This is an Amazon-made craft." She patted the control panel lovingly. "You'll knock him silly before he knows what hit him."

"An ancient weapon against energy beams." Eagleman cawed. "Should be interesting."

"You don't know how fearsome you look, diving into battle with that thing." Amazon Woman squeezed his feathered knee. "I have confidence his skull will yield to your old-fashioned bludgeoning."

"If you can fake him out, that is."

***

Rannin Nord found them first and commenced firing.

Amazon Woman drew him over the Atlantic Ocean where he blasted her with energy beams. The Silver Machine shook, and the duo proceeded with the plan. Amazon Woman killed the engine and dropped from the sky. "Go, man."

Eagleman tumbled from the door, wings folded to make a smaller target for the attacker. Weapon secure in his belt, Eagleman threw out his arms and legs like a skydiver escaping certain death as he fell from the spiraling plane.

Rannin Nord turned to check his handiwork. The aircraft was doomed.

Eagleman maneuvered behind the invader and unfurled his wings, which made the *blamf* sound of an opening parachute.

The alien turned in time to see Eagleman diving toward him, swinging the morning star. He connected. Other than producing a dull thud, it had no damaging effect.

A blast of energy was the invader's unemotional response. Eagleman evaded the beam, and as promised, he performed aerial maneuvers the Silver Machine couldn't match.

The invader was fast but the avian defied gravity.

Eagleman wasn't sure how the second beam of energy managed to wing him, but he was not so lucky with the third. He saw a burst of light, bright as the sun. Stunned, he was knocked backwards. There was heat. There was force. The null gravity material woven into his costume kept him from plummeting, but the eagle became a sitting duck. He was hanging in the air, blacked out. If a blast should shred his costume, he would no longer float. The invader shot another blast of energy.

Eagleman was defenseless.

Out of nowhere, a gold medieval shield of energy appeared in front of Eagleman. It was Golden Ring. His ring sparkled, and a golden catcher's mitt caught the falling morning star.

"I got your back," Golden Ring shouted.

Amazon Woman pulled out of the dive, came about, and zoomed toward the alien.

This unexpected complication distracted Rannin Nord from attacking Golden Ring. He knew then he had been had.

She closed in, willing to sacrifice herself to rid the world of this menace. The Silver Machine was too big a target to miss.

The invader blasted her. The Silver Machine rocked, a wing ablaze. Unlike Eagleman, it couldn't float in defiance of gravity. This time the downward spiral was for real.

Golden Ring willed the shield into a rope and lassoed Eagleman. The winged man came to, mad to the bone. One blast wasn't going to stop him.

Golden Ring opened the catcher's mitt. "Your trusty morning star, sir."

Eagleman took it then saw the Silver Machine's death spiral. "Amazon Woman's been hit."

"She'll ride the air currents down. Meanwhile, we've got to stop this guy."

Fighting inertia in the spinning jet, Amazon Woman realized her confidence might have been misplaced. The Silver Machine turned out to be no match for the alien. Her controls were useless, a safe emergency landing impossible. Now she had to bail out. With teeth gritted, she stabbed a button and shouted into her mic, "Mayday. Mayday. I'm going down in the drink. Mayday. Mayday."

That call was heard by Aquamarine in his Airphibian.

She followed up by pressing her personal communication device with the team's EMERGENCY signal beacon. The whole team received an alarm. She slapped the eject button.

Aquamarine called back, "Princess, take your boots off."

The canopy blew off and her seat jetted into the air. As the parachute deployed, her first thought was: *boots*? In all matters *ocean*, she trusted Aquamarine.

Riding the wind currents gave her time to yank off her prized boots and drop them to the ocean below. Soon after, she would hit the water, and her life-saving seat would become her doom, as it would drag her under, and she'd keep going down. Bracing for impact, she grabbed the seat harness release latch and filled her lungs with air.

Above, Golden Ring watched the Silver Machine slam into the waves with a horrendous splash and a ball of fire. "Where is she?"

Rannin Nord blasted the heroes.

Golden Ring threw up the shield again. Energy particles ricocheted off in a dazzling display of arcs and sparks.

"Blazing suns," the shining man cursed. *But* there was a phrase he had learned during his encounter with the Atoms Family. It now echoed in his mind.

One down.

He flashed away at supersonic speed.

**

The Silver Machine hit the water surface ahead of Amazon Woman. There was a sickening sound of crunching metal, a geyser of white water, and a red-hot fireball. The ocean swallowed it whole. She turned away, saddened as if she'd just witnessed a death in the family.

Now to save herself. Her tunic would soak up water and weigh her down. She grasped her whip from her belt with her free hand and unsnapped the belt. It fell away, and as the waves reached up to greet her, she unlatched the harness and ripped off the tunic, leaving her dressed in a blue body stocking. The seat hit the water, throwing her off and into the cold waves. With the whip clenched in her teeth, she swam unimpeded.

Aquamarine set the Airphibian's course toward Amazon Woman's last position. He spotted floating debris...and her red tunic tossed by the waves. His heart sank. He was too late. After engaging the retractable floats, he set down on the water, then dove in. His eyes easily pierced the inky depths, saw the sinking seat and parachute, but no sign of Amazon Woman. Parts of the jet already lay on the bottom.

"Where are you?" he spouted aloud in the Atlantica way of talking underwater. He looked up to the surface, and there, maybe a hundred yards away, a woman in blue was treading water with powerful strokes. He knew she had good lung capacity, but he didn't know how long she'd last trying to stay afloat.

Aquamarine angled toward her. Then the sea king surfaced and grasped her in his strong arms.

"Took you long enough." She wasn't accustomed to being rescued.

"Your chariot awaits." He guided her onto his plane.

Eagerly, she accepted the blanket he took from a cabinet and sank her face into, sobbing. "My beautiful jet."

"Leave it to me." He pressed a button marked SEND. "Tadpole. Aquamarine here. Imperative you and your team of Atlanticans salvage Amazon Woman's jet. Bring all you can find to headquarters for reassembly and repairs, if feasible."

"10-4, boss."

"Thank you," Amazon Woman said softly. "I must look a fright." She dragged a tuft of sopping hair from her face.

"Now you see why I wear short hair." Aquamarine ran a hand through his buzz-cut. "You're alive. That's all that matters."

"I'm grateful for that." She shook her waterlogged head. "Once I'm back on dry land, I'm getting one of those mod pixie cuts." *And maybe get it dyed jet black.*

Aquamarine requested medical stand by for their arrival.

CHAPTER 9

Superior Man was about to enter the rift into another world when the activity on Earth sidetracked him. His visual powers revealed Aquamarine's rescue of Amazon Woman, and the battle with the disc, which was fleeing the scene. Rift forgotten, he took chase.

I hope I can catch him. Got to really move.

Over the ocean, there was nobody to be unnerved by sonic booms. And so it was at supersonic speed that Superior Man slammed into the invader. Thrown from the disc, the shining silica man fell, but the disc quickly returned to catch him. The alien scrambled back onto it, stood upright, then as if surfing on air, he shot off, riding higher into the atmosphere, going supersonic himself.

Superior Man was on his tail.

Like cold on ice.

He flew in behind and, this time, grabbed the disc. As expected, the alien rider kept going, flew off and began to fall. That's when the disc reversed and slammed into the hero's midsection. Although not painful, the move surprised Superior Man enough that he released it.

"What the hey?" Superior Man sputtered. "It's alive."

The disc swooped after its master, catching him in mid-fall. And again, Superior Man flew to the invader. He dealt one of Ratman's karate chops to the shining man's neck. That had no effect.

The alien flung a line of energy at him then sped away. A blinding blast shocked Superior Man. Air was knocked from his lungs as the force pushed him back. But Superior Man didn't need air; all he needed was a yellow sun. Subsequent blasts the invader cast back were almost unbearable. His costume, of course, was indestructible. Determinedly, Superior Man flew in pursuit. After kicking into supersonic flight, he X-rayed his opponent.

No bones, no organs. He's an energy sponge.

Superior Man once more slammed into the alien invader. This time, as he was separated from the disc, Superior Man grabbed the shining man's wrist. And squeezed. Though the joint collapsed, this had no effect on the invader's stoic expression, however, he finally gave forth a grunted, "Uhh."

"Now you won't be blasting me again."

Rannin Nord's other hand pointed up to his pilotless disc. Incredibly, it swung around and battered itself against Superior Man. He turned heat vision on the thing, hoping more power and closer range would be effective...but no such luck. The disc kept up its attack.

Superior Man swung his captive like a club and slammed him into the disc. The hand on the end of the crushed wrist flopped like a broken toy. Superior Man did not like this sadistic tactic but then saw the hand pop back to normal and claw at him. Surprised, he released his grip on the invader.

"Maybe I'll knock some sense into you yet." Superior Man turned to deal out a punch. He landed one on the shining man's jaw but got nothing for his efforts. Then the alien and his disc reunited and flew off. Superior Man withstood another blast as a parting shot.

This is getting monotonous. He took off after the alien again, wondering what was next.

A giant gold net appeared out of nowhere and snagged the invader. Golden Ring was at the other end of it. Energy blasts shot out. Golden Ring imagined a blocking shield, and it materialized, but he was forced to drop the net to double the shield. It held off the beams, but just barely. The alien poured the energy on. Golden Ring was pushed back in the air but remained unharmed. Dissatisfied, the alien generated white hot rays. He meant to roast this golden warrior right through the shield.

Superior Man put an end to that. He gripped his enemy in a full-nelson. Superior Man had scoffed at the hand-to-hand combat tips he'd received from Ratman. The masked detective insisted his teammates be prepared for an enemy with equal strength. Superior Man never thought that would actually happen.

As he expected, the disc hammered him. He flew close to Golden Ring with his captive still in a headlock "You okay, Goldie?"

"Fine. Any ideas?"

"See if you can trap the disc. I'm going through the hole with this yahoo."

"Will do."

Superior Man rose up into the thin atmosphere and sought the rift. His visuals found it again. He flew through it with his captive then floated in front of the opening on the other side. Tightening his grip on the invader, Superior Man violently spun him around and around, then released him. Though the high-speed spinning didn't affect him, Rannin Nord couldn't control his acceleration. The disc wasn't there to intercept him. Rannin Nord was hurtling through the solar system of his home universe, tracing a trajectory away from the plane of the celestial equator. There wouldn't be any planets to land on. No moons or asteroids, either. Rannin Nord, defeated and without his disc, was relegated to an infinity of moving through outer space. Exhausted from battle, he entered a sleep-like meditation to dream of revenge to come.

Back on the other side, the disc was a loyal dog, trying to break through to follow its master. Ineffectively, but annoyingly, it battered Superior Man. When he moved away from the rift, the disc shot forward, through the hole, but Golden Ring was there; he willed a gold net into which the disc flew.

Superior Man flew to the other side and saw the disc flailing back and forth, trying to get free like a giant bird in a butterfly net. He gave Golden Ring a signal. Although he could smell the metallic scent of space, speech was impossible in a vacuum. Responding to Superior Man's gesture, Golden Ring imagined headsets that formed around his and Superior Man's heads, which enabled conversation.

"Drop the net." Superior Man grasped the disc. "We have to dispose of this thing for good, otherwise, it'll find Shiny Man and they'll be back." He struggled to keep a hold on the wild disc.

"What do you propose?"

"Stand back."

Like an Olympic discus thrower, Superior Man wheeled around and flung the disc toward the sun. Between that and gravity, within minutes the disc would become nuclear ash.

***

Back at headquarters, the team, less Superior Man and Golden Ring, were sorting through problems. "It's the scent of ionized air," Eagleman said. "The same harsh scent I picked up when I first got transported to this planet."

Aquamarine asked, "Are you confirming Merlin has perfected his own personal transportation beam...that he used it to escape death?"

"I think so. He must have engaged it as the silica guy blasted him. Otherwise, there'd be a heap of smoldering ash. That invader left the Mecha-men a molten mass. Merlin's likely alive."

Aquamarine had it figured. "Split second timing."

"He might be able to send me back to Iukkoth."

"Let's not get ahead of ourselves, Eagleman. We've

still got this menace to deal with. And you're needed here."

"I bet you want to tell Eaglette," Amazon Woman put in. She had a new outfit: blue shorts with stars, red lace-up sandals and bustier with an American eagle on it. A golden tiara kept her hair under control. She had scavenged it from odds and ends Superior Girl left after abandoning the idea of making a new costume. There was even a magnificent red cape. Amazon Woman wore it inside out, to obscure the yellow "SG" crest. Wrapped in it, she felt nice and toasty.

"I don't know about you..." Aquamarine let out a sigh, "but this waiting is killing me."

"As team chair..." Amazon Woman rose. "I say we take action."

Eagleman had doubts. "Are you suggesting dimension hopping?"

***

Superior Man watched the disc spin toward the other world's sun.

Golden Ring clapped him on the back. "Right on target."

Minutes passed. Then a solar flare arched up on the sun's surface.

"That's it. I can't see it anymore," Superior Man reported. "I still want to find what my friends here know about that shining man. What if there's another one?"

"The Assemblers." Golden Ring winced. "And the Atoms Family. What awful names for superheroes."

They got an unexpected delayed reaction from the sun. An eruption of magnetized plasma, a coronal mass ejection, exploded away from the sun and flared into space. It was a scorching stream flowing outward at a speed approaching a million miles an hour. Only twenty milliseconds long, the resulting release of energy knocked both heroes for a loop. Golden Ring's last thought revolved around this being worse than a sonic boom. He was knocked unconscious. The ring automatically protected him. An opaque sphere blocked out the extreme luminosity, but the concussion had sent him spinning.

Superior Man, tumbling, quickly recovered. He X-rayed the energy envelope but couldn't penetrate it.

"Golden Ring," he shouted soundlessly, the headsets gone. He caught up to his teammate and stabilized the roll. Superior as he might be, it would be hard to navigate space and hold unto a human in an energy field. Superior Man untied his cape and slung it around his companion, then gathered the corners and flung him over his shoulder, Santa Claus style.

I know the only girl who can help with this.

He set off for the other Earth and the Atoms Family. Superior Man traveled fast. He took a chance that Golden Ring could stand the extreme G-forces. Within minutes, he descended to Earth A and their United States. He located New York City, still unbelieving that name belonged to a major city. As Ken Clarke, his first newspaper job, he recalled, was with *The New York Star* in New Guernsey. He located the Leland Building.

They did say to drop in whenever I'm in town, Superior Man mused.

But this was serious. His friend was out of it. Even his super powers couldn't confirm if he was alive or dead. A different super power might. Intangible Girl could pass through this field and check Golden Ring.

***

At that very building, on East 42nd St and Madison Avenue, Golem and Flaming Youth were enjoying free time. After all, their teammates were away. Superior Man scanned and found the pair relaxing in their Recreation Room. Over blue trunks, Golem wore a smoking jacket.

Flaming Youth was in a blue bathrobe bearing an "A" on the right-front panel.

Holding Golden Ring with one hand, he knocked at the window.

"Superior Man," Golem exclaimed. Springing up to greet the visitor, a deep impression on the couch showed. "If I'd known you were coming I'd have baked a cake."

"No cake for me if I'm going to fit into this costume." Superior Man used his free hand to shake Golem's gravelly mitt. Despite his acute mental abilities, he couldn't remember the civilian names of the members of the Atoms Family. "One power I don't have is superior metabolism."

"Yeah. I guess flyin' doesn't burn many calories if you ain't flappin' wings."

"You've got someone here who flies by flapping wings? Oh, yes." Superior Man snapped his fingers. "One of the Tomorrow Men. Eagleman's wings are artificial. Hawk's wings are real."

"Yep. Born with wings," Flaming Youth said. "I wonder what that was like for his parents."

"Hey, how'd you get here? I didn't hear De'ath's gizmo."

"There's a hole between our universes. It's a rift high above the respective atmospheres of our Earths. I can easily fly to it."

"What's that in your sack?"

"A teammate from my Earth, Golden Ring. He's on the Superior Squadron. I organized them after I met you folks."

"Why is he glowing?"

"That's a protective field his ring created. We were caught in a blast from the sun."

"Yeah? Which one?"

"Your sun. Actually, I think we caused it."

Flaming Youth looked out the window. "So that's what caused the radio blackout over the Northern

Hemisphere."

Golem grumbled. "Poor kid missed the Top Ten survey on W.B.E.X. Gimme Jack Conrad's big band any day. They don't play that kind of music on the radio no more. Er...is Golden Ring on the shy side?"

"We got walloped pretty bad. The ring threw the glow around him as protection. I don't know if he's dead or alive." Superior Man walked to a couch. "I came to find out if he's okay in there."

"Oh, you can't see through it?"

"Nor can I hear through it. Mind if I put him down here?"

"Sure, go ahead." Flaming Youth moved the throw pillows.

Superior Man set him down and sat next to him. "I was wondering if Intangible Girl would mind peeking through the barrier to check on him."

"No can do," Golem said. "She and Rich went to Cape Kennedy with Man Machine. They're going to take a close look at that hole."

"I could have saved them the trouble."

"Rich is a scientist," Flaming Youth threw in. "He wanted a looksee himself, might be a nexus to all realities."

"As if we're not enough proof it's there."

Golem pondered the glowing figure under the cape. "So, he's got a golden ring, huh?"

"One of a kind."

"Nah. Counselor Claw in China got rings like that. Nasty customer, according to Man Machine."

"It creates anything Golden Ring can imagine."

"Same with C.C. but he's got an evil imagination."

Superior Man looked at Golden Ring and wondered why he hadn't come out of his shell. Could his powers be different on this side of the rift? Might be a good idea to take him back to the other side, see if he comes around. "Golem, tell me...Intangible Girl and Rich...they got a rocket waiting there, or a space plane, something to get them up to the hole? What about the Time Oscillator?"

Golem cleared rocks from his throat. "We keep the Time Oscillator in an impregnable cell in Storage and Supply. The black diamond that Dr. De'ath used for power means it's always on. Anyone coming through from another place is locked inside until we determine their threat level."

"What about that spark plug thing? Don't you remove it to make it inop?"

"Not if we want to use it in a hurry, or if *you* wanted to come through."

"Plus, we didn't want to misplace it," Flaming Youth added.

"Rich keeps a lot of doohickeys around here. Trust me, nobody from another dimension is going to bust out of *that* room."

"The kid is right," Golem said. "Even I couldn't do it."

That's not very practical. But he didn't want to reprimand his friends. Friends, he knew, who genuinely wanted to make it easy for him to transverse freely between universes. He tapped his glowing cape. "We're the only two people in my universe who can get to that rift." He didn't need the Time Oscillator. "And I can easily find it. Question is...who else knows about it?"

"You see why we keep the damned thing locked up."

"No I don't. The hole is what started this when Dr. De'ath thought he could time travel. He punched a hole and traveled to my universe," Superior Man huffed. "Golden Ring stumbled on the hole—"

"*That's* the guy? Man Machine told us about him."

"Problem is, someone else might do the same thing...the Time Oscillator has nothing to do with it anymore."

"We never thought it punched a portal between

Steven Trent

universes."

"Rich thought it might be access to a *world of limitless dimensions*." Flaming Youth quoted him.

"A furshlugginer *crossroads of infinity...the junction to everywhere*." Golem doubled over with laughter. "Ah, that Rich...he's too much."

Flaming Youth joined in. "The joke is on him."

Laughter broke the tension.

"You fellows seem ready for the beach."

"Naw, I sink like a rock," Golem said.

Flaming Youth roared.

"I was going to read this." Golem presented a paperback copy of Doc Caliban's adventure, *Terror Under the Sea*.

"Doc Caliban?"

"You got his books over there?"

"Books? I know his *son*."

"He has a son?"

"Caliban authorized a magazine back in the '30s to fictionalize his adventures, so long as they changed his name." Superior Man saw no reason to reveal Doc left his fortress to him.

"He's real there? Wow. Anyway, you're welcome to wait here until Suzette gets back. I take it if Golden Ring was dead, the energy field wouldn't still be...glowing."

"That's what I'm hoping. It's up, he's alive, but he could still be hurt. We just had a knock-down drag-out fight with a shiny being, flying on a disc." Here Superior Man's hand made the shape of it.

He saw something pass between the two men.

"What is it? What did I say?"

"Flying on a disc? That's bad," Golem said. "You should have told us that sooner. That's Rannin Nord."

"Or as we call him, the Silica Rider," Flaming Youth added. "Yeah, he's from here. Well, from somewhere in our universe. He's the herald of Faculus."

"Herald? Who is Faculus? Why does he rate a herald?"

"He's got more than one," Golem said. "You oughta see that four-armed enforcer he keeps on a chain."

"Faculus is an immortal space being." Flaming Youth this time. "A god, you might say."

"He wanted to eat Earth." Golem hit the homerun.

Superior Man nearly choked. "Th-the whole thing?"

"We tricked him into pledging he'd never try that again."

"The whole thing?" Superior Man's needle was stuck in a groove. "The whole thing?"

"That's what he does...feeds on planets. Earth to him is a tasty snack."

Superior Man felt a chill, which he seldom did. "Faculus found a loophole in his pledge. If not this Earth, then my Earth. Rannin Nord coming into my universe means Faculus is aware of our Earth."

"Maybe he created that hole," Golem muttered.

"You dirt clod." Flaming Youth whacked Golem's stony arm. "Why would a giant make a *small* hole?"

"Dr. De'ath's machine caused the rip," Superior Man jumped in before somebody got stomped or fried. "He made a hole in the fabric between the two universes."

"I get it. When De'ath crossed over, there had to be a spatial consequence somewhere." Golem seemed rock-solid sure of himself. "Something had to give. Result was a forever rift."

"Rich's theorizing has rubbed off on you, Golem," Flaming Youth said. "You sound just like him."

"Roast me alive if I ever say anything like that again, kid."

"De'ath did something unnatural to the order of natural things, and it had a consequence." Superior Man latched on to that line of reasoning.

"De'ath stretched the cosmic rubber band too far and

it snapped." Flaming Youth grinned.

"Quit playin' with words," Golem said.

"No, that's a good analogy. Whatever the cause, Faculus took advantage of it and sent his *herald* through the hole." Superior Man's fingers made air quotes, still in wonder that one of this universe's menaces had a herald. *I'm a good guy and I don't have a herald.* "He attacked the super teams on my Earth."

"Faculus gets to stick to his pledge by consuming *your* Earth, not ours." Flaming Youth was flaming mad and exploded. Literally, for in his anger, flame briefly flared. "Silica Rider runs point for him, eliminates your Earth's protectors, and gives his boss a red-carpet ride to dinner. At least you came out on top of your rumble with him."

"I sent him packing, all right." Superior Man wasn't boasting. He did what he had to do. "I'm heading over to the Assemblers."

"Wait," Golem said. "You should know they changed since you met them. Guy named Sergeant-at-Arms leads a new bunch. Besides Man Machine, you'd only know King Bee and Hornette."

"No more Behemoth, huh?"

"He was getting harder to control. They ought to let me handle him. I'd show him a thing or two or three."

"Last time you met the Behemoth, he fought you to a standstill," Flaming Youth said.

"I fought *him* to a standstill," Golem countered. The crunch of his rock knuckles cracking was nothing like Superior Man had ever heard before. "Behemoth got real wound up after meeting *you* and took off."

"He did seem a bit belligerent." Superior Man shuddered, wondering if he could handle that monster in an all-out fight. His grip had been a warning. "Watch my friend for me." He retrieved his cape from the glowing cocoon. "If he comes out of it, tell him what happened."

"We'll call you at the Assemblers' Mansion."

At that moment, a voice emanated from a speaker. *"Mr. Mike Murdaugh will be exiting the main elevator."*

"So...I interrupted something?"

"Naw, just our lawyer with some documents." Golem gave a dismissive wave.

Flaming Youth's eyes showed a flicker. "Yeah, in all this excitement, I totally forgot Murdaugh was cleared through our security checkpoint twenty minutes ago. Must have had a long wait for an elevator."

"He's blind. That's why we didn't bother dressing up."

An elevator door whooshed open and in walked a slim, red-headed young man in a black suit, sunglasses, and a white cane clearing the way. He carried a briefcase.

"Hey, Counselor Murdaugh," Golem chirped. "Meet the new superhero in town, Superior Man."

"Another one?" the lawyer kidded. Tapping the cane ahead of him, he stepped forward. "He smells like burnt ozone."

"Pleased to meet you, sir."

The cane came to rest on his booted foot. "Ah, there you are." Murdaugh tucked the cane under his arm and stuck out a hand.

The two shared a handshake.

Superior Man thought the blind man moved with all the confidence of the sighted. Faking? An X-ray revealed burned out optic nerves. In turn, Murdaugh sensed something pass through his head. A beam of some kind, like an X-ray. There was something decidedly otherworldly about this man, superior or not.

Suspicion allayed, Superior Man stepped to the window. "Well, I'll be off."

Murdaugh's sensitive hearing detected the swoosh of a cape. But it didn't sound like any material he had ever heard before.

Superior Man flew out the window, reluctantly

leaving Golden Ring in the care of the Atoms Family.

Murdaugh wondered if Red Devil should investigate this *superior man.* "Is he gone? I didn't hear a door close."

***

Amazon Woman undid her cape and hung it over her chair. She, Eagleman, and Aquamarine prepared to jump to the other Earth via S.O.L.A.R. Labs' device. They stepped onto the platform. Shrinking Man, full sized and in his civilian identity as scientist Paul Pymer, took charge of the machine. One stipulation for S.O.L.A.R. Labs' presence at the warehouse was that Pymer be employed there. A crackle sounded and the Superior Squadron was gone. Pymer settled in, reluctantly getting back to Kurt Gottfried's *Quantum Mechanics: Fundamentals.* He didn't like missing the action.

But I might just learn something about this, he mused, opening the textbook.

***

Landing at the front entrance of Assembler Mansion, Superior Man strode to the door. He was about to knock when Penniman the butler opened it. "Greetings, sir."

"Oh, er, Penniman. Nice to see you again."

There was no offer to take his cape this time. Penniman led his guest into the meeting room. Present were two Assemblers Superior Man knew, Hornette and King Bee. Or maybe not. He was a giant in a semblance of King Bee's costume and reclined in a gigantic chair. Hood down, the superhero looked like a fair-haired Robert Culp.

Maybe on this Earth the actor had been diverted into superheroing, Superior Man thought.

"You're not King Bee."

"Not when I'm supersized. All I had to do was reverse

the shrinking process to become Kingsize." He offered a giant handshake. Superior Man's hand disappeared in Kingsize's appendage.

"I'll suggest that process to my team's tiny member."

"Nice to see you again," Hornette said.

The pair sat with an archer. "Marksman at your service." Arms crossed, he didn't look like he was ready to serve anyone.

"Oh, on my Earth we're considering an archer for membership."

"Yeah? He any good? Heads up, big guy." Marksman shot an arrow at Kingsize.

In response, he merely shrunk.

Hornette groaned. "You guys need a new routine."

"Enough showing off, mister," a commanding voice rang out. "You think those things grow on trees?"

"Actually, Sarge, they do." Marksman retrieved his spent wooden arrow. "Hey, did you lose your shield? I thought it always came back to you."

"It's being polished, smart guy." Sergeant-at-Arms was accompanied by a beauteous brunette in a caped bathing suit and a wimple in red. Trailing was a prematurely gray youth in green with a lightning bolt running across his shirt.

Pointing to the adornment on the shirt, Superior Man couldn't help but ask, "Let me guess...superspeed, right?"

***

The Superior Squadron was smooshed together inside the Time Oscillator. The trio materialized in a small cluttered room. A small light was burning. This was where the Time Oscillator was mothballed.

"Ladies first," Eagleman said to Amazon Woman.

"Remember, you will know the Atoms Family by their matching blue costumes."

"Sort of like the Challengers of the Fantastic," Aquamarine noted. "On our Earth."

"Quite, except with the letter A enclosed by an atomic whirl on their shirt fronts."

She traced one on Aquamarine's chest.

"Four guys in matching costumes? Should be easy to spot."

"Three men and one woman." Amazon Woman was interested in asking another female how she liked superheroing with men. She stepped off the oscillator. Her teammates followed.

Trying the door, they found themselves locked in. Eagleman swung his morning star at it, which produced no effect.

"Stand clear." Amazon Woman punched the door of the secure room. It didn't budge.

Aquamarine added his strength to hers.

No luck. They were trapped.

***

Elsewhere in the building, Golem and Flaming Youth were enjoying their free time. They sipped iced tea from a pitcher. Flaming Youth said, "If I applied heat, we could have hot tea."

"I thought you liked hot coffee."

"Anything hot is what I like."

"Well, I don't want hot tea. I want *iced* tea."

The kid, in an effort to get some sun, had doffed his bathrobe to reveal swim trunks. Somehow, the kid had scored a pair patterned in garish orange and yellow flames. Catching his friend's eyeroll, he felt the need to boast. "Come on, these baggies are what actual surfers wear."

"Surfers? There must be easier ways to commit suicide." Golem pulled a cigar from one of his pockets. "Got a light, kid?"

They turned to each other upon hearing a commotion. While Amazon Woman's fist merely produced a *thump*, Eagleman's morning star created a racket.

"That came from the storage room." Flaming Youth allowed the flame on his forefinger to proceed up his arm.

The pair stared at each other over who would investigate.

Golem grunted. "Is it wise to get lit in them shorts?"

"They're made with unstable atoms, natch. Just like my costume."

Now completely conflagrated, Flaming Youth's flying ability kicked in. He rose in the air, leaving a fiery trail hanging in the air below him.

"Someone came through the gizmo. I'll moider da bum!"

"Naw, you don't have to get off your cushy seat and lose your place in that easy reader. After all, you worked so hard learning to read."

"I'm a-comin'," Golem grumped. "Ya ain't leavin' me here to miss no action. I bet it's some super criminal from the other universe. What was that guy Superior Man mentioned?"

"Alex Lugar," Flaming Youth said. "I hear he's in prison."

When they arrived at the storage room and reached to unlatch the door, they got a surprise. It flew off the hinges. A winged man was mid-swing with an archaic weapon. His companions spilled out.

"Who are these monsters?" Eagleman blurted.

"A guy with wings is calling *me* a monster?" Golem griped.

"Look at that one." Aquamarine pointed to the flaming man, particularly wary.

"What are you doin' in there?" Golem demanded. "That's a restricted area."

Amazon Woman unfurled her whip and lashed the

man of rock.

"Ow, that hurt," Golem bellowed. "You asked for it, lady. It's cryin' time."

"You will be doing the crying, monster." Amazon Woman showed him a fist. "Routine six, Eagleman."

Flaming Youth gasped. "Routine six? What's routine six? We don't have a routine six...but they do."

The winged man flew around the room, swooped in behind Golem and clamped onto the back of his robe. Wings thrashing, he started to lift the rock man.

"You'll never do it, buddy. I weight five hunret pounds."

Indeed, the fabric tore and Golem fell loose of the garment. Eagleman gave up and gripped Golem's rocky ankles. With that burden, he ascended. It seemed an impossible feat of strength. Eagleman, in fact, defied gravity by manipulating the disc on this wing straps.

With Golem off his feet, Amazon Woman sallied forth with a punch. The rocky man saw stars and went out. Her punch raised tiny pebbles from his jaw. Flaming Youth blasted out a line of flame that singed Eagleman's wings.

"Let go of that dumb ox," the kid bleated.

Eagleman dropped Golem, creating a crater in the floor. The avian flapped furiously, hoping to put out the flames.

"Man. That guy could teach me a few things about flying." Flaming Youth landed to check his teammate. His flaming hands reverted to normal.

Floating in one spot, Eagleman aimed the downdraft from his beating wings.

The kid yelled, "Flame up."

There was a *FOOM*. His body inflamed more intensely than before. Aquamarine, with unexpected speed, grasped a pipe the crater had exposed and broke it with one pull. Water shot out, and he directed the flow to the ignited young man, but the stream quickly faltered to a dribble.

The now wet face of Flaming Youth sneered. "The rest of me is still flaming." He rose in the air. "Your goose is cooked, Bird Beak."

"I ain't no goose." Eagleman kicked a large multi-gallon plastic Culligan water bottle off its dispenser toward Amazon Woman.

Flaming Youth could only sputter, "What the..."

She caught the bottle. Effortlessly, she squeezed it and water jetted at the now aloft Flaming Youth. "Cool it," Amazon Woman quipped.

Flames sizzled out. With no fire, Flaming Youth couldn't remain aloft. He fell and hit the floor. "Hey. No fair."

Aquamarine locked him in a full nelson.

Eagleman flew in with a knockout punch to the jaw.

"He has to be on fire to fly," Aquamarine said. "Weird."

"I'll leave you to ponder it." Eagleman flew off to explore.

Amazon Woman assessed their situation. "A flaming man and rocky monstrosity. This can't be a good sign. Who are they? What have they done to the Atoms Family?"

"Be a while before these two will be answering questions." Aquamarine yanked up the unconscious kid by a hank of hair. "This boy has a lot to learn."

Eagleman returned. "I found an aircraft that suits our needs."

His companions hurried to see it. Unknown to them by its name, this was the AtomiCar. In it, the Atoms Family could cross an ocean. The craft was some twenty feet long. On the top sat a tailfin with wings. Behind the pilot's compartment on either side, a pair of bubble-topped and matching pods housed jet engines. A short corridor gave access to each of the sections. The craft was also equipped with turbine boosters. However, unknown to Eagleman was its ability to fly over five hundred miles an hour, with an altitude of thirty-thousand feet and a range of over four thousand miles. A transparent windscreen covered the entire craft, allowing four riders to converse.

"Blast proof," the winged man said, knocking on solid titanium...or some similar compound.

Amazon Woman, the most experienced pilot of the group, made other observations. "See the bolts on their inner wings? Those side pods jettison for independent flight. They have their own wings and tails."

Aquamarine examined a rear pod. "Looks like the rear section doesn't jettison, though."

The seat at the rear was non-detachable, with an obvious exit hatch covering the back and top.

"I call rumble seat," Eagleman shouted, flipping up the hatch. This opened like a Mohs Ostentatienne Opera Sedan 3 he used in his day job, assisting archaeologist Malcolm Bietak. If they had Mohs in this parallel world. Its top was supported by a pair of struts, bottom having both a seat and steps.

"She's fueled up," Aquamarine reported.

Amazon Woman claimed the pilot seat and familiarized herself with the controls.

"Take a look at that world map on the dash," Eagleman pointed out. "I switched it on earlier."

Consulting the map, Amazon Woman stated, "Ruritania here is approximately where Calbia is in our universe."

"Who were those freaks?" Aquamarine asked. The nations of his own Earth hardly interested him. The ones on this Earth not at all.

Amazon Woman looked up. "No idea. De'ath may have sworn off killing the Atoms Family, but maybe others haven't made a truce with them."

"Or they might be De'ath's agents..." Eagleman put in, "and he thinks they can't be traced back to him."

"He's supposed to be an Alex Lugar level genius,"

Aquamarine said. "Do you think he somehow created that rock monster and flaming freak?"

Amazon Woman scoffed. "*Created?* That seems far-fetched. Superior Man said this world has people *born* with super abilities." She fired up the turbines and maneuvered the controls. The craft lifted, nose slightly tilted down. There was a faint whine and hum of operating jets.

Aquamarine looked down at the wreckage they left in the floor and noticed a gold glow. "What's that?"

Eagleman ruffled his feathers. "You think there's a Golden Ring in this universe?"

"Could there be an evil Golden Ring?" Aquamarine asked.

Amazon Woman put an end to their speculation. "If there is, I don't want to lose a second finding out what Dr. De'ath has done to Superior Man."

"And the Atoms Family."

She flipped a dashboard toggle marked ROOF. A panel opened above, letting in daylight. "Next stop, Ruritania." She throttled up the thrusters.

They did not know the wonderous ring had extended its field of protection for Golden Ring. Their teammate, left behind, was oblivious to the action here. Back there, nobody was around to watch over him.

CHAPTER 10

T arantula-Man eagerly undertook his assignment to hunt Red Devil. With Assembler membership looming, no task was too big. That particular costumed crusader operated in Hell's Kitchen, Tarantula-Man knew. He'd gotten action shots of Red Devil there for *The New York Daily Press*, Tarantula-Man's employer in civilian life. He had stopped off, snuck into the paper's building, and raided the files there. Knowing the layout, he got in and out undetected. Now Tarantula-Man had photo references. He looked over his own work and reacquainted himself with the target: an athletic man in a yellow and red costume with little horns atop his hooded mask. He wielded some sort of stick-like weapon.

Hell's Kitchen was where Tarantula-Man now headed. Sometimes he leapt great distances between buildings, other times spanning gaps with webs shot from tiny devices at his wrists.

The presence of the supposed lawbreaker was not unknown to Red Devil. He stood, stock still, on a darkened rooftop and listened to sounds only he could hear. Without moving his hooded head, Red Devil followed Tarantula-Man's every move. He'd considered how he might boost his own standing with the police. They tolerated Red Devil on these streets. Capturing Tarantula-Man might elevate his stock with them. Finding Superior Man could wait.

Yes, just the thing. He smiled to himself.

The world did not know Red Devil was truly blind. He possessed super senses that more than compensated. Acute hearing told him the leaping figure was Tarantula-

Man. His breathing, Red Devil heard, was muffled by a full-face covering. Who else adhered to walls, easily leapt great expanses, and swung on a line that made a *thwip*?

So acute was Red Devil's hearing that he could perceive flaps of webbing under Tarantula-Man's arms. All this exertion was hardly taxing Tarantula-Man. He was a mere youth whose heart was beating at a rate that should have killed him. Red Devil was reminded of the time he heard Man Machine's irregular heartbeat.

Red Devil spoke softly, "How is it possible?"

He wanted to bring in this lawbreaker. Now the hunter was accosted by the prey.

Tarantula-Man stopped. He seemed to sense being watched.

A body landed lightly behind him. "Hold it, you," rang out.

Tarantula-Man turned. "You're just the guy I'm looking for."

Red Devil, almost invisible in the shadows, had swapped his red and yellow costume for one of all red.

In the dark, Tarantula-Man couldn't even make out the details of what Red Devil wore. It might have been a three-piece suit, for all he could see.

"Okay, arachnid, you found me." Red Devil grinned. "The cops have outstanding warrants on you. I'm taking you in."

"I just want to talk," Tarantula-Man said.

"Forget it. You're coming with me."

"I don't mean to fight you."

"Scared? Typical crook."

"Now you're making me mad," Tarantula-Man spat.

While Red Devil heard the adjustment Tarantula-Man made to his web shooters, he didn't know that meant a net would shoot out with the next shot.

When he tried to snare Red Devil, the prey moved like he had advance warning.

The battle was on.

***

"Better call the Assemblers," Golem groaned. Groggily, he pushed himself up off the floor.

"Why?" Flaming Youth dried himself with a towel emblazoned with his team's symbol. "We can take care of ourselves."

"Like we took care of this? Those villains from Superior Man's universe probably got the Assemblers in their sights next." Golem staggered to the video phone and made the call himself since the kid was still wet. Kingsize answered.

"When Superior Man gets there, tell him super villains from his world attacked us."

"Superior Man is right here." Kingsize adjusted the camera to bring the visitor into range.

"Villains?" Superior Man echoed, looking into a tiny camera as good as the ones Louis Wemyss designed. Alex Lugar must have escaped prison and found a way to traverse universes. "Can you describe them?"

"Blond guy with short hair and another one with wings. He had no shirt. Plus, a dame strong enough to knock me silly. I don't mean just by looks, but she had those, too."

"Aquamarine, Eagleman and Amazon Woman." Superior Man breathed with relief. "They're tough customers, all right."

"You've fought them?"

"They're my friends."

"Those are your *friends*?" Golem was taken aback. "I'd hate to see your enemies."

"You never will. The Superior Squadron managed to banish all, or most, of the bad guys. Some met untimely accidental deaths at the hands of Ratman."

Sergeant-at-Arms entered the room, this time bearing his shield. Now his questions would be answered. Maybe the rest of these people believed what every guy in a costume told them about another universe. He wanted proof and stepped up to their guest. "Superior Man. I want to ask you—"

Superior Man groaned and collapsed.

"Hey, what's with Superior Man?" Golem boomed.

"Something's got to him." Marksman came into camera range.

"Wasn't he caught in a solar flare?" Flaming Youth craned his neck past the bulk of his teammate. "It registered amperes in the millions."

"Yeah." Golem agreed. "The sky turned scarlet, shot through with plumes of yellow and orange."

Superior Man managed to sit up, nodding, his breaths labored. "That...must be...it."

The sun was the source of his power. Was this Earth's sun different? Trying to stand, numerous gloved hands, more than he wanted to count, gently forced him to lay back. Lying back seemed to help.

"My friends...used S.O.L.A.R. Labs' platform. Ended in your secure room." He gasped. "Worried about me. Told them I'd be...right back."

"Sure. They think your absence is De'ath's doing." Sergeant-at-Arms' tune changed seeing Superior Man in pain. "Don't try to talk, fella. C'mon, get him to Medical."

"They mean...confront De'ath," Superior Man managed then passed out.

Kingsize grew to fifteen feet and gently carted off Superior Man.

"Can you get 'em to bring back the AtomiCar?" Golem asked. "I'd say in one piece, but it splits apart."

"We'll go after them," Sergeant-at-Arms assured the rocky man. He had wanted to quiz Superior Man further. Right now, that was on hold. "We should be able to catch your kite."

"Take care of my buddy from the universe next door," Golem called.

Flaming Youth reappeared to give the Assemblers the transponder setting of their errant craft. With that, the Assemblers could track the AtomiCar while out of visual range.

Marksman sneered. "They don't make heroes quite so super in that other universe."

"If he really *is* from another universe." Sergeant-at-Arms still wasn't convinced.

Ferro had a nice, new green Brasinca Uirapuru in the garage for team use, but this trip required real speed. He turned to Galloping Gazelle. "You're up."

"Roger."

Off sped the mutated human. His assigned destination was the boat the U.S. Navy maintained for the Assemblers at their East River dock. Once there, he was to cross the river to the small Belmont Island. There, he would initiate takeoff prep for their modified Blackbird SR-71. Like David Glickman's purchase of Red Rock Island in San Francisco Bay a couple of years ago for $49,000, Johnny Ferro owned it. Every Assembler was required to be a qualified pilot. Galloping Gazelle's speed gave him the chore of prepping the craft.

Meanwhile, Sergeant-at-Arms buzzed the Special Projects Agency. "Rock, we're going after the stolen AtomiCar. It's headed to Ruritania—"

"Whoa, slow down," the colonel shouted. "Atoms Family suddenly got it in for Dr. De'ath? That could start a war."

"I won't allow an international incident to happen." Sergeant-at-Arms snapped his fingers, not easy through his protective gloves. "Request all the countries of the League of, er, the United Nations to clear a path for that bird. Don't let anyone else approach her except us."

"Can do. Keep me posted." Kent's screen went blank, ignorant that this related to the footage he had shown the Assemblers.

A new signal on the console buzzed and lit. Galloping Gazelle's voice spoke, "Blackbird prepped."

Leaving Superior Man in Penniman's capable hands, Sergeant-at-Arms barked, arms extended, "What are you waiting for, people? We have an international incident to prevent. Double-time it to the elevator. Move."

Red Rose, Kingsize, and Marksman jolted into action and ascended to their rooftop hangar. Sergeant-at-Arms brought up the rear. Kingsize's long legs ate distance. Hornette shrunk and flew on tiny wings.

In the rooftop hangar, half a dozen Hiller VZ-1 Pawnee flying platforms awaited. These were for transport to the island hangar. They bore twin counter-rotating propellers below the cockpit. To fly it, the pilot leaned and the platform followed in the desired direction. For size-changing Assemblers, the platforms worked best with them at normal height.

It was a short hop to the island.

Sergeant-at-Arms hailed, "Every second counts."

Once there, the team dashed from the devices. A U.S. Navy Shore Patrol squad took possession of the platforms to ready them for their next use.

"Marksman, take the controls," Sergeant-at-Arms ordered.

Galloping Gazelle had the craft warmed up and humming. He gave up his seat to the archer. Modified to seat six, the Blackbird was capable of transcontinental flight. The airframe could withstand bullets. Bullets were the least of their worries. The team crowded the cockpit.

"Keep a sharp look out for a/c." Sergeant-at-Arms slid into the copilot seat.

"Why do I know you don't mean *air conditioning*?" Hornette stated.

"Air craft," Sergeant-at-Arms elaborated.

"Do you think we can take them?" Marksman asked, more worried than Sergeant-at-Arms had ever seen him.

"There may well be a fight. We'll try negotiations first."

"You got a plan?"

"We'll fly low and stay behind them. Kingsize, Hornette, Red Rose and Galloping Gazelle, rest up. When we engage them, I want Gazelle on the controls. His quick reflexes could decide whether this turns into an international incident or not."

"Then what?" Galloping Gazelle frowned. "We're not armed."

"Oh, we're armed, all right." Sergeant-at-Arms smiled. "Red Rose, think one of your hexes would affect them from here? Ever toss one this distance?"

"Cast, you mean. It should work, but I've never cast one from one moving plane to another. I'll need a clear visual."

"You'll get one," Sergeant-at-Arms assured her. "Sooner or later, they'll know we're after them. I don't want them entering Ruritanian airspace."

"They won't know who *we* are," Galloping Gazelle put in.

"Superior Man told his teammates about us," Kingsize said.

"Yeah? Well, they still might shoot first and ask questions later," Marksman said. "I sure would."

***

By now, the two heroes facing off in Hell's Kitchen were at street level. Unbelievable to Tarantula-Man, Red Devil had expertly blocked every blow.

"Like I telegraphed every punch," muttered the arachnid, under his mask.

Heard by Red Devil, that made him chuckle. Tarantula-Man's superior strength was for naught. Red Devil was superbly conditioned. Red Devil, in turn, noted his opponent still wasn't breathing hard. In the distance, sirens wailed.

"Did you forget devils eat spiders, Tarantula-Man?" Red Devil taunted him. He heard his opponent's vitals fly into a rage. It was time for heavy artillery. He kept a bludgeon. Tarantula-Man had gotten a shot of it but didn't know what it could do. In fact, the weapon began life as a rifle hidden in the shaft of a cane. He had taken it from a criminal and, with the precision his super senses provided, rigged the workings of a retractable whipcord into one end. That gave him a bludgeon, a line for swinging and a single shot rifle in one weapon. He made a show of aiming with sightless eyes at Tarantula Man...with the rifle end. His radar sense was better than eyes.

Then he stopped. "Hear that?" Red Devil lowered his weapon. "The police are coming. Not for me. They're coming for you."

"You sound pretty sure about that." Tarantula-Man cocked his head. The outlaw's tarantula-sense was tingling.

"Who's the lawbreaker here? I work with the cops," Red Devil said. "Surrender and they won't shoot you. Maybe."

"Because you'll shoot me first?" Tarantula Man knew Red Devil was right. The cops were likely to open fire on a perceived outlaw.

Red Devil sensed a racing heart. His opponent was in fight or flight mode. *He's just a kid...too young to die.* He collapsed the weapon and holstered it.

On the ground, a cop rushed up. He took aim at Tarantula-Man, a sitting duck on a wall.

Red Devil called out, "No. Don't shoot."

"Is that you. Red Devil?"

"Hold your fire, everyone."

The cop saw Red Devil's horns, which identified him in the gloom. "He's got warrants."

"I think he's innocent."

"You win this round, bub," Tarantula-Man said, and a line of web shot out. He swung right over a green and black Chevrolet Biscayne police car. He would report to the Assemblers that Red Devil did not play well with others.

In the scuffle, Red Devil's super hearing had caught something. His accurate hearing pinpointed the spot where it landed. There, he picked up a small card. Back to the cops, Red Devil removed a glove. Pretending to read, Red Devil ran his fingers over the printing. His touch was so acute, the printing was like braille. Super sensitive touch revealed the writing.

"Assemblers Priority Identicard? What's Tarantula-Man got to do with the Assemblers?"

He couldn't ponder that long, however. Mike Murdaugh had papers to review for clients, but he might be paying the Assemblers a visit...soon.

***

Hours later, over the Atlantic, Marksman called, "Hey. The AtomiCar's transponder cut out."

Sergeant-at-Arms got on the interphone. "This is it. Gazelle, take over. Drop to seven hundred feet. Get us to one-hundred seventy miles an hour."

"That's kind of low." Galloping Gazelle was a flash to the cockpit. "Even for reflexes like mine."

"Don't worry. Ferro installed Dan Bateman's ground proximity warning system."

The superfast mutated human scowled. "Sarge, even with that, do you really think this is safe?"

"No. But safety has no bearing on this chase."

***

"We got company," Eagleman reported from the back. Amazon Woman and Aquamarine turned to follow the winged man's pointing finger.

"They've been shadowing us for some time," Amazon Woman said. "Almost the whole of the Atlantic Ocean. If this advanced radar is to be believed."

"That's some sleek jet," Aquamarine chimed in.

A voice came over their radio. "This is Sergeant-at-Arms calling. You are to land immediately."

"Fasten your seatbelts, boys." Amazon Woman checked her buckles. "It's going to be a bumpy ride."

"I represent the Assemblers."

"Leave this to me!" Eagleman grasped his weapon, jumped out, and flew toward the menacing jet.

***

"I have a visual, Sarge," Galloping Gazelle shouted. "And you won't believe it."

Kingsize gaped out the cockpit window. "Some kind of freaky bird."

"Like you should talk," Marksman said.

"Kingsize and Hornette, shrink." Sergeant-at-Arms marched down the aisle. There, he stood at a sliding door on the plane's side. "Red Rose, you're starting with him. Kingsize and Hornette will be tiny enough not to block you. They'll hold your ankles while you hex. Don't forget, they retain their full-size strength."

Red Rose blanched, but she was an Assembler. She might have to give her life to save her universe. If she were to die, it would be as a superhero. "Now that my cape is short, I won't have to doff it."

"You arthropods ready?"

"She's not going anywhere," King Bee grunted in a small voice. He clutched a booted ankle. "Right, Janice?"

"I'm hanging on for this dear's life," the tiny woman

responded, grasping an ankle of her own.

"Marksman, stand by," Sergeant-at-Arms ordered. "You're on deck."

"Huh," the archer huffed. "Under it, you mean?"

Red Rose got into position.

Sergeant-at-Arms yanked back the sliding door on the side of the Blackbird. It was eerie to see a woman standing in a plane's open door. Red Rose leaned out, gestured, and cast a hex at the AtomiCar.

***

Seconds later, on the opposing craft, there was a shudder as its electrical systems shut down.

"Hey. Who turned out the lights?" Aquamarine shouted.

Amazon Woman noted from the controls, "Backup batteries just kicked in. Whoever designed this craft was a genius."

***

"You missed him but got them. Now we switch it up." Sergeant-at-Arms turned to the bowman. "You got something for that Hawk imitator?"

"How about I brighten his day with a flare arrow?"

"To your battle station. Fire at will."

Marksman relocated to a modified ball turret below the jet. Taking a fetal position within, back and head against the rear wall, hips at the bottom and legs aloft in footrests, used a handle to rotate it toward Eagleman.

"Come to papa." Marksman grinned and loaded a crossbow set. "That guy is fast."

As Eagleman approached, the archer let loose. "Flare arrow away."

The Assemblers covered their eyes; Eagleman did not.

He was caught by the burst. Blinded, he stopped, hung motionless in the sky. Aware of his vulnerability, he lowered himself to Earth by adjusting the anti-gravity dial on his wing straps. It was an Earth he didn't know. He shuddered. The Blackbird whizzed above him.

"How's he doing that?" King Bee asked. "I got wings and I can't do that."

"Never mind him." Sergeant-at-Arms called over the craft's interphone. "Marksman, do you think King Bee can ride an arrow?"

"Gee, I never thought about it."

"Start thinking about it. Launch him when I give the signal."

"Now what?" Galloping Gazelle asked.

"Let's see." Sergeant-at-Arms headed to the cockpit. The patriot had his hand over the handset of the radio. "We don't know who's listening in. We don't want De'ath to know these are superheroes from the other Earth."

"Why not?"

"He'd find some way to exploit it."

"I got it. Make it sound like they're trying out for the Assemblers. Everyone knows we're recruiting. Amazon Woman impulsively took the AtomiCar to prove herself to all us chauvinistic males."

"Good." The leader turned to the mic. "Sergeant-at-Arms here. Your Assembler membership is hereby revoked."

He covered the radio mic, and spoke into the interphone. "The rear hatch is open. Marksman, if they don't do as instructed, put King Bee in that craft. King Bee, when you get there, introduce them to your other self, and I don't mean Hiram Pymer."

King Bee took this assignment well. After all, he had wings. He flew to the ball turret. Marksman readied a second arrow. King Bee straddled it. "What if you miss?"

"In that case, flap them wings like crazy."

"If I fall, maybe if I grow big it won't hurt much when I land."

"I won't bother wishing you luck since I never miss." Marksman grinned. "Ready, tiny?"

"Fire away."

***

"Eagleman's caught in a flare," Aquamarine reported. "They're gaining."

"Take over here," Amazon Woman said. "These controls are no harder than your Airphibian." She moved along the narrow aisle. The sea king left his pod and claimed Amazon Woman's place at the controls. She looked down. Her winged teammate was now a dot.

Amazon Woman came back to the pilot chair. "Aquamarine, take your pod and harass them."

"With pleasure."

He was on his way when suddenly an unknown added weight played havoc with the craft's attitude stabilization.

Kingsize, not King Bee, appeared in the AtomiCar. "We asked you nicely," he said. "We're through asking."

Aquamarine seethed. "You're big but you don't order us around."

Kingsize grew again, this time large enough to swat Aquamarine.

Angered at the sight of blood when he pulled his glove back from his face, Aquamarine doubled his fists.

Amazon Woman shouted, "No. The pod and get De'ath. One of us must accomplish the mission."

"*You're* the chairperson." Aquamarine grumbled. *This month. Next month it's my turn.*

The aircraft was hit by another hex and the pods fell off.

"I've jumped from planes, but this time I'm taking High Pockets with me," Aquamarine bellowed. Faster than expected, he grabbed Kingsize. It was a grip the giant couldn't believe.

"Nice night for a swim." The sea king pushed open a door, and out they went.

Kingsize shrunk, escaping Aquamarine's grasp, and he disappeared.

"What the... Where'd that big oaf go?"

Unknown to Aquamarine, insect wings sprouted on King Bee's back as he shrunk. Taking Marksman's advice, he flapped them furiously. It was a long flight back to the Blackbird for a tiny man buffeted by powerful winds. "I'm not going to make it."

Now in free fall, Aquamarine effortlessly turned. In perfect form, he aimed for what he had seen on the map, Lake Ruritania below. He had a full view of his surroundings.

His form would make any cliff diver jealous. He hit the water surface.

***

At that moment, Dr. De'ath's image appeared onboard the Blackbird. This was via his Ultimate Display hologram projector. "Assemblers. You are in Ruritanian airspace. That is an act of war."

Sergeant-at-Arms first presumed this was a two-way transmission.

"That's just a hologram image..." Marksman clarified, "he can't see or hear us."

Sergeant-at-Arms blinked. "Oh, yeah. Now I see. They've been playing with this idea since the late '30s."

"De'ath refined it to a wonderous level, pops."

At the plane's open door, Red Rose cast one more hex. She observed her handiwork. The AtomiCar started to shake. She couldn't admire her work for long.

Planes bore down on her.

***

From the cockpit, Sergeant-at-Arms barked, "Bandits at twelve o'clock." They had the markings of Ruritania.

Sergeant-at-Arms recognized the attackers. "Heinkel He 162A Spatz jets from 1945." These had jet engines aft of the cockpit, centered over the wings. Tails were made of two vertical stabilizers with horizontal elevators mounted below. "They must be from a stock of a hundred or so delivered to airfields but never flown during the war."

Red Rose's eyes widened as a fighter approached their opened door.

Galloping Gazelle yelled, "Look out." He snatched up Sergeant-at-Arms' shield and, in a flash, held it in front of his cousin...just as bullets sprayed.

"You are safe." The speedster zipped back to the controls.

"Fast thinking, kid." Sergeant-at-Arms held up his gloved hand. His shield flew back to his gauntlet.

Red Rose peeked around the door. She tossed hexes at the fighters. One lost a wing. A pilot ejected unplanned. Another plane sprouted a fuel leak. Sundered, the rest flew off.

Sergeant-at-Arms stabbed the radio transmission button. "Dr. De'ath, the Assemblers are pursuing a stolen craft and errant members. This is not an act of aggression. Acknowledge."

"We have another problem, Sarge," Galloping Gazelle called.

"Don't make me guess. Give."

"It's the retractable tricycle landing gear. The two midplane are down and locked, but the nose gear isn't responding. We're in for a rough landing."

Sergeant-at-Arms punched a gloved palm. "That chatterbox fubared us. I'll go out there and manually adjust the gubbins."

"And perhaps provide a translation," Galloping Gazelle suggested.

"No." That came from Hornette. "It's not safe for you to go out there. When I shrink, not only do I retain my full strength, I've got wings. I'll go."

"No," Marksman countered. "I'm doing it. If I die, all you've lost is a lousy archer."

"You're not that bad." Galloping Gazelle smirked. "At least you try."

"I'm strong enough to jar the landing gear loose," Hornette said. "Besides, it'll take you forever to get that quiver off."

The girl flew out the sliding door. She fought against winds to the damaged gear. There they were, folded across the belly. The pair was massive, with dual wheels on each unit. Hornette landed on the damaged strut. It wouldn't budge. She kept at it. If she failed, her friends would die a fiery death.

Back inside, Marksman asked, "Who said I'd take off my quiver?"

Sergeant-at-Arms silenced him with a wave. "We've got nothing to lose. I'm going to settle this."

"Sheesh. We got *us* to lose."

"I have every faith in Hornette," Sergeant-at-Arms said. "Bring us in close to the AtomiCar." He went back to the plane's sliding door. Galloping Gazelle flew as instructed. Marksman took the copilot seat.

"With any luck, I'll see you on the ground," Sergeant-at-Arms called. "If not, you were fine Assemblers."

The two craft were now dangerously close. Sergeant-at-Arms aimed for the AtomiCar's rear hatch. This might be his only chance. Slinging his shield onto his back, he leapt. With the AtomiCar only feet away, he encountered unexpected turbulence.

"I'm falling," he called.

***

With a firm hold, Hornette realized she could spread her ninety pounds more evenly over more of the contraption at full size. She chanced growing, at the price of her wings retracting. The damn thing still wouldn't move.

"Awp," she cried out, tugging. Hornette also pushed and pleaded. "Come on, you. Move, damn it."

There was no flying power now. The ground seemed closer than it had before. That set of gear stayed put.

She blanched. "Hero's death."

CHAPTER 11

Hanging precariously from the edge of the AtomiCar, Sergeant-at-Arms looked up helplessly. If not for his protective gauntlets, the skin on his hands would have been shredded. He found a tall woman in a scandalously brief costume, menacing whip in hand, gazing down at him.

She reached down to his wrist. Her grip was iron. Effortlessly, Amazon Woman hefted him like he was a ragdoll. As Sergeant-at-Arms scrambled to his feet, she stepped back, sizing him up.

"Thanks." He pulled his shield off his back. "I'm Sergeant-at-Arms from the super team, the Assemblers."

"You didn't look too super hanging there."

"You must be Amazon Woman."

"I must be." She laughed.

He pondered handling Amazon Woman without striking her. But she struck first. Her blow was met with his shield. Each punch was blocked. Displeased with her results, she dashed back to the cockpit.

"Lady, don't make me fight you."

"You'll have to catch me before that." She turned off the autopilot. "You'll be busy keeping this craft out of Dr. De'ath's living room."

"That would be an act of war."

"It's already war." Amazon Woman leapt out of the craft. She hadn't expected to test the aerodynamics of her new outfit under real battle conditions quite so soon.

Sergeant-at-Arms watched her descending body.

Amazon Woman was gently spiraling to the ground in

wide circles, pleased with the costume.

"Well, I'll be. She did that as a distraction." Sergeant-at-Arms looked up and saw no pilot. Meanwhile, De'ath's battery of defending cannons let loose. The Assembler dashed to the cockpit. As he did, a body grew there. It was Kingsize, resizing to normal height. He seized the controls and swung the AtomiCar away from the line of fire. Still, the fuselage caught flak.

"Pymer," Sergeant-at-Arms shouted. "You still on board?"

"Yeah, but I almost wasn't. Hitting the ground as a giant wouldn't help me, and those winds kept me from reaching the Blackbird."

"When we land, shrink and stay aboard. You and Janice will be our reserves." Sergeant-at-Arms dreaded silently, but hoped Hornette was still alive.

The AtomiCar was coming in for a landing. The Blackbird was coming in for a landing, too. They were at the airstrip on the grounds of De'ath's castle. It had a walled yard, covering twice as much real estate as the castle itself. Once on the ground, Marksman, Red Rose, and Galloping Gazelle warily peeped out the door.

Seeing the reception of soldiers, Marksman nocked an arrow. "I'll give them a plain one." He smirked. "No reason to advertise I pack specialized ones."

He shot an arrow into the barrel of a soldier's rifle before diving back inside. A hail of bullets was the response.

The hologram of Dr. De'ath spoke again, hanging in the air. "Attention. Cease this fighting."

Sergeant-at-Arms walked to the Assembler craft. With his blue and white shield hefted, he feared no bullet. He faced-down the soldiers. Seeing him, the Assemblers exited the craft. He managed to gesture to Hornette. Shrunken again, she flew to him.

"Good job on the landing gear," he whispered. "Stay

small, get back aboard the Blackbird, and sit tight."

The tiny woman maneuvered near Sergeant-at-Arms' uncovered ear. "Understood. After what I just did, I don't mind sitting."

She flew to her assigned post.

A contingent of soldiers covered Sergeant-at-Arms, unnerved by his lack of fear. A crashing sound in the distance was Amazon Woman. She was involved in a vicious fight with eerie skeletal robots. Effortlessly, she would grab one and bludgeon his fellows with him. Then her whip unfurled and struck. Amazon Woman looked up to find herself surrounded by a patrol of human soldiers. They were in shock seeing what short work she had made of their mechanical reinforcements.

Bringing up the rear were a patrol of Vespa 150 TAPs. Sergeant-at-Arms couldn't have known they were made for French paratroops in the '50s as an anti-tank response. In their heyday, he was still frozen. The bazooka wasn't used while riding. Rather, they'd park, mount it on a tripod, and fire. "That's enough," he barked.

Maybe the soldiers didn't speak English, but they understood his tone. They may have been dazzled by his spinning shield. Even Amazon Woman stopped fighting.

"You heard Dr. De'ath. Take us to him now. Marksman, cover our new member. Galloping Gazelle, watch her closely. Red Rose, pat her down."

A steamed Amazon Woman held her arms apart. "Do you think I'm hiding something in this skimpy outfit?"

This was merely Sergeant-at-Arms' clever way of introducing Amazon Woman to the team she was supposedly part of. He meant to obscure the fact she had never met them. Amazon Woman and the balance of the Assemblers followed him. To her, Galloping Gazelle resembled Barry Frankoff, Jet Man. Other than the prematurely gray hair, anyway.

After a walk through the castle, they were ushered

into Dr. De'ath's throne room.

"Well, well." Dr. De'ath stepped from his Ultimate Display. "I expected the Atoms Family to emerge from the AtomiCar, not the leader of the Assemblers."

A beautiful brunette stood by De'ath's side. She wore a black veil, cocktail dress, high heels, fur stole and elbow-length velvet gloves that made Red Rose envious. In fact, every stich of clothing on her was black.

Dr. De'ath introduced her. "Svetlana Yurakivetsky."

Sergeant-at-Arms controlled his surprise. He had seen her before. Then he knew. Jimmy Yen showed him a file on Mrs. Yurakivetsky. So. The KGB planted an operative into Ruritania. Sergeant-at-Arms wondered how he might play these two off each other.

De'ath laughed. "Struck by Svetlana's beauty, Sergeant-at-Arms, you're speechless?"

He wanted to say he was sad the Soviets were the enemy now. That wouldn't do. Instead, he dodged the question. "Our new members rather impulsively took the AtomiCar. I apologize for that. They were wrong. As we are on Ruritanian soil, I am formally requesting permission to take custody of the prisoner."

"Ah. Granted," Dr. De'ath grumbled. "No doubt, they did this in an effort to prove their worth. By hunting me."

"Very perceptive of you."

"Apology accepted." De'ath waved off formalities. "It was a bit of excitement, eh? I did not catch the name of this ravishing creature."

Sergeant-at-Arms doubted that. There was little Dr. De'ath did not catch.

She stiffened. "I am—"

"Hold up, lady," Sergeant-at-Arms said. "Let *me* do the honors. Amazon Woman is a new superhero. One of our tryout members."

Inwardly, she acceded to this. Sergeant-at-Arms didn't want De'ath to know she was from Earth One. Now she knew not to ask about Superior Man, for De'ath knew he came from there.

"Lovely." De'ath looked her over. "Did you really think you could *apprehend* a head of state? Do silly do-gooder notions fog your judgement?"

Amazon Woman picked up on Sergeant-at-Arms' ruse. "I wanted to see what villainy you were up to. The Assemblers wouldn't do it. We took this craft—"

"Dear lady..." De'ath stopped her, "I do not engage in villainy. Running this nation takes all my time. I am but a humble servant of my people. Still, you shall be welcomed. It is the Ruritanian way. I retain a household staff of three hundred. They will arrange refreshments." He touched an intercom and spouted an order in his native language. Then: "You've had a long journey." De'ath turned back to his guests. "Rest yourselves. My lackies will bring the repast."

Sergeant-at-Arms agreed. "Yes, we indeed had an eventful, tiring trip. Perhaps we could stay the night."

"Indubitably. My airstaff will attend to your planes. I will send the bill to Assembler Mansion." He led the heroes to a heavy wooden door, which creaked uninvitedly, then gestured them to enter the cozy room. The door soon groaned again as he left. Food quickly followed via a retinue of servants bearing plates, bottles, and a rolling tea tray. Efficiently, they put up tables and draped tablecloths over them, then an impressive spread of food and drink was laid out. There was cold beef, cheese, loaves of bread, wine, beer, a pot of coffee, tea, and enough greens to concoct a salad.

Red Rose shrugged and made herself at home. Marksman began to juggle knives. Galloping Gazelle had to show off by snatching one from Marksman.

"Hey. You threw off my rhythm. I could have been cut."

"I need one to cut the ham." Galloping Gazelle readied sandwiches for he and his friends at top speed.

Then he sat and helped himself to some red wine.

"You think that's a good idea?" Marksman chided. "With your speed power, and all—"

"He gets a buzz," Red Rose explained.

The speedster added, "Then I sober up at super speed."

"What if it's poisoned wine?"

"*I* can't be poisoned," Sergeant-at-Arms declared and reached for the bottle. "I'll taste it for you."

Red Rose poured herself tea. "Some for you, archer?"

"I don't drink tea *or* coffee." He waved off the girl's offer. "I don't want anything to interfere with my nerves. A life could depend on it. My own, for one."

"Your concern for mankind is touching." Sergeant-at-Arms was being facetious.

"Mankind?" Galloping Gazelle smirked, inebriation taking hold. "What about other forms of life? Like mutated humans? Or are Americans the only people you care about?"

Before Sergeant-at-Arms could answer, a fanfare of trumpets interrupted. Again, the chamber door flew back.

"His Majesty, Dr. De'ath," a lackey sang.

De'ath strode in. "I trust you find my humble accommodations acceptable."

"We wondered if you might try to drug us," Marksman said. "Or poison us."

"Oh? Point at any item, bowman."

Sergeant-at-Arms indicated a hunk of Swiss cheese.

De'ath took a knife and cut off a piece then popped it into his mouth. "Delicious. Satisfied? Or shall we do this *ad infinitum* while you starve?"

"Take a drink," Galloping Gazelle suggested.

De'ath snarled. "Didn't those buffoons bring you any white?"

The speedster found a bottle of German beer and opened it. Sergeant-at-Arms noted it was Trappist brew, not easily found in the U.S.

"Repugnant stuff." De'ath's voice soured. "But the social lubricant of my university days." He took a sip.

"I'm satisfied," Marksman grumbled. "For the moment."

"Good." De'ath flung the knife at Marksman, which he expertly caught. Was that De'ath's way of saying he had observed the juggling? "Now, Red Rose must stay in this country."

"What?" she gasped.

"Red Rose is a citizen who left Ruritania in an unauthorized manner. She will be my bride. The AtomiCar is forfeit. Since it is not useful evidence of a crime, I will accept it as a wedding present from the former owners."

Galloping Gazelle rushed toward Dr. De'ath. "If you think you can hold—"

"Not so fast, Gazelle." Sergeant-at-Arms stood.

"That phrase isn't in my lexicon," the speedster noted.

"Striking Dr. De'ath would precipitate the international incident we're trying to prevent." Sergeant-at-Arms set a hand on his shoulder. "You're still on my payroll, kid."

Galloping Gazelle shoved Sergeant-at-Arms back. "Are you going to let him get away with this?"

"Play along," he whispered.

***

Getting his bearings in the lake, Aquamarine thought he saw a form dart. He peered into the inky water. Lake or ocean, his eyes had evolved for such viewing. Whatever it was, it was gone now. He hoped he wasn't being stalked.

Aquamarine saw it again. Now, strong hands arrested his progress. Then those hands swooped him out of the lake. After being dropped on the lakeshore, Aquamarine beheld a man with pointed ears, upswept eyebrows, and jet-black hair combed to a widow's peak. He recognized something of himself in those features. The man wore green swim trunks and gold wristbands.

"Who are you?" the odd man demanded. Having a hard time grasping Aquamarine's skintight shirt front, he switched to Aquamarine's wrist. The grip was tremendous. "You are not of my people. They have a bluish complexion."

Aquamarine landed a powerful punch to the arrogant face with his free hand.

"Impressive." The blow had no effect.

"Your people are blue?"

"They alone absorb oxygen from water. How can *you*? Who are you?" A killing blow in return was about to be dealt, dependent on the answer.

"Funny. You don't look bluish," Aquamarine stated.

"What? Oh, ha, ha." The newcomer doubled over in laughter, releasing his captive.

Aquamarine rubbed his wrist. "What's so funny?"

"Have you never heard of Prince Neptune, the Sub-Merger? Ruler of Atlantica." He thumped his chest. "Do the Tomorrow Men keep you in seclusion?"

"Atlantica?" This universe also had an Atlantica. Aquamarine asked, "Who are the Tomorrow Men?"

"Or were you bred by Dr. De'ath to fight me? He has tried creating super-powered beings. My intention was only to beat him insensate. Now I shall kill him for this mockery."

Before the point could be disputed, a voice shouted, "Hold it, Ears."

Sub-Merger turned to see a winged man headed at him. Eagleman drove his feet right at the newcomer's chest. This proved fruitless. The winged man bounced off Sub-Merger. Eagleman grimaced in pain and hovered in the air. Sub-Merger's hand sped out to grasp the ankle above Eagleman's claw. "Not only do you fly, but you defy gravity."

Eagleman reacted fast. With astounding flexibility, he swung his morning star. "You pass the eye test. Let's try reflexes."

This, too, merely bounced off Sub-Merger's hand. He grasped the morning star as easily as a tennis racquet. The amphibian yanked it from Eagleman and flung it over his shoulder.

"Wait." Aquamarine scurried to his feet. "He's from Atlantica."

"Atlantica?" Eagleman echoed. "But that's—"

Aquamarine shot him a *shut up* sneer.

The winged man fell silent. No need to admit there was another Atlantica on another Earth.

"Yes, it is real," Sub-Merger bellowed.

Eagleman gasped. "I thought Atlantica was a legend."

"It is no legend," Sub-Merger said. "You changed costumes again, Hawk?"

"Hawk?" Eagleman asked.

"Ah, I see now you are not Hawk. Too old. He is a teenager. The Tomorrow Men dared ask me to join them in their recruitment of mutated humans."

"What have you got against, er, mutated humans?" Aquamarine asked.

"Nothing, fool. I am one myself. You see?" He lifted a leg to present a heel with a pair of small wings.

"We're not Tomorrow Men, whoever they are. And I'm not Hawk. I'm Eagleman." He wondered at Sub-Merger's apparent invulnerability. This ocean-bred being was far stronger than Aquamarine.

Aquamarine tipped his head to Eagleman. "He's with me. We have no argument with you."

"You surface dwellers are fond of talking...talk fast. Now. What are you doing here?"

"We're after a guy named Dr. De'ath," Eagleman said.

"He runs this whole country. I am here for him, too. Keep talking. Perhaps I will let you live."

"Oh, thanks a lot," Aquamarine growled out.

"Yes, I can use you as a distraction when I attack."

"Another friend is in De'ath's castle," Eagleman added. "His air force attacked us."

"Boon companions, then," Sub-Merger said. "Since we have a common enemy, we will work together. Under my command, of course."

"Don't worry about that." Eagleman retrieved his morning star. "Aquamarine and I are like a well-oiled machine. Neither you nor De'ath can handle us."

"Then what are you waiting for?" Sub-Merger laughed. With that, he flew toward the castle.

This impetuous move was caught on camera. An alarm sounded. Red Rose, now under Dr. De'ath's orders, was dispatched to the castle's battlements. She hurled hexes. They caused Eagleman and Sub-Merger to fly into each other. The latter was only dazed. A squad of robot soldiers appeared and pounded Sub-Merger and Aquamarine into unconsciousness. De'ath's human forces made sure Eagleman was subdued. The super-beings were taken into custody.

"Bring them to Dr. De'ath's lab," a human squad leader commanded.

Aquamarine broke free and came face to face with the human officer. He fired point blank. Aquamarine could not dodge bullets.

***

King Bee, hidden on the AtomiCar, got an eyeful. Under the pretext of making repairs, De'ath's men bugged the aircraft. He checked their handiwork. No bombs or gas canisters were installed, just listening devices. He flew to his partner on the Blackbird. Holding a finger to his lips,

King Bee got close to Hornette and whispered, "Don't flap a thing, lady bug. Not your lovely lips or your wings."

She gestured, pointing outside. King Bee nodded he understood. Silently, she flew off to warn her teammates.

***

After the impressive *smorgasbord*, the Assemblers collected around a huge couch. The flunkies had removed the remnants, the service, the table and chairs. Hornette flew to each Assembler's ear with her warning. Then she returned to her assigned station.

"What are we supposed to do about my cousin?" Galloping Gazelle asked.

Sergeant-at-Arms weighed what could be said aloud about the situation. Suddenly, the floor opened. Galloping Gazelle saw the movement first. Before he could yell a warning he, Sergeant-at-Arms, Marksman and Amazon Woman dropped into a pit.

"Go limp," Sergeant-at-Arms barked. "It's—"

"Save it, pops," Marksman snapped. "I tumbled with the circus."

Above them, the trapdoor began to close. The speedster attempted running up the wall, but the trap closed too quickly. He fell backward. Their spill landed on a chute, which funneled them to four separate rooms.

Dr. De'ath's voice crackled over a loudspeaker: "Perhaps you will fight to get your teammate back. Do well in my tests and I may yet issue a visa for your friend. If you live."

Amazon Woman landed on her back. The quickness with which she regained her feet indicated she was unhurt. Amazon Woman found herself in a cramped compartment. Except for spouts high up on the walls, it was empty.

This puzzled her. "What can that mean?"

In answer, the spouts began ejecting a torrent of

cement. She drew back her fist for a punch. The wall she connected with cracked. But it held.

Muscle is not going to work.

Changing tactics, she pulled out her whip, lassoed one spout, and tugged. That snapped it off the wall, but now cement gushed out faster.

Out of the frying pan. She took the broken spout and crumpled it like paper. By leaping, she jammed it into another one. Although that spout was blocked, those remaining still belched their deadly mixture. She had merely bought time. Amazon Woman grasped her whip for another strike. The flow of cement was relentless.

***

Sergeant-at-Arms dodged metal bars. Any of them sliding along, he knew, was capable of piercing him. He not only dodged but blocked with his shield. A resounding *clang* sounded. No sooner would he grab one to swing over, another would slide toward him, ceiling or floor, this wall, that wall.

"I can do this all day, De'ath," he yelled with more bravado than he felt.

That bravado was squelched when one bar caught him in the midsection. The belly band was great for blunting knives, but the force was still transferred to his body like a sledgehammer.

"Oof." He gasped.

He wouldn't let this slow him. That blow set him up for another that slammed his head. The leathery helmet gave some protection, but not much. More moving bars threatened him. As long as they moved one at a time, he had a chance, but now, the bars began moving *two* at a time.

***

For Galloping Gazelle, it was another story. The room with a fan-driven whirlwind proved to be no challenge for him. In fact, he managed to match the speed of the spinning blades and gain momentum. The speedster ran along the four walls. With the right implement, he knew, it would be possible to rapidly dig through a wall and escape. But no implement presented itself. Except for the spinning blades themselves causing the wind. Those blades, he considered, would do. Galloping Gazelle was about to find out how fast he really was.

Even if it cost him a hand.

***

Marksman's room featured a floor that was slowly withdrawing over a black pit.

"Think fast, archer," he ordered himself.

His fingers found his grapple arrow-and-line. He nocked it and aimed ceilingward. It hooked onto the ceiling. Then he shimmied up the line.

***

Amazon Woman had not been idle. Feet now immobilized in cement, she pounded that spot on the wall again. More cracks appeared, but breaking through was taking too long. The wall buckled but wouldn't give. She took a deep breath before the gooey mass engulfed her.

***

Sergeant-at-Arms saw the new set of bars were sharpened. It was now or never. Taking a chance, he hooked his shield onto an oncoming bar. This left him no protection, but it slammed the wall with his impervious weapon. The impact produced a prestigious crack. From then on, he returned to that spot and pounded full force with fists, feet, shoulder and shield.

***

Marksman, momentarily safe, realized he couldn't hang around there all day. He reached for an explosive arrow head in the strap on his jerkin. With accuracy, he blew the wall out. It happened to be the wall Amazon Woman was pounding from the other side. The blast blew her out of her would-be cement tomb, knocked her over, but left her unhurt.

Marksman offered her a hand up. "Here, let me."

"So gallant." She smiled. Once on her feet, she retained her grip on Marksman's arm and lifted *him*.

"Point," he grumbled.

"Beg pardon?"

"I'll tell you all about it later."

"May I?" Amazon Woman asked, taking his bow. She scraped cement off herself.

"Let's get out of here, lady."

***

Speeding up, Galloping Gazelle had to maintain his pace. Matching the speed, the fan blades seemed motionless to him. He increased his speed. The first order of business was to loosen a blade. He had to strike the weakest part of the joint. Finally, Galloping Gazelle grabbed the blade from its hub and yanked. Immediately, the whirlwind diminished. Do it wrong, he knew, *and I lose a finger.* Fast healing would not help Galloping Gazelle if that happened. But it was better than getting a hand cut off completely.

"Feet, don't fail me now."

He used the blade to attack the wall. Pleased with the results, he went back for another. His high-speed digging broke through the wall.

"Child's play," he muttered.

Galloping Gazelle found himself in Sergeant-at-Arms' death trap. He turned, becoming the target of a sharpened bar. The speedster saw his captain about to be perforated by metal skewers coming from two directions. He dashed for his exhausted compatriot, all the while dodging the shifting bars of doom with ease. He grabbed Sergeant-at-Arms and launched himself at the cracked wall, feet first. There wasn't time for high-speed scraping. Sergeant-at-Arms' pounding had weakened the wall. Galloping Gazelle broke through, but he lost his grip on Sergeant-at-Arms. He now deftly tumbled and rolled to his feet. They found themselves in a corridor.

"Thanks, kid," Sergeant-at-Arms grunted.

They surged forward. The next corner they turned gave them a surprise.

***

A cement splattered Amazon Woman stood. Behind her, Marksman was using the bow on her back.

"Gotta get this off you before it hardens."

Galloping Gazelle said, "I can help." He ran the flats of the blades over her. Done, the speedster tucked the blades into the back of his lightning-bolt belt.

At that moment, Dr. De'ath announced over a hidden loudspeaker, "You have escaped just as I expected you would."

"De'ath, stop this now," Amazon Woman demanded. A flex of muscles flung off the last bits of cement.

"Those toys were meant for others," he shot back. "Now the cat-and-mouse game truly begins."

Sergeant-at-Arms yelled, "You're not dealing with the Atoms Family now, you fiend."

"I have other challenges for you. I shall test the mettle

of this girl—"

"Girl?" Amazon Woman shouted. "I was born in 2000 B.C."

Marksman's hawk-eye vision found the speaker. He gritted his teeth. "Doc, you talk too much." Impressively, he snapped a weighted arrow at the loudspeaker, silencing De'ath on impact.

"You're too quick, mister," Sergeant-at-Arms said. "I wanted to hear that last remark."

"You will when I catch up with him," Marksman countered. "He won't *stop* yappin'."

From the other direction came fierce barking.

Amazon Woman gasped. "Dogs!"

"De'ath wants us to fight dogs?" Marksman fumed. He chose an arrowhead and snapped it onto a shaft. "I ain't hurting no dumb animals." He shot in front of the approaching canines. One by one, a whimpering pack of wolves, not dogs, keeled over and went to sleep.

"There's probably more coming," Sergeant-at-Arms said. "Maybe more than your gas arrows can handle. This way."

He pointed to a stream. Into the drink they went. It was icy cold.

Cold doesn't bother me. Sergeant-at-Arms flashed back to his time in the glacier. He stopped to yank up his cuffed boots.

Bubbling indicated the stream was now boiling. Amazon Woman seemed barely fazed as she entered. Pretty soon, the two were up to their hips.

"Whoa," Marksman bleated. "Parboiling I can handle, but I can't get these arrows wet."

Amazon Woman offered a solution. "Throw me your quiver, Marksman. Then jump."

He did so.

"She's right. It's not too bad," Marksman said and turned toward Galloping Gazelle. "You gonna super-speed swim?"

Not only could every Assembler pilot, but János Urbancsok had been retained to instruct them in swimming. Galloping Gazelle estimated the narrowest part. He backpedaled and ran across the surface like a skipping stone.

Part way across, the stream came to a rolling boil. Marksman quickly changed his tune and expression as the water heated up.

"Yeow! Get me outta here."

"Use your circus tumbling, smart guy," Sergeant-at-Arms suggested then submerged.

On the other side, the speedster presented a hand to Amazon Woman. "Dear lady."

She let him yank her up. But the price for that was a vise-like grip. It reminded him who she was. Marksman reached out with his bow. Amazon Woman turned and grasped it, pulling the archer out.

Sergeant-at-Arms broke the surface of the water, wearing a tiny rebreather. The Special Projects Agency lent it to him on a semi-permanent basis as long as he reported on its function. "Water is clean, so it's pumped in from somewhere." He took off the device. "The channel is newly built. That sadist engineered this whole torture chamber. There's even a stopper in a drain."

"Did you try pulling it out?" Marksman asked.

"I managed to break it." Sergeant-at-Arms hefted his shield.

The water level was lowering. The patriot got on the bank and rolled down his boots back to their usual state. A squad of robots approached. The commando knife might come in handy right about now. Amazon Woman didn't hesitate. She plowed into them. Marksman unleashed a variety of arrows. Galloping Gazelle was upon them. His fans sliced. The speedster turned on a dime, cutting them at super speed.

"Couldn't you have saved some for me?" Sergeant-at-Arms tucked the knife away.

Steel doors slid open. A massive tank clanked forward.

"You hadda ask," Marksman yelped.

"A Fiat 2000," he bellowed. "Developed in Italy. Weighs over forty tons."

A turret zeroed in on the heroes. Sergeant-at-Arms didn't like the looks of this.

He hefted his shield. "Get behind me, archer. Damn thing has twenty millimeters of armor."

"Language, Sarge," Marksman said. "There's a lady present."

The tank fired. Ball bearings bounced off Amazon Woman's bracelets. Galloping Gazelle was untouchable.

From behind the shield, Marksman steamed. "Okay. That's it." He loosed an arrow down the gun barrel on the turret. This one carried another explosive arrowhead. Seconds later, it blew.

"Whatcha think of my arrows now, Sarge?"

"Nicely done."

Amazon Woman dashed to the tank, dealing punches on a soldier evacuating it. She lassoed the fleeing tank driver with her whip before he got very far. Sergeant-at-Arms strode up to him, grasped the soldier's shirt front, and pulled him close. "Where is the control room?"

Silently, the tank driver pointed.

Amazon Woman rushed to the wall the tank came from. It wasn't hard to determine the exact spot. There were telltale tread marks on the ground. She battered the wall until it crumbled. Galloping Gazelle ran up to it, chopping with the fan blades. Together, they beat the hole bigger and climbed through.

The speedster shot ahead. Amazon Woman followed; Sergeant-at-Arms and Marksman brought up the rear. The latter walked backward, nocked arrow at the ready. His companions laid waste to those on duty. Galloping Gazelle did most of the damage, super-fast fan blades applied to their guns. Sergeant-at-Arms' shield careened off the walls, ricocheting into the men.

A door slid back. Dr. De'ath appeared. "Stop!"

Marksman spun. He let loose an arrow. It was deflected from De'ath by an invisible force field.

"Hold it, Marksman," Sergeant-at-Arms said. "Start talking, Dr. De'ath."

"Bah! I was merely playing with you. Had I meant to kill you, I could have done so at any time." He sneered. "You have won the girl's freedom."

Red Rose stepped forward. De'ath dismissed his men with a pointed finger.

Galloping Gazelle shot to his cousin. "You all right?"

"I am unharmed," Red Rose answered. "But I was forced to fight Sub-Merger and his allies. A man with wings and another—"

"Wings?" Amazon Woman perked up. "That has to be Eagleman."

"Either that or Hawk," Marksman countered.

Amazon Woman broke into a run through the control room, deep into a corridor. "Where?"

"Gazelle! After her," Sergeant-at-Arms commanded.

The speedster lit out.

"Will you strike a woman?" Amazon Woman loosened the whip from her belt.

"Stay back, my cousin," Red Rose shouted. "I'll handle her."

As Amazon Woman raised her whip, Red Rose's hex launched. Swinging the whip, it spun back to Amazon Woman, entangling her. *This girl is a witch.*

De'ath had a hearty laugh. "Come. Dessert awaits."

CHAPTER 12

Gradually, Aquamarine regained consciousness. He played dead. Still groggy, he watched through half-lidded eyes. A scientific team in lab coats seemed fascinated by the unconscious Eagleman. Like Aquamarine, he was strapped to a gurney. They couldn't budge his helmet. Indeed, it was locked in place by some manner known only to Eagleman. If the thing stymied them, his wings were another story. The circular disc holding them piqued their curiosity. They slipped the harness off Eagleman. With the wings off, they twisted the dial. The whole harness rose.

De'ath can't get hold of Eagleman's antigravity device, Aquamarine thought. There was a soft snap. He looked over and saw Sub-Merger in the midst of bursting his bonds. Another quiet snap went unheard by their captors. Aquamarine shook himself, indicating his desire to be free. Sitting up, Sub-Merger waved the request away.

"C'mon, we helped you," Aquamarine said *sotto voce.* He pointed with his chin. "That device can't fall into the wrong hands."

Sub-Merger remained unimpressed. He swung his feet off the gurney to leave.

"Dr. De'ath can cause a lot of trouble with that," Aquamarine pressed.

Sub-Merger soundlessly glided back. "How do you know *I* am not the wrong hands?"

"You already fly," Aquamarine noted, too loudly.

De'ath's science staff turned. They saw their prisoners awake.

"They're loose," a scientist bellowed in Ruritanian.

The aquatic man didn't understand the language, but the meaning was clear. The scientists forgot all about Eagleman. Sub-Merger reached over and effortlessly tore off Aquamarine's bonds. Free, Aquamarine dispatched two of the human scientists. Sub-Merger handled three more.

"Thanks, Subby."

"You will call me Sub-Merger or Prince Neptune. Failing that, Neptune McCurry."

That surname struck a chord with Aquamarine. It was one he shared. "Is that a common surname in Atlantica?"

"Ignorant fool. My father was an American," Sub-Merger grumbled testily then shrugged. "As De'ath has Red Rose working for him, I shall deal with him another day. Perhaps, I will see you in the seven seas."

"We'll pass like two ships." Aquamarine suggested.

With that the man from the other Atlantica burst through a window and flew off. Neither glass shards nor broken window frame seemed to affect him. Aquamarine was looking for Eagleman's harness. It took him a few seconds to spot it floating up by the ceiling. With a tremendous leap, he snagged it.

The thump of his landing stirred Eagleman. He bolted upright. "What's that?"

Although an alien being within that human body, Eagleman had fabricated the sturdiest physique possible for a human. Aquamarine went to help his avian friend. "A dip in the water would do you a world of good."

"Maybe two worlds." Eagleman smiled while strapping on his wings. "I had a morning star when I came in."

"Here." Aquamarine reached back and presented it.

Eagleman hefted the weapon. "We'd better get going. When they see that flying galoot streaking through the sky, they'll know we're free."

"You've got some nerve calling anyone a flying

galoot." Aquamarine smirked. "What are we going to do about that girl? I can survive gunfire like it was rocks, but that chick knocked me for a loop with a wave of her hands."

***

"De'ath," Sergeant-at-Arms called out. "Produce her friends or there really *will* be an international incident."

"Are you prepared to incite such? You would bring America into a war."

"I am a private citizen. The Assemblers work for no single nation—"

"Calm yourself, Sergeant-at-Arms." De'ath turned to check a monitor. "It would appear they have escaped my custody. They are now fugitives. Behold, Assemblers. My flying cameras have picked up those you seek."

Various screens flashed on. Different angles showed Sub-Merger zooming away into the distance, diminishing in size as he went. Within a few seconds, Aquamarine and Eagleman zipped by, appearing on one screen. They would go off camera range of one, then appear on another at a different angle.

"I suppose the Assemblers are on a recruiting drive," De'ath said. "Those costumed clowns will not replace your pet monster, your Norse god and Ferro's metallic flunky."

Sergeant-at-Arms did not like Dr. De'ath knowing that much about Assembler doings. "De'ath, back off," he ordered. "Find them. Then we'll leave peacefully. There will be no interference from you, or I will chop up that armor with this shield and feed you the pieces."

"Such insolence."

"Try me, Doctor."

De'ath grunted and stalked off to find solace with Svetlana. A door clicked shut.

"It appears we are free to go," Galloping Gazelle said.

"I'll take a look for those two."

***

"A most tiring day. So weary, must sleep. Damnedable force field drains so much power." Dr. De'ath said to Svetlana, once inside. "There is wine. Help yourself, my dear."

He clicked off the force field, unfastened his holster, and sat. Within seconds, he was snoring.

Svetlana crept up. Suddenly, she picked up the Mauser and fired and fired, producing only clicks.

"So," De'ath roared, now fully awake. "My suspicions were correct. A Soviet assassin. No wonder Sergeant-at-Arms' gaze lingered on you so. He recognized you."

The girl was fast. She threw the gun at De'ath and ran.

***

The Assemblers made it to the Blackbird. Sergeant-at-Arms said, "Sorry we restrained you with your own whip, Amazon Woman."

"Think nothing of it." She waved the incident off. "I just want to find my friends."

Marksman gripped Sergeant-at-Arms' bicep. "Say, why don't we let Amazon Woman fly the AtomiCar back? She can look for her boyfriends along the way."

She saw something intangible pass between Sergeant-at-Arms and Marksman.

The carny was up to something, Sergeant-at-Arms realized. He knew what Marksman was trying *not* to say.

"Oh, Sergeant-at-Arms, could I?" Amazon Woman played along. "Of course, I am still in your custody and swear on my honor as an Amazon to return this craft to the rightful owner."

"Ah, yes." The Assembler looked over to the

bowman. He nodded. "Let me show you our radio frequency."

She knew the frequency. Still, she walked over to the AtomiCar with him. In a low voice, Sergeant-at-Arms said, "When you find your friends, say nothing sensitive. He's listening."

"But how?"

King Bee flew near her ear. "De'ath bugged both ships, lady."

"We have small friends in tight places." Sergeant-at-Arms chuckled. "Easy to miss."

"Ah, might you grow as well as shrink?" she whispered.

"He gets points for using both powers."

"Points? Marksman alluded to points."

"It's a long story."

"So, that's how a giant appeared in the AtomiCar and quickly disappeared. Another teammate of mine shrinks. But he does not grow to a giant."

"All he has to do is reverse the—"

"Not now." Sergeant-at-Arms stopped King Bee. "If we destroy his bugs, De'ath will know we're on to him. Instead, we'll feed him Grade A baloney. I guess the gold fellow hails from your universe. Superior Man mentioned him."

She brightened at the mention of her companion. "Yes, that's my teammate Golden—"

"Assemblers. Please take me with you."

Svetlana suddenly appeared, running. She did not seem a bit winded. Her high heels were gone, however.

"What? But you're—"

"I want to defect."

"And just who *are* you, lady?" Sergeant-at-Arms asked. He'd give her asylum but the Russkie was going to be made to work for it.

"To save my life, I must break cover. I am KGB,

assigned to get close to De'ath. I took my best shot at him, but he tricked me with an unloaded gun."

"Oldest trick in the book." Sergeant-at-Arms smirked.

"The KGB's penalty for failure is execution. Now De'ath is after me. I am between rocks and the hard place," she pleaded, mangling the Americanism. "Let me come with you."

"I'd be required to turn you over to Special Projects," the patriot warned.

"That is preferrable to death."

"I have another question, lady. And you better tell the truth." Sergeant-at-Arms gripped her wrist in an ungentlemanly way. He didn't like it, but he meant to show her who was boss. "Are your Soviets masters of deceit holding an American nuclear physicist from Caltech named Robert Bannion?"

"What? No, of course not." The girl jerked her arm back with surprising strength. "We already have the best nuclear brains in the world."

"That's debatable." Sergeant-at-Arms allowed the Soviet to board.

Impulsively, she turned and kissed him. "Thank you."

She could have easily snapped his neck. Conflicted, Sergeant-at-Arms smiled, knowing she was a cobra. That was a kiss of gratitude she'd practiced. He noticed the Assemblers were smiling at him. Red-faced, Sergeant-at-Arms rushed to the cockpit and started the craft.

Grinning Assemblers strapped themselves in. Sergeant-at-Arms taxied. The team kept quiet. King Bee pointed out the offending device. Marksman signaled a leave-it-to-me response. Removing his quiver, he carefully dumped the arrows.

"Easy with the trinitrotoluene." King Bee reminded him.

"Trinitrotoluene?" Svetlana gasped.

Marksman slipped the quiver over the device. He

zipped up his newly attached lid. It enclosed the device almost totally, muffling the sound at the other end. Now the group could talk freely.

Sergeant-at-Arms stopped the craft and returned from the cockpit to examine the quiver.

"Like that?" Marksman asked Sergeant-at-Arms.

"I love it, archer. I move we call this meeting to order."

King Bee, at human size, asked, "Mind if I fly this contraption." He was unwilling to do any further idle sitting.

"Permission granted."

Hornette, just as bored, grew to normal size and claimed the co-pilot seat. The ground crew cleared them for takeoff. It would be a long flight back.

"Do you really think we can fool Dr. De'ath?" Red Rose asked.

"Possibly." Sergeant-at-Arms turned to Marksman. "Remove the quiver. We'll start feeding him a story, beginning with our *tryout* members. Marksman, you have an opinion on everything and frequently give it, even if unasked. Hit it."

Marksman was busy eyeing the shapely Soviet agent. She wouldn't be going back to her Commie masters. The archer nodded, musing aloud, "Aquamarine showed he could box Sub-Merger's pointy ears. He's got my vote."

"And think, with Eagleman," Galloping Gazelle expounded, "we'll have our own Hawk. How I miss fighting him."

Svetlana picked up on what they were up to. "So, Sergeant-at-Arms, you're not going to hold Amazon Woman's impulsive move against her pending membership, are you? It wouldn't be very...American."

"I second that," Red Rose added, turning. "We could use more girls on the team. Don't you agree, Hornette?"

"Yes. And she simply must tell me who does her hair

lately."

Luckily, the eye-rolling from Sergeant-at-Arms was inaudible to the bug. Still, it gave him an idea. "I know of another superhero we should recruit. He's not local but I'm sure Superior Man would jump at the chance to sign on."

Svetlana was puzzled. "We do not have that name in our files."

***

In his castle, De'ath was stumped by the information he was receiving. He decided not to send his hologram to the Assembler jet with a demand for Svetlana's return. They could have the assassin.

"She is your problem now," he muttered. But the thought of the Assemblers recruiting Superior Man disturbed him greatly.

"He must have a weakness."

***

Amazon Woman was curious. Would the Superior Squadron signal belts work on this Earth? Between the conditions the team exposed them to and the scraps they got into, they were forever getting damaged beyond repair. Moving at super speeds, exposure to the vacuum of outer space, size-shifting and bone-shattering adventures didn't allow the communication devices to survive long. It was why Superior Man didn't carry one and Aquamarine kept his built into the Airphibian's dashboard. This universe was no less fraught with mishaps that would likely destroy electronics. She tuned the AtomiCar radio to the obscure frequency her team used, as her belt radio was rusting at the bottom of her own universe's sea. Amazon Woman was pleasantly surprised to establish contact.

"Eagleman here." His voice crackled. "Why didn't I

think of this before?"

"There was a lot of excitement. Give me your position. I'll pick you two up. I'm in the Atoms Family's aircraft."

Soon, she was taking her companions aboard. It was a tight squeeze with the two side pods gone.

Aquamarine made himself comfortable. "Why don't we have one of—"

A finger to her lips made Aquamarine clam up. Amazon Woman turned to Eagleman. "Do you remember when you coached us?"

Her face seemed to be pleading to say something else entirely. Alien Eagleman might not be getting the human trait of deception. Aquamarine got it. He pointed to his ear and Amazon Woman nodded.

"Sure, I do," Eagleman said. "But why—"

"We can make good use of our time in the air getting a refresher in it."

There was much ear pulling and pointing about the inside of the craft on her part. Finally, Eagleman got the message: Dr. De'ath was listening.

Switching to the Iukkothian language, Amazon Woman managed to get out, "Golden Ring was spotted when he appeared in this universe. That's how our new friends got involved."

She was careful to avoid words that couldn't be translated by unauthorized ears. Then, Amazon Woman increased speed. She could fill her teammates in on the long flight back to New York. New York, she shook her head, a hick town in her world. Amazon Woman had to remember it was the equivalent of Mascouten, New Waukee.

***

"Want to see how it's done, Man Machine?" Suzette

Frost asked. The girl was piloting Reide's rocket plane.

Man Machine jolted in his new astro-armor. Coppery red, his arms and legs were gold. The gold parts were flexible metal. Resembling the high-altitude full-pressure suits the Royal Air Force developed for prolonged flights, it was semi-rigid. The whole of his back was a solar panel. His helmet was coppery red and yellow. He could hinge up the faceplate to breathe the air around him. Inspired by Tarantula-Man's feats, electromagnetic coils were in his boot soles. For this space journey, Man Machine packed auxiliary tanks of rocket fuel and oxygen he could easily attach to his armor at the appropriate time.

"Lady, you don't have to ask me twice."

The girl showed him the controls, then let him pilot the rest of the way. Before long, Cape Kennedy spread out before them. Once they landed, the two men transferred to their space transport. Rich Reide donned a blue spacesuit designed like his costume. They took the place of a pair of astronauts on a scheduled rocket mission. NASA didn't much care who checked the LES1 satellite or what they rode up on. Reide and Man Machine would do the checking. By this means, the pair could cover their observation of the rift.

Reide nearly didn't get his own rocket launch off the ground in the radioactive incident that granted his team their powers. But his modified aerospaceplane was different.

"I picked the *Coléoptère* up cheaply. We'll mount it atop a NASA's Saturn 1-B rocket."

"Isn't that 'beetle' in French?" Man Machine asked.

"Yes, it is. Notice the unusual angular wing. It's a vertical takeoff and landing aircraft designed by Snecma and manufactured by Nord Aviation in the '50s. The thing requires no runway and very little space to land."

"Looks like a plug for a socket," Man Machine said. "Except for the kooky wheels on the end of those landing struts."

"You won't be mocking those wheels when we land back on Earth standing up."

Suzette kissed Reide goodbye. "You fellas have a safe journey. Man Machine, I'm relying on you to return him alive."

Launch seemed to take forever. Finally there was ignition. Ascending, Man Machine turned to see a blast of blinding light. Earth fell away. The G force was terrific. He'd previously only flown high in the atmosphere. This was old hat to Reide. That guy held degrees in electrical engineering, aerospace mechanics, chemistry, physics and biology. How does he even find time to lecture at Triborough University? He recalled that demonstration Reide gave, exposing a spider to radiation.

Low orbit was three hundred miles over the Earth's von Kármán line. First, they docked with the dead satellite. Reide opened the hatch. Air vented out of the airlock, Reide followed standard procedure, yawning to equalize the pressure between his middle ears and atmosphere of four point three pounds per square inch. He exited and looked the satellite over. Reide beamed a message to Man Machine: "A lost cause. She'll never transmit again."

That part of their mission accomplished, they sought the rift. This wasn't so hard, knowing it was there. A patch of space blacker than the space surrounding it, and a vortex of sparkling lights in a pinwheel pattern would describe it. Reide again went out to look it over. Coming back in, he reported, "It's amazing. This is like a barrier door."

Man Machine got ready for his own spacewalk. He followed the same procedures then stepped outside into space. Momentarily, he was stunned. The emptiness, the beauty, stars everywhere. Out there, it was minus two hundred forty-five degrees Fahrenheit.

"Ferro, old boy," he said to himself. "You've done it again."

Inside Man Machine's astro-armor suit, the cold made his teeth chatter even through his insulation. He peered through the rift, fascinated. Against the black of space floated a curving ball with blue fringe. Earth of the other universe looked just like his own.

Man Machine's joy was short lived, however. He caught a glimpse of the space plane through the hole. And it was tiny. Unknowingly, Man Machine had gone through the rift. He was moving farther away. In fact, he couldn't even locate it without the craft passing by to mark it. The gravity of the other Earth was tugging on him.

"Reide," he called over the radio. Man Machine operated the rockets in his boot heels. In his panic, he overshot where he meant to be. He disengaged them but, of course, momentum kept him going.

"Reide. Mr. Atoms."

There was no response. Again, he glimpsed the spacecraft. It was moving away.

A song he heard on the radio came into his head. This peculiar hole in the sky would be the cause of his death.

***

Paul Pymer put down his book as a thought occurred to him. He sent out a signal for Jet Man. As usual with the speedster, his response was in person.

A purple streaking motion solidified to a human shape. "What's up, Paul?"

"Just this. I've been boning up. From what I read, you might be able to vibrate to this other universe."

"Vibrate there? How?"

"Simple, our two universes occupy the same space. Otherwise, De'ath's machine couldn't have brought him here. But they're vibrating at different speeds."

"Ah, I see. You speculate with my speed I can match the vibrational speed of the other universe. And come out on the other Earth, is that it?"

"Theoretically, it's possible."

"Theoretically, anything is possible," Jet Man held. "I don't think I can generate enough speed for that."

"With Jet Boy's help you could. Can you get him to assist?"

"You know, we *should* have an alternate way to traverse the universes." Jet Man nodded. "All right, I'm game to try."

"While you're at it, have him put the Wonderkind on standby."

"That's a good idea. Despite being teenagers, their powers might come in handy with this crisis."

The Wonderkind were sidekicks of the members of the Superior Squadron, organized into their own superhero team. Jet Man radioed Jet Boy. He and Pymer didn't have long to wait before another purple blur solidified at headquarters.

"Irene wants to know if you'll be home for supper." The kid sported a duplicate of Jet Man's outfit, right down to the last lightning bolt. "Mercury passed the word to us that Ratman resigned. What's happenin'?"

"Jet Boy, do you remember Paul Pymer?"

"Sure."

Pymer offered a handshake. "Nice to see you, Jet Boy."

"Hey, Dr. Pymer." He accepted the offered hand.

Jet Boy, Pymer knew, was faster than any boy ever.

"He thinks crooks might see an opportunity to strike while we're busy with something else," Jet Man said. "Put them on alert."

"I'll send out a signal to them right now." Jet Boy pressed his belt, sending to Mercury, Amazon Girl and Tadpole. Now the Wonderkind was on standby.

"I have to trust you with something confidential. Maybe you should sit down."

"Aw. I can take it. What is it?"

"There's another universe."

Jet Boy squinted at Pymer. Then he looked at Jet Man. He was deadly serious. "I think I better sit down."

"Yeah, but don't tell anyone about it. Not even the Wonderkind. Now, with your help, we should be able to vibrate there."

"Another universe." Jet Boy's eyes filled with wonder. "Are they barbarians with swords? Elves, maybe?"

"It's just like this Earth," Pymer said.

"But their heroes are different," Jet Man added.

"That sounds crazy, brother-in-law o' mine."

"You won't help me get there?" Jet Man asked.

"Heck, yeah, I'll do it."

Jet Man figured it was best they hook up like collegiate wrestlers ready to compete.

"Maybe you better shrink to a safe distance," Jet Man advised Pymer.

"Shrink? You must have me confused with Shrinking Man." Pymer saw them begin to vibrate.

"We can trust him," Jet Man called. "He's my—"

Pymer saw the pair become silent, indistinct smears of purple. Then they were gone.

***

Superior Man was feeling back to normal. There was no pain or nausea. He rose a few inches in the air. His super hearing worked, so did his stomach; he felt hungry. Right at that moment, Penniman appeared. Superior Man was still reminded of someone. Then he got it. He snapped his fingers. Penniman had a duplicate in his universe. His boss at *The Daily Globe* had a butler also named Penniman. Superior Man thought, briefly, of Capgras syndrome.

"Something, sir?"

"Ah, well, I *am* a bit hungry. Golem joked about

baking me a cake. Now I wish I had some cake."

"I would advise even a superior man not to eat Golem's baking, sir."

"At this point, I could eat anything."

While that was literally true, Superior Man craved actual food.

"I shall rustle up something, sir. Perhaps a delicacy not found in your, er, universe."

Superior Man took the opportunity to scan his choices in the kitchen. It was a good excuse to confirm that his X-ray vision was restored. He saw foodstuffs that were familiar, but he pondered what had sickened him. It was as if he'd been exposed to hercolubite. That was pure poison to him, remnants of his home planet that had landed on Earth. Superior Man wondered if there could be hercolubite on *this* Earth.

"Impossible," he dismissed aloud.

***

At the Leland Building, Eagleman, Amazon Woman, and Aquamarine sheepishly turned the AtomiCar over to Golem and Flaming Youth.

"If there are any repairs you'd like us to make," Amazon Woman began, "Eagleman has quite advanced tech. Aquamarine and I worked on our own respective craft."

Those two Squadron Supreme members avoided looking Golem and Flaming Youth in the eye.

"Naw, forget it," Golem grumbled, waving a rocky hand. "Ya gave De'ath what for, so all is forgiven."

He wasn't very convincing. Amazon Woman could tell Golem was sore.

"Yeah," Flaming Youth piped up. "The damage was worth it if De'ath got his lumps."

"We don't want to cause any further trouble."

Amazon Woman wished she could shrink like her teammate and those two insect-like superheroes on this Earth.

"In that case, we'll all feel better after I send ya back to your own Terra Firmer," Golem said.

"We're ready. C'mon, boys."

"If there's any more beatin' on De'ath, I'll be doing it."

He led the trio to the Time Oscillator, crooking a chunky finger. Without a word, he engaged the controls. There was a crackle of energy and the three visitors disappeared.

"Not a minute too soon." Flaming Youth wasn't too keen on the three, either.

"For once I agree with you." The rocky man pulled out a stogie. Without a word, Flaming Youth lit it.

***

All talked out from their marathon bull session, the Assemblers exited the Blackbird on their island. In fact, they were grinning, proud about pulling the wool over Dr. De'ath's eyes.

Sergeant-at-Arms turned to Svetlana. "Not you. You wait aboard until Special Projects can collect you." Then: "Sailor."

A Navy man snapped to.

"Watch her." Sergeant-at-Arms turned to Svetlana. "I'll have some food sent to you."

This was met with an indifferent shrug from Svetlana. At least she was alive and free to watch these superheroes. Svetlana liked how they could use their talents and abilities right out in the open, not hiding in shadows. She watched as they transferred to their flying platforms for the hop to Assembler Mansion.

"The Soviet Union has better flying platforms, of

course," she told her guard.

"I wouldn't know, ma'am. I'm a sailor."

***

Within a few minutes, the Assemblers landed on their townhouse roof and descended.

"Superior Man," Marksman called, spotting their visitor from another world. "You all right?"

"Yes, perfectly fine." Superior Man had a milk mustache from the tall glass Penniman gave him.

Marksman tapped his own philtrum. The guest grabbed a napkin and wiped the spot on his face. Maybe they didn't get milk mustaches in their universe, Marksman thought.

Meanwhile, Red Rose was jumping out of her skin with an idea. Finally, on the ground and away from bugs and secret agents, she set her hand on Sergeant-at-Arms' chest. "Sarge, don't get too close to Superior Man."

"Huh?" The patriot gaped.

"I noticed Superior Man weaken whenever you are near."

"You're not saying I make him sick, are you?"

"Only when you have your shield. You weren't carrying it the first time you two met."

"That's right. I came down to greet him without it. No ill effects."

Superior Man remembered. "That's it. Flash that shield and boom...I keel over."

"All right. I'll keep my shield clear of you," Sergeant-at-Arms said. "Right now, we have more pressing issues."

Marksman led off. "We sure did a bang-up job with De'ath's games and making a monkey out of him."

"We may have stopped an international incident," Galloping Gazelle said. "But a menace from our universe still wants to eat Superior Man's Earth."

"And we're at a low ebb without Man Machine and Týr," Sergeant-at-Arms said. "We're going to need allies on this. Our new friend here and I can't get too close, we now know."

"Maybe we can enlist Sub-Merger," Kingsize suggested, at his new preferred height of seven feet.

"No, not that guy. I know him. Despite our old alliance fighting Nazis, Prince Neptune is unpredictable."

"The Tomorrow Men. They aren't a menace," Red Rose put forth, looking to her cousin. "We fought them under the sway of Solenoid. Goodness, we were the menace, not them."

"Right," Galloping Gazelle added. "Let's get their help."

Red Rose headed to the communication room. It wasn't long before she returned with a report; the Tomorrow Men were flying to Japan, following a lead about the fiery mutation, Rising Son.

"That name isn't ominous," Sergeant-at-Arms said. "Much."

"Aw, relax, gramps," Marksman put in. "Japan's cool these days."

"Yeah," Kingsize said. "Should there be another war, Norse god forbid, they'll be on our side."

"And they got a nifty form of archery called *kyūdō*," Marksman chimed in. "At least, from what I read in Eugen Herrigel's book."

"Isn't that a German name?" Sergeant-at-Arms asked.

"I'm amazed you don't dig they're our friends now, too."

"I am amazed Marksman read a book," Galloping Gazelle quipped.

Superior Man finally saw his chance to ask, "Sergeant-at-Arms, what is your shield made of?"

"Orichalcum, from Kosawa in Africa. In fact, we have an Assembler there: Black Leopard. Special Projects gave me this one after I came out of the ice."

"The ice?"

"Oh, right. You don't know. I'm not just some cheerleader wearing the flag. Back during the war, I led the troops fighting Nazis, using my super athletic skills. In those days, I had a triangular shield. Near the end of the war, I took a tumble into the Arctic Ocean and froze."

"You're revived from another age?"

"Right," Sergeant-at-Arms agreed. "That serum the government gave me to make this American super, acted like anti-freeze. The condition even has a name, cryptobiosis."

Sergeant-at-Arms seemed too young to have served in World War II, as anything more than a camp mascot, Superior Man thought. Had he really survived being frozen in ice? Could he be delusional? Superior Man employed his super hearing. The patriot's vital signs were at peak efficiency. Casually, Superior Man followed up with a scan. He found a man of indeterminate age, wearing chain mail. His arteries had no plaque.

"The Assemblers came upon me and thawed me out. I took on missions for Special Projects. When that creep, Mysterious Laser, melted my shield, Special Projects replaced it with this one."

But Superior Man was preoccupied with this material, not thawed out Assemblers. Orichalcum affected him like hercolubite. Hercolubite could only be here if his home planet, Hercólubus, preceded it.

***

Man Machine had been outside too long. He searched for stars. All he saw was enveloping darkness. One hundred seventy miles above Earth, Man Machine became a human satellite. Despite traveling at twenty-three times the speed of sound, he felt no sense of movement. Then he looked down and saw Earth rotating beneath his booted feet. It was a pin-sharp relief map unspooling at four miles per second. Suddenly, a blue arm came stretching out of the blackness of space.

In his helmet, Man Machine heard a jovial, "Let me give you a hand."

Bands of blue reached for Man Machine. There were fingers, stretched out in an impossible manner.

"How can you stretch in that outfit?"

"Spacesuit's made of unstable atoms, just like our team costumes. It does what I do."

Elongated fingers pulled Man Machine back through the rift. He never felt so good to be in the cold vacuum of space. Because it was his own space.

Rich Reide had something else to ponder. The voice that came over to him via Man Machine's radio link was one he knew. It was Johnny Ferro's. But how could that be? Man Machine, he'd been told, was Ferro's employee. Had the boss, eager to ride to space, donned this new armor?

***

Late evening commuters in New York City's midtown were startled to see a purple glow. It made the news. At Assemblers Mansion, Penniman rushed from the kitchen to the heroes' meeting room.

"There's something you should see," he shouted and hurried to the television console. "On the T.V., channel 7."

"This is no time to be watching *Ratman*," Sergeant-at-Arms stated.

"They've broken away from it, sir."

"Ratman is on T.V. here?" Superior Man gulped. "Is it, um, a documentary news program?"

He didn't think Ratman of any universe would allow himself to be filmed.

"You don't have that show?" Hornette asked.

"No," Superior Man said.

"He's so dreamy," Red Rose purred. "It's all about his adventures. Fiction, of course. Nobody could really do all those things he does."

"Especially with no powers." Galloping Gazelle smirked. "I plan to marry you off to someone with superpowers, cousin. Be he *lusus naturae* or Mancestor."

"Some of us can do those things, I beg to differ." Marksman derived great satisfaction that Ratman was last seen in a cliffhanging deathtrap set by an archer.

"We've got Ratman, all right," Superior Man added. "He's on our team. Well, formerly. He resigned over, well, me not mentioning this universe."

"Never mind that. What is *this*?" Sergeant-at-Arms pointed to a purple glow on the set.

"It's a friend." Superior Man bolted. "Another teammate, Jet Man. They must have found some other method of traveling here. Be funny if he brought Ratman."

"Hilarious," Sergeant-at-Arms said drolly.

"Ooh?" Hornette let out. "You think he might be coming here?"

"Well, I'd like to meet Ratman," Red Rose purred.

David Chetley's voice came from the set, describing the scene. Superior Man picked out it was Jet Boy, not Ratman, with Jet Man. His super visuals had no trouble separating the two similarly adorned heroes even through a television transmission.

Marksman asked, "How does your guy do that?"

"He moves at superspeed. Quite like—"

If he meant Galloping Gazelle, the speedster was already in motion. "I shall welcome them."

***

On that Manhattan street, Jet Man and Jet Boy were

solidifying.

"Keep at it, kid," Jet Man called, "until we're locked in place, maintain internal vibrations."

The teen was awed by what he saw. Around him, a duplicate of his world shimmered into existence.

"Mascouten," he mistakenly called. "They have it here, too."

Jet Boy stopped vibrating too soon. From Jet Man's point of view, his sidekick seemed to shrink as he fell back across the dimensions.

Galloping Gazelle arrived in time to see that. "Jet Man?"

Jet Man turned. "Did you arrive by super speed?"

"Yes, I—"

"We have to get him," Jet Man interrupted. "C'mon, lock up collar and elbow. Then shake at super speed."

Galloping Gazelle did so. "How did you get here?"

"We moved fast enough to match the vibration of your universe."

The pair began to vibrate. All a gathering crowd saw were washes of purple and green.

"If anything happens to him, my wife will never speak to me again."

"Why?"

"He's her brother," Jet Man exclaimed. "I can see it now. 'Oh, by the way, honey, I lost your brother superheroing.'"

"A super-fast lad can take care of himself," Galloping Gazelle said.

"On another Earth? That's a chance I can't take." Jet Man looked around. New Yorkers saw them disappear. Another city materialized before the pair. "There, that purple glow."

They found him all right, but where? Jet Man saw signs in a foreign language. "Does your Earth have a country called Japan?"

CHAPTER 13

W aiting for Galloping Gazelle to return, the Assemblers settled in to watch *Ratman* on television. This newfound information of him being real in the other universe fascinated them. Superior Man stood, uninterested in the fictional exploits of someone he'd been in action alongside of. "I feel just about back to normal."

Perhaps watching adventures made him want to have ones of his own. Superior Man, moreover, wanted to clear his head. Flight should do it. He headed to the backdoor.

"Perhaps something to eat, sir?" Penniman asked, appearing at his elbow. "One glass of milk is hardly enough for a superhero."

Superior Man's olfactory senses told him there was food in the oven. X-ray vision confirmed it. "Ah, turkey."

"The one thing everybody will eat."

"Thus explaining the turkey leg Behemoth had."

"Oh, yes, sir," Penniman said. "We quickly realized food made him docile. It was a welcome relief from the others pounding him into submission."

"Say, could you put me in touch with this Black Leopard fellow? The Assemblers seem to have every conceivable method of communication. Right now, they're absorbed in Ratman's adventures."

"Oh, yes, sir. That they do." Penniman untied his apron. "It would be my great pleasure."

He led his guest to the communications room. The butler quickly raised Black Leopard via video phone.

Superior Man beheld a regal black man on the screen.

"Hello, Black Leopard. I'm, er, well, a new superhero around here. They call me Superior Man."

"A white man named *superior*? How interesting." Black Leopard had responded with only a trace of sarcasm. "Just what the world needs."

"Oh, thank you." The object of that sarcasm missed it entirely.

"Are you a new inductee into the Assemblers?"

"No, just visiting. However, I'm curious about orichalcum."

"Orichalcum? Odd you mention it. I've lately suffered a theft of it. A very unusual heist. Do you have some insight into that?"

"A theft? Yes, I may. You see, hercolu, er, orichalcum is harmful to me."

"Harmful? I assure you the stuff is quite harmless."

"It robs me of my super abilities. You see, I can fly, I'm invulnerable, and I have super strength."

"Thus, Superior Man," Black Leopard finished for him.

"Right. But exposure to, er, orichalcum, weakens me. It could even kill me."

"Extraordinary." Black Leopard grumped. "Never would have thought it could have that effect on someone."

Superior Man didn't need special powers to know Black Leopard found it amusing that an inanimate object was his great weakness. "Any leads on the theft?"

Black Leopard described the details of that crime.

"That's someone I've dealt with," Superior Man shouted. "He's no garden variety crook. And he knows how the material affects me."

"In that case, keep out of Sergeant-at-Arms' way." Black Leopard wondered how superior this fellow was if that thief had eluded him so far. "His shield is made of it."

"Too late for that information," Superior Man said. "We found out the hard way."

"You will have to steer clear of my country, too."

"That's what I wanted to ask you about specifically. How does your nation come to have it?"

"Legends say that many, many years ago, a rock fell from the sky into Kosawa."

Superior Man felt a chill. So...orichalcum was hercolubite. Then there must have been a Hercólubus in this universe. One that sundered apart, just as his had. Pieces of it came to this Earth. Braindroid knew this and was harvesting it. Could Faculus have consumed this universe's Hercólubus? If the two are working together, might have Faculus advised Braindroid to hunt for the material on Earth? Yes. It was just as Golem speculated. Those two menaces were collaborating.

***

NASA insisted they were morally obligated to prevent potential contamination. They put Reide and Man Machine in an isolation booth. Once out, they got a Presidential reception.

"Man Machine..." A Texan drawl issued from the President's lips. "You should be awarded astronaut wings for what you have done today."

"Aw, shucks, sir." Man Machine blushed within his helmet. "Reide did all the real work."

"Sir," Reide cut in. "What is the most secure room you have here?"

"Most secure? That room."

"Would you take us to it, please?"

They ended up in the bathroom. There, he gave them what he called the Presidential Treatment. "What's on your mind, Professor Richards?" He got up close to them and cajoled answers from the two heroes, who gave a report about the rift. After that, there wasn't more to be said. Air Force One was approved to take Man Machine and Mr.

Atoms back to New York.

Suzette flew Reid's craft back solo.

The President reverted to his true form. "This changes everything," the alien Krull muttered.

***

Superior Man found the Assemblers discussing the *Ratman* episode. "I just spoke to Black Leopard. The thief behind the orichalcum heist is someone from my universe."

"What?" Sergeant-at-Arms bleated.

"An evil genius named Braindroid. It just figures if anyone in my universe could do it, he'd find the rift. He knows orichalcum is hercolubite. I think Dr. De'ath tried to take you out so you wouldn't interfere in this scheme to let Faculus consume my Earth. Remember, he only pledged not to harm the Atoms Family's Earth, not anyone else's."

"De'ath wouldn't let his own planet be eaten," Kingsize said. "Even *he* has some honor."

"I'd like to make sure. If you'll excuse me, I'm going to take flight."

"It's not like we can stop you," Red Rose uttered.

Superior Man went out the front door and shot into the air. Once safely over the Atlantic Ocean, he accelerated to supersonic speeds. He had questions for the dictator. Superior Man scanned for De'ath, found him and then politely knocked at his window.

"Good evening, Superior Man." Dr. De'ath spoke dramatically and gestured to a lackey to let the visitor in. "This is truly an historic meeting. Leave us, you."

The lackey did so.

"I want answers, De'ath. I know you're doing something big. What are you up to?"

Superior Man didn't have to scan with his superior sense to know there wasn't any hercolubite nearby. Surreptitiously, he engaged them and found no trace of

Braindroid or Faculus ever having been there.

"Up to? Why, nothing. For above all things I am a reasonable man," De'ath chirped. "Ever since you, ah, rallied I call off my vendetta against the Atoms Family, I have had more time to devote to my people."

"Looks like there's been quite a to-do here." Superior Man scowled. "Time spent devoted to your people?"

"Unruly visitors."

"Is this when you tried to kill Amazon Woman and the Assemblers?"

"Why ask when you already know? Bah! I was bored and sought amusement. Those bumblers are hardly the *real* Assemblers. As for the maiden, she is quite indestructible."

"Bored?"

"I have kept my promise not to kill the Atoms Family. Naturally, that leaves a gap in my time. I had a lovely array of death traps going to waste. Alas, the lady and those pretenders acquitted themselves with flying colors. I'm sure it was she who made the difference."

Superior Man's acute hearing detected the dictator's heart rate. He was not lying.

"The whole thing did me good. It flushed out a Soviet assassin in my midst. Now, will these crossings be a regular event? I could have a repast set out."

"Don't worry about that."

De'ath turned somber. "You know, you ought to make up for incinerating my files and melting my gun. That was an antique from 1914."

"Surely, those are minor things to you."

"True, I have other guns and know the contents of the files back and forth." De'ath stood his ground. "It is the principle of the thing. You manhandle me and destroy my possessions without a word of protest from me."

Superior Man huffed. "What is it you want, De'ath?"

"Sub-Merger means to kill me."

"Oh?" Superior Man recalled that name from the files.

The Assemblers mentioned him but didn't elaborate beyond his hatred for De'ath. "Why would he want you dead?"

"A failed partnership. Nothing you need concern yourself with. But killing me would create a power vacuum here. There would be chaos. Thousands would die. You must convince him to leave me be."

"Me? Why me?"

"Because none of the heroes will. Your strength rivals his. And he flies. He is invulnerable. Should I be deposed by that buffoon, my country would fall into civil war. None of these do-gooders care."

"After all, you've only tried to kill them," Superior Man put in.

"Laugh if you like. You must convince Sub-Merger not to attack me. I am quite sure he is hiding in Lake Ruritania. My flying cameras can only range so far."

"You have flying cameras?"

Dr. De'ath shrugged like they were the easiest things ever to invent. "No doubt, he would annex this country for Atlantica."

"Atlantica? But that's—"

"It is real. Not a legend. I may be a tyrant, Superior Man, but I keep the peace. He has already attacked and was only repelled by Red Rose."

"She being compelled to fight for you," Superior Man noted.

"I admit that. But she kept me alive."

"All right." Superior Man imagined this favor could quickly be completed. "I'll hunt up Sub-Merger." He took off, out through the same window he entered. Maybe innocent lives *will* be saved. His superior hearing did not catch Dr. De'ath's parting exclamation.

"The Image Duplicator." He stabbed a button on an intercom. "Ready my swiftest jet."

***

Although he had the problem of a hole between universes to consider, Superior Man realized De'ath was right. Sub-Merger deposing him would create a power vacuum in Ruritania. De'ath didn't hold Red Rose anymore. Superior Man flew over the lake and scanned. *No man there.*

Figuring the aquatic Sub-Merger would naturally head for the most water, Superior Man flew over the rest of Europe, heading to the Atlantic Ocean. He X-rayed miles of ocean. Then: "Ah, ha!"

Superior Man homed in on a muscular man. The files hadn't mentioned he wore only green swim trunks. He was cavorting with dolphins. Sub-Merger had tiny flying fish wings at his feet. Surely they couldn't lift him the way Eagleman's wings did. Sub-Merger must have the power of levitation, the wings being merely incidental vestiges. His ears were another matter. They were pointed. Superior Man dove in after the king of Atlantica. *Well, this world's version, at any rate,* he mused.

"Sub-Merger," Superior Man called...or he tried. Water rushed into his mouth and he could no longer speak. He descended into the depths.

His quarry literally swam circles around him. "So, another water breather, eh? You will find speaking here impossible." Sub-Merger grasped the interloper by the arm and shot upward. Up he went, until he broke the surface. "Who are you?" Sub-Merger demanded and continued his ascent in flight. "What do you want? How is it you thrive in the ocean? This is an alarming trend."

A clear reference to Aquamarine, Superior Man thought. Unexpectedly, but gently, he broke free and noted Sub-Merger's tiny wings really did flap.

"My name is Superior Man. And, well, I'm superior. I've just come from Dr. De'ath—"

"De'ath?" Sub-Merger parroted. With that he attacked.

His blows packed a wallop, but Superior Man quickly recovered and casually asked, "You done?"

"Done?" Sub-Merger raged. "I will show you done."

"Nope. My turn," Superior Man said. Hands on his hips, he beamed heat vision all over the flying amphibian, guessing this water being wouldn't like being dried out. Still, Sub-Merger flew at him, launching blows that got weaker and weaker. They were nothing like his initial barrage that actually stung.

"Would you quit, for gosh sakes," the superhero pleaded, and then caught a wrist in an iron grip. "I'm not friends with De'ath. I've just got a message from him."

"What does he want of me?" Sub-Merger grated out as he tried to break free of the iron grip. He would have if his skin had not dried out.

"Leave Dr. De'ath alone," Superior Man stated. "Kill him and his whole country is thrown into a tizzy. Innocent people will die."

"Do I look like I care about Ruritanians?"

"Oh? And what if he kills *you* during an attack? Justified self-defense. How would things stand in Atlantica? Are things so stable there?"

"Your logic, if not your grip, is unassailable, Superior Man." The flying fishman grumbled. "I shall concede."

With that assurance, Superior Man released his captive.

Sub-Merger dove into the ocean.

"I guess there's irony that escapee from *Galaxy Quest* talks of logic." Superior Man grinned as he floated contemplatively above the surface.

Seconds later, hands rose from the ocean. Sub-Merger, now refreshed, skin already restored to normal, grasped Superior Man's ankles and pulled him into the depths.

"I desire a rematch." Sub-Merger spoke effortlessly underwater. "We'll meet on dry land or in the air. You strike me as a man of honor, like me. I will abstain from the reviving ocean. You will refrain from heat beams. Then we will settle this man to man."

With that he released Superior Man and plunged into the murky ocean depths.

"Like I've got time to deal with that water-logged prima donna." Superior Man was steamed as he broke the surface.

***

Jet Boy's arrival was foretold by the glow of purple hanging in the air. Then he fell out of the sky. As he fell, he caught sight of a bullet train. Stationmasters were making announcements and station staff were cramming passengers into train cars. "Japan," he exclaimed. "But my Japan or theirs? I can't just ask someone which world this is."

It was only a few feet to solid ground. Wonderkind teammate Mercury had taught him the fundamentals of falling safely. Unfortunately, his fall included landing on a salaryman on his way to the bullet train. The man's briefcase went flying, scattering papers.

"Sorry, sir," Jet Boy spouted in response to the man's yammering in Japanese. At superspeed, he gathered the papers, some still floating. Done, he slid them neatly into the briefcase. This he snapped shut and presented to the accident victim. "Here you go."

The man took the briefcase.

Jet Boy hauled up the man and brushed him off.

The salaryman adjusted his sunglasses, then asked in Japanese, "What are you doing? What is the meaning of this? Who are you?"

"Look, I'm not hip to the lingo, but I can guess what you mean." The teen slapped his chest insignia. "Jet Boy.

Jet...Boy. I tag team with Jet Man."

This, too, got no response from the salaryman.

Jet Boy wondered, *hey, maybe they won the war in this universe.*

The salaryman began howling for the police. A crowd gathered. The teen was battered with questions in Japanese.

"Please, calm down, pops," Jet Boy pleaded. "It was an accident."

This must be the other Earth. *Nobody recognizes world-famous Jet Boy.*

A pair of representatives of the National Police Agency appeared, pushing their way through the gathered throng.

"Uh oh." The superhero gulped.

The cops didn't look happy to see him. The victim was gesturing and going on in Japanese. One of them approached Jet Boy, handcuffs at the ready.

"Great. They think I'm a supervillain."

The cop reached for Jet Boy's wrist and swept the handcuffs toward him. Jet Boy was too quick, and as he pulled away, the cuffs ended up on the cop's wrists. Laughter rang out from the crowd. The other cop didn't like that. He moved in on the speedster.

"Hey," the teen called, hands cupped around his mouth. "Anyone here speak English?"

A Negro with a flute case pushed forward. "I speak English."

The teen rock 'n' roller didn't recognize this universe's version of American jazz great Corny Fortune. "Would you please tell the fuzz I'm no crook."

"You need a translator, huh? You got to learn the language if you come here," Fortune said.

"I'm, er, just passing through."

Fortune relayed all that in Japanese. However, the salaryman was nowhere to be seen. He'd bolted for the bullet train, which had already left the station. Fortune kept an eye on the cops. "Son, it might be best to go with them. They think you helped that man steal some documents and get away."

But Fortune was talking to air. Jet Boy needed only to see a New Nambu M60 being brandished to dash off, running at top speed. He heard the gunshot. A bullet was no match for Jet Boy, though. But evading them was not how he wanted to spend his time here.

Contemptuously, he smirked and simply outran it. "Geez, I thought this Earth had superheroes. These people act like they've never seen one before."

Maybe I can find the U.S. Embassy.

"No... They won't know me either."

A mountain in the distance caught his eye.

***

A world away, Dr. De'ath's jet landed in New York's Idlewild Airport. A limo took him to his embassy. Nearing midtown, he and a lackey with an attaché case got out and walked the streets of the city. Coming to a subway entrance, the pair descended. He remembered the configuration of this one from his college days. You could go down one staircase and, via another, emerge across the street. Like once before, De'ath gave his cloak and holster to the lackey. These went into the case. While the latter purchased a token and entered the subway system, De'ath continued on to the corresponding set of stairs. As he walked, he flicked on the Image Duplicator. It was Man Machine in gleaming gunmetal armor who exited that subway. On the street, De'ath engaged the rocket pack on his back and flew. His destination was Assemblers Mansion. He was lucky the real Man Machine was still in transit aboard Air Force One.

Minutes later, Dr. De'ath came in for a landing. Realizing he did not know what protocols the Assemblers used for entry to their headquarters, he improvised. De'ath smiled inside his helmet. "Easily solved," he said to himself.

Landing on the sidewalk in front of the townhouse, De'ath allowed for a crowd to build. They approached him. Fans of Man Machine gathered. The fake shook their hands, clapped their backs, and signed autographs. Before long, the front door swung open and a butler called to him.

"Sir! You've returned from space?"

"Well, I, ah, did all I could there." De'ath strode to the door. "Confidential matters, you know. In space."

"And back to your old armor, I see." Penniman scoffed.

"Yes, much more, er, comfortable." De'ath entered the townhouse, wondering what new armor Man Machine might possess.

"Something to eat, sir?"

"No, nothing, my good fellow. I had some, er, space food."

"Tang, sir?"

"Yes and very filling."

"Quite a bit of excitement we had here, sir," Penniman said, wondering how Tang could be filling.

"Oh?"

"Yes, apparently the orichalcum in Sergeant-at-Arms' shield is harmful to Superior Man."

"What? Why, that's—"

"Yes, sir. We shall have to keep them apart."

"Well, well," De'ath gleefully said. "Perhaps we should have a supply of this orichalcum on hand."

"Sir?"

"Just thinking aloud. In the event Superior Man should ever become a menace." De'ath was suddenly lost in thought. Delightful thought. *So, there's a substance that can hurt that meddler. A takeover of Kosawa, perhaps?*

"The Assemblers are waiting for you, sir."

"I must see to my armor first. This suit is not working correctly. Don't know why I, er, ever went back to it." With that, Dr. De'ath flew off.

Vaguely, Penniman wondered why Man Machine didn't just retire to his private chamber here. "Curious."

***

Superior Man ascended beyond the high atmosphere and found the rift. He just chanced to see something that startled him. Showing no reaction whatsoever, he went through and flew to his Earth. He dived toward Superior Squadron headquarters. Once inside, Superior Man activated the team signal device.

Bzzrmmm sounded via an attachment on all member phones at home. A small red light lit, and stayed lit, until the recipient called in. He followed up by notifying members via the radios in their belts. Shrinking Man, no longer in his civilian guise of physicist Paul Pymer, entered. For once not via the phone.

"Paul, are you the only one here?"

"Hey. Don't forget the rule," he said. Bad enough Jet Man let his identity slip out to the kid.

"Yes, yes, *Shrinking Man.*" Superior Man sighed, thinking: *How could I forget Ratman's rule?*

"Everyone's gone to that universe."

"We're in trouble," Superior Man said. "Coming through the rift, I spotted a giant on an asteroid in space there. Faculus. He's an interstellar menace."

"In what way?"

"He has to eat planets to live."

"That sure qualifies." Shrinking Man shuddered. "Did he seem interested in this one?"

"I dared not scan him with my opticals. Faculus might be able to detect X-rays. It would alert him. He's watching the rift from 269 Justitia."

"The biggest object in the Asteroid Belt?"

"He may have seen me go through. It looks like Golem was right. Faculus wants to eat our Earth."

"Not the other one? It's right there in his universe."

"If you can believe it, Faculus pledged not to consume that one. On top of that, Braindroid was spotted in that universe. And you'll never guess what he was doing."

"Try me," Shrinking Man said. "What was he doing?"

"Harvesting hercolubite."

Shrinking Man gasped. "How can they have hercolubite?"

"It's obvious Faculus consumed the Hercólubus of that universe. Pieces of it fell to that Earth, just like here."

A world, Shrinking Man wondered. *He consumed a whole world.*

"If only I could confront him," Superior Man said. "But he'd see me coming through the rift and be ready for me."

"It's not like you'd sneak up on him."

"That's only honorable."

"Since it involves our planet being eaten, how about forgetting honor? Travel to the other universe via S.O.L.A.R. Labs' device and come up behind him. You said he's watching the rift."

"Why, Shrinking Man..." Superior Man grinned. "That is downright sneaky."

"I hope you settle his hash," Shrinking Man floated.

***

Japan again experienced a cast of purple, this time mixed with green. Galloping Gazelle and Jet Man materialized. The police had been alerted to deal with these superpowered criminals. That young speedster had outrun bullets, after all. So they called for help. This time, the police were waiting with superpowered backup.

Jet Man and Galloping Gazelle materialized above the ground. Jet Man churned his legs. This braked him, creating a compressed blanket of air that cushioned his descent. Galloping Gazelle didn't have the speed to do that, so he expertly tumbled to a landing.

"I wish Sarge saw that," he trumpeted while straightening up. His glee was short lived, however.

"More, eh? Hands up, invaders. On your feet," a costumed crusader ordered in English.

"If we're *more*..." Jet Man said, "then the kid must have come through here."

Galloping Gazelle gestured he would do the talking. Jet Man shrugged.

"Rising Son," Galloping Gazelle said, having recognized the *lusus naturae*. Japan's protector was resplendent in a costume of white and red tights. The design suggested the nation's rising sun flag. A full facemask left only his chin exposed. "I see you're working for the National Police Agency now? I am—"

"I know who you are. You are one of Solenoid's lieutenants. The sensitive work here was sure to attract the villainous."

"*Once* I stood with Solenoid. Not anymore." Galloping Gazelle clapped his chest. "I am an Assembler now."

"Silence," Rising Son demanded. "Do you think you can just warp into Japan as you wish with no documentation?"

Jet Man, coming to a boil over his lost partner, stepped forward. "We just want to find the boy who appeared here. Then we'll leave."

"Ask him how they got here," a cop suggested.

"Yes. How *did* you get here?"

Galloping Gazelle didn't miss that obvious cue. "We're speedsters."

"You won't be so disrespectful in a minute," Rising

Son responded. Knowing Galloping Gazelle's speed, Rising Son struck first. He gestured. A superheated puff of plasma, more solid than blazingly hot, shot from his hands. Galloping Gazelle was felled by the flow. Instantly, his super-fast hands patted his smoking costume down before much damage could be done. He suffered not much more than soot on his face and costume. Tendrils of his hair got singed. The costume was durable, resistant to the heat of friction. A tongue of pulsating flame burned itself out as it fell from the speedster. The last thing that filled Galloping Gazelle's vision before lapsing into unconsciousness was a second blast of blinding white light.

Jet Man was too fast for Rising Son. He grabbed his companion's arm, shaking him back to consciousness. "Let's go."

To Jet Man's surprise, Rising Son took to the air. From that vantage point, he blasted again. The speedsters dodged the plasma streams.

"Wait." Galloping Gazelle halted. "We will never find the kid with Rising Son on our backs."

"I can ground him." Jet Man waved both arms, flinging a compressed wall of air at Rising Son. The Japanese hero was hurled head over heels. He used his flight ability to manage an unsteady braking and landing. He was stunned but scrambled to his feet.

Galloping Gazelle ran up to him and held down his arms.

Jet Man, going along with his host, dashed up and added his weight.

"I told you...I am an Assembler now." Galloping Gazelle reached for the team's I.D. card, kept in his belt pocket. Pulling it out, he found the card was blackened, unreadable. "You burned up my identification."

"Do you think we are stupid?" Rising Son demanded. "You're in cahoots with that salaryman."

A police detective huffed up to them. "He got clean

away with sensitive documents."

"Let me up," Rising Son shouted. "I have to go after him."

"Will you listen to reason? We just want to find that kid. We won't harm your precious country."

"Time's wasting," Jet Man said. "Who's coming with me?"

"We are at a stalemate," Rising Son conceded.

"I'll remain here until you get back." Galloping Gazelle released his captive.

Rising Son rose toward Jet Man.

"Try to keep up, Rising Son." Jet Man took off.

Galloping Gazelle turned to the policeman and held out his wrists. "Hold me as hostage, a material witness, whatever you like, until they get back with your documents."

The police seemed mollified with this win. At least, their own superpowered guy was with the other one. No loss of face.

***

The two heroes spotted a crowd at a Shinkansen station. Seven bullet trains had already left this morning, they learned. The trains would speed up to over two hundred miles an hour, twelve cars. The first one would be freight only.

"There he is." Jet Man slowed for Rising Son's benefit. "That's who we're after."

As trains pulled away to Nagoya and Osaka, they saw Jet Boy trying to communicate across a language barrier. The two heroes pulled even with the kid.

"Jet Man," the kid yelled. "Am I glad to see you. Who's your buddy?"

Jet Man explained the situation. "So, it's up to us to find that guy," he concluded. "All we have to do is catch some trains and recover the documents. Easy work for us."

"Oh, yeah? Like the ad for Crackly Pops. We're faster than some cartoonish advertising mascot."

"We'll split up and cover the trains way ahead," Jet Man said. "Leave those slower ones for the flying slowpoke."

That slowpoke spoke up. "How will we know him?"

"He was the only salaryman wearing shades," Jet Boy said. "And he had a pencil-thin moustache. It's like Central Casting found him filed under 'Spy.'" Then he and Jet Man took off down the tracks. Rising Son was left in the dust to check the connecting Toei Subway Line 1, a slower line.

"That one's just my speed." Rising Son rose in the air.

The speedsters had already caught up to most of their targets and came up empty. Two were left. At the second to last train, Jet Boy spotted the spy. He came to a halt in front of him. "Remember me?"

The spy produced a gun. He got off a shot. Jet Boy not only dodged it, he slapped the bullet away.

Jet Man got the gun in his hand.

"We got him."

"Kid, I just realized we have to let him go." Jet Man took charge of the gun.

"What? Why?"

"This isn't our universe."

"It's not like we're messing with the timeline."

"True, but we're not supposed to be here. It must be fate that he got away with those documents."

Reluctantly, Jet Man gave the spy back his gun and the briefcase with schematics for a certain widget.

Jet Boy was steaming. There must be *some* reason their vibrations brought them to Japan. Maybe some greater power didn't want those schematics in the wrong hands. Surely, they didn't materialize in Japan just so this crook could get away with his crime.

The spy dashed out...and ran right into Rising Son.

Now the gun was pointed at that hero. He flashed a blast of superheated plasma at it. The weapon became impossible to hold. Rising Son followed up with a haymaker to the jaw of the spy. He went down.

"What did you mean by this not being your universe?"

"Maybe we better let Galloping Gazelle explain," Jet Man said.

***

Man Machine maintained a private room at Assemblers Mansion. Stealthily, he entered the roof access hatch, using the key built into the finger of his gauntlet. After removing his helmet, the handsome, mustached industrialist ran a bath. Ferro got out his shaving kit while the water heated up. Then he sat at a radio and made a call. This was to the Assemblers themselves and meant as a cover story. Penniman answered.

"Ferro here. Has Man Machine checked in? I haven't heard from him in days."

"Good day, sir. He hitched a ride on a NASA rocket ship, if you can believe it, then—"

"What?" Ferro feigned an overreaction. "Well, knowing him, I believe it."

"He returned a few minutes ago, sir, but flew off to attend to his armor."

Ferro was taken aback. "If he comes back, call me immediately."

"Yes, sir... Oh, he reverted to his old armor."

"Really?" Ferro knew it was an imposter. Of course, he couldn't accuse anyone of masquerading as Man Machine without giving away his secret. Ferro could see it now: *He can't be Man Machine. I'm Man Machine.* No, that wouldn't do. He ran to his vault and checked his arsenal. The gunmetal armor was there, untouched since he left it. That told him, at least, the imposter was not up to date. Who in holy hell could have fabricated his old armor?

"Are you still there, sir?"

"Oh... Just lost in thought, Penniman. Signing off."

At his end, Penniman was puzzled. He thought radio communication was temporarily out due to a solar flare.

***

Jail cells on this Earth were no different from the ones Galloping Gazelle had occupied on his own Earth. This one was exceptionally clean, however. The guard appeared and took the speedster to an office. Rising Son was waiting for him. Only telling the truth would get Japan's protector to cooperate. Rising Son believed the explanation. It was hard to deny when he had seen the speedsters warp into his city. They walked outside. There, Jet Man and his sidekick waited. Galloping Gazelle made his offer. It was mostly to keep Rising Son from blabbing.

"Come with us to America. Your powers would be a boon for the Assemblers."

"My place is here, protecting Japan." Rising Son waved off the offer. "Besides, what do you need me for? In America, you have Flaming Youth."

"But an extra set of flaming hands would be appreciated."

Jet Man jumped in. "You were quite impressive."

Still fuming, Jet Boy made his own point. "Hey, we're not even supposed to be here, we let the spy go, and you're weighing in again?"

"That's the way it had to be," Jet Man explained. "Besides, Rising Son caught that guy."

Rising Son scoffed. "I am not much for teams. I protect Japan. I'm not joining the Assemblers or even the Tomorrow Men. Besides, America is a land of smug and smirking insects."

Galloping Gazelle wondered if Rising Son meant

Tarantula-Man, King Bee, or—

"Too bad you feel that way," a voice rang out. "We would have welcomed you in a heartbeat."

Heads swiveled. Galloping Gazelle yelped, "The Tomorrow Men."

"Nice to be remembered, Gazelle," a masked redhead purred. She and two men wore matching black and yellow costumes, complete with yellow gauntlets and boots. Tight hoods left their lower faces exposed. One man, with wings, wore a red and blue costume that deviated from the others. His shirt had slits from where wings jutted, which unlike Eagleman's, were real. A fifth man was covered in a layer of frost. Jet Man guessed the frosty one never worried about being cold.

"How did you get here?" Galloping Gazelle asked.

"Our Gulfstream II jet," a five-by-five beast of a man answered. Another one's costume made no allowances to cover his hairy feet or hands.

The thinnest guy added, "Don't forget the transport the Japanese government lent us." His hooded mask was altered to host an impressive visor, rivaling anything an Inuit might wear as protection against the sun. He pointed.

The speedsters turned to see an old deuce and a half U.S. Army truck.

The simian addressed Rising Son. "By the by, my good fellow, might I peruse the documents that were saved from the proverbial wrong hands?"

"Since when do your refinements extend to reading Japanese, Animal?"

"There is such a thing as the universal language of schematics." He grinned.

"Yeah, he's not just another pretty face." The icy youth smirked.

"Indeed, I hold several degrees."

Grudgingly, Rising Son handed the briefcase over to Animal, which he opened. A worried look crossed his face.

The power core the papers delineated had nothing but sinister purposes.

Rising Son said, "You shall return those to me when you are done."

***

At the Ruritanian embassy in New York, the master issued an order. Hari Balay was to be contacted and rushed here directly. He lived in New York. While Balay had retained his liberty, he was to be immediately available for any job Dr. De'ath might have for him. Once there, Balay was brought before De'ath.

"Greetings, Balay. I know you have been well because you cannot be harmed." He laughed heartily and clapped the visitor on the shoulder.

"Thanks to you, Dr. De'ath." Balay humbly bowed. He was an Indian man of indeterminate age. In fact, he was older than he looked. Bearded, he wore a turban with otherwise conventional western clothing.

"I have a task for you, Hari." Dr. De'ath's tone was serious. "Come."

The pair went to Dr. De'ath's study. After unlocking a closet, a mirror was revealed.

"Simple enough but potentially dangerous," Dr. De'ath explained. "Perhaps not to one with your abilities."

"A mirror?"

"This mirror is not what it seems. Research has paid off." De'ath tapped a musty tome. "I shall utter, and teach you, an incantation. That will allow you to walk through the Mystic Mirror. I expect you will come out in a duplicate Earth."

"Are you serious?"

"As a heart attack. I never believed the legends...until now. I have already visited it and its inhabitants have been here. But not through this. I do not know what you will encounter. Unknown forces might defeat my electronic and mechanical weapons. Your powers will protect you."

"What must I do?"

"This is merely an exploratory mission. You go through, come back and report. I will then make a determination as to whether it's clear for me to make the same journey. Hari, I must be frank with you. You might not come back. Even with the power I gave you, you could die."

"Doctor, you have done much for me," Balay stated. "I would have died if you had not given me my great strength. Of course, I will undertake this journey."

"Good. I realize you will have to take time to comprehend all I have told you. My servants will bring you a hearty meal. Then you will begin."

"My curiosity runs wild, Dr. De'ath. I would like to start now."

"Excellent. Memorize this chant. For it, and only it, will give you egress from the opposite mirror on the other Earth and allow you to come back to this one."

Incanting in Latin, De'ath made obscure gestures. The mirror shimmered like water, no longer a hard surface. De'ath nodded. Balay knew this was his cue to go through.

Once through, Balay had the impression he was walking through a cave with rounded walls. The darkness, cold and deathly silence did not scare him, but impressed him. Shadows loomed, disappearing when he spun to them.

"Who's there?"

Fists balled showed he was ready to fight whatever eldritch horror was there. After what seemed like some long distance, Balay saw the glimmer of glass ahead. Its shape corresponded to the mirror he came through. An ordinary room beyond. He fumbled the incantation. Frantically, he banged on the mirror.

Coming to the room was a young woman. She was dressed like a clichéd stage magician. Black top hat, tails, high heels, fishnet stockings, purple shorts and vest, with a white blouse and bow tie. Through the glass, she could not hear Balay. She didn't have to be an expert at lip reading to perceive "please" and "help." Her expression was one of amazement. She reached out and grasped the mirror by the frame. Finally, Balay composed himself and uttered that incantation correctly, the glass parted like water. He passed through and into the room.

"Who are you? How can you be coming through this old mirror?"

"Many thanks, kind miss. My name is Hari Balay. I am exploring this mirror for my master. I am from another Earth."

"My name is Pandora," she answered, looking thoughtful. Suddenly, she knew what had happened to her missing father. This was his mirror. "Tell me, in your world have you met a man named John Pandopoulos?"

"I know of no such man, Miss Pandora. There are, of course, billions of people there. There must be several hundred men bearing that name."

"Compose yourself, Hari. We are going back to your Earth."

The girl doffed her top hat and picked up a trench coat. Balay uttered the incantation. With surprisingly firm hands, the girl took Balay and fairly pushed him through the now liquid mirror surface. She had saved him. It was his turn to protect her. After a time, they came to its opposite mirror.

Pandora peered through. "Who is that sleeping man?"

"That is my master, Dr. De'ath. He has fallen asleep waiting for my return."

"Why is he wearing armor?"

"Ah, the results of an unfortunate accident. He has quite the hair trigger, miss. We will wake him carefully."

Balay gave forth the chant, and the pair exited the mirror. With trepidation, he woke De'ath. De'ath was elated to see Balay. "And who is this child? I trust you have a good explanation for changing the mission."

"My name is Pandora Pandopoulos. Your friend was trapped in my father's mirror. He has been missing for years. I believe he went through it to this world."

"No person has come through here," De'ath said.

Of course, someone *could* have while it was in the possession of others. Could that be why Stephen Merlin kept it locked in that closet? Secured, but easy enough to check on. Anyone coming through would announce himself by banging on the inside of the door.

Vaguely, he considered killing the girl. Nobody would know. Then, oddly, De'ath felt obliged to help her. After all, she saved Balay and confirmed travel was possible between the two Earths with the mirror. And she owned its twin.

"Where are we?"

"This is the Ruritanian embassy in New York, my dear. I am the reigning monarch of this nation. It is one not found on your Earth."

"But New York is just—"

"Yes, I know." De'ath dismissed her with a wave of his hand. "On *your* Earth the city of New York is inconsequential. Here, it is a major city, quite like, oh, Isola on yours. I have been there."

"My father is somewhere on your world. I just know it." Pandora strode to a window. Looking out, she confirmed what De'ath said. "He might be hurt."

This poor girl, De'ath thought. *She has set herself an impossible task: seeking her father who wandered across dimensions.* "Hush, child. I will help you find your father."

"Where did you get this mirror?"

"From a dealer in unusual objects."

"May I examine it?"

"Of course, dear girl. Of course."

Pandora ran her hands over it and looked at it from

every angle. A tab of white caught her eye. It was a postcard stuck to a crevice in the back. With practiced sleight of hand skill, she palmed it. *Ah, the old Pandora shuffle. I still got it.* Surreptitiously, she managed a peek at it. She would go to the addressee.

"Hari, have you yet retained your talent for drawing?" Dr. De'ath picked up a lab book, presented it to Balay, along with a pencil.

Pandora secreted the card into a pocket.

"Our guest will describe her father. You will sketch the details as described. Then we will have an idea of her father's appearance. What do you say, my dear?"

"By all means." Pandora bowed.

The two got to it. Balay followed the girl's descriptions, penciling, crossing out. He stopped once. "Eraser, sir."

De'ath plopped one into Belay's hand. He went back to drawing and erasing until:

"That's him. That's my father."

Balay turned it to his master. "I have never seen this man."

"Nor have I," Dr. De'ath lied, for he recognized the face.

"Doctor, I will go home and make arrangements to be away, cancel all my appointments." Pandora studied the drawing. "Then I will return to search for my father."

"As you wish. Hari will accompany you. You will stay in this embassy, of course. The staff shall be at your beck and call. I will make it clear to them your every request is to be treated as if I spoke it."

CHAPTER 14

Animal handed the documents back to Rising Son. "We might put that precise query to you, old chum." He seemed jovial, but inwardly Animal was worried. Those were no ordinary schematics. The item it described, a single silicon transistor, usually sold for the hefty sum of one-hundred fifty dollars.

Chatter clarified names for Jet Man. Polar Man, Astro Lass, and Hawk were easy to figure. The latter's maverick costume harkened back to his days fighting crime solo. Polyphemus sported the visor. Polar Man was icy. The frosty façade couldn't hide he was no older than Jet Boy. Astro Lass, of course, was the redhead.

Polyphemus said, "Nothing more we can do here. Wasted trip. Okay, people, we're heading back to New York."

"Not a complete waste," Galloping Gazelle pointed out.

"Oh?"

"You can give us a lift back on your Gulfstream."

"Okay..." Hawk spoke up, "but you'll have to ride in the pokey we reserve for bad guys."

"You just wanted to finally herd me into that." Galloping Gazelle smirked.

"Ah," Animal noted with a wave of his hand. "You cannot escape past crimes. Come, your aerial paddy-wagon awaits. Since we know you, we'll leave the cell door unlocked."

They rode the Army truck to an airfield. The swept low-wing monoplane with a T-tail could easily exceed

Mach 1. Wingtip tanks added an extra four thousand pounds of fuel capacity with a corresponding increase in range. The airframe was of aluminum monocoque construction, with armor plating. A standup-cabin held a dozen passengers. One side had bench seating behind cell bars, the other boasted swivel chairs.

The speedsters filed aboard. They were escorted to the bench seat, and the cell door was closed.

Jet Man told Galloping Gazelle, "You escaped a Japanese police jail. Now you're in the Tomorrow Men's cell."

"And you're in here with me."

"Oops," Astro Lass yelped, dramatically overacting to locking the gate by looking at it. "Well, it's too late to do anything but buckle up and enjoy the ride. We'll release you boys later."

The Tomorrow Men cackled.

"Seriously, people, let's settle in," Polyphemus added. "We got more than six thousand miles to cover. At five hundred miles an hour, we'll be in the air for twelve hours."

The captors found seats and strapped in.

Animal bent to all fours. "Excuse my quadrupedalism, people." In that manner, he made his way to the pilot's seat in the cockpit. Within minutes, they were airborne.

Galloping Gazelle turned to his companions. "What if they don't let us out of here?"

"Should I show him or will you?" Jet Boy asked Jet Man.

"Show me what?"

"This." Jet Man began to vibrate. Then he went through the cell bars. Next, he was fully solid on the other side.

Galloping Gazelle gasped. "How did you do that?"

"It's something Superior Man discovered back in the '50s," Jet Man said.

"Nothing to it," Jet Boy piped up. "We can vibrate our molecules fast enough to go right through solid structures. Anything we carry passes with us. With a little practice, you could master it."

Jet Man repeated the process and was back with his companions.

"I doubt it. You fellows are far swifter than me."

Jet Man shrugged. "Yeah, well, when I first got this superpower, I practiced running downhill. It improved my pace."

"Did it ever," Jet Boy exclaimed. "You ought to try that, G.G."

"That's all right for you, but how do I get out?"

"We'd take you with us."

"Take me with..." Galloping Gazelle stopped. "Alright, I'm going to sit right here and think about that."

Jet Man buckled in next to Galloping Gazelle. "I thought you were the only speedster on this Earth."

"So, you noticed the salaryman's fast reflexes, too?"

"We tend to spot things other people miss." Jet Boy tapped his temple. "The hand isn't always faster than the eye."

"I'm not the only speedster on this Earth. There's a villainous *lusus naturae*, the Human Whirlwind. Charles Cannon is his real name. And, oh, yes, Frank Roberts, a retired superhero from the '40s called Turbo Man. Neither of them was the salaryman in disguise."

"Geez," Jet Boy said. "We're the only speedsters on *our* Earth."

"But we were still faster than that guy. He was like a semi-speedster. He's definitely not one of our mutated humans."

"Could someone have, I don't know, artificially given him speed?" Jet Man asked. "Take an ordinary guy and purposely give him the power that I got by accident?"

"That's a distinct possibility. When I was with

Solenoid, he tried creating mutated humans." Galloping Gazelle nodded forward. "He meant to copy the cells of Hawk's parents, ordinary people who gave birth to a super-powered child."

When he could arrange it, Galloping Gazelle meant to visit his old boss in prison. *Should I get out of this cell,* he mused, *without having to pass through the bars.*

"You move at friction burn velocity," Galloping Gazelle commented to Jet Man. "Don't you ever get burnt?"

"I wondered about that. We had Superior Man scan us. He detected we have protective auras that keep us from burning up."

***

The Tomorrow Men had no intention of keeping the speedsters locked up. Once in the air, Astro Lass mentally unlocked the cell. She let it clank loudly so they'd know. They got up and stretched their legs.

"We'd heard you and your cousin turned good," the girl stated to Galloping Gazelle. She was sewing. "Joined the Assemblers."

"You've heard right, but none of you have answered my question. I was in Japan on official Assembler business. The world thinks you're a menace. Why were you there?"

"We came to recruit Rising Son," Polyphemus jerked a thumb back toward Japan.

"Another thing. How did you manage to fly this craft into Japan?"

"If you can keep a secret between *lusus naturae.*" Hawk grinned. "Some humans trust us. A National Guard general and an Air Force general vouched for us. Air Force brass arranged this jet for us."

Polyphemus added, "They realized we're not a menace when we intervened that time in Washington. The rest of mankind doesn't feel that way, though. Professor Z is Program Director of the Special Projects Agency's PSI Division. He pulled a few strings."

"That's our chief, Francis Zyfos," Astro Lass put in.

"Yeah," Polar Man chimed in. "The prof's got them convinced he's keeping us under control so they can use us."

Ice on the teen began to melt. This left the kid in trunks and boots that matched his teammates' colors. Even when not iced up, cold was no impediment to him, for he wore no shirt.

"We can't do this alone, you know," Polyphemus stated. "Z calls the shots."

"I don't get it," Hawk bellowed. "I'll never get it. It's like Gazelle said. The world thinks we're a menace. But the Atoms Family have super powers. The Assemblers have former criminals in their ranks. Why aren't they menaces?"

"How do you fly with that chip on your shoulder?" Jet Boy asked.

The Hawk turned to him, ready to unload.

Jet Man zipped between them. "Let's save it for the bad guys. Er, how many superhero teams do you have on this, um, Earth?"

"You must be new. Three. Us, the Assemblers, and the Atoms Family." Astro Lass's expression told Hawk to stand down.

He did so, knowing the girl could telekinetically pin him to the ceiling if she wanted. He, of course, would stand down his own way. The Hawk glided forward. It was an impressive maneuver in the enclosed space.

The girl said, "It's like the three television networks."

"But we get the worst ratings." Polar Man chuckled, now completely free of ice and moisture. He bent to touch a puddle on the floor and absorb it.

"And just who *are* you fellows?" the winged youth asked from down the aisle. "I don't recognize you. I was fighting crime as Green Hawk long before the Tomorrow Men recruited me. I thought I knew all the superheroes."

"We're just new in town," Jet Man said.

"Well, not exactly," Jet Boy countered.

Superspeed would not have been necessary to account for how fast Jet Man and Galloping Gazelle swung their heads to him.

"We're from good old New York," Jet Boy added. "That big city they have over there. In the United States. New York, yeah."

"These fellows helped me recover those papers," Galloping Gazelle explained. He hoped the Tomorrow Men wouldn't ask how *they* got to Japan. "Might recommend them for Assembler membership."

"Say, what are your powers?" Jet Boy inquired.

"Mine should be obvious." Hawk sneered. He seemed to have a particular disdain for Jet Boy. Hawk saw Jet Man was part of the older generation, but Jet Boy, was indeed, a boy. "Whatcha got here, a father-and-son act?"

"Father and... No. He's my brother-in-law. Why the heck are you being so nosy?"

"Gazelle says you're okay," Hawk said. "Maybe you'd like to try our Doom Room?"

"Doom Room? Sounds groovy, cat." Jet Boy flashed to the winged man, extending a hand in a gesture of fellowship. "I'm always game for friendly competition."

Contemptuously, Hawk took it. "You ain't scared of much, kid, are you?"

"Wings against speed?" Jet Boy figured. "You don't have a chance."

Galloping Gazelle turned to his fellow speedsters. "The Tomorrow Men operate somewhat more secretly than the Assemblers. They have a mission to vet *lusus naturae*. But because of their inborn powers, they're feared by mankind. My cousin and I battled them under the influence of Solenoid."

"You want to know who does what, eh?" Hawk asked. "Polyphemus shoots force beams from his eyes, Astro Lass can move objects with her thoughts."

"The object she's moving is my head," Jet Boy commented. Then his mask, untouched by hands, sharply rotated sideways until he couldn't see.

"Are you faster than thought, little boy?" Astro Lass ribbed him. "You might not fare so well in the Doom Room."

Laughter filled the air. Jet Boy didn't find it funny, but he held his tongue.

"Polar Man is the Rising Son of ice," Galloping Gazelle said. The kid illustrated by making a brinicle emerge from his hands.

"He can use his powers even when not iced up," Hawk noted.

The kid had formed snowballs and was now juggling them.

"And Animal, despite his refinements, is more agile and stronger than any ape."

"Spoken like a true enemy." Apparently, Animal also had sharp hearing.

Jet Boy, mask back to normal, sped to Astro Lass. "Listen, I'm sorry about that wisecrack."

She was working on an upswept eye-covering mask so feminine it could only be for herself. Jet Boy thought it wiser not to comment that it would leave more of her pretty face uncovered than the hood. Astro Lass might actually put his foot in his mouth. And he'd tread in some pretty filthy places.

She looked up. "Apology accepted. Hey, do you want a new costume?"

The feminine mask floated into a bag.

"New?" Jet Boy pulled his shirt back and looked at it. "What's wrong with this one?"

"Why wear a duplicate of daddy-o's? I almost shifted

the wrong guy's mask before. I make costumes for the team. Look, here's a yellow shirt Polar Man didn't want and this is a mask Hawk rejected."

The girl floated them mentally. His hair would be left exposed, Jet Boy saw.

"What do you say? Drive all the chickies wild by showing your manly mane."

"Gee, would it take long?"

"Well, we've got quite a long trip. Plus, I can think my sewing *and* use my hands at the same time."

"Oh, yeah. You must be great at threading needles."

"Thread goes right where I think it to go. I might be done by the time we land in New York. How about it, kid?"

"I'd dig a new costume."

With that, the threads holding the lightning bolt symbol on his uniform began to unravel.

"That we'll reuse on your new one," Astro Lass said.

"We?"

"You're going to help, speedster."

***

Things were happening in New York that had nothing to do with new costumes. After parting with Man Machine, Mr. Atoms and the Intangible Girl arrived at the Leland Building. There, they found Flaming Youth and Golem attempting to restore their headquarters to normal. Or to a semblance of normal, given it was a haven for the superpowered.

"What happened here?" Reide asked, taking in the damage. He wasn't very surprised. Their headquarters was often attacked and reduced to shambles. He remembered when they fought the Mancestors.

"We had a punch up with villains from that other universe." Golem stopped to lean on a broom. Hearing the wood protest, he straightened up. "Except they was superheroes."

"Three against two," Flaming Youth complained. "They took the AtomiCar."

"They were superheroes?" Intangible Girl frowned. "Who?"

"Superior Man's pals. I forget their names. There's something else. Superior Man showed up with a sick friend," the rocky hero added. Golem led them to the glowing figure on their couch.

"Supes brought him here for safe keeping. They had a fight with the Silica Rider and threw his flying disc into the sun."

"Making the sun belch," Flaming Youth added.

"Silica Rider?" Reide gasped. "But—"

"I know. Faculus pledged to never attack Earth. *Our* Earth," Golem explained. "But he found out about the other Earth. It's obvious he means to eat it, using Silica Rider to clear a path."

"Extraordinary." Reide lit a pipe and indicated the human shape aglow on the couch. "What is this fellow's name?"

Flaming Youth jumped in. "Golden Ring. His ring created that glowing field as protection. Superior Man can't see or hear through it. He wanted to know if Suzette could pass through it and check on him."

"From one crisis to another." She dropped her travel bag. "Okay, here goes."

The girl touched the glowing field and concentrated on entering it. Nothing happened. "I can't get through."

"Try it again," her husband urged.

It didn't matter. For at that moment, the golden warrior's barrier dropped. "You're the Atoms Family," he guessed, taking in his hosts. "What happened?"

Golem said, "Superior Man brung you here after you guys was caught in a solar flare. Don't you remember?"

"Oh, yeah... Where is he now?"

"He flew off to see the Assemblers," Golem answered.

"How are you feeling?" Suzette asked.

"Bit of nausea. I ache all over and there's spots before my eyes."

"Cherish the feeling, friend." Reide offered a stretched-out hand. "Means you're alive."

"I should be getting back to my own universe," Golden Ring said, returning the handshake. Reide's stretching power reminded him about nominating Plastic Freak for squadron membership. He dreaded that superhero's turn as chair, though, knowing he would form himself into an actual chair just to be funny. "Thanks for your hospitality."

Reide sighed. "You're going? I've got a million questions for our second visitor from another universe."

"I'd love to stay and answer them, but I've got to go before my ring runs out of juice."

With that, he strode to a window, opened it, and flew out. Airborne, Golden Ring decided top speed was called for.

***

Back on her own Earth, Pandora considered the purloined postcard again. Its addressee was "Dr. Steven Merlin, 177B Bleek St., New York City, N.Y." Odd, she couldn't get it out of her head; New York City was an insignificant part of New Guernsey. On her Earth, that is. She made arrangements with a neighbor to feed her cat and check on her home intermittently.

Then Pandora affixed the mirror to the *inside* of the closet. After this, she chose the most ordinary clothing she had. A plain black mid-calf skirt, a gray windbreaker, comfortable loafers, and a plain jersey in blue. Further, Pandora packed an overnight bag and a backpack with everything else she might need. The girl went before the mirror. She watched herself intone the incantation De'ath taught her. The surface rippled like water and she stepped through the mirror. Something about the chant was familiar. Then, in a flash, it came to her. She'd once heard her father use that incantation.

***

Aboard the Tomorrow Men's aircraft, the team discussed more individuated costumes. Uninterested, Jet Man left them and made his way to the cockpit. Animal was at the controls. Jet Man was surprised to find their pilot steering with his feet, perusing a book. Reading glasses perched on the end of his nose. *So much for sharp vision,* Jet Man thought.

"About that stolen item, Animal. I noticed your look of concern."

"Ah..." Animal looked up. "Another master of science, eh?"

"Chemistry," Jet Man said.

"The item in question is a mechanism that has very few practical applications." Animal straightened up and put down his book. Their conversation was interrupted by Jet Boy.

"Hey, that dude won't talk," he reported, meaning their prisoner.

"Don't worry about that." Hawk sneered as he poked his nose into the cockpit. "We've got someone who can easily overcome that."

"Oh?

"Professor Z."

"Buckle up, lads," Animal ordered. "I'm coming in for a landing. We'll see the prof soon."

"Back to your cell, smart guy." Hawk chuckled, looking at Jet Boy. "Mush!"

***

It wasn't long before the stratojet was landing at a specially reserved runway at the Westchester County Airport. The team had their own hangar. This was guarded and maintained by members of the Special Projects Agency.

Astro Lass was as good as her word. Jet Boy now had the original purple replaced with a costume that consisted of a yellow shirt to contrast his purple leggings, gloves and lightning bolt emblem. He found a room in the hangar to change. As promised, the yellow mask left his ginger hair run as wild as he did.

"Looks cool," Polar Man said. "That was fast."

"And he ought to know." The girl smiled, looking at Jet Boy.

Polar Man raised a frosted eyebrow. Tiny icicles adhered to his lashes.

"She took over my hands with thought, and I used super speed to sew. Only I don't know how to sew. Hey, speaking of cool, you ever get tired of looking like a snowman?"

"What do you mean?"

"I bet if I massaged you while your snow comes out, I could make you look like ice. Ice is groovier than snow."

"Why don't you try it?" Astro Lass suggested.

Polar Man iced up. Jet Boy ran his hands over Polar Man's arms, legs, torso and head. The desired affect was achieved. Polar Man gleamed like an ice sculpture; his head squared off like an ice cube.

"Ginchy," Polar Man called. "What am I supposed to do when you aren't around?"

"Do it yourself," Jet Boy said. "All I did was use super speed. It should work even at normal speed."

From there, they drove a black limousine to a Westchester mansion.

"The old Halliday place," Polyphemus said.

Jet Man and Jet Boy met their host. He was the wheelchair-bound Francis Zyfos, Professor Z. Of course, he and Galloping Gazelle knew each other.

"You seem well, Pyotr," Zyfos said. "Obviously, being an Assembler agrees with you. Who are your brightly garbed friends? New Assemblers? I've heard your team is recruiting."

"Ah, yes." Galloping Gazelle smiled. "Allow me to introduce Jet Man and Jet Boy."

"One doesn't have to be a mind reader to know who is who. And I recognize Astro Lass's handiwork. She finally foisted that unwanted mask on someone."

"I'll leave you gentlemen to get acquainted with the prof." Galloping Gazelle bowed out.

Jet Boy wheeled around comically, as if looking for the gentlemen.

Galloping Gazelle was eager to make time with Astro Lass. A fellow mutant would be his only choice for a wife.

"She's no *fellow*," Zyfos called after him.

The two Jets exchanged looks.

He spoke to them. "It's unusual that Cerebrum hadn't detected you."

"Cerebrum?" Jet Man asked.

"A device I use to help me find mutated humans. You must not be *lusus naturae*."

"That's right. Our powers came from a lab accident," Jet Boy proclaimed proudly.

"Something about you two... Odd."

"Oh, it's just that we've never been to Westchester before."

"You know, I don't like pressuring friends and allies, but I have a way of getting the truth."

"You can really read minds?" Jet Man nodded back toward Galloping Gazelle in reference.

"Gazelle was being a bit too...eager. I couldn't *help*

but pick up his thoughts. But I have carefully scanned your prisoner."

"You have? But he only speaks—"

"Japanese. He's imagining his punishment from Dr. De'ath."

"Dr. De'ath? That guy with his own country?" Jet Man scratched his head.

"Yes, he is outside the reach of the law. Now, you will forgive me if I do not take your statements at mask value. I feel the need to—"

Jet Man didn't hesitate. He took off, grabbing Jet Boy's wrist. They covered the grounds of the mansion, looking for the third of the speedy triumvirate.

Zyfos pushed out a mental command: "Attention, Tomorrow Men! Stop Jet Man and Jet Boy. Bring them to me."

Immediately, Hawk unfurled his wings and took to the air. "Now we'll see how speed does against flight."

Jet Man found Galloping Gazelle with Astro Lass. The girl had been using a damp cloth to wipe soot from his face. This was to the chagrin of Polyphemus.

The two Tomorrow Men stopped as if listening. Jet Man and Jet Boy bore down on them. Together, the two Jets yanked their fellow speedster backwards by the arms and bundled him off. Astro Lass telekinetically caught the falling cloth. Hands on hips, she asked, "Now, what is going on?"

"I could have used a damp cloth, too, you know." Polyphemus got off a blast at the trio, but they were too fast. They dodged, and it merely dug up a patch of ground.

Within seconds, they were on the Saw Mill River Parkway, headed to New York City. The pair, used to evading moving cars like they were parked, easily navigated the highway. They stopped beneath an underpass, though they weren't tired or out of breath.

Jet Man exclaimed, "Gazelle, you didn't tell us he was

a mind reader."

"Of course, he is. How do you think he detects mutated humans?" Galloping Gazelle broke away from his erstwhile captors.

"We don't have them back home." Jet Man turned to his young partner. "Let's go. That fly boy is going to be here any second. I don't want to fight with a fellow good guy."

"What do you think you're doing?" Galloping Gazelle pointed back to the mansion. "Those are my friends."

"Baldie is no friend of mine," Jet Man spat. "Now let's go before he scans us and finds out there's another universe."

"You might be right about that."

"Yeah," Jet Boy added. "No more people should know about that than necessary."

The three took off again without the Jets hauling Galloping Gazelle along. He got the feeling these two were not running at top speed...so he could keep up. They soon approached Manhattan and Assemblers Mansion.

Galloping Gazelle came to a halt at the gate. "My Assembler I.D. card won't be accepted by the electric reader. It was fried."

"Oh, we'll get you in," Jet Man assured him.

Jet Boy nodded. "G.G., speed up."

Again, the pair grasped Galloping Gazelle. He waved them away. "No. No, don't..."

Jet Man poured it on, as did Jet Boy. They vibrated through the gate, continued on toward the front door and, once more, vibrated. The trio came to rest in the living room.

Galloping Gazelle collapsed into a chair. "Did we just pass through solid matter?"

"Congratulations." Jet Boy grinned. "You no longer need training wheels."

"Listen, this has been quite a lot for me." Galloping

Gazelle closed his eyes. "I'm going to change out of this damaged costume, ponder warping to Japan and passing through matter."

"Maybe we should go back to our universe," Jet Man threw out.

"That might be for the best." Galloping Gazelle sighed. "I'm sure your wife and teammates are worried about you."

"We'll leave you to deal with Zyfos scanning minds," Jet Man said.

"I'll manage. Solenoid taught me a jingle to stymie his mind reading." Galloping Gazelle began the thought: *Tenser, said the Tensor. Tenser, said the Tensor.*

Jet Man said, "Yeah, now that we've proven inter-dimension travel can be done by vibrating, we'll just vibrate home."

The two visitors once more hooked up like collegiate wrestlers and began to shake. Galloping Gazelle wondered how long before the phone call from Zyfos would come. Then he brightened. He'd take that call. Mind reading couldn't work over the phone, the speedster pondered. "Could it?" He started to write up a report for Sergeant-at-Arms.

Penniman appeared. "I couldn't help but overhear you, sir. Your cousin has a new costume for you."

The speedster took the duplicate costume and held it up. "My cousin made this?"

"No, sir. She ordered it from a shop in Flushing, Queens."

"Blue?" Galloping Gazelle asked. "That's going to clash with Sarge's outfit."

"But it is better than scorch marks, sir."

CHAPTER 15

Braindroid maneuvered his spacefaring lifeboat near the rift. He went through, beginning the journey back to 269 Justitia. Landing, Braindroid rested his miniaturizing ray across his knees. Faculus was waiting.

Impatiently gesturing his guest inside the hollowed-out asteroid, Faculus said, "I am ready. Begin the process."

Braindroid got the giant in his sights and squeezed the trigger.

"Strange." Faculus gazed at his outstretched hands as he shrunk to tiny size. "I feel no different." His voice got tinier, however.

"That is to be expected," Braindroid explained. He, as instructed, shrunk Faculus's mysterious equipment, one piece, a man-sized box. "Your cells are now packed closer together. Everything else is the same."

The tiny conqueror took the equipment and walked alongside Braindroid to the lifeboat. There, Braindroid plugged the lifeboat into a gridwork of red diodes on his head. They accelerated to the rift. It was some time before they reached it. Once through, they flew to Braindroid's orbiter, mocked up like an Earthly satellite. The inhuman pair docked with the female mothership. Braindroid exited the lifeboat. Faculus remained aboard.

"This will be delicious," Braindroid crowed, checking his visual screen. "You enter their atmosphere too small to be seen. There will be burn in reentry, of course. That's no harm to a being such as yourself, nor your machinery within."

"And you have checked and double checked your

restorative devise?"

"Triple checked. Upon impact you will be bathed in radiation that regrows you. Then, they will *see* you."

"Indeed. They shall all see me." Faculus was eager to feed and tired of Braindroid's rantings.

"Your landing will be spectacular. This Earth will be yours, yours will be mine. None of their heroes are capable of stopping either of us. Humans call this *the old switcheroo.*"

"The plan is well known to me."

Braindroid locked on the target with his teleoptics. He had an ideal spot picked out. But he didn't want any of the humans killed in the landing. No. Death would come later as Earth was sapped. They all had to witness this.

"I simply must see their reaction."

Now I can do what I wish to that other Earth, Braindroid imagined with glee. After all, he was frustrated with how Superior Man or Golden Ring could fly to space and interfere. This other Earth had no Superior Man or Golden Ring. *Perhaps they will kill each other,* Braindroid speculated. Then he would have *two* Earths to rule.

He hummed a human song that mentioned his foes he'd heard while monitoring Earthly radio signals, adding his out of tune vocalizing, "Superior Man and Golden Ring/Ain't got nothing on me."

The target was Mascouten's oasis of green, Center Park.

***

On Earth One, in Center Park, the respective softball teams of Federal Comics and Wonder Comics were limbering up for their weekly game.

"Curt, you've really got to bring back pirate comics," Jim Dennis said.

"What's wrong with our comics?" Jack "Curt" Curtiss

asked.

"Some of the stuff in your hero comics is too crazy."

"Er, what's that?" a third player asked, pointed finger stabbed skyward. A brilliant light was like a second sun. What looked like a flaming meteor had appeared above them. It was a reddish streak that grew and grew. Finally, it became obvious it was crashing to Earth. In particular, right *here*.

"Come on. It's not the end of the world," Curtiss held.

The teams scattered. The resulting impact was deep. Buildings shook. Window glass shattered. Alarms went off; emergency vehicles scrambled. Inside the ship, impact triggered the restoration device, spreading rays out onto Faculus and his cargo. He began growing to his full size.

"So much like the Earth I know." Faculus's voice echoed around the skyscrapers of Mascouten. He pivoted, taking it all in.

***

Focusing through his scanner, Braindroid saw, but could not hear. Eagerly, he awaited the arrival of authorities and the Superior Squadron. Rannin Nord had winnowed out the lesser teams. Faculus had declared that Superior Man had neutralized his herald and would pay.

"I just have to see their faces," Braindroid yelped. "Who do you think will respond first? Jet Man? Superior Man? They're the fastest."

The ship did lightning-fast calculations and reported, *"There is a high probability Jet Man and Jet Boy will arrive first."*

"Jet *Boy*? Are the Wonderkind involved?" Braindroid gaped. "I hadn't factored them in."

"I can factor them in, if you like, darling."

"Bah! Faculus has nothing to fear from those lightweights. A team of sidekicks. Ratman's little helper doesn't even have superpowers."

Braindroid didn't have long to wait. As calculated, Jet Man was first on the scene, closely followed by Jet Boy. They didn't stop to ask questions. They simply began attacking Faculus. Golden Ring was next to arrive. He noticed everything he threw at the invader had no effect.

"Oh, no." He groaned.

***

Watching from above, Braindroid was most anxious for the arrival of Superior Man. Finally, the hated superhero zoomed in. And instantly he was felled by radiation deadly to him. Braindroid squealed with delight. Bouncing up and down in his chair tested its durability.

Superior Man's vector toward the invader resulted in an ignominious tumble from the sky. He skidded across the grass, leaving a trailing gash. Superior Man rose shakily. He had the wherewithal to turn his heat vision toward the giant. The hero gaped as the beams petered out well before incinerating the intended target.

Braindroid cackled.

***

"Golden Ring," Superior Man called, knowing what was up. "You'll have to take him. The giant is wearing hercolubite."

Golden Ring said, "No can do. He's all gray."

"Your ring can't affect gray." Superior Man scowled. "This is turning into a monster movie." With that, he collapsed.

"Superior Man." Golden Ring landed beside him. "Are you—"

"Radiation...so strong. Weakening me..."

Several yards away, an outdoor phone in a kiosk rang

impatiently. Then the handset jumped off its hook. Out came Shrinking Man, gradually growing. He hit the ground at his preferred six-inch height. The sight of his felled teammate made him shout, "Hey. Superior Man."

He expected the object of his shout would hear him. Shrinking Man had a pretty good idea what the problem was: hercolubite.

Golden Ring turned toward the mighty mite. "What'll I do?"

"First, move him back."

Golden Ring imagined a stretcher. With it, he flew Superior Man out of range of the hercolubite. He knelt over his comrade. "There's no heartbeat."

"Restart his heart," the pocket-sized hero ordered. "Give him a real whomp."

Golden Ring imagined a massive mallet and made it strike the prone hero's chest.

"Try for a pulse," Shrinking Man advised.

"What's the pulse of a man from Hercólubus?" Golden Ring found none at all.

"Dead," Shrinking Man yelled. "Superior Man is dead."

***

High above them, Braindroid watched with glee. He even hit "record" so he could watch Superior Man die again and again.

"I finally did it."

"Not only are you handsome, you are smart and ruthless," the ship said.

***

"Do it again," the tiny hero advised, jumping away. "Next, shield him like you do for space travel."

Golden Ring did as instructed. Superior Man, in turn, jerked. He stirred, groaning. Superior Man got to his feet, careful not to tread on Shrinking Man. Golden Ring enclosed his friend in a radiation-proof globe.

"Guy's covered in hercolubite, isn't he," the tiny hero said.

"Lots of it," Superior Man answered. "Thanks, Goldie."

"Shrink thought of it."

"In that case, I owe you both."

"No thanks are necessary." Golden Ring beamed.

"Yeah, that's what heroes do," Shrinking Man said.

"I hope you're here with some bright ideas, little guy."

"I just came from headquarters. The S.O.L.A.R. crew alerted me when they spotted something in the sky that shouldn't be there. Ratman is on his way."

"I thought he was through with us." Superior Man turned to the rustle of bushes his teammates hadn't heard.

"Feeling better?" Ratman was unfastening a shoulder block on his right side that would not be out of place on a member of the Gothic City Titans football team. He transferred it to his head in the manner of a helmet. Of course, it had rat ears.

"Somewhat. Change your mind about leaving?"

"No," Ratman said. "I'll get Vest Man and False Dave some other time. This is for the sake of the whole planet."

"You got here fast."

"I was hiding from overly amorous debutantes at the decommissioned firehouse owned by my butler," Ratman explained. "S.O.L.A.R. traced that giant's path back to what looked like a satellite. It's holding stationary and too low to be genuine."

Superior Man's gaze followed Ratman's pointed finger, assessing as he scanned. "Lead lined. Braindroid?"

"I have no file on him," Ratman said.

"He *is* unaccounted for," Shrinking Man added.

"Remember his protection against you?" Golden Ring asked Superior Man.

"Yeah, that amulet of hercolubite."

"We have a bigger problem than Braindroid." Shrinking Man's chin indicated the giant. "And I *do* mean bigger."

They turned and saw the speedsters continuing their attack. After the first blast of cosmic energy, they knew to keep up a distraction. Like a well-oiled machine, they circled the giant's legs or alternately ran up his body. In response, furrows were displaced along the green by his hand blasts. The speedsters kept moving, got in close and pulled back. All of this was done while avoiding annihilation. Jet Man had caught Superior Man's reaction and guessed what was up.

It was during one of these retreats that Jet Man called to his partner, "Keep him away from Superior Man."

He dashed out to the open where Superior Man could see him, yelling, "You guys have any ideas?"

Superior Man looked up.

"That's the Airphibian," he shouted. Jet Man probably couldn't hear, so he pointed and made a swimming motion. Against the sun, he might not recognize the plane.

Jet Man followed his finger. He shot back to Faculus. His move was just in time, as the giant aimed a blast of energy to where Jet Man had stood.

Amazon Woman, Superior Man saw, was with Aquamarine, ready to jump. Tuning in, he heard Aquamarine shout, "This didn't work against the silica guy."

"I'm no morning star." The Amazon leapt.

Faculus's follow up blast was momentarily spoiled by Amazon Woman landing atop his helmet. Its flatness had practically dared her to use it to land on. Immediately, she began pounding his skull, thankful to be out of range of his energy blasts. He couldn't very well risk blasting himself. At the least, her attack kept Faculus from blasting Aquamarine, plane and all, out of the sky.

Superior Man heard, "I have withstood the onslaught of asteroids. Your blows cannot hope to affect me, female."

Abandoning cosmic blasts, Faculus dislodged her the old-fashioned way. His enormous hand swiped Amazon Woman.

Superior Man gasped and started to move.

Ratman clamped his arm. "Easy. Remember what she can do."

They watched. Her fall was gentle, riding air currents to the ground.

Superior Man heard, "It is well I have the Handler," the invader announced.

A massive foot released a latch on the restored casket-like box. A panel flew back and there appeared an ugly cuss, vaguely resembling a man. But if a man was five-by-five, with four arms and hand-like feet. Like Faculus, he was draped in hercolubite tinted gray. The giant pointed to Amazon Woman. No sooner had she gotten her feet under her, that the creature charged. He dealt out punches. She fought back, but four arms were too much for her to handle.

Superior Man snapped his fingers. "Shrink, can you reverse your process?"

"Grow giant size?"

"Yeah. The other Earth has a shrinker who does that. He waffles between being King Bee and Kingsize."

"Oh, that's clever," Shrinking Man said.

"While tiny, you move in on the giant. He won't notice you. Then you grow and surprise him. Get that armor off him, then we'll move in."

"Should work," Shrinking Man said.

"Good idea." Ratman signaled Jet Man over their linked communication system. Almost instantly, the superfast hero appeared.

"Jet Man, carry Shrinking Man close to the giant. When Shrink gives you the signal, you and the kid start getting that armor off him. It's hercolubite."

"I figured. What signal?"

"You'll know it when you see it," Shrinking Man answered. "Drop me by his foot."

Jet Man caught the leaping tiny hero and took off. He was just in time. Jet Boy wasn't doing well against Faculus solo.

"We're going to unbuckle that armor," Jet Man said to his young partner. "It's hercolubite."

"Right on. What's hercolubite?"

"Oh, you don't know. I have to trust you. It's a substance fatal to Superior Man."

"Now, that's interesting. Yeah, I'll keep it under my mask."

Beneath the gigantic boot, Shrinking Man rolled unseen. There, he initiated the growing process. He kept on growing. With that growth, Faculus was abruptly upended. The invader went over with an Earth-shaking *thump*. Now horizontal, the speedsters could attack without having to defy gravity.

"Shrinking Man." Amazon Woman gestured to Handler. "Help!"

With Faculus momentarily distracted, a giant-sized Shrinking Man reached down. "The princess has a big brother watching over her." He grabbed the Handler and wound up like a major league baseball pitcher. He flung Handler into Center Park Lake.

"Ha! Still got the old Pymer pitch."

"Thank the gods," Amazon Woman let out, woozily. The whip fell to her feet.

Aquamarine, aware his flying plane was a target, landed. He lit out for the action on foot.

"That ain't gonna stop Four Arms for long." Shrinking Man's voice boomed through cupped hands.

"Your element, Aquamarine."

Aquamarine heard. "I'll fix his wagon."

He ran to the lake. At the same moment, Shrinking Man reversed size before Faculus could incinerate him as a larger target. Trees behind him were not so fortunate.

***

Faculus was first baffled by the appearance of his equal in size, and then by his disappearance. Now the giant Shrinking Man was back, this time bigger than Faculus. He slapped a full nelson onto him. Faculus possessed the superior physical strength to break out of it, but the Earthly maneuver stymied him.

Before Faculus deduced how to break free, Shrinking Man staggered, yelping, "Eh, grew too fast."

He released Faculus and reversed to tiny size. That move saved him from a fiery death. Jet Man saw this and ran in to rescue his small pal. Jet Boy and Amazon Woman, whip in hand, continued the attack. At the very least, Faculus was kept off balance.

Jet Man sped Shrinking Man to Ratman and Superior Man holed up at the outdoor phones. "He's out of the fight."

"I grew too fast." Shrinking Man groaned.

"I suppose it'll take some practice," Superior Man said.

"Once I got small again, I felt okay."

Superior Man scanned his teammate. "You have an instant form of altitude sickness."

"Plan B," Ratman said. "The giant has Superior Man neutralized. So we set him on Braindroid. You two burst in on him. You'll be out of range of the big guy's radiation. Once up there, Superior Man will overact the effect of the hercolubite in the amulet, really selling it. With Braindroid distracted, Shrinking Man takes possession of it. That'll free up Superior Man to strike. Secure his miniaturizing ray and use it on the giant."

"I've got a mind to use it on Braindroid," Superior Man stated. "He shrunk a whole city of my people. He's got a lot to answer for."

"Line forms behind me, pal," Shrinking Man put in. "I'd like to sock him after I shrink him."

"How about it, little guy? Ready to ride?" Superior Man bent, holding open the pouch on the inside of his cape.

"Let's go." Shrinking Man jumped into the pouch.

Ratman added, "Try not to rend the ship too much. Once it's on Earth, we'll salvage the lead and have the Jets wrap it around the giant. Then you and Golden Ring attack him while encased in one of his bubbles."

"Good thinking. The force of my blows will be transferred to the giant while the bubble blocks the hercolubite, like it protects Golden Ring in space."

"Right," Ratman replied. "Without that armor, you can handle him."

The pair took off.

***

At the lake, Aquamarine found Handler. Frantic thrashing gave him away. He was already climbing out of the lake. Aquamarine leaped, launched a flying kick he'd learned from Ratman. It staggered the alien. From there, it was child's play for Aquamarine to dodge the alien's appendages.

"You're not beating up a woman now, Four Arms," he taunted as he pounded the alien into submission.

He pulled off the hercolubite layer from the alien, let it sink and moved to rejoin his team. Unfortunately, the only thing Aquamarine could do with the alien was leave him to sink to the lake bottom. Then he caught himself.

"No, I can't do it," Aquamarine spouted. Superheroes

don't kill, he reminded himself silently. "Even hideous aliens are spared death."

He dove back into the lake to retrieve the alien. The Handler, still unconscious, was deposited on a lawn. Eyes shut, he gasped irregularly. Aquamarine hurried back to his teammates, wishing there was some of that tough seaweed around to bind him up with. He had to take a chance and leave the alien there. For now, he was out of the fight.

Aquamarine dashed for his plane.

***

Superior Man ascended to the ersatz satellite, careful not to cause motion harmful to his rider. He had to move fast before air got too thin and too cold for Shrinking Man. Superior Man's hearing came into play. Lead countered his visual powers but didn't hinder super hearing. What they suspected was confirmed. This was no satellite. Carefully, Superior Man tore off the side of the craft with a tormented wrench of metal.

"So, you finally pierced my camouflage." Braindroid sneered, like he was expecting a visitor. "For all the good it will do you."

Climbing aboard, Superior Man hoped Braindroid didn't notice he carefully preserved that lead. Superior Man blew Shrinking Man to the alien. Microscopic vision confirmed the tiny hero latched onto Braindroid's ear. A good handhold. Braindroid looked around like he heard something.

"You *should* be worried," Superior Man said, approaching menacingly to distract Braindroid. He made a gesture of invitation.

"Worry is an emotion I'm not burdened with." Braindroid reached for his throat to open his amulet. Instead, he clutched at empty air.

"My amulet." Braindroid howled. "Where is my

amulet?"

"You're not the only deceiver here." Superior Man grinned. "I brought a friend."

Shrinking Man was in the midst of growing in a leap. Now full sized, he presented the amulet.

"Looking for this?" Shrinking Man smirked. He had to push through the dizziness of all the shrinking and growing. But it was imperative he distract Braindroid for the next step, no matter how damaging it might be.

"Shrinking Man," Braindroid bellowed. "I should have miniaturized myself and beaten you for sport long ago."

So preoccupied was Braindroid with this blasphemous sight, he didn't notice the sudden flash of light momentarily bathing him.

"You're welcome to try." Shrinking Man put up his dukes.

"Miniaturize yourself with this?" Superior Man asked.

Braindroid turned to find himself covered with his own miniaturing ray gun.

"Phooey on hercolubite and rays." He clicked a toggle on his belt. "Once I activate my force field—"

"I burned it out while you were spouting invectives," Superior Man stated. "Along with all your personal weapons systems."

"What? I—"

Superior Man pulled the trigger and Braindroid shrank. In a burst of speed, Superior Man grabbed him. With the tiny Braindroid in one hand and Shrinking Man having hopped into the other, Superior Man leapt out the torn-off entryway. "Remember when you shrunk Hercólubus City? You'll get a fair trial there."

They were airborne.

"I have a surprise for you," Braindroid boasted. "Coppélia is armed. Fire, my love."

"Is he talking to his spaceship?" Shrinking Man

blurted out.

A panel opened, a barrel swung over, aiming at Superior Man. Beams of hercolubite belted him. Powers gone, Superior Man fell from the sky.

"Yow," Shrinking Man yelled. No amount of getting smaller was going to make hitting the ground from this height survivable. Alien cyborg Braindroid wouldn't be harmed.

CHAPTER 16

I ntangible Girl snapped her fingers. "Seventh Son."

"Seventh Son?" Golem asked.

"More specifically, his canine companion. He can teleport us to the other universe."

"That's right," Reide said. "Lockhorn can traverse dimensions, bypassing the Superior Squadron's headquarters. He'll take us right to where the action is."

"That mangy mutt?" Flaming Youth scowled.

"Hey! That's the dog I happen to love," Golem barked. "But we shouldn't let them Mancestors know there's another universe. They'd want to move there to avoid being hassled by humanity."

"Golem's right." Reide again. "We can't let that happen. Who knows what havoc would break loose if the Mancestors suddenly appeared on the other Earth. We need Lockhorn, but we can't tell them why."

Intangible Girl pointed. "Richard Reide, you go to the Radio Sending and Receiving Room, get on the hyper radio and call them this minute."

Her teammates exchanged looks.

"We won't do it," Reide said, standing his ground.

"Men!" Intangible Girl stamped through the walls to their communication room. Her brother, husband, and their old friend followed her via a more conventional route.

Flaming Youth asked, "Do you even know how to operate that thing, sis?"

"Of course I do." She was already dialing for the frequency to the Mancestors' hidden city in the Himalayas.

An image formed on the screen. No less than Seventh Son, the leader of the Mancestors himself, had answered the call.

"Greetings from the Atoms Family in New York," Intangible Girl said. "I trust all is well with the Mancestors."

Seventh Son did not speak. Rather he chose not to. Perhaps it was for the better. His very voice could shatter mountains. Instead, he gestured greetings and understanding. This man was dressed completely in black: hooded mask, gauntlets and tights. These were decorated with bolts of crackling energy. Folded up gliders, louvered like window shades, hung under his arms. The mask featured a jutting aerial. Intangible Girl recalled how that aerial would glow and carry him aloft. The gliders allowed flight. In all, it was a less dangerous method than how her brother flew.

"We have a problem," she went on. "It is not safe to discuss it even over this line. But we have great need of Lockhorn."

Seventh Son might as well have been a wooden Indian guarding a tobacco shop, for all the emotion he displayed. Then the camera tilted, revealing a gigantic brown bulldog that could have doubled as a horse. On his head was an aerial matching that of Seventh Son's. As the dog turned to look up at his master, now off-camera, a faint vein of energy crackled between the two antennae. The dog barked once, like he understood.

The camera tilted back to Seventh Son. Still unsmiling, he waved a gesture like he was wiping the screen. It went dark.

"You talked him into it, Suzette." Golem cheered. As he went to clap her on the back, she became intangible enough for his stony hand to pass through her.

She became solid again.

Reide simply kissed his wife.

"Yeah," Flaming Youth added. "Good for you, sis." In

his excitement, he flamed.

"Not too close, little brother. I'm the Intangible Girl, not the Intangible Grill."

Seconds later, the air shimmered. There was a pop, air being displaced, and there stood Lockhorn. He was accompanied by the young Mancestor named Jewel. She was a beauty in a yellow leotard costume accessorized with little black boots. A black hairband held back ginger locks. The girl was smitten with Flaming Youth. Jewel took every opportunity to be around him. She knew he had the latest records from the Tolling Bells and the Beastials.

"Greetings Atoms Family." She smiled. "We will lend you Lockhorn. What is your problem?"

"We can't tell you that," Reide said.

"In that case, the offer is rescinded." Jewel turned to the dog. "Lockhorn—"

"Wait," Reide yelled. "I'll tell you but you must keep this revelation a secret...even from Seventh Son and the other Mancestors."

"We don't keep secrets from each other."

"You Mancestors owe us that much...or have you forgotten—"

"All right. So, like..." she sounded like an American teenager, "what's the big secret?"

***

In free fall, Braindroid sprang from Superior Man's limp grip. The tiny menace engaged his rockets. On his back, they'd been unaffected by Superior Man's heat ray blast. Small wonder, as Superior Man had only fried the gizmos on his front. "I live to fight another day...on another Earth." Braindroid made the human gesture of throwing a kiss, and then secured the hoodlike glassine helmet over his head. "Faculus will make you heroes his appetizer before he eats your planet."

"Yow," the tiny Shrinking Man let out. This looked like the end for him. And Superior Man, as well.

Eagleman swooped in and caught them. Thanks to his anti-gravity controls, his arms weren't jerked from their sockets. Shrinking Man might have looked easy to catch, but even small, he retained his full-size weight.

"Don't worry, guys," Eagleman announced. "I'll set you down nice and safe."

The easiest and quickest place to do that was back aboard Braindroid's ship. Eagleman took his burden there. Superior Man slumped unmoving from his second exposure to hercolubite that day.

"I'll leave you here and go after that creep."

"The ship is alive," Shrinking Man managed. "She speaks and she'll blast Supes again."

"In that case..." Eagleman looked around, "I've got some pounding to do." He took the morning star from the loop on his belt and bashed the controls of the ship. She wailed with an electronic voice, "They're killing meeeeee..."

The ship immediately began to shake and falter. Sparks flew. Bludgeoning done, Eagleman returned his weapon to his belt and picked up his passengers anew.

Superior Man came fully awake. "Braindroid won't be standing trial after all. We were this close to nailing him."

"Forget him," Shrinking Man said. "We have to deal with a giant wrecking your adopted home."

"You're right. I'll find Braindroid some other day." Superior Man held out the miniaturization ray. "Eagleman, take this. Use it on the giant."

"I've only got two claws, guys."

"Just get me close in and *I'll* do it," Shrinking Man shouted. "I want another crack at that big goof."

Below them, they witnessed Amazon Woman trip up Faculus with her whip before he could blast her. Had the speedsters not been so preternaturally swift, they would have been dead from all the blasting. To their credit, they had loosened most of the giant's layer of hercolubite armor. Overhead, American military fighters streaked into the battle. Faculus raised an arm to pick them off.

"Oh, hell no," Golden Ring yelled. He flew in, projecting a shield between the invader and the jets. The energy blasts couldn't penetrate the barrier. Eagleman descended with his passengers. Faculus turned to him. The wings caught his attention. Faculus saw something he recognized, the miniaturization gun clutched in Shrinking Man's hand. He knew what was coming.

He boomed: "You cannot..."

Shrinking Man aimed while holding onto Superior Man's cape.

Faculus raised his arm.

Shrinking Man fired.

Faculus felt a familiar tingle and began to shrink.

The canyons of Mascouten resounded with an agonized, "No!"

Shrinking Man smirked. "I bet they heard that in New Guernsey."

Eagleman spotted the airborne Airphibian. He matched his speed with it. Aquamarine slid the door open.

"Hey! Room for passengers?" Eagleman called.

"If the little guy stays little."

Eagleman bundled Superior Man and Shrinking Man aboard. He meant to get Braindroid's ship and land it. Braindroid's craft couldn't be any harder to pilot than those he had flown on Iukkoth. Except this one had wrecked controls.

Golden Ring arrested its descent before it crashed into buildings bordering the park.

***

Above them, Braindroid poured on the speed. "Next

stop, other Earth." He cackled.

Approaching the rift, he took a look back at Earth One. The combatants would soon kill each other. His elation was short lived, however. A terrific blow smashed him.

Týr came through the rift. He had shifted in midair and caught the flying alien with his warclub.

"I thee smite!" he shouted, unheard in the thin atmosphere.

He had to contort back to flying position. Týr caught the tumbling Braindroid. The god squeezed. Enclosed by Týr's hand, the alien struggled. There was a burst of flame as Braindroid's rocket fuel exploded. Týr grimaced. He didn't expect his grip to produce that result. It was the hand bitten off by Fenrisúlfr. The explosion tore open where the wolf wounded him, but losing a hand to save two universes would be worth it.

**

Golden Ring imagined a hand that gently set the spaceship in Center Park. There, the shrunken Faculus still wouldn't be held. His remaining hercolubite seemed, when miniaturized, less effective against Superior Man. Even tiny, Faculus dealt out deadly blasts from his hands. Superior Man attacked anew, leading with heat rays. These had no effect on Faculus who cast bolts of energy into Superior Man. He felt excruciating pain but shook it off.

Amazon Woman unfurled her whip and coiled Faculus in it. Not just a foot this time, his whole body.

Faculus didn't like that. He pulled on the whip. With a burst of strength, he snapped it.

"No, no, no," Amazon Woman cried out.

Shrinking Man called to Eagleman. "Bring me in closer to him. I'll distract him or die trying."

"You'll catch his eye, all right, at his size," Eagleman

replied. "Shrink fast if he blasts."

Now the same size, Shrinking Man ran up to Faculus. "Remember me?" He dealt the alien a punch Ratman would have been proud of. The haymaker, while textbook, had no effect. As the alien raised his other hand to blast the tiny titan, Golden Ring encased him in a protective sphere.

The speedsters ran in again, continuing their attack. Their physical pounding on the alien still didn't seem to have much effect, other than keeping him preoccupied. Once more, Faculus brought his arm around and tried to belt the speedsters with energy. Then he was caught up in a swirling funnel of air the speedsters wove around him. They ran off and returned with slabs of lead.

Together, the speedsters encased Faculus in the material.

Superior Man flew in, tightening the prison of lead, using his super-fast hands to create friction that melted it. He molded it, then blew air to super cool it. Superior Man next applied heat vision to solder the gaps in place.

Faculus applied tremendous strength to the lead, expanding it.

Ratman, adverse to appearing in daylight, had quickly dashed to a small two-seater Chinook with "Pan Am" displayed on its side. From the air, an observer would think it was a full-size model flying between airfields.

Golden Ring flipped his energy globe from Shrinking Man to Faculus. The collapsing glowing globe locked the lead in place. Now Faculus couldn't walk through the globe like it wasn't there. Golden Ring tightened it further. The Superior Squadron had Faculus in check.

"I'll settle this," Golden Ring declared. "The other Earth's sun made a fine blast furnace, Superior Man. So will ours."

"We're really doing this?" Superior Man countered.

At that moment, Týr landed behind him, dropped the alien cyborg and used his foot to hold him down.

"I say thee nay," Týr called. He was amazed to see these heroes had managed to shrink Faculus.

"I...will kill...you." Braindroid struggled impotently. "Overload...my circuits...explode...take you with me..."

Týr bent, swinging Hval. The impact was thunderous. Gears, springs, pieces of Braindroid went flying in every direction. Braindroid seemed to have been abruptly deactivated. He tumbled, head over what was left of his heels. The avenging god picked up the stunned, broken invader.

"Who the heck are you?" Superior Man asked.

"My name be Týr! I be of yon other realm." He pointed upward with the warclub. "I will dispatch yon giant from there."

"So Faculus is one of yours?" Golden Ring asked.

"Aye. With his power, even tiny Faculus will break free no matter what shackles ye bind him with. Surely not the glow of alien science. *Thee* shall attend to this one."

Týr handed Braindroid to Superior Man. "I leave the fate of this machine to thou. Auric ringbearer, come. Thou art needed on mine own Earth."

"Now, wait a minute." Superior Man tossed Braindroid to the ground. "Who put you in charge?"

"Superior Man's right." Amazon Woman grabbed a shoulder of the stranger. "You can't just—"

"Unhand me. It is unwise to touch a vengeful god."

"Oh, you're a god, are you?" Superior Man stood firm. "And we're just playthings of the gods? Or do you only talk to women that way?"

"Thou might be smite as easily as I have done the creature."

"Hey..." Eagleman descended, swinging morning star. "If there's smiting to be done, I'll be doing it."

Týr's battle-hardened reflexes swung his warclub up. It smacked Eagleman's incoming morning star, which shattered. Not being on solid ground, the impact propelled

Eagleman back. He spun, then he floated.

Týr gasped. "Repelled yet he still be airborne."

"Tyr!" Superior Man illustrated his distaste for Týr by grabbing his arm with a paralyzing grip of iron.

Týr turned while raising Hval in the other, but before he could strike, Superior Man shot out a fist faster than Týr had ever seen Galloping Gazelle punch. The god was rocked but managed to block the next blow. There was an audible snap as Superior Man's arm broke.

"Argh!" Superior Man screamed.

The god smiled at this folly, but his face turned to shock as Superior Man grasped his own arm and, guided by X-ray vision, forced the broken bone back in place. Recovered, he grabbed the club. It took him to the ground. Hval was too heavy to lift. *That's impossible,* Superior Man thought.

"Ye may tug to thine contentment," Týr said. "But never will ye raise Hval. For enchantment allows only mine own self to wield it."

Gritting his teeth, Superior Man kept up his fruitless task. He tried his flying power. The results were the same.

"Ye try mine patience. Enough!" Týr aimed his damaged fist at Superior Man.

The blow landed on his sternum, causing him to grunt.

"How do ye go unscathed?" Týr bellowed. "Behemoth hath been felled by this hand."

Braindroid stirred and rose to a crouch. "I...Will... Kill... You... All."

"Guys," Amazon Woman shouted. "Can we decide who's top dog another time?"

Golden Ring willed a glowing wall between the two combatants. Týr and Superior Man stood down. The wall reshaped to enclose Braindroid.

Týr addressed Amazon Woman. "I sense great power and, aye, great good in thee, valkyrja." He perceived the woman and his erstwhile opponent had some bond. Týr raised his warclub. "Upon my return, we shall settle this. But not anon. These two must come first. That one belongs to mine own realm."

Golden Ring asked, "How did you know to intercept Braindroid?"

"Wotan of the Aesir wisely advised me to journey here," Týr stated, as if that settled who put him in charge. "These villains needs be given their final reward. Now!"

He again beckoned Golden Ring to join him. The gold guardian looked at his teammates.

"Do it," Superior Man said.

With Faculus locked in the glowing gold globe, Týr swung his club to fly. Golden Ring rose with him.

CHAPTER 17

Galloping Gazelle, as a former member of Solenoid's criminal gang, required special permission to visit his old boss. He was justly proud of having achieved a cross-country jaunt, encouraged by speedsters from the other universe. He was at the maximum-security prison on Alcatraz Island in California. The prison had divested its human inmates, now holding only super-powered criminals, *lusus naturae* or otherwise. The mutated human's magnetic powers were such that they should have thrown away the key after locking up Solenoid, Galloping Gazelle mused.

Assembler I.D. card burnt, Rocco Kent had to vouch for the speedster. But when it came time to leave, would the warden heed Kent? Maybe they'd just decide to lock him up, as well. After all, Galloping Gazelle had abetted Solenoid longer than he helped mankind with the Assemblers.

Inwardly, he shuddered at that possibility.

Galloping Gazelle doffed the windbreaker he had traveled in. Underneath was his new costume. Blue, modeled on his old green one, it had the same jagged lightning bolt straps. He could claim the jacket at reception upon leaving, he was informed. The metallic parts had to be kept out of range of Solenoid's influence. The master of magnetism could turn a zipper, a tie clip, or the screws on eyeglasses into deadly weapons.

A guard, plastic rifle at the ready, loaded with wooden bullets, stopped Galloping Gazelle. "Do not approach the prisoner closely. Do not touch the prisoner."

To the speedster, this was a stupid and unnecessary stipulation. He could grab that guard before he got off a shot, pounded the rifle into plastic crumbs, put the guard in the cell, and run off with the prisoner.

Apprehensively, the speedster entered into his audience with Solenoid. The criminal had a large cell. Because of his powers, it was far easier to usher visitors to him than to magnet-proof the visiting area. There was no trace, not one, of anything metal. His axiom that he who controlled magnetism controlled the universe may have been right.

"I have heard you joined the Assemblers," Solenoid said. He was a fit, middle-aged man, gray hair growing unruly. His bright orange, ill-fitting jumpsuit had not one metallic part to fasten it. Canvas deck shoes were on his feet. "Have you come to gloat?"

"I came for your help."

"Help? After abandoning me, you want my help? And for the Assemblers, not even for a team of *lusus naturae*. Not the damned Tomorrow Men? At least, they're your own people. Now you take orders from a man out of time, live with humans who shrink, and an archer..."

Galloping Gazelle knew enough to let his old boss vent. Then: "If you're of service to me, my standing as an Assembler might get you some leniency."

"There is no leniency you can secure for me."

"You certainly seem comfortable enough here."

"They've taken pity on me. I can't visit the prison library so they bring me books. But I miss browsing. I am as comfortable as one can be in a prison made solely of plastic, wood and ceramic. The upside is I cannot be eavesdropped on electronically. Do you suppose a guard is on the other side of this cell wall with a plastic cup on his ear listening?"

"No plastic cup is necessary. A guard need only stand within earshot."

"No metal," Solenoid shouted, as if he hadn't been heard. "I wish I knew who told them my power's effectiveness declined after fifty feet."

"What would you do to him?" The speedster asked carefully to avoid saying "or her" in an effort to deflect suspicion from his cousin. After all, one of the conditions of their parole was to tell the Special Projects Agency everything they knew about the mutated human underworld boss.

"I would curse him, but not kill him. That girl advocating for me, Nancy Nevelloff, recommended a legal journal. It comes with the staples removed. Apparently, I am a political prisoner. Violence is no longer my way. What kind of help are you seeking? I'm just bored enough that I might indulge you."

"When you sold Dr. De'ath your Image Duplicator—"

"What do you know of my Image Duplicator?" Solenoid shouted. Perhaps his swearing off violence was just a ruse.

"Only to confirm you gave it to him. When that happened, did you also share with him your method of creating *lusus naturae*? I'm thinking of your scheme to use the genes of Hawk's parents for that."

"In fact, I did. Sort of a trade. Superlicates, I called them. I used his body cell analyzer to fabricate super-powered duplicates created from human genes. Homunculi, as it were. An alchemist who studied creating homunculi, De'ath was the one to consult."

"Dr. De'ath combines such arcane knowledge with science."

"That is his genius. He is smart for a human. De'ath used it to give extraordinary abilities to living humans. He must have analyzed the cells of the Atoms Family as I did with Hawk's parents. With two of them married now, the offspring of the Reides will be *lusus naturae*."

"Likely." Galloping Gazelle was thinking about a

supplicate with fast reflexes. Now he was sure Dr. De'ath had augmented that Japanese spy. There might be others like him out there. Not true mutated *lusus naturae*, their brain waves would not be detected by Zyfos' device.

"It was working. Superbly. Until Polar Man broke in and spoiled it. Iced up the machinery. Crystalized it. The other Tomorrow Men intervened before I could kill him. I couldn't win without my Brotherhood of Mutated Humans. You, your cousin and those others."

"Do you really hold that against us?"

"At first I did..." Solenoid sighed, "but not now. Not really. I agree my quest is political. I want only for all *lusus naturae* to live free without fear from humans."

"With you as their leader?"

"Do you doubt I am the one most worthy?"

"I think you have a messiah complex."

"And your fellow heroes don't?" Solenoid countered. "Going around doing good deeds, whereas I envision a perfect world with no crime."

"Those with great gifts should put them to better ends. People, mutated or not, don't want a dictator."

"Well, if you ever reconsider, there will be a place for you in the homeland of ours I will make. Think of it, Pyotr. Your experience in the Assemblers would be of great value."

"Do you really think you can escape this prison? The guards on the towers have wooden bullets that can splinter in your body."

"I am aware it would be more painful than a standard bullet. No surgeon with metallic instruments would operate to save my life. Ah, but I shall be released soon. My cause is just. When the time comes, I will go quietly to live apart from mankind. Humans won't hunt our kind anymore. Did you get what you came for?"

"Yes, I am satisfied. De'ath has succeeded in creating his own mutated humans."

"Of course, you cannot detain him. He will claim diplomatic immunity."

"We have no current conflict with De'ath," Galloping Gazelle stated. "Now, in return, what do you want, short of your freedom?"

"You know what I really miss in here? Movies. See if you can arrange some way I might view movies. Any movie. Well, not today's trash."

CHAPTER 18

The impact woke Bob Bannion. "What the..?"

Bannion had left the hippies, thankful for the poncho and sandals they'd gifted him. After all, he had fixed many of their scavenged devices. Bannion never would have guessed he'd one day repair a guitar amplifier. If they were going to start giving concerts of *rock* music, it was time to move on.

Scrambling to his feet, he peered around a boulder. He was surprised to see an old teammate. Týr was straightening up from a landing. With him was some guy in gold and black tights. A new superhero? A fellow god? Or was he some criminal mastermind? A glowing golden dome seemed to trail from his hand. Within was a tiny figure in purple. The mite looked wrung out. *Is that King Bee,* Bannion wondered, *in yet another new costume?*

"Who is he now, Violet Vespa?" Bannion snorted. It was hard to see clearly without his glasses. "Maybe it's the girl."

The pair talked; Týr spoke commandingly. Bannion overheard: "Upon my word, you will remove your barrier so I might strike."

The pair turned their attention to the globe. Týr glared at it. He raised the warclub over his head, poised. This was serious. Was he about to kill Hiram Pymer? Bannion wondered, did this gold guy have control of the Norse god? And Pymer, if it was him, was a fellow scientist. Had something happened to him to make *him* a menace? Could all that shrinking, reverting to normal, then growing to giant size have affected his mind?

I can relate.

He pulled back. Maybe that wasn't Pymer at all, but some being who had the power to detect Behemoth's gamma radiation trail. Whatever they were doing, it made Bannion tense.

"They know I'm here." He gasped. To that god, the Behemoth was just another monster to be slain. Was that tiny figure some kind of bloodhound?

His thoughts raced: *they're here for the Behemoth. Or me. End the menace of the Behemoth while he was human.* No! They couldn't know he was the Behemoth. He'd kept that secret. Smitty wouldn't have told.

Bannion chanced another peek. If his secret was out, would Týr really kill him, his human self? He didn't wonder long. Without realizing it, Bannion started changing. The fading mind of Bannion looked down and saw his clothing in shreds, skin gray. He had convulsed into his other self. Then he bellowed, "Pick on someone your own size!"

He sundered the boulder and barreled toward the god.

"Behemoth," Týr yelled, shifting Hval. He knew now the Behemoth had not, as feared, aported through a hole to the other universe. "Verily, we have sought thee."

"Now ya got me."

"You know this guy?" his companion sputtered. A ring on his hand began to glow.

"Aye, once an Assembler. Man Machine hast told me Behemoth be awash in gamma radiation."

"*That* thing was an Assembler?"

"Can't ya leave me be?" Behemoth screamed.

There was a blast of energy. The tiny man was free. Maintaining the globe had been forgotten.

"Faculus is loose." Týr cast the war club after the tiny man.

"Get him, Týr," Golden Ring called, ascending. "I'll handle this joker."

"Some skinny guy is gonna handle *me*?"

The gold warrior raised his arm, and a wall shimmered into existence.

Behemoth ran into it and continued through like it wasn't there. "That the best you can do?"

"But how?" Golden Ring landed a safe distance away. "Oh, no. He's gray."

"'Course I'm gray," Behemoth yelled.

Golden Ring took flight. "I know what I *can* affect."

He imagined a giant shovel. It appeared and scooped up mounds of earth, then covered the gray monster.

"Usin' dirt?" Behemoth raged. His low estimate of Golden Ring's tactic didn't stop it from being effective.

Týr caught his returning warclub. "Thou must buy me time while I—"

"Did your club just fly into your hand?" Golden Ring asked as he landed.

"Scatter, Golden Ring," the god shouted. "We must not stand so—"

The Behemoth pounded the ground, and shockwaves rocked the heroes.

"Uhh!" Golden Ring grunted as he tumbled.

At that moment, Faculus projected beams at Týr and Golden Ring. His ring protected him automatically, while Týr blocked with Hval. In fact, it seemed to absorb the beams.

Behemoth dug himself out of mounds of soil. Seeing the gold man was protected, the Behemoth might be able to move the whole glowing barrier. He clapped his hands together. The shock wave rocked Golden Ring. Týr now took his club in a vicious swing. The tiny conqueror doubled his blasts of energy. Twin beams were too much for the warclub. The god was knocked over. Another found the Behemoth. Golden Ring forgot about burying the Behemoth and willed a sphere around Faculus. Inside, a fireworks display erupted. Golden Ring willed it to contract around Faculus. Now it was closer to him than before, like a second skin. Faculus's own blasts of energy stunned him.

At that moment, the Behemoth broke free of his burial mound. "The little guy is blastin' everybody."

Now he had a more interesting challenge.

Týr readied Hval to cast. "We be like fire." He hoped Behemoth remembered they were once allies now that they had a common enemy.

The bestial man grunted. "Behemoth raging fire. You smoldering fire."

He leapt at the alien, going right through the protective barrier and onto Faculus. There was a blast. The whole world broke into flame. The release of energy swept Týr and the Behemoth backward. The shock did things to them. Unexpected things. Golden Ring took to the air, unharmed. The blast lasted only a split second, but for the beings caught up, it seemed an eternity.

***

"Well, if everything is under control here, I'm off to Fort Superior." Superior Man wanted another shot at that god. He scanned Braindroid. "This jerk is in a coma. I've got a city full of tiny people who want to see justice served. Shrinking Man, you can be his defense."

"I might at that. Then he couldn't say he was railroaded." Shrinking Man nursed a sore fist.

Amazon Woman strode to Superior Man, strutting in her new costume. "Well, what do you think?"

"Isn't it a bit, I don't know, brief?"

"These are castoffs from Superior Girl's costumes. You never said anything bad about her looking brief."

"I'm not in a relationship with her. You look like a go-go girl in that getup."

"It gives me freedom of movement." She flexed a curve here and a curve there. "Besides, they're super under the yellow sun. This will never shred."

"We'll talk about it later. Alone." Superior Man huffed and flew off with his prisoner.

"Ooh, sometimes he can be so...superior." Amazon Woman stamped a foot. Inadvertently, she smashed the miniaturization gun.

Shrinking Man called, "I wanted to study that."

None of the Superior Squadron noticed the Handler's approach. Now *he* would have the advantage as his feet firmly gripped solid ground. These Earthlings would fall to his deadly vengeance.

The Handler roared his disapproval with the human in blue. With no master to control him, the Handler sought death, not just punishment. He almost had the blue one within his deadly four-armed grasp. Until an arrow struck.

Rather, a series of them.

The first bore a weighted tip that delivered a concussive blow to the alien's chin. It staggered the Handler but did not stop him. He turned to see who perpetrated this trick with a primitive weapon. The second was a bolo arrow. This wrapped a cord around the Handler. Meant for a foe with two arms, it was only half effective. Growling, he snapped the snare.

The Superior Squadron turned to see a blond man wearing a brown jerkin, tights and Colombina mask. His boots and archery gloves were gold. Lastly, a bycocket in brown sat upon his head. This bore a feather. There was a quiver on his hip. With amazing speed his next arrow was nestled on his recurve bow. This had pulleys at each end.

"It can't be," Amazon Woman cried.

That arrow discharged a noxious cloud of gas, which merely made the Handler cough. As far as his alien body chemistry went, this might well have been aftershave. A final arrow was stocked with batteries, like something from Jules Verne. It delivered an electric shock to the alien. The Handler was finally settled.

"Sue me for battery," a high voice piped. They didn't know Gold Arrow's sidekick had a penchant for puns.

"Good shooting," Jet Man said.

"It's just Zen. Gold Arrow at your service." The archer introduced himself with an elaborate display of bowing. "Some of that belonged to my second, Swifty."

Swifty clicked his boot heels. He wore a duplicate of Gold Arrow's costume, albeit in green and red.

Amazon Woman asked, "How ever did you just happen to show up here?"

"Your millionaire benefactor recruited me as a replacement for Ratman," Gold Arrow explained. The group exchanged looks. "He gave me a card for entry to your clubhouse. Some eggheads there sent us here."

"Don't you operate down in Florida?" a tiny voice chimed in.

Gold Arrow pivoted until his sharp eyes settled on Shrinking Man. "I flew up. Didn't you folks send for me?"

"Well, we scouted you. They let you take your archery weapons on a flight?" Eagleman asked, ignoring Gold Arrow's question.

"Are these questions part of the interview process?" Gold Arrow bristled. "I assume Wemyss told you my real name and status. A private jet is not unexpected, right? Anyway, at your warehouse, I flashed the card. Got my mask on under the hat and coat. The bycocket unfolds from an ordinary rain hat. My bow was folded up, natch."

"Same goes for me," Swifty added.

"Natch." Shrinking Man nodded.

In the distance, emergency vehicles began entering Center Park.

"Those scientists said you were by the phone bank. We hopped into a cab, shucked out of my coat and found Four Arms menacing you. That was a good coat."

"You sure know how to make an entrance." Eagleman beamed. "Welcome aboard."

Jet Man said, "I'll find your coat for you."

He ran off.

"My coat? It's gone. Anyway, I figured out Wemyss's secret."

The Superior Squadron collectively blanched. The archer was about to reveal Ratman's real name in public. Jet Man wasn't here to clamp a hand over his mouth.

"He's your talent scout," Gold Arrow stated. "Got the time and money to travel around recruiting for you."

"Why, yes..." Shrinking Man exhaled. "You've pierced his secret precisely."

Amazon Woman only had eyes for the archer's bow. "I have never before seen one such as that. May I?"

"You shoot?" Gold Arrow asked.

"Used to. Not in, ah, years."

"Oh. In my civilian identity I financed this for Holless Wilbur Allen." The archer handed the weapon to her. "Seeing how well it worked, I'm giving him the go-ahead to apply for a patent."

The female took the thing, hefted it, plucked it and sited an imaginary arrow. Swifty, ever the gentleman, took a real one from the quiver on his hip and offered it. She took it and sighted across to the outdoor telephone bank. Releasing the arrow, she hit the handset Shrinking Man's entrance had left dangling.

Jet Boy dashed around to Swifty, who was marveling at her shot. "We could use a joker like you in the Wonderkind. We asked Superior Girl to join, but she didn't respond."

"Cool," the junior archer replied. "Think you can catch an arrow?"

"That's a good question."

"Looks like we'll be fitting you for a new pair of boots, with ankle support and extra-grip soles." Amazon Woman smiled at Gold Arrow. "Standard issue."

"Fine, fine. So, what *is* that living coat of arms?" Gold

Arrow jerked his head at the Handler.

"He was the least of our worries." Amazon Woman returned the bow. "But a dangerous ally of a cosmic threat."

"The Handler, to put a name to him," a voice called. "Strong-arm for Faculus."

"Don't cha mean 'strong *arms*,' Reide?" a rocky man farther back grumbled.

The Superior Squadron and the archers pivoted as one. The latter pair instinctively loosed arrows. One was incinerated with a line of shooting flame. A stretching blue-gloved hand slung out and stopped the other one. Then the pillow-like shape reverted to the form of a hand in a gesture of greeting. Walking with the man in blue were two women. Hanging back stood the rocky ocher man and the youth who had shot the flame. He was in his own blue costume. A giant dog panted beside them.

"Now what?" Aquamarine groaned.

"Plastic Freak, right?" Gold Arrow presumed behind his bow. "Without his crazy goggles."

"I'm Richard Reide, Mr. Atoms of the Atoms Family." He indicated the woman with him. "This is the Intangible Girl."

Amazon Woman stepped up. "Flaming Youth and Golem. Hello. Who is your new member? That yellow is a nice contrast to all the blue."

"Jewel's not a member, just a friend." Reide shook the hands of the Squadron members.

"Why are the others hanging back?" Amazon Woman asked.

"I think they're still hurting from your last encounter," Intangible Girl said. "If only their male pride."

"That's right, sis." Flaming Youth folded his arms across his chest. He and Golem plopped down on the grass with Lockhorn. He chewed playfully on the latter's rocky big toe. "We're staging a sit-in protest."

"Nice park for it, too," the rocky man said.

"Anyway," Reide continued, "I theorize the Handler is a human Faculus mutated. Otherwise, he couldn't breathe your air or move under your—"

"Skip the lecture," Golem cut in. "Things seem okay here. We proved Lockhorn can get us here. Now, the faster we get home the better. I'm missing *The Jason Taverner Show*."

There was a whoosh. Jewel pivoted. "Look. Up in the sky. Is that a bird?"

Superior Man landed, grasping Braindroid. He was still comatose. "I chanced a look back and heard my friends from the other universe. I had to come back here."

"You heard us?" Jewel was in the dark about Superior Man's range of powers.

"Trust me, kid," Golem said in a gravelly voice. "He did." Flaming Youth and Golem finally ambled over. "Hiya, Superior Man." Flaming Youth flashed a fiery peace sign. Still, neither looked at nor greeted the Superior Squadron members that beat them.

"So, that creature caused all this, huh?" Reide appraised Braindroid.

"None other," Superior Man said. "And you're right about the four-armed guy. I was curious and x-rayed him. Human, with signs of having been genetically altered."

"At any rate," Reide went on, "we can't just kill Handler. And we shouldn't lock him up in your universe."

"Your universe?" Gold Arrow frowned. "What does he mean?"

"We'll tell you later," Amazon Woman said. "Maybe we should retire to our headquarters."

"He didn't know? Oh. Well, the Handler belongs in our universe," Reide said. "Jewel, do you think the Mancestors would hold him for us? Any of them, with their awesome abilities, could keep him in line."

"Another superhero team on your Earth?" Superior

Man asked. "Dr. De'ath's files didn't mention any Mancestors."

"We Mancestors are superpowered. But we are not superheroes." Jewel turned to Reide. "I will arrange your request on one condition."

"Name it."

"This woman has given me an idea." Jewel nodded toward Amazon Woman. "I join the Atoms Family. Life among the Mancestors is quite boring. Also, I yearn to hear more of Flaming Youth's records."

The team looked at each other. There was whispering.

"Well? What is your decision? Lockhorn hasn't been fed yet."

Reide spoke up. "Yes, of course. We *could* make good use of your elemental powers in our work. But not a word about this other universe to the Mancestors."

"I agree to your condition." Jewel offered a hand.

Instead of a handshake, the Atoms Family joined their hands together atop hers.

"Oh, force of habit," Golem said.

"So, what happened here?" Intangible Girl asked, taking in the park and the spaceship.

"A giant from your universe fell out of the sky."

"Faculus?" Reide scowled. "He isn't the type to fall out of the sky."

"Was that his name?" Jet Boy shrugged. "He was wearing hercolubite and in gray, so neither Superior Man nor Golden Ring could battle him."

"Teamwork stopped him," Superior Man added. "We shrunk him."

Gold Arrow exchanged looks with Swifty, then: "What are you folks talking about?"

"Oh, no, no! You can't shrink a being like Faculus without repercussions." Reide's eyes were filled with shock. "He's full of energy. Anything could happen."

Jewel asked, "Where is he now?"

Eagleman offered up the answer. "A guy from your Earth, Týr, took him and our guy, Golden Ring, back through the rift."

Mr. Reide Atoms huffed. "We should go after them. I'd feel better knowing where Faculus is."

"How exactly did you get here, anyway?" Shrinking Man asked.

"Like this." Reide turned to Jewel. "New member, here's your first assignment. Can you coax Lockhorn to take us to the golden man?"

The girl turned to the dog. Lockhorn whined in either agreement or hunger.

"The dog," Reide whispered to Shrinking Man.

"Oh, you travel by dog." Shrinking Man blinked. "I've done that."

"Not like this you haven't."

"Lockhorn will need an image," Jewel said. "Those of you who know this golden man, picture him in your mind."

The members of Superior Squadron looked at each other, shrugged and thought about Golden Ring.

Lockhorn barked.

"Good." Jewel embraced the dog. "Gather round, new teammates."

They did so. The canine panted. The air shimmered and the five members of the Atoms Family and the dog were gone. Jet Man returned with Gold Arrow's coat just in time. He remarked to Jet Boy, "Sure beats trying to hit the right vibration."

"Sure does."

***

Golden Ring opened his eyes. He saw blue sky. Blinking, he found both eyes intact and working. He felt his face for a nose. It was there. Slowly, he tried moving. Then he looked around. Golden Ring heard neither Elizabethan

English nor hoarse roaring. Týr and Behemoth were not in sight.

Instead, he saw a blond man in an immaculate business suit unconscious on the ground. Golden Ring imagined a pincer. He used it to pull back his suit jacket. He extracted a wallet and brought it close to his face. His vision was still blurry. Opening it, he read the I.D. aloud: "Donner Sigmundson."

Hearing that, Sigmundson sat up. Golden Ring willed the pincer into a serving plate and sent the wallet back on it. "You okay, sir?"

"Yes, I'm fine." Sigmundson tucked away the wallet. "Except for the ringing in my ears. It's so loud you should be able to hear it. Why are you dressed like that?"

"Oh, I'm Golden Ring."

"Golden Ring?" Sigmundson retained all of Týr's memories and knew that. Týr was now in his human form. Sigmundson could move among humans undetected. To preserve this, Sigmundson lied about not knowing this interdimensional visitor.

"Refers to this." The gold-clad man displayed the ring on his gloved hand.

"You're named after a ring?" Sigmundson asked, now crawling around and slapping the ground like he lost something.

"It materializes anything I can imagine." Golden Ring heard groaning and craned his neck. A man in tattered clothing lay across the way. "Who's that?"

"I'm a physician." Sigmundson stood up. "I'll help him."

Golden Ring noted Sigmundson's limp as he walked. "You're hurt."

"A bad leg I've always had."

"Let me give you a hand." An oversize gold hand formed, steadied, then lifted the doctor to the downed man. Sigmundson feigned surprise. "Hey, that's pretty cool. Like the kids say."

He knelt to examine the dirty man in rags. No broken bones. The state of his clothing, or lack of them, made him wonder if this was a victim of the Behemoth. While dirty, there was not a bruise on him. He was slight, with dark hair that showed flecks of gray. Sigmundson did not know Bob Bannion was the Behemoth. Golden Ring, of course, could not guess these men before him were counterparts of the now missing individuals. He did not know, either, that the blast triggered their change to human form.

Sigmundson roused Bannion. "Who are you, bud? Are you all right?"

There was no answer.

He felt for a pulse. "He's dead!"

***

At Superior Squadron headquarters, the team sat around their meeting table. Superior Man spoke. "We may have ended the threats of Braindroid and Faculus, but we still have that rift between universes. I can't see how we, even with all our powers, can close it."

"Right." Eagleman agreed "Any spacefaring person, good or evil, from either universe, might go through it."

"As could any piece of space rock," Aquamarine added, pondering the impact crater he discovered near the Yucatán Peninsula in Mexico, near Chicxulub. "What about those *space elevators* I've been hearing about?"

"I know how we fix this," a tiny voice piped up. They all swiveled to Shrinking Man's miniature chair. "Your fellow Hercólubusians are super, like you, under our yellow sun, right? They can help. I believe they owe you a big, fat favor."

"What's your angle?" Superior Man asked, interested.

"We post a small rotating patrol of them up there, near the rift. They won't let anyone in or out."

"No. I can't ask the Hercólubusians to do that."

"I guess they have their own lives, huh?"

"Yes and they don't speak English, for another thing. Plus, their powers are new to them. Besides, they're restoring their tiny city. We should put something of our own up there to monitor the rift."

"That's a good idea," Eagleman said. "We could monitor all of Earth from a satellite."

"Who's going to gift us something like the Manned Orbiting Laboratory?" Jet Man countered. "How would we get there? Easy for you, not so easy for us."

Shrinking Man had another suggestion. "We cannibalize Braindroid's satellite and launch it in orbit."

Amazon Woman chimed in. "Noah Merlin's beam could get us there and back."

"If he'll share it with us," Shrinking Man pointed out.

"I let him have Braindroid's spare rocket pack and laser gun to study," Superior Man said. "I think he might agree to a trade."

"Merlin can send me back to Iukkoth."

"He told me your world is a wreck."

Eagleman took the news rather stoically. "So, I'm not only stranded here, there's nothing to go back to if I could get there. Looks like I'll be here for a while."

Jet Man wanted to brighten him up, keep Eagleman busy with a project. He snapped his fingers. "Say, how about you use your tech to rig up a way for this satellite to have normal gravity?"

Eagleman nodded. "I could do that."

Amazon Woman had a question. "What about on the other side of the rift?"

"The Special Projects Agency there keeps their advanced carrier at some thirty thousand feet. I think they can be convinced to double that altitude to surveil the rift." Superior Man made a note to himself. "I'll visit the Atoms Family and get them to suggest it to the head man there."

"So, more people will know about us." Jet Man moaned.

"The Special Projects Agency can be trusted."

"They'll have to be," Jet Man said. "The rift can't be left unattended on their side, either."

"On our side, it's just us," Shrinking Man put in. "That's what we should rename ourselves, the Just Us League."

"But what created the rift?" Eagleman probed.

"I don't know." Superior Man lied to avoid a lengthy explanation. "I looked it over with my visuals and learned nothing."

"However it was created, someone *will* find a way to exploit it."

Superior Man tilted his head as if listening to a sound no one else could hear. "Aquamarine. Your communicator onboard the Airphibian is beeping."

Aquamarine did not wear his communication unit upon his person. No radio waves would penetrate underwater. Water and undersea pressure would quickly make short work of such a device. But whenever the craft surfaced, it could send and receive. The sea king ran off to check it.

***

Golden Ring sprung into action. Once again he formed a mallet. With this he hammered the disheveled man's bare chest. Bannion opened his eyes.

"Ah, the precordial hammer thump. Quick thinking." Sigmundson breathed. "You've taken a first aid class?"

"Not formally, but I'm getting to be an expert at this." Golden Ring formed a gold stethoscope around the doctor's neck.

"Thanks," Sigmundson said, taking it up.

"What? What happened? Where am I?" The

disheveled man groaned and tried to sit up.

Sigmundson stopped him. "Take it easy, fella. You've had a shock. I'm just trying to see if you're all right. What's your name?"

"Er..."

"Do you know your name?"

"Oh, yes, my name is, er..." he paused in thought, then: "No, I don't know my name."

The doctor set the stethoscope on the man's chest. "Your heart sounds good. You seem to be all right."

Bannion grumped. "If you call being stranded in the desert, covered in dirt and wearing tatters all right, well, I guess so then."

"And just where did *you* come from?" Golden Ring asked Sigmundson. "I didn't think there was another person around for miles."

Sigmundson needed a story. Fast. "Er, the last thing I remember was, ah, walking along the trail—"

"You hike dressed like that?"

"I'll have you know in my profession I'm considered quite the dandy."

There wasn't any way for Golden Ring to fact check that.

"What about him?" He nodded to Bannion.

"A hermit caught in the Behemoth's path." Sigmundson brushed dirt off the victim and sat him up.

Golden Ring noted Sigmundson scouring the ground for something.

The doctor pulled back with a gnarled stick. It was his own cane, but the golden guy did not have to know that.

"Maybe I can just use this old stick to help me walk." Sigmundson improvised a story to throw suspicion off it being Hval in another form.

"Spring for a real cane when you're back in civilization," Golden Ring advised him.

"Of course."

He had a question, but already knew the answer. "Why are you dressed like that?"

"I'm a superhero. New in this sector, er, town. What I *really* want to know is what happened to Týr and that Behemoth guy?"

The two ordinary humans exchanged baffled looks.

"Týr was here? *And* the Behemoth?" Sigmundson gaped, close to overacting. "Man! We must have wandered into them. These fellows always have to fight."

"There was an explosion and everything went dark. Faculus is gone, too. Look, I've got to fly back to, er, New York before I'm out of power."

"You should see a doctor about that. Take one of my cards." He patted his pockets.

"No, not me. This ring." Golden Ring couldn't risk it running out of juice. Besides the flight up to the rift, he had to fly back down to his own Earth. "Can I drop you fellows anywhere?"

A two-seater gold glider appeared.

"Don't worry about it." Bannion's memory came back. He had been the Behemoth again, cursed by science to be a monster. "There's a hippie commune over that way. They know me."

"Maybe they can remind you of your name," Sigmundson suggested. "If they're not so, er, uptight about names."

"I'll send help." Golden Ring collapsed the glider and took off in flight. "I'll have a lock from the air, see if I can spot that Behemoth guy."

"Wow, he flies," Bannion noted. "How about that?"

"Looks like it's just you and me, pal. How far is it to that commune?"

"About a mile, Doc. I'm Robert, by the way. Robert Bannion."

"Do they ever call you Bob?"

"Sometimes." Bannion shrugged. *You should hear*

what else they call me.

"Nice to meet you, Bob. I'm Donner. Everyone calls me Don. I feel like we're old pals."

"You look familiar," Bannion said. Then: "I saw you in the newspaper. You're that doctor who gave up his practice to tend to the Assemblers."

"Why, yes. That's right."

"So, what's a Faculus?" Bannion was worried. A friend of the Assemblers was here. Could they be far behind? Now more than ever, Bannion had to be careful. The two started off. He was wondering about that blast. Could Bannion dare hope he was cured of being the Behemoth?

Sigmundson meant to get away as soon as he could and find if he could still transform into Týr. Both men were so preoccupied with their thoughts to notice the air shimmering as they walked.

***

Flight wasn't all the ring could do. High above the wonderstruck pair, Golden Ring spoke. "Ring, tell me about the rift over the Earth."

Why didn't I think of this before?

A cold, inhuman voice emanated from the ring: *"The rift is a rip in the fabric of space. It is the result of a man-made mass moving from one universe to the other. We are currently heading directly toward it."*

"Can it be closed?"

"Negative."

Pondering this, Golden Ring continued on toward the rift.

***

Aquamarine skimmed his Airphibian on the ocean

surface near Atlantica. From the waters burst a red and blue form. He recognized Superior Girl, despite her outfit of fishnet stockings and bustier crafted from seashells. While the garb was of Atlantica, she seemed to favor those particular hues. He moved to one of the plane's pontoons and sat. The girl landed gracefully next to him.

"So, *you're* the surface woman my people recovered," Aquamarine stated.

"They took excellent care of me."

"What exactly happened that a superior girl needed care?"

"I don't know. I was flying along—"

"Minding your own business..."

"Actually, I was looking for Braindroid." She chuckled. "Not sure if you know—"

"I'm quite familiar with the cyborg." Aquamarine grunted. "No need to look for him anymore."

"The Superior Squadron caught him?"

"Oh, yes. Justice was served."

"Well, like a bolt from the blue, my powers faded. I hit the water. I was in bad shape. Good thing my powers returned."

"That explains not drowning."

"I broke a lot of bones. Of course, they quickly healed. It was like my powers shut off. I'm fine now. Your friends kept an eye on me until I regained my senses, though. Outside of not knowing who I was or why I was in a costume, which shredded upon impact with the surface. They gave me this to wear." She indicated her Atlantician garb. "Luckily, I have odds and ends packed away."

"Not anymore." Aquamarine decided to fill the girl in. "Amazon Woman pieced together a costume out of your castoffs."

Braindroid must have tested his hercolubite ray on Superior Girl. She didn't have to be tormented that Superior Man suffered the same fate. Twice, in fact.

"I was never happy with that skirt but I've always liked mermaids. Now your people dressed me like one. I didn't realize you were who they meant by King Andrew."

"I haven't used Andrew McCurry lately."

"Is there a Mrs. McCurry?"

"There isn't." Aquamarine sighed. "Perhaps you should stay on here while you recuperate. You can breathe under water. I'll show you the sights."

"I've seen the sights." Superior Girl tapped her temples.

"In that case, I'll teach you how to talk under water."

"Great Hercólubus! The first time I tried, I got a mouthful of ocean. Your people must have thought I was a mute."

"They're used to the foibles of surface people. Even Superior Man hasn't mastered that skill. Do you have a name besides Superior Girl?"

"I live as a human under the name Marlene Denville." She took his hand. "On Hercólubus, I was Meerah. What would you like to do on our first date?"

"How would you like to help me salvage Amazon Woman's jet?"

"Sounds romantic, but...are you sure you're not just using me for my super strength?"

***

The Atoms Family, Jewel, Lockhorn, and their prisoner found themselves in the California desert. Around them, it was a scene of destruction. The hills, the ground, the shrubbery and boulders were scorched. Distant sirens sounded. A military helicopter hovered overhead.

Reide stretched the top half of his body over what looked like a new blast pit that radiated out from the center. He kept one stretchy arm tightly coiled around the Handler. Flaming Youth took to the air and spotted a highway patrolman. Landing, he hailed the cop. "Hello."

The cop got out of his car. "Hey. You're Flaming Youth from the Atoms Family." He had the features of Flaming Youth's college roommate. After all, Crawbuck's tribe lived near here. He wondered if he should mention that name. "Where the heck did you come from? I just checked the area. There was no one around."

"If I told you, you wouldn't believe it." He shut down his flame. "What happened here?"

"Got a report of an explosion."

Reide, Jewel, Intangible Girl, and Golem approached them.

"I've got to check in." The amazed patrolman headed back to his car. "Wow. The Atoms Family. They're never going to believe it."

Reide turned to Jewel. "Can Lockhorn pick up Golden Ring's trail from here?"

"He can."

"Wait," Golem said. "Golden Ring is able to go into space. We may end up there without our spacesuits."

Reide considered this, then: "Okay, let's get Four Arms to the Mancestors."

The Handler had acquiesced to his fate. He'd been beaten by those superheroes and knew the Atoms Family could beat him again. Perhaps now he could finally be free of Faculus.

Jewel gathered together the Atoms Family and their prisoner. She reached out to the dog. Lockhorn sniffed her hand. They seemed to be in communication. Then, with a shimmer, they were gone.

The highway patrolman returned to the place they'd been standing. With a gulp, he realized he was alone. "Maybe Red Bear should take a look into this."

He began unbuttoning his uniform shirt.

***

On the same Earth, Hari Balay greeted Pandora Pandopoulos. "Dr. De'ath has arranged a Ruritanian passport for you." He slapped it into the girl's hand.

Pandora had been resting at the embassy. This was in Manhattan's Lenox Hill on Lexington Avenue. The girl found it quite like Mascouten's own neighborhood of the same name. Pandora had found her room was locked; the windows were wired to an alarm system. After eating a catered breakfast, inspiration struck, and she packed the essentials she'd need, photos of her father among them. The room had its own laundry chute. That was her way out. It was like she was performing her escape artist act again. Outside the embassy, she had to ask about the subway. Pandora managed to find her way to Bleek Street and Stephen Merlin's house.

His manservant answered the door. "Yes?"

"I must see Mr. Merlin. It is a matter of great urgency."

"*Doctor* Merlin is not currently receiving visitors," the man stated, and as he began to close the door:

"Please! Show him this." Pandora presented the postcard.

He took it and showed her in. "Sit here."

She sat in the vestibule's only chair.

Within minutes, a distinguished middle-aged man with gray streaks in his jet-black hair and a pencil-thin mustache, appeared. "I am Dr. Merlin. Where did you get this? It's from my late wife."

"It was among my father's things. He is missing. I have photos of him and me." Pandora showed these to her host.

Merlin looked them over. That was the girl, at various ages. Merlin stood frozen. The man with Pandora was someone he knew. "This is truly your father?"

The girl nodded.

"He is an evil man."

"What?"

"I said he was evil. He tried to kill me, my ancient mentor, my love, and even the man who let you in here." Merlin pointed with his chin to the servant.

"You must be mistaken. My father is a good man. Where is he? Do you know?"

"He is being held in a safe location."

"Held?" The girl jumped up. "You're wrong. My father would never do anything evil."

"I assure you it is true." Merlin took up one of the photos. "This is Count Pandemonium. A very evil man."

"Count Pandemonium?" Pandora furrowed her brows. "His name is John Pandopoulos."

Merlin sighed. "Very well. I will show you."

He moved to a large glass ball. His hands made elaborate gestures over it. "The lights, Chang."

The manservant flipped a wall switch; the room went dark.

Within the globe, images appeared. There was John Pandopoulos. There were a variety of images. All showed Pandopoulos engaged in battles, with her host, the servant, an ancient man, and a silver-haired girl in purple.

"Where was this?" Pandora demanded, though she recognized some of this very house. She wondered if Merlin could see her Earth with this crystal ball.

"In Shangri-La, here, various locations," Chang said.

From her father's hands, and from the hands of Merlin and Chang, brilliant flashes of light emerged. Sometimes they coalesced to shields, other times they were bolts of energy. They were different colors. Each time, Pandopoulos was either stalemated or defeated. But she could see he was vicious. Kill crazy!

"Please..." she sobbed, "where is he?"

"Come with me," Dr. Merlin said. "Chang?"

The three of them moved deeper into the house. The presence of the manservant made Pandora realize Chang was more than just a butler but merely posed as one.

The group wound down a curving staircase to a cold basement. Chang unlocked a room. Within, a transparent casket was set upon a bier. Inside, a bearded middle-aged man lay, dark hair receding, hands atop his chest. He looked like he was resting peacefully. Pandora rushed to the casket, sobbing. "Father. Father, what happened to you, father? How did you die?"

"He is alive," Merlin said. "But in the state of suspended animation."

"Like a coma?"

"You may not be familiar with the term. Alive, but in stasis. I cast such a spell on him. He had meant that fate for me, but under more degrading circumstances."

"What could be more degrading than this?"

"After he separated my astral being from my physical body, I was to be displayed in a wax museum. At the very least, I have shown him mercy he wouldn't have shown me or my friends. I would not like being displayed as a *lifelike* wax figure."

"Dr. Merlin," Pandora sobbed out. "Don't you see? Some*thing*...has twisted his mind. I should like to take him."

"That is not possible."

"In that case, I ask to be allowed to watch over him."

Chang spoke up. "Dr. Merlin, I believe...perhaps this girl can take over my duties while I continue my studies with you."

Merlin searched for something in his pocket. Finding it, he took the girl's hand and placed a ring on one of her fingers.

She held it to the light, watched it glimmer.

Merlin grunted. "She is telling the truth."

***

With Fort Superior now a crater, determined to be a total loss, Superior Man's tiny Hercólubusians, superpowered, had scouted out a new location in the Adirondack Mountains. With his approval, they had quickly taken to rebuilding the fort and, within it, their miniature city. Superior Man and Amazon Woman flew in on Ratman's Goblin craft and stopped to tour the work.

"Greetings, Lo-Kar," their designated spokesman called out. He got the job because he spoke the best English. "These new powers are...strange."

Superior Man turned abruptly, not used to hearing his real name spoken.

"Oh," the Hercólubusian breathed. "Did I blunder using your real name in front of this Earthwoman?"

"No, no blunder. She is my special lady. I am through with secrets."

"Well, I have one to reveal to you," Amazon Woman said. "I'll be working as a civilian private eye for the military."

"Regina, why?"

To Superior Man, she was Regina when they were alone.

"With the Silver Machine sundered by that disc rider, my whip destroyed, my old costume in shreds, and you not approving of my new one," she ticked off a laundry list, "I mean to do something different with my life."

"What a-about us?" Superior Man sputtered. "When will I see you?"

"I don't know. But I've signed a lease for a shop in Mascouten. Stop in if you're in the neighborhood."

"But we need you in the Superior Squadron."

"Admit Eaglette," Amazon Woman suggested. "She'll add a woman's touch. Well, Lo-Kar, I'll see you around."

She strode back to Ratman's Goblin craft.

***

Solenoid was alerted to a message over his cell's primitive communication system that wouldn't have been out of place on an old naval vessel.

"Prisoner 5271009," a voice rang from the horn. "In recognition for services rendered you shall view a movie."

Then *The Wizard of Oz* began in a phantasmic manner via Dr. De'ath's Ultimate Display. Solenoid pondered this miracle. Maybe, after Galloping Gazelle had contacted someone, a deal was struck, allowing the Ultimate Display to be used for his entertainment. A sympathetic guard had even brought in a bucket of popcorn.

EPILOGUE

O verjoyed that her father was at least alive, Pandora left Merlin's townhouse. She needed help. *Only Dr. De'ath can fix this.*

Inside, Merlin turned to his manservant. "Chang, get your hat and coat." Dr. Merlin was watching the girl through a window. "Follow her. Slip up at some point, let her see you. Once she thinks she has lost you, I will trail her."

Chang went for the garments. Merlin retired to the sitting room. He made himself comfortable in an overstuffed chair and seemed to fall into a trance. What could not be seen was his invisible astral image rising from his body. Merlin's image went through the walls and followed Chang as he stalked behind Pandora. He saw the girl give Chang the slip. Her next move surprised him.

At the Ruritanian embassy, the girl requested a call to be put through to Dr. De'ath.

"I have found my father. He is in a state of stasis in the possession of a man named Stephen Merlin. I think the transit between worlds must have driven my father insane. He began calling himself Count Pandemonium and tried to kill Merlin and his associates."

"I am quite impressed with your detective work." De'ath's reply buzzed over the wire. "What will you do now?"

"I will join you in Ruritania and go home. There I will make further arrangements to stay here for an extended period."

"If you wish, I could assign Hari to watch your

home."

"Oh, if you could, Doctor, I'd be forever grateful."

Dr. Merlin's astral form was unaware of De'ath's part of the exchange. Nor could he guess his own mirror was involved. He seemed not even to have missed it yet. Satisfied with what he had learned, Merlin floated back to his body.

In Ruritania, Dr. De'ath summoned Hari Balay.

"Dr. Death," Balay said. "I was just about to call you. Listen to this headline. It comes from the clipping service you employ. "Man Machine debuts new armor. Says...if you have questions about it, ask Mr. Ferro."

"So, that is his way of saying my deception is found out. He knows the Man Machine that appeared at Assembler Mansion while he was in space was an imposter."

"But Man Machine doesn't know *who* was masquerading as him."

"True, Hari. I need only kill Man Machine and use the Image Duplicator to appear as him. Bah! Killing Man Machine is hardly worth the effort. Nonetheless, I have won this round. You will be taking care of Miss Pandopoulos's apartment on her Earth."

"I am ready to leave immediately, sir."

"Guard that mirror with your life, Hari. I have a little surprise for Superior Man. Soon I shall be invincible."

He turned and surveyed his supply of hercolubite. Laughter echoed through his chamber.

***

Wotan turned to Lokke from the pool through which he watched mankind. "It is good thou had advised me to take a hand."

"Yes, All-Father. Yes, indeed," Lokke purred.

"For thou hast forestalled Ragnarök!"

And that is another story.

Steven Trent

About the Author

Steven Trent has variously been a journalist, a publishing professional, an editor, and a book dealer. Most of his writing time is spent compiling notes for the next installment of "The Superior Squadron" series. An accomplished artist, he sketches drawings of the cast to help him visualize them in the storytelling. He splits his time between New York and New Waukee.

Steven Trent

https://www.twbpress.com

**Science Fiction – Horror – Supernatural – Thriller –
Romance – and More**

www.ingramcontent.com/pod-product-compliance
Lightning Source LLC
Chambersburg PA
CBHW051242260626
47162CB00002B/557